A Perfect Proposal

Katie Fforde lives in Gloucestershire with her husband and some of her three children. Recently her old hobbies of ironing and housework have given way to singing, Flamenco dancing and husky racing. She claims this keeps her fit. *A Perfect Proposal* is her sixteenth novel.

Praise for Katie Fforde

'A great fun countryside romp with engaging characters and a narrative thrust that had me hooked to the end'
Daily Mail

'A funny, fresh and lively read' *heat*

'A witty and generous romance . . . Katie Fforde is on sparkling form . . . Jilly Cooper for the grown-ups'
Independent

'Deliciously readable' *Sun*

'A heart-warming tale of female friendship, fizzing with Fforde's distinctive brand of humour' *Sunday Express*

'Acute and funny observations of the social scene' *The Times*

'Old-fashioned romance of the best sort . . . funny, comforting' *Elle*

'A fa   30131 05737117 8   varming –
                                             olitan'

Further praise for Katie Fforde

'The mother-daughter bond the women develop is endearing and the heartache caused by a failed long marriage is touchingly conveyed' *Sunday Telegraph*

'A sweet and endearing read' *News of the World*

'Delicious – gorgeous humour and the lightest of touches' *Sunday Times*

'Fforde's light touch succeeds in making this a sweet and breezy read – the ideal accompaniment to a long summer's evening' *Daily Mail*

'The romance fizzes along with good humour and is a good, fat, summery read' *Sunday Mirror*

'Joanna Trollope crossed with Tom Sharpe' *Mail on Sunday*

'A spirited summer read that's got to be Fforde's best yet' *Woman & Home*

'Can be scoffed at one sitting . . . Tasty' *Cosmopolitan*

'Perfect holiday reading. Pack it with the swimsuit and suntan lotion' *Irish Independent*

'Fforde is blessed with a lightness of touch, careful observation and a sure sense of the funny side of life' *Ideal Home*

Katie FFORDE

A
Perfect
Proposal

arrow books

13

Arrow Books
20 Vauxhall Bridge Road
London SW1V 2SA

Arrow Books is part of the Penguin Random House group of companies whose
addresses can be found at global.penguinrandomhouse.com

Penguin
Random House
UK

First published in the United Kingdom by Century in 2010
Published by Arrow Books in 2011

www.penguin.co.uk

A CIP catalogue record for this book is available from the British Library

ISBN 9780099525066

Typeset by SX Composing DTP, Rayleigh, Essex

Penguin Random House is committed to a sustainable future for our business,
our readers and our planet. This book is made from Forest Stewardship
Council® certified paper.

Printed and bound in Great Britain by Clays Ltd, Elcograf S.p.A.

To my family, all generations,
past and present, who all helped
with this book.

And to the Romantic Novelists' Association,
for being Fabulous at 50 – thank you!

To my family, all generations
past and present, who all helped
with this book

And to the Romantic Novelists' Association
for being a revelation — thank you

Acknowledgements

Truth is always stranger than fiction and the idea for this book came from something in my own family – the inheritance of some drilling rights that over the years had been widely dispersed. My cousin Elizabeth Varvill has worked incredibly hard trying to co-ordinate these which makes herding cats seem like a pleasant afternoon activity. And she didn't have the lovely assistant I gave my heroine. So enormous thanks to her, and not only for a wonderful idea for a book.

To my American consultants, most of whom are actually American! Maggie Dana, writer, Nora Neibergall, Lisa Bernhard and Liz Fenwick – although Liz is part of the Cornish consultation team that is also writer Judy Astley.

To Pete and Mary Donkin and Amanda Shouler who between them got me onto a Gulfstream – relieved it didn't leave the ground but wow – and thank you so much!

Also the wonderful Smug Sisters – aka writers Sara Craven, Jenny Haddon, Kate Lace and Joanna Maitland. They not only gave me huge plot pointers and assistance but their good example around me meant I got twice as much done as I usually do in a day. Also thanks to Amanda Craig whose generous prize to the Pen Quiz raffle meant that the Smug Sisters could spend a week in a little piece of heaven, writing.

To Bill Hamilton and Sarah Molloy at A M Heath for being Rottweiler-like to the world but wonderful to me. Thank you so much.

To my truly amazing editors at Cornerstone, Random House – Kate Elton and Georgina Hawtrey-Woore – who have such inspiring ideas and infinite patience. I really couldn't do it without you!

To Charlotte Bush and Amelia Harvell who obviously have dirt on all the people likely to help sell my books because every year they do more. They also make author tours seem like holidays with especially jolly guides.

To the miraculous sales and marketing departments who every year are more ingenious, more cunning and more hard working at getting my books sold. They include Claire Round, Louisa Gibbs, Rob Waddington, Oliver Malcolm and Jen Wilson. Thank you!

To Alun Owen who coped with the traffic jams so calmly, and as ever, Richenda Todd who spots and prevents more blunders every year but who never tells me off.

Really, producing novels is a team effort and I have a wonderful team.

Chapter One

❧❧

'So, remind me, who's this "Evil Uncle Eric" then? I'm sure you've told me but I can't keep track of my own relations, let alone other people's.'

Sophie laid her teaspoon down in her saucer and looked thoughtfully across the table at one of her two best friends. 'He's some relation of Dad's, Mands, but as I've never met him either – or if I have, I was too young to remember – it's hardly surprising you've forgotten. I'm not quite sure if he's really an uncle or just an older cousin. There was some sort of falling out which apparently is all sorted now.'

They were in their favourite coffee shop, at their favourite table by the window where they could watch the passers-by, and, if appropriate, comment on their clothes. Sophie, from habit, mopped up some spilled coffee with a napkin.

'And remind me why you're going to look after him? You're only twenty-two. Not quite old enough to be palmed off as a spinster and sent to look after single male relatives.' Amanda's disapproval was evident in the way she was carving patterns on the top of her cappuccino in choppy downward movements.

Sophie narrowed her eyes in mock disapproval. 'You read too much historical fiction, Mandy, although I must say it does sound as if the unattached daughter is being sent to live with the rich uncle in the hope that he'll leave her all his money.' She frowned. 'It's not really that at all.'

Her friend raised her eyebrows sceptically.

'It's not!' protested Sophie.

'So your family aren't using you as a dogsbody – yet again? While this random relative's minder goes on holiday?'

Sophie shrugged. 'She's not a minder! She's a house-keeper, or a carer or something. Minder sounds awful.'

Amanda looked Sophie in the eye. 'Why you? Why not anyone else in your family? Your mother, for example?'

'Oh, Amanda! You know why! No one else would do it and, to be fair, I am currently between jobs.' Sophie was aware that her friend was much more outraged by her going to look after an aged relative than she was. Maybe she did let herself get pushed around by her family. 'I am going to make him pay me.'

'And do you think he will? Surely if he wanted to, he could just get someone from an agency to look after him. He wouldn't be insisting on getting a family member to do it. He must be mean. That's why they call him "evil".'

Sophie considered. 'Well, as I said, I've never met him personally, but the family do all say he's terribly tight-fisted. Apparently they tried to borrow some money during some financial crisis or other and he sent them out of the house uttering Shakespearean texts about borrowers and lenders and not being one.' She laughed. She was imagining the irritation her parents must have felt. 'It was years and years ago though.'

'Well, he must be penny-pinching to ask you to care for him if he can afford a professional.'

Sophie bit her lip. She didn't want to tell Amanda that her mother had offered Sophie's services, possibly to sweeten Uncle Eric now he was so much nearer to death than he had been years before. If he wouldn't lend them the money, he might still leave them some, given that he didn't have many other relations. And Sophie's family had always been desperately short of money.

But Amanda had known Sophie since primary school and was well aware of how Sophie's family regarded its youngest member. 'Don't tell me, your mother said you'd do it.'

'Well, I won't then!' Sophie twinkled at her friend over her coffee cup. 'It's OK! I know you think they all bully me dreadfully, but I do have my way more often than they think I do. Being thought stupid by people – even your family – does give you a bit of power, you know.' She felt she had to explain her lack of indignation. 'I know I always seem to take it on the chin, but I never do anything I really don't want to.'

Amanda sighed. 'Well, if you say so, but what I've never really got is why your family think you're thick?'

Sophie shrugged. 'I suppose because I'm not academic like they all are, and being the youngest and all. It's partly habit and partly because they don't see my strengths as useful.' She sighed. 'Although they do get the benefit of them. In my family if it doesn't involve letters after your name, it doesn't count.'

Amanda humphed. 'Well, I'd like to hear what Milly has to say on the subject.'

Milly, the third of the trio known at school as 'Milly-Molly-Mandy' – unfairly, according to Sophie, who didn't awfully like being called Molly – lived in New York. A couple of years older than the other two, she was the head of the gang and spoke her mind even more than Amanda did.

'I haven't bothered Mills with this, although I am due to ring her. But now I must fly. I've got to find some half-decent plastic glasses for the children. People are turning up at about one.' She made a face. 'My mother is insisting

3

we make a children's room upstairs in the old playroom. She says it's because it'll be more fun for them, but really she doesn't want kids cluttering up her party.'

'You see! There you are again, doing loads to help your mother have a party and they still treat you as a second-class citizen.'

Sophie giggled. 'It's not about class, darling, it's about brains! I do have the former, but my exam results indicated I didn't have many of the latter.'

'You sound just like your mother!'

'Do I? That's not good!'

'It's inevitable. And to be fair to your mother, I think she has a point about the children's room. Parents' parties can be frightfully dull when you're little. And your father is prone to demanding if people are learning Latin – if you're a child, anyway.'

Sophie raised an eyebrow. 'They're quite dull when you're five foot six, which is why you're not coming. Unlike last year. And he doesn't ask you about Latin any more. He knows you went to the same school as I did, and didn't.'

Amanda obviously now felt guilty. 'Do you really want me to come? I will. We did used to have fun at your parents' annual bash.'

'When we three used to cover each other in face paint and play with the hose in the garden.' They both sighed reminiscently and then Sophie went on: 'No, you're fine. I'll do this one on my own. After all, I'm used to my ghastly family. I can cope with them.' She frowned slightly. She hadn't been entirely truthful with Amanda. Although she always appeared to accept her lot in the family pecking order it had irked her more lately. Especially during these hard times, when her skill with turning shabby into chic was particularly useful, she could have done with the occasional pat on the back.

4

Sophie found the shop selling party favours tucked down a side street in the old part of the town. As it had a sale on, she added some extras to her list: sparklers, face paint and some tinsel wigs, and then walked up the hill to the big old Victorian house where she lived.

She often thought that if her parents really minded about being short of money, they would have either moved into something smaller or converted part of it into a flat. For the cost of putting a bathroom and a galley kitchen into the attics they could have had some regular extra income for years. As it was, the family who still lived there – Sophie, her older brother Michael and her parents – all bumbled about, arguing over the only bathroom and filling the spare rooms with clutter.

Sophie's mother, who'd given up her life as a teacher to become an artist, had taken up a lot of the space to have a studio and to store her paintings. Her father, an academic, was a compulsive book buyer. He needed a study and a library. Michael, who was also an academic, needed the same. Sophie had once enquired tentatively about them sharing a library so that maybe she could have a room to do her sewing in but was patronised into submission. 'Art' was 'arty', whereas sewing was either 'mending' or entirely frivolous. When her sister Joanna left home when Sophie was fifteen, Sophie took over her room for her sewing machine and all the bits and pieces she needed for her creations.

Now, the downstairs rooms had been cleared for her parents' party, which took a lot of Sophie's talent. The house had grace and charm but the carpets were threadbare, there were patches of damp that required huge floral arrangements to conceal them and Sophie had had to fling tablecloths over the tables to disguise the rings caused by careless academic people, who put their hot mugs down just anywhere.

The kitchen had been taken over by the caterers, Linda and Bob, for whom Sophie often did waitressing. This was a large room, which had the sort of free-standing furniture that was so fashionable these days, simply because it had missed out when fitted kitchens were all the rage. Sophie sometimes contemplated selling off the utensils as 'kitchenalia', replacing them with newer items and making a nice little amount of money. But new things wouldn't fit into their gently decaying family home.

She dumped her bag on to the counter. 'OK, lemons, limes, crisps and bits and pieces for the children. Was there anything else?'

'Don't think so,' said Linda, taking the lemons and limes. 'The salads are all assembled and I've garnished the salmon and the cold meats. Everything hot is in the oven, so we're pretty well on track, really.'

'So, what would you like me to do?' Sophie was good at reading body language and could tell that her friend needed something, if not very much, and she'd always helped out when her family entertained. She'd always helped out, full stop. She found a lot of satisfaction in being useful, unlike the male members of the family, who always seemed affronted if anyone asked them to do anything remotely domestic. Her mother obviously didn't feel she had to offer: she was currently soaking in the bath, having exhausted herself remodelling part of the garden. (Her artistic sensibilities had taken against a particular colour combination.)

'Could you set out the glasses in the dining room? And maybe give them a polish? Your brother picked them up from the wine merchant's but I had a look and they don't seem all that clean to me.'

'OK.' Sophie found a clean tea towel and put it over her shoulder, then she carried the boxes of glasses into the dining room. Here French doors looked on to the garden; with the finest October on record, they hoped to be able to open them and let people spill out on to the paving and on into the wilderness.

The garden, like the house, was lovely if you didn't look too closely at the details. There were lots of huge shrubs – unpruned for years – and massive clumps of shocking pink phlox, flowering late, against the orange crocosmia. (It was these that had caused her mother's last-minute attack with a fork.)

Now, still a little red and shiny from the bath, her mother found Sophie in the dining room holding the glasses over a bowl of hot water and polishing them.

'Oh, darling, don't do that! They're perfectly clean. I need you to do some flowers for the hall. I hadn't noticed that frightful damp patch just opposite the front door. A big vase of flowers would hide it. Another one of your mad creations – just what we need.'

'Hm, I'll need to find a table or something to put them on. Oh I know! There's a good solid cardboard box upstairs. I'll find a bit of fabric. Leave it to me, Mum.'

'Thank you, darling,' said her mother, catching up escaping locks of hair, and wandering back upstairs, presumably to finish getting ready.

Sophie went to find the secateurs.

Sophie, after setting up the largest attic room as a space for children – which could mean anyone under twenty-five – had found herself running from one minor crisis (no clean hand towels) to another (no loo paper), and so had little time to get ready for the party herself. She just pulled on a white blouse because it was clean and a little black skirt

7

because her mother would prefer that to jeans. Then she ran downstairs to help her parents and brother serve drinks. Not that her brother did serve them. The moment someone arrived whom he wanted to talk to he did just that; having made sure he and his victim had full glasses, he led them to his study where they could chat in peace.

Things were soon well under way; food was being served, people were standing on the terrace, and Sophie was beginning to wish she was upstairs with the younger crowd. She was tired of explaining that yes, she was very much younger than her clever older siblings and no, she wasn't at uni and had no plans to go; she was perfectly happy doing what she did, thank you. (She was very polite.)

Sometimes she yearned to tell her interlocutor that she really wanted to learn tailoring, but her parents dismissed this as not being a proper subject and something she would 'grow out of' so she didn't. She was beginning to seethe inside though, something Milly and Amanda would have thoroughly approved of.

She was just wondering if she should steal a whole bowl of chocolate mousse to take upstairs when some connection of her mother's she'd met several times – she was a member of the same art class – tapped her on the shoulder.

'Could you get me a clean glass. This one's filthy.'

The woman didn't add a smile to her request, let alone a please or a thank you, and Sophie, who'd personally polished all the glasses and couldn't imagine which dark cupboard that one had been lurking in, took offence. The woman didn't realise she had, of course, because Sophie just gave her a tight smile and took the offending glass. She went to the kitchen, washed the glass, dried it and then took it back to the woman.

'Oh, and white wine, please. Not Chardonnay,' said the woman. 'Something decent.'

8

Only when the woman had the wine she wanted, and had deigned to acknowledge Sophie's helpfulness with an incline of her head, did Sophie decide she'd had enough of being an unpaid waitress for one day and would escape.

She stole the chocolate mousse and a handful of spoons, knowing there were paper plates upstairs in the children's room. She would share it out among everyone who was up there, sort them out with a game and then she would phone Milly in New York.

'And then,' Sophie went on, her mobile captured between her ear and her shoulder as she sorted playing cards, 'some evil old biddy thought I was a waitress! At my parents' party! I've met her loads of times! It got too much for me so I've taken refuge up here. Far more fun.'

'That's so horrid.' From the other side of the Atlantic, her friend's voice sounded croaky.

'Oh, sorry, Milly! Have I woken you up? I've been meaning to ring you for ages and I forgot the time difference.'

''S all right, I'm awake now. I was having a lie-in, but never mind.' There was a short, expensive pause during which Sophie could almost hear her friend rubbing her eyes and settling in for a gossip. 'So no one nice at the party?'

'Not if you mean men, no. It's my parents' annual summer bash – a bit delayed. You remember, you and Amanda always used to come – it's full of family and their old friends. I've come upstairs to the nursery where the kids are. I'm fed up with being treated as staff. My family are bad enough, but when the guests start doing it . . .'

'To be fair, Soph, you do do waitressing.'

'I know! And I'm proud to be a waitress, but this woman was so rude, I'd've objected even if I *was* working. So I've organised this lot into finding enough packs of cards to play Racing Demon and we're going to have brilliant fun.'

9

Milly's lack of agreement as to what amounted to 'fun' was somehow audible. There was a moment's silence, a rustle of bedclothes and then Milly said, 'Look, why don't you come to New York? I know I'm always asking you but now would be the perfect time. You've left your nannying job, haven't you? You're free? It's lovely here just now and Thanksgiving's only a month away.'

'It sounds heaven! But I don't want to spend the money. I'm saving up for a course.'

'Doing what?'

'I can't quite decide. Either tailoring, or running a small business. Whichever seems more useful when I've got a chunk of money, I suppose.'

'Won't your parents pay for you to study?' Milly didn't hide her indignation. 'You didn't go to uni, you must have saved them a fortune.'

'Well, yes, but they won't pay for anything they consider "recreational" like bookbinding or stained-glass making and I'm afraid tailoring comes under that heading for them. Art is different,' she added quickly, reading her friend's thoughts. 'And the small-business thing would too, probably. They don't understand people working for themselves.' She sighed. 'Although to be fair they haven't got much money either.'

'Then come to New York! It needn't cost much. You can get really cheap deals on the fare and you could stay with me.'

'Um . . .' Sophie had put off saying this; Milly would respond just as Amanda had. However, it paid to be honest where her friend was concerned; she'd only get it out of her eventually anyway. 'I've got to go and look after an aged relative. But it's fine! He's going to pay me.' She crossed her fingers because she didn't know this for a fact yet.

As expected, Milly's (low) opinion of her friend's family

whooshed across the Atlantic. 'Oh, Sophie! You mustn't let your family push you into doing something that benefits them and not you. You know what they're like.'

'None better.'

'They've always made you fit in with what they want for you and never given you the space to follow your own dreams. It's time to take control and follow your star!'

Sophie hesitated. 'Did you get that from a self-help book or an inspirational television programme?'

Sophie could imagine Milly's rueful expression. 'Well, OK, I probably did, but just because it's a cliché doesn't mean it's not true.'

'I know. And I will try and brace up and not be a doormat.'

'You're not a doormat, Soph, but they are bossy and you are a bit too helpful and obliging for your own good. Now, I'm going to try and find you some sort of job that can get you over here without a green card.'

'Thank you, Milly. I'll overlook the fact that you're the one being bossy now. And how did you get a green card anyway?'

'My boss sorted it all out. I have unique skills.'

'Oh. Is that being bossy?'

'But I'm being bossy for your good!' insisted Milly.

'That's what they all say,' said Sophie.

'Sophie!' said one of the twelve-year-olds waiting patiently for her to finish sorting the cards. 'The little ones are getting fed up. Can we play now?'

'Sure,' said Sophie. 'Mills, got to go. I'm needed. I'll ring again.'

'And I'll see about finding you a job over here. We'd have such fun together. I'll show you all the sights – the best shops – it'll be brilliant! I'll email you,' said Milly, who now sounded wide-awake.

'Cool! And thanks for listening. What time is it with you?'

'Just before ten o'clock in the morning. But it's Sunday.'

'Oh, no need for me to feel guilty then.'

Sophie disconnected from the second of her two best mates with a sigh and turned her attention to various cousins and the children of her parents' friends. 'OK, guys, have you all got a pack of cards each?'

One of the older 'children' had smuggled a couple of bottles of wine upstairs and now Sophie found her glass being filled. She may have been the 'less bright' (no one wanted to actually say she was stupid) member of the Apperly family, but she was the pretty one and by far the kindest, which was why she was now sitting on the floor, her long legs crossed and her toffee-coloured hair done up in a knot on top of her head. After being mistaken for a waitress she had quickly changed out of her tiny black skirt and white blouse into jeans and a V-necked top she had edged with mother-of-pearl buttons salvaged from a jumble-sale bargain.

'Let's go through the rules, shall we?' she said now.

As several of them hadn't played before there was a lot of explanation as to how the game was played, account taken of the youth and inexperience of some, and penalties awarded to Racing Demon experts. Then the game began. Hands and cards flew, squeaks of indignation and yells of triumph drowned each other out. When the first round was over, Sophie comforted the youngest player.

'This time,' she explained, her arm round the nearly tearful six-year-old, 'you only have to put out ten cards and everyone else has to put twelve, and your big brother has to put out fourteen because he won!'

'Sophie,' complained the big brother in question, 'I think you're making the rules up as you go along.'

'Absolutely. My privilege.'

There were a few moans, but since Sophie was their favourite cousin and all of them had a crush on her to some degree, a full mutiny was avoided.

'Right, fill up the glasses. Toby, you can have some wine in your lemonade, but only I can have it neat,' she declared.

'Not fair!' said Toby, backed up by the others.

'I know.' Sophie feigned sorrow. 'Tough, isn't it?' Easygoing she might be but she wasn't going to be responsible for her younger cousins overdoing it and being sick.

Sophie continued playing until the youngest player, with a pile of only five cards to get rid of, eventually won. Honour satisfied, she got up from the floor, brushed at her jeans and went back downstairs, having checked there was no more alcohol for her cousins to get their hands on.

As she had hoped, only the family remained, gathered in little clusters round the house. The caterers were clearing up. Sophie started gathering glasses, partly from habit, partly because she knew no one else in her family would.

'Darling!' said her mother, pretty, artistic and now ever so slightly drunk, putting her arm round her youngest child as she went past. 'I've hardly seen you. Have you been keeping an eye on the little ones?'

'Some of them are quite old now,' Sophie said, 'but yes.'

'Such a sweet girl!' Sophie's mother started stroking her hair, which made it tumble further out of its clip. 'Always so good with children.'

'Glad to be of service,' said Sophie, trying not to feel damned with faint praise. 'I think I'll give Linda and Bob a hand in the kitchen.'

'See if there's another bottle of fizz while you're there,' said a crisper voice from the hallway, 'I've been talking to some boring old friend of Dad's and haven't had a drink for ages.'

13

Sophie's older sister Joanna was her favourite sibling. While they all treated Sophie as if she was slightly simple, Joanna did at least realise she was no longer a child.

Sophie found a bottle of champagne and a couple of clean glasses and returned to look for her sister. She tracked her down in the conservatory, having a sneaky fag. 'Do you want me to open the bottle for you?' Sophie asked.

'I've been opening bottles of champagne since before you were born,' her sister said, putting down her cigarette.

'What, since you were fifteen? I'm shocked!'

Joanna took no notice. 'Are you joining me?'

'I'll just help them clear up a bit. They're all really tired in the kitchen and they've got another do on this evening.' Sophie paused, not sure if she was ready to see the funny side yet. 'Did you know? That old cow who used to go to art class with Mum thought I was a waitress! Asked for a clean glass and then was picky about what sort of wine she got.'

Joanna shrugged. 'Well, you do rather throw yourself into helpful mode. I'll save some champagne for you. The cousins and their offspring will be going in a minute. We can put our feet up and have a chat. I can't believe they've talked you into looking after Evil-Uncle-Eric.'

As Sophie couldn't either, she retreated to the kitchen; the sooner everything was cleared up the sooner she could have a quiet drink with her sister and relax.

Chapter Two

❧

Alas, a quiet drink wasn't on anyone's agenda. Although all the aunts, uncles and cousins went home, the remaining family members, the host and hostess's children, became combative. It often happened and Sophie could never quite decide if it was alcohol induced or just because they were naturally argumentative and jealous and didn't bother to hide it when they were together as a family.

First, Sophie's eldest brother came storming into the conservatory. Stephen worked for an environmental charity and Sophie felt he gave saving the planet a bad name. He was preachy and bombastic and boring. Already annoyed because he'd discovered his children playing poker, he was looking for someone to blame now the cousins were out of reach. He found new fuel for his anger in the slight smell of smoke that lingered among the plumbago and weeping figs.

'Honestly, Jo, you haven't been letting Sophie smoke, have you?' he said.

Sophie didn't react. There was no point in reminding her brother that she was old enough to smoke if she wanted to.

'Of course not,' said Joanna, her feet up on the sofa, puffing away. 'And I only let her have a small glass of champagne.'

'I've been legally allowed to drink in pubs for four years now, Stephen,' said Sophie, who was curled up in a chair, almost hidden by jasmine.

He ignored this. In his eyes Sophie was too young to do anything remotely fun but quite old enough to be a scapegoat. He stood over her, hands on hips. 'Was it you who started them playing cards? I found my two gambling!'

'Only with matches,' Sophie said. 'The poor things had to do something. It's terribly boring being a child at a grown-up party, you know. Especially when the guests are so stuffy.'

'Poor old Soph got mistaken for a waitress,' explained Joanna, tipping the remains of the bottle into her glass.

'I thought you were supposed to be looking after them?' her brother stormed on, determined to fight with someone and finding his much younger sister the easiest target.

'I played Racing Demon with them all for a bit, but then I came back down,' said Sophie. 'They must have carried on playing cards when the others left with their parents. They are your children, you know. Your responsibility, not mine.'

This pressed his guilt button, as it was supposed to. Stephen took his responsibilities seriously. 'I just wasn't pleased to find my children playing games of chance—'

'For matches,' said Joanna and Sophie together.

'Where's Hermione?' asked Sophie, referring to his wife.

'She's having a chat with Myrtle and Rue about the perils of gambling.'

The sisters exchanged glances.

'I'm sure you think it's very funny,' Stephen went on, correctly reading his sisters' expressions, 'but we work very hard to instil a proper moral code in our children. We don't want it all undone in an afternoon.'

'Well, either you should supervise your children better,' said Joanna, who always enjoyed a ruckus with her big brother, 'or you should trust that you have instilled a moral code into them – along with the home-knitted muesli and yoghurt.'

'Just because we've chosen to have a sustainable lifestyle there is absolutely no need to mock!'

'But, darling, there is!' insisted Joanna.

'Shall I make some tea?' said Sophie, wanting five minutes to herself. Her family always left her needing tea. Champagne made Joanna quarrelsome but as she didn't come home often and they had champagne even less often, Sophie always forgot not to let her have it. Tea might help her, too. Sometimes she felt she must have been swapped at the hospital, she was so different from the rest of her family. But as she did look very like her mother she accepted she must have inherited her character and skills from some ancestor. These things often skipped a generation.

The caterers had left the kitchen immaculate but Sophie used the time the kettle took to boil to empty the dishwasher. By the time she'd done this, made tea, found some alcohol-blotting biscuits and headed back to the conservatory, Michael and her parents had joined the group and the mood was escalating from argumentative to blood-drawing. Sophie immediately turned tail, muttering, 'More mugs,' as she retreated.

She came back with more mugs and more hot water, and as everyone had been too busy arguing to notice the pot of tea, she began to pour.

'Does anyone take sugar?' she said, raising her voice to be heard.

There was a silence. 'You'd think you'd know that by now,' said Stephen, 'but the answer is no. And I don't want cow's milk, either.'

'Oh, darling,' said his mother, 'we've only got cow's milk.'

17

'Cow's milk is crueller than eating meat,' said Hermione. Her two children, Myrtle and Rue, were clutching on to her hand-woven skirt, thoroughly subdued by their recent lecture. Whether this was because they were truly grateful to have been rescued from an occasion of sin, or because they'd been ordered to clutch it, Sophie couldn't tell. She felt very sorry for her niece and nephew; having her bossy brother for a father and her self-righteous sister-in-law for a mother couldn't much fun.

'Biscuit?' Sophie held out the plate to them.

'No thank you!' Hermione snapped on their behalf. 'Full of sugar and trans fats.'

'Well, they have got sugar in them, but I made them myself, with butter,' said Sophie.

'Did you?' said her mother. 'With butter? That sounds very extravagant.'

'I'll have one,' said Michael, the second eldest of the family, 'Sophie makes great biscuits.'

Sophie smiled.

'You should know,' said Joanna, 'you always eat them all. Isn't it time you moved out?'

'No,' said Michael, 'I'd miss Sophie's baking too much.'

'Darling,' their mother addressed Joanna, who asked this question every time she came home. 'I've told you lots of times, there's no point in him paying rent somewhere when there's so much room here for him.'

'I pay rent,' said Sophie quietly. She knew it wasn't fair but she preferred to feel right about herself than freeload on her not-wealthy parents. When she first offered her mother money for her keep, her mother, vague as usual, just said, 'Thank you, darling,' and put it in a tin on the dresser. She never actually asked for it, but Sophie put it in the tin every week. Quite often Sophie raided it for money to buy light-bulbs or loo paper or some other household essential.

'That's different,' said Michael. 'You're not doing important work like I am.'

'But that's terrible!' Joanna leapt in to defend her sister, although more to goad her brother than for Sophie's sake. 'She earns peanuts compared to you and yet you live here for nothing!'

'But she only has jobs!' declared Michael, like Joanna ignoring the fact that Sophie was present. 'I have a career!'

'And she hasn't much to spend her money on except fripperies,' said Stephen, who always sided with Michael against Joanna. 'Look at her! She looks like a wig or a wag or whatever it is!'

Sophie, who customised her charity-shop and jumble-sale finds, combining her eye for detail with her sewing ability, was annoyed and pleased at the same time. She also wondered if her limited budget would allow her to buy her niece Myrtle a subscription to *heat* magazine for her birthday. Having that 'symbol of everything that's wrong with the twenty-first century' coming into his house every week would drive her brother mad. Joanna could afford it – maybe she'd pass on her idea.

'It's Wag, Steve,' said Joanna, who knew he hated having his name shortened. 'It stands for Wives and Girlfriends. Unless there's something she's not telling us, Sophie doesn't qualify.'

'I only said she looked like one, not that she was one.' Stephen snatched a biscuit, irritation causing him to forget he didn't eat anything that wasn't organic and stone-ground.

'Which does rather prove she's less use than ornament,' said Michael. 'Baking, while delicious, isn't really that useful.'

'Especially not when the products are made of white flour and refined sugar,' put in Hermione. 'We always use

19

honey in preferences to the "pure white and deadly". And of course we use wholemeal flour, brown rice, brown pasta, nothing at all refined.'

'Your dentist bills must be frightening!' said Joanna, who, like the rest of the family, had heard Hermione relating their perfect diet once too often.

'Why should that be?' asked Hermione. 'It's sugar that rots your teeth, you know.'

'I didn't mean your teeth would need filling,' explained Joanna. She hated Hermione and didn't often bother to hide it. 'I just meant that bits must keep breaking off, trying to get through the slabs of cement you serve.'

Sophie noticed her brother unconsciously putting his tongue to his upper jaw, which indicated Joanna was right. But Sophie felt she should do her best to make peace. 'Don't you think we should all stop bickering?' she said now. 'We're not often all together, we shouldn't fight.'

'The trouble with you, Sophie,' said Michael, 'is that you can't tell the difference between bickering and meaningful discussion.'

'Yes I can,' she retorted instantly, 'and what you're doing is bickering.'

'But what do you know about anything?' said Stephen, coming in on his brother's side now that his wife's cooking was no longer under attack. 'You hardly ever say anything meaningful.'

'That's a bit unkind!' objected Joanna, who had found half a bottle of white wine behind a plant and had poured most of it into her glass.

'Sophie knows I didn't mean it unkindly. And we all know it's the truth,' said Michael, sounding self-righteous. 'Sophie is a sweet girl, a brilliant cook, but not the sharpest knife in the box.'

'I have always wondered why,' muttered Sophie, 'when

you're all so bloody clever, none of you ever have any money. This family is full of brainboxes but you're all as poor as church mice.'

'That's not necessarily a bad thing,' explained Hermione. 'Material wealth is nothing in the scheme of things.'

'Unless you've got bills to pay,' said Sophie, whose sweet nature was rapidly dissolving.

'We do keep our expenditure right down,' said Hermione, sounding smug. 'It's quite easy to live within one's means if one isn't hooked into the materialism of modern life.'

'I don't think I'm hooked into materialism,' said Sophie, 'but I think you lot are!'

Sophie's immediate family looked at her, all of them appalled except Joanna, who looked amused and pleased that she was speaking up for herself.

'What makes you say that, darling?' asked her mother.

'Because why else would you be sending me off to Evil-Uncle-Eric?'

There was a collective sigh of relief. 'You know why, darling,' her mother went on, as if explaining something to a child, 'it's because his carer is on holiday, he must have someone, and you're free.'

'Don't get "free" muddled up with "available" please, Mum,' said Sophie. 'I'm insisting on being paid, even if it is only a fiver a week. But that's not the real reason I'm going, is it?'

There was some shifting about and looking into empty tea mugs in response.

'You're sending me because you want me to get some money out of him!'

The shuffling and eye-contact avoidance became more extreme.

'It's true!' Sophie persisted. 'You all want his money.'

Joanna produced a cigarette from her bag. 'I think you'll find the technical term for it is the "redistribution of wealth".'

'It's not for selfish reasons, sweetheart,' her mother explained kindly. 'We need money to repair the roof, and Uncle Eric has got pots of it.'

'You don't know that,' said Sophie, hoping she wasn't expected to go through his bank account and check.

'We do actually,' said her father, who'd kept out of it all until now, nursing a whisky and watching the floor show with mild amusement. 'I saw his father's will. The old man's loaded.'

'And has no one to leave it to,' put in Michael.

'Apart from the fact that Eric might have spent all his father's money, I think you should wait till he's dead before trying to get hold of it,' Sophie went on. 'While I can't undertake to poison him for you, I don't suppose he's going to live too much longer.'

'We can't guarantee he'll leave any money to the family,' said Sophie's mother. 'He could leave it to a cats' home or something.'

'That is his privilege,' Sophie agreed, immediately deciding to put other suitable good causes under his nose to encourage him to disinherit her greedy family.

'We need the money more than a cats' home does,' said Stephen.

'I thought you—' began Sophie.

'Oh, don't be ridiculous! I want to spend the money on a reed bed, so we can deal with our own sewage,' snapped her brother.

'Yuck!' said Joanna.

'Yes, Sophie, don't be silly,' added her mother, ignoring Joanna. 'And I think it's very selfish of you not to try and help your family!'

22

'Oh, for goodness' sake!' Sophie unlinked her legs and got up from where she'd been sitting on the floor. 'You lot are unbelievable! You mock me because I only do "little part-time jobs"; you complain that the things I bake aren't "useful", although you're all quite happy to stuff your faces with them – even you, Stephen. None of you would cross the street to help Uncle Eric—'

'Well, he's not called "evil" for nothing,' put in Joanna.

'And you expect me not only to look after him, but to get his money out of him too!'

'Well, let's face it,' said Michael. 'You haven't got much else to do.'

That decided it for Sophie – she *would* have something else to do. The moment she'd finished looking after Uncle Eric, she would go to New York and visit Milly. She'd always wanted to; now her family had pretty much made it a necessity.

'Well, that may change,' she said and left the room, pulling her mobile phone out of her pocket.

'Milly? You know you said you might be able to find me a job in New York? Could you do that? Or even if you can't, I'll come! I think if I don't leave my wretched family soon, I might just go mad!'

Chapter Three

❦

The train may have been going to Worcester, but throughout the entire train journey to Uncle Eric's, Sophie thought about going to New York. She, Milly and Amanda had all watched *Friends* and *Sex and the City* together, and all dreamed of wearing those shoes, visiting those shops, and drinking in those bars. They had also speculated about meeting those men, but since no one in either show seemed to go out with anyone absolutely gorgeous who didn't have some major flaw, such as being gay, they confined their daydreams to more material fantasies.

And since Milly had gone to work there (without Sophie and Amanda! How dare she?), the two left behind had planned to go on a girly trip one day, so the three of them could live the dream together, if only for a few days.

But shortage of money, other commitments and, probably, good sense, had always stopped them actually going. However, after her stint at Uncle Eric's, Sophie decided that she wouldn't let the money issue stand in her way. She was brilliant at doing things on the cheap – always had been – and somehow she would get there.

It would do her family good to be without her, she decided, looking out of the train window but not really seeing the passing scenery. They took her utterly for granted. It would only be when she wasn't there to do all the little things that made a house run smoothly – the replacing of lightbulbs, the household repairs, the little errands – that her family would realise they missed her. And she would do something with her life that made them see that she wasn't just a pretty face with a talent for needlework.

She considered. It would be better if she could go to New York and not blow all her savings doing it. She would have to come home after her holiday and when she did, she would have to start again from scratch to save for her course.

Which course, she still couldn't quite decide. Ideally it should involve both tailoring and pattern-cutting, and combine fashion and business skills so she could actually make a business out of what she loved to do – remaking jumble-sale buys into quirky, interesting items. One day she would make her family sit up and admit that she was perfectly bright, and that her practical skills were more useful than all their academic qualifications put together.

By the time the train pulled in, Sophie was fired up with passion – for going to New York, for doing something for herself, and for making her family think for once. She pulled on her backpack and, glancing at the map she'd taken off the internet, she set off towards Uncle Eric's house almost fizzing with determination to better herself.

To their mutual surprise, for Sophie and Uncle Eric, it was almost love at first sight. Uncle Eric had assumed Sophie would be like the rest of her family, who he was convinced were idle and money-grubbing. He had only agreed to have Sophie as a holiday replacement for his regular house-keeper because it would save him the trouble of finding a more suitable candidate.

Sophie had assumed he would be crotchety, set in his

ways and 'evil' as described by her family, although she soon began to wonder why she'd believed them. They were so often wrong about things that mattered. But the moment the elderly gentleman opened the door to Sophie, in her skinny jeans with her hair in some sort of nest on top of her head, she saw that while he might well be set in his ways and possibly a little bored, he certainly wasn't evil. Sophie, expecting a combination of Fagin and Scrooge with a bit of Child-Catcher thrown in, saw a kindly old person, in a slightly shabby but once well-cut suit, a cardigan with a hole in it and a tie that needed a good press. She instantly wanted to darn him – if not literally, emotionally. He needed her practical skills and she determined he would get them.

He led her into the sitting room and gave her a wine glass full of sherry. 'You'll need it, my housekeeper is going to give you a very long list of instructions about how I like my life to be organised.' He sighed. 'Not sure she's got it right, actually.'

Sophie took a sip of the sherry, which she decided she rather liked, and then went to find Mrs Brown, who, as foretold, had a timetable and a list of instructions that went on for several pages.

Sophie scanned the pages and then looked up. 'I don't see much exercise on this list. Can he leave the house? Get about OK?'

Mrs Brown nodded. 'Oh yes, but he just prefers to read the paper and listen to the wireless. And very simple food. Nothing fancy. Good plain cooking, like I've always given him. I know how old people like things done.'

Sophie had no idea how old people liked things done but she knew she wouldn't much fancy such a restricted life. Maybe Uncle Eric needed a bit of a change. She took another speculative sip of her sherry.

She was shown to a bedroom which had a single bed made up with sheets, blankets and a paisley eiderdown. There was a bookcase full of old-fashioned books by authors Sophie had never heard of: Ethel M. Dell, Jeffery Farnol and Charles Morgan. A silver dressing-table set comprising a hand mirror, hairbrush, clothes brush and comb was arranged in front of a three-part mirror on which hung a little cardboard cone which Sophie realised was a hair tidy – somewhere to put the bits of hair you pulled out of the brush. It was sweet and appealed to Sophie, who liked old-fashioned things, aware that in some ways she was quite old-fashioned herself. At bedtime she snuggled down into the bed, which didn't have the most comfortable mattress, and started reading one of the books. Two lines in she decided she should go to sleep instead.

Mrs Brown called in at breakfast-time the following morning to make sure Sophie knew what she was doing.

She explained, obviously feeling guilty for taking a long-overdue break: 'I've been with Mr Kirkpatric for a long time and it suits me, but when my daughter in Australia arranged for me to visit I felt I must take the opportunity. My daughter says two weeks isn't long enough really, but it seemed long enough to me. I don't like leaving him.'

'We'll be fine,' said Sophie firmly. 'You just enjoy your trip. I promise I'll look after him and hand him back to you in perfect condition.'

'It's porridge for breakfast—'

'I know. It's on the list. You've given me wonderful instructions. Uncle Eric and I will be just fine.'

Mrs Brown still wasn't convinced. 'The number of the agency is on the bottom of the final page. I felt it would be better to have someone qualified, but he wasn't willing to pay the agency and wages. He likes to watch the pennies.'

As her family had described him as a mean old skinflint, this wasn't a great revelation to Sophie. 'We'll be fine. I like to watch the pennies myself.' With this, she ushered Mrs Brown out of the door, waving merrily at her from the step when she got to the pavement.

Then she offered a silent prayer that nothing would go wrong and he wouldn't fall down and break a hip or anything ghastly, before going back to talk to her aged relation.

Porridge (made with water, no sugar, just a dribble of milk, don't let him have extra salt) was what she was expected to produce, but when she mentioned this to Uncle Eric, who was already spreading the newspaper around him in the dining room, he didn't seem enthusiastic.

'Muesli then? I brought some with me.'

'Good God, girl! Are you trying to kill me? Invented by dentists to increase trade! They put those damned nuts in that break the strongest teeth. Give it to the birds!'

'OK, so what would you like? Toast? Maybe with scrambled eggs?'

A wistful expression crossed Uncle Eric's well-worn face. 'Boiled eggs with soldiers?'

Sophie made a face. 'Well, I'll do my best, but it's very hard to get boiled eggs just right. But if it turns out too hard, we can have egg sandwiches for lunch.'

As Sophie managed to get Uncle Eric's eggs – she made him have two – exactly right, boiled eggs and soldiers became a breakfast favourite.

Sophie had to cook Uncle Eric four small meals a day, see he took his pills, and do some housework, but that didn't take all day. When the weather was fine she explored the local area for charity shops and cafés; when it wasn't, to keep herself amused she sorted him out. Accompanied by Radio Four – the only radio station Uncle Eric would permit – she went through the hidden corners of his house, clearing cupboards, washing and sorting, cleaning and rearranging. By the end of the first week, having investigated every cupboard, she had found enough bric-à-brac to furnish a small shop. As he wouldn't let her book a stall at the local market and sell the bric-à-brac, she wanted to start on his muddle of a desk.

She'd already been through his wardrobe, darned his favourite cardigan (pointing out she was one of the few girls of her generation who knew how to do it), sewn the pocket back on his dressing gown and put fleecy insoles into his slippers.

In the evenings, over supper, and afterwards, they chatted. Sophie asked Uncle Eric about the 'olden days' until he got bored with this; eventually he asked her about her love life.

'So, young Sophie, you're moderately good-looking, I suppose, have you got a chap?'

It took Sophie a moment or two to work out what he meant. 'Oh, you mean a boyfriend? No, not currently. Thank goodness.' She momentarily thought of Doug, her particularly clingy ex, but dismissed him just as quickly.

'I thought girls liked having a man around to take them dancing, on picnics, that sort of thing.'

'Well, I would if my boyfriends ever did that, but they didn't. The best I could hope for was a half of lager in a gloomy pub.' She sighed. 'I seem to attract dreadfully boring men.' Then she considered. 'Although my girlfriends say it's because I'm too soft-hearted to tell them to pi—— go away. If they ask me out for a drink I always say yes and go, if I want to or not.'

'Sounds like sheer lunacy! And pretty damn boring!'

'Yes, it was. Awfully boring. I'm planning to stay single for a bit, anyway. I have much more fun with my female friends than I do with most of the men I know.'

'You don't know the right sort of men, obviously.'

'Well, no. You're not the first to say that.'

'Hmph. And what's your father and brothers doing about it? Making sure you meet the right sort?'

Horror and hysteria at the thought of any of her male relations finding her suitable men caused to Sophie to choke with laughter. She took a large sip of tea to calm herself down.

'I'll take that as a no, then?' said Uncle Eric.

'Uncle Eric!' Sophie was shocked. 'That's a very modern expression!'

Uncle Eric looked extremely pleased with himself. 'I like to keep up with modern times.'

'No you don't!' said Sophie, reaching over and patting his hand. 'You just like to shock people, same as I do.'

'I've washed all the ornaments and put them back on the mantelpiece,' said Sophie later, after Uncle Eric had woken from what he described as his 'postprandial nap'. 'Now what can I do?'

'Goodness, child, you need constant entertainment! What is the matter with you? Mrs Thing doesn't need things to do all the time!' Uncle Eric tried to appear displeased with Sophie but she wasn't fooled. He was thriving on the disruption to his very circumscribed life. One week into her visit and Sophie had had a visible effect, both on Uncle Eric and on his house.

'Mrs Thing – Mrs Brown even – must have a high boredom threshold.'

This time he looked hurt. 'Some people find caring for an elderly gentleman a very satisfying and fulfilling task. A privilege to stay in my lovely house! Should do it for nothing.'

'Of course it's a privilege to count out your pills and make sure you don't overdo the nightcaps and fall down the stairs, but it isn't enough to keep me occupied. And your house is large, but it is not lovely! You should pay me extra for having to walk such long distances. As you're not going to do that, you mustn't object if I need projects.' She paused. 'I'll start sorting out your desk if you like.'

'Absolutely over my dead body! I'm not having my valuable documents pored over by a flibbertigibbet who won't understand their significance!'

Sophie was unfazed. 'I won't throw anything away. I'll sort everything into neat piles. Then you can file or recycle them, or even burn them.' She smiled at him encouragingly. 'In fact, that's a good idea. They'll help you keep warm until you get your winter-fuel allowance.' Her great-uncle made the sort of face that encouraged her to go on. 'After all, there can't be anything that recent, the papers are all covered in dust. And the rest of the room looks quite tidy. The desk spoils it.'

He harrumphed, frowned and snorted but then said, 'Oh, very well, child, if you must. But you have to promise not to read the papers, just sort them.'

Uncle Eric was wearing a very moth-eaten cardigan Sophie had begged to throw away but he had refused to be parted from it. The sight of it now made her rebel a little. 'I can't sort them if I don't read them. Don't be silly, Uncle-Eric-dear.' She used her pet name for him, devised so she wouldn't accidentally call him Evil-Uncle-Eric.

He sighed, having made his token protest. 'Well, please yourself then, child, as you always do.'

'I abandoned my iPod for you, didn't I?' said Sophie. 'I only listen to Radio Four now.' She actually found she

31

enjoyed it, picking up bits of information that otherwise she would never have known, but she didn't want to tell him that. Their game depended on each maintaining their chosen stance.

'You mean the machine that makes buzzing noises? You should be grateful.'

'It doesn't make buzzing noises if you've got the earpieces in, you hear the music. Maybe you should get one?'

Uncle Eric tutted appropriately. 'Well, I'm going for my nap now, and maybe finish the crossword.'

'Would you like me to put the heater on for you?'

'I'm quite capable of switching a switch,' he snapped. 'I'm not senile yet.'

Sophie gave him the sunny smile he was after. 'Oh good. When I've finished this lot I'll help you with those last clues.'

'Huh!' said Uncle Eric with a derisive snort and pottered out.

Sophie sighed fondly. She had never even looked at a crossword until she'd come here – her family whistled through them without ever giving her a chance. Uncle Eric, although very quick, was quite pleased to have someone to mull things over with. Now Sophie had learned some of the rules, she found she could get clues quite often. Staying with Uncle Eric had been good for her in many ways, and not only because his area was populated by excellent charity shops; her wardrobe was expanding.

She took the vase off the round table in the middle of the room and straightened the chenille tablecloth. She needed space if she was going to sort out the desk. Unlike her siblings, who seemed to covet everything, the only thing Sophie wanted to inherit was his desk. As it was unlikely that she would, she wanted to at least clear it, dust it and polish it now. Then she could really admire the plethora of little drawers and pigeonholes, the possible-secret compartment and the craftsmanship that had gone into producing it. It might never be hers, but she could enjoy it for a few days.

By the time Sophie went downstairs to give Uncle Eric his pills, she'd made a good start but there was still a mound of papers to go through. Cheating, really, she had emptied out all the papers on to the table so she could get to the dusting and polishing stage almost immediately. Now she had to go through all the old bills, bank statements, expired insurance certificates, estimates for work done on cars long gone and all the other bits of paper trivia that people kept. But the desk itself looked beautiful.

The following day, when she'd done all she could for Uncle Eric, including dragging him for a short, invigorating walk and separating him from his cardigan so she could wash it, Sophie went back to her task. She liked sorting things, putting into order that which had been chaotic. While she worked, she daydreamed about going to New York, shopping with Milly, visiting art galleries and museums, getting away from her family.

At first when she saw the name New York on a wodge of papers that were stapled together, she thought she'd imagined it, but a moment's inspection told her that she had read correctly. Unlike everything else on the table, this looked interesting. She was about to start reading them when she remembered that these were Uncle Eric's private papers so, instead, she took them downstairs with her.

'What's this, Uncle Eric?' she asked him, handing him the papers.

'How the hell should I know!' he said, having peered at

33

them through the glasses round his neck. 'Is it suppertime? I'm hungry!'

This was a good sign. Uncle Eric didn't have much appetite, but Sophie had noticed that since she'd been cooking small but tasty little snacks, he'd been eating more. She planned to leave Mrs Brown some recipes.

'I'll start cooking when I've given you your pills. You can have a look at those papers while I do it. You've finished the crossword, presumably?'

'Oh yes. Didn't need your help today.'

'Then you'll need something to keep you occupied. Why don't you get a television? You'd love it.'

'Dear child, you know perfectly well how I feel about television. Give me the papers and I'll have a look.'

Patting his shoulder as she left the room, Sophie said, 'I'll take you to the library tomorrow, to get you something else to read. Or maybe we could arrange for the travelling library to come a bit nearer?'

While they were eating scrambled eggs with Marmite on the toast that evening, Uncle Eric said, 'You know that bunch of papers you wanted me to look at?'

'Yes?' Sophie picked up the teapot and began to pour. Uncle Eric would have no truck with teabags and mugs; he liked tea from a pot.

'They might amuse you.'

'What are they?'

'They're to do with part of my inheritance – your family's too. Drilling rights.'

'What? Do you want another slice of toast? It wouldn't take a minute.'

'Well, I would, actually. I like this brown stuff on it.'

'Marmite, Uncle-Eric-dear. It's been around for centuries. Even you must have experienced it before.'

'I've probably forgotten. Anyway, go and make the toast,

34

and then I'll tell you the story.'

When Sophie returned with a fresh supply of toast, he began. 'Ages ago, about four generations, our family owned the drilling rights to a bit of Texas. They're not worth anything because they're on the only bit of Texas that doesn't have oil in it – either that or it's far too expensive to get out.'

'Shame,' said Sophie, buttering a crust. 'I'd love to own part of an oil well. I could do with the cash.'

'Couldn't we all? But even if there was oil, the rights were turned into shares and they've been left to different people over the years.'

'So why was New York written on the top of the paper?'

'Oh, that's the address of my cousin Rowena who tried to get everyone who owns any of it to form a group, so one person could speak for us all and make it possible to negotiate renting the rights.'

'Oh. But she didn't manage to get everyone to do it?'

'I have no idea. She also bought the rights from some people who thought they'd never be worth anything, but I haven't heard from her in centuries. I expect she's in a care home or something. I wrote to her a couple of years ago. Got no reply. Perhaps she's dead.'

'You don't sound very sad.' Sophie crunched into her toast.

'Most of my friends are dead, Sophie. At my age you get used to that,' he said matter-of-factly.

'So you don't think the drilling rights are worth anything?'

Uncle Eric became thoughtful. 'They never have been before but it's possible that, with newfangled equipment, they are now. Maybe.'

'So there's a possibility that you, and other members of your family, could be sitting on a gold mine – or rather an oil well?'

'There's a possibility, but not one I'm really prepared to pursue.'

'Well, would you mind if I read through the papers? It might be interesting.' She paused. 'You should see your desk. It looks amazing! All ready for the *Antiques Roadshow*!' Then she remembered that Uncle Eric didn't have a television and wouldn't get the reference.

'If you've nothing better to do with your time, but I'm sure you'll find it very tedious. Dry as dust, that sort of thing.'

'But it might lead to something. Oil wells are quite interesting, aren't they?'

'True. If you want to look into it further there's nothing stopping you. But no taking the papers back to your family! They'll get all sorts of daft ideas and it'll all come to nothing, you mark my words.'

'You go back to your Sudoku,' she said. 'I'll tell you if there's anything worth pursuing.'

'So, did you come up with anything?' asked Uncle Eric as they drank hot chocolate and ate digestive biscuits before bed.

Sophie had expected him to have forgotten all about her investigations. 'Only really that address in New York, but there was an ancient letter, which obviously everyone affected received, suggesting that people got together to form a syndicate or something, just like you said.'

'Hm. Don't think we did though. Can't remember why not. Long time ago.'

Something in the way he said this created a flicker of excitement. 'Would you like me to look into it?'

'Well, if you've got the energy and enthusiasm to investigate, it could be worth your while. Maybe not you *personally*, of course.'

'No?'

'It depends to whom the shares have been left. It's possible that your grandfather left them to you and your siblings. Otherwise it'll just be your father who'll benefit. Do you want him and your mother becoming oil millionaires?'

Sophie chuckled. 'Well, it's unlikely they'd be millionaires, but I'd be happy for them to have a few extra thousand. They could get the house put in order, repair the roof. That would be good.'

'Then go to it! If you had something to really get your teeth into, it would stop you bothering me.' He frowned. 'There may be some more papers in the loft, but I had a bad leak up there some years ago, so I expect they've all been ruined.'

'I could look—'

'No you can't. There's nothing of use there, I'm certain. You work on the papers you've got. Quite enough for your purposes.'

'But I'd have to go to New York.'

'You told me you wanted to go anyway. See your friend Molly.'

'Milly,' said Sophie. 'Yes. I'm hoping she can get me a job. It would be dreadfully extravagant to just go for a holiday.'

'I'm sure you'll find a way to get there. You're a resourceful girl.'

At the end of her stay, Sophie hugged Uncle Eric hard. From his reaction she got the impression that no one had ever hugged him hard before. He was rather frail in her arms but she knew it was good for him to feel loved.

'Goodbye, you scamp,' he said. 'Keep in touch. And let me know if you find out anything useful about those drilling rights. I might need to go into a care home myself one day, if Mrs Brown can't cope with me.'

'I'll come and look after you,' said Sophie, and realised she meant it.

On the train journey home Sophie daydreamed about announcing to everyone that she'd saved the family fortunes. It would be brilliant being the one who actually made a difference to the family, without having been to university, or passed dozens of A levels. Then she realised she couldn't say anything until she'd got somewhere with the project or they'd tease her unmercifully.

A couple of days later she found herself helping out in a café where she'd worked on and off since school. While it was fun seeing all her old friends, and discovering that the same customers still went there and all remembered her, it did make her feel very claustrophobic. There must be more to life than this!

Every day she went home and headed straight to her laptop hoping for an email from Milly. Sometimes there was one but it was only news and chat. Then one day, at last, there was an email headed 'Possible work opportunity'.

It's only holiday cover, but they're lovely people. Hugely rich, but going on what Jess says (she's their regular nanny) generous with it. Jess says they'll pay your fare as long as you don't mind going cattle class. I think you'll be fine with that! Let me know if you're interested ASAP and I'll tell Jess. She'd be thrilled if you'd come. It would be big brownie points for her if she found her own replacement while she goes back home.

The email went on about needing references and other details.

A quick glance at her watch told her she could ring Milly immediately. Then she checked the balance on her mobile phone; she had hardly any credit left. She decided to email instead: *Brilliant news! No, I don't mind going cattle class. I'll go online and find out about a visa and things.*

When she went downstairs later to join her family for supper she was feeling very positive.

Her brother noticed. 'You're looking very chipper, Soph. Don't tell me Uncle Eric just sent you a huge cheque.'

'Nothing like that.' Sophie was having to fight down the smile that was drawing her family's attention to her.

'You didn't manage to find out where he's leaving his money, did you?' asked her mother. 'If it's a cats' home, I think we'll have to contest the will.'

'No, I don't know who he's leaving his money to. I don't think he's got much, actually,' said Sophie. 'This looks lovely, Mum.' She indicated the cottage pie that graced the table. With her away, her mother had had to get back into cooking.

'Thank you, darling!' Her mother was distracted by Sophie's praise, as she was supposed to be.

'But, Sophie, you look as if you're the cat who's got the cream,' said her brother. 'There must be some reason.'

'Sophie's always had a sunny disposition, darling,' said her mother, putting the serving spoon into the mashed potato.

'She doesn't usually look smug,' said Michael.

'Glad to hear it!' said Sophie, not really wanting to share her news just now. She wanted to have time to get used to the idea herself before she told her family, who were bound to have lots of reasons why it wasn't a good idea to escape them all.

'So, what's up, Sophie?' asked her father. 'Are you feeling smug? Or just looking it?'

'Do tell us if you've got something to say,' said her mother, handing her a plate.

Realising there was nothing to be gained from holding out on them any longer, Sophie launched in. 'OK,' she said. 'It's nothing really. I've just had an email from Milly. She's got me a job in New York.'

Chapter Four

❧

'New York!' said her brother and father, practically simultaneously. 'What would you want to go there for?'

'Lovely shopping,' said Sophie, giving them the answer they expected, knowing they'd be disappointed if she said anything else.

'How on earth could you finance a trip to New York?' asked Michael, checking his plate against everyone else's to make sure he'd got enough.

'I've saved up,' said Sophie, 'and I'll be working when I get there.'

'Can't do that without a green card,' said her father, pointing out the obvious as usual.

'I'm being a nanny for a month. I'm not planning to stay there for ever.' Her lack of green card did concern Sophie a bit but her employers hadn't been worried about it so she supposed she could get away with it, for such a short time.

'Oh, a nanny!' Sophie's father made his opinion of this means of making a living predictably clear.

'Yes. It's nothing to be ashamed of. Children do have to be looked after,' said Sophie. This was a perennial topic of conversation and she waited for her mother's well-rehearsed response.

'I never had a nanny for you lot,' said her mother. 'I looked after you myself.'

'That's partly because you didn't have a job outside the home,' said Sophie, feeling a little unkind.

41

'I had my work!' said her mother, as she always did, referring to her painting, which she'd used as an excuse to get out of anything she didn't want to do with her children; if Sophie's older siblings hadn't taken her to the local pool, Sophie would never have learnt to swim.

'Well, anyway, I'm going to New York,' said Sophie, not wanting a re-run of her mother's Life in Art, including the time she'd nearly exhibited with someone who'd nearly won the Turner prize.

'Where will you get the money for the fare from?' her father demanded. 'You can't go to New York for nothing!'

'I know! I said, I've been saving up. Uncle Eric turned out to be a nice little earner.'

'So Evil-Uncle-Eric did pay you?' said Michael. 'How did you get money out of the old skinflint?'

'You know perfectly well I worked for him: he gave me my wages. And he's not evil, he's really quite sweet when you get to know him.' She thought fondly of the good times they'd had together. He might play the part of a grumpy old man, the old fraud, but at least he didn't patronise her, as the rest of her family did.

'He wouldn't give you the drip off the end of his nose,' muttered her mother. 'When I asked him to sponsor an exhibition for me he flatly refused.' The fact that he wasn't the only one didn't lessen his parsimoniousness in her eyes.

'He gave me the same as he pays Mrs Brown. I still worked out cheaper than going through an agency.'

'Told you he was mean.' Her mother helped herself to more vegetables, having tucked up a strand of hair into its comb.

'So what are you going to do in New York?' said her brother. 'It's a very expensive place for a holiday.'

'I've told you, I'm not going to be on holiday,' said

Sophie patiently, 'I've got a job.'

'But how will we manage without you here?' complained her father. 'I don't know what the young are coming to. They just go about, pleasing themselves.'

'Have some more pie, dear,' said her mother, putting more food on her husband's plate. 'I made it.'

As her father tucked in Sophie realised with relief that her family had lost interest in her goings-on and she wouldn't be forced to divulge her ulterior, most recent reason for going to New York. She wasn't ready to do so yet.

Having loaded the dishwasher and tidied up the kitchen (her mother was a talented but untidy cook) she went upstairs to find another email from Milly. *Just heard from the lovely family you'll be working for. They're really thrilled to be having a real English nanny while their regular one visits her family. But they do want references. Here's the email address; they can't wait to hear from you.*

Sophie punched the air before writing her introductory email and deciding which of her recent employers would provide a reference at such short notice.

After several good-humoured exchanges the family took her on as their nanny and promised to pay for her fares when she got there. It was all going exactly to plan! Sophie could hardly sleep for excitement. She went through her clothes several times in her head, sorting out the perfect capsule wardrobe. She was determined to travel light and then, if she got the opportunity, buy something in New York. You couldn't go to New York and not buy clothes. She had just decided she had to buy a new pair of jeans when she finally dropped off.

All through work the next day, while she smiled, served coffee, cleared tables and made industrial quantities of scones, she thought about New York and the fact that she was actually going there! Skyscrapers, yellow cabs, fire hydrants and wonderful shops: she could hardly contain herself. Every now and then she reminded herself that she was going to be working and that her family lived in the country somewhere, but she was sure she'd be able to tack on a couple of days with Milly, either before her time working or after.

A couple of nights later she arranged to meet Amanda.

'Oh God, I'm so excited!' said Sophie as she and Amanda waited by the bar. 'I can't believe I'm actually going!'

Amanda ordered a bottle of white wine and a bottle of sparkling water. 'So have you got your ticket and everything?'

Sophie nodded. 'Yes. I got it all online, including my visa. Thank goodness I had a newish passport. And obviously no convictions for terrorism or anything.' She paused. 'What is "moral turpitude"?'

'What on earth are you talking about?' Amanda looked bewildered.

'It was mentioned on the visa application. I think I said the right thing.'

'Thank goodness they didn't finger you for some car bomb or other, or they wouldn't let you in,' said Amanda, handing over some money to the barman.

'Noo! Don't joke! That's something you must never do,' said Sophie anxiously. 'The immigration people won't get it and will put you straight into jail!'

Amanda chuckled and collected her change. Then they picked up their bottle and glasses and headed for their favourite table. 'Don't mind me, I'm just jealous.'

'It would be so much more fun if you were coming with me,' said Sophie, when they'd taken their first sip. 'Although you'd have to get a job too.'

'And I have a job here.' Amanda sighed. 'Have you thought about clothes?'

'Continually, but basically, I'll be a nanny, so I'll take casual things. I gather they're very outdoorsy so I won't need any dresses.'

'Do you need to borrow a case or anything?'

Sophie shook her head. 'It's kind of you but I think I'll just use a rucksack. I may want to travel around a bit and it would be easier.'

Amanda sighed. 'I can't believe you and Milly are both going to be in New York and I'm not with you!'

'It is a bit of a waste of New York, isn't it? But I'm not going to America for long,' said Sophie, 'it's only a temporary job. I'll be back before Christmas. And nothing would drag you away from your doctors anyway.'

Amanda had done work experience in a doctors' surgery and almost had to be surgically removed when her fortnight was up, she loved it so much. Fortunately they loved her too and offered her a full-time job as soon as she'd finished university. 'Well, yes.'

'And you've got a lovely boyfriend.'

'I know! I've wasted my youth already.' She'd once told Sophie that she felt her life had become too settled, too young, but she loved it, so what was she to do?

'Silly! We could arrange to go again, together. I'm going to have my fare paid back when I arrive. I won't have to find that money again.' She pushed away the thought that her employers might forget to pay her back. It was such a large amount of money to spend all at one time. Although maybe, if the drilling rights came to anything . . . It was desperately unlikely, of course, but maybe possible enough to daydream about? She'd made a dossier for herself with all the papers photocopied and made sure she'd got every scrap of information from

45

Uncle Eric before she left. If only she could bring this off. Anxiety about the possibility of trying to track down Cousin Rowena while she was working shaded her enthusiasm a little. She had set herself a very difficult task.

Amanda, unaware of Sophie's private thoughts, said, 'At least you going to New York will get Doug off your back finally. I've never known anyone so clingy. You finished with him months ago and he still moons around after you, trying to get you back.'

Sophie eyed her friend. Any minute now would come the usual lecture about her being too soft. 'Soft-hearted-Soph' had been her nickname when they'd stopped dressing up and experimenting with make-up and begun to go out with real boys. 'I didn't take him back though,' she said now, a touch indignantly.

'No, but you do go for long walks with him, which is just encouraging him to think he's got hope!' Amanda didn't approve of Sophie's habit of staying friends with her exes.

Sophie sighed. 'Well, you know, I hate letting people down.'

'It's fine to be kind, Soph, but with you it's all one way – you're always there for them but they're not there for you! You even pay for everything!'

'I've learnt my lesson. I'm never going out with a hopeless, hard-up weakling again. Promise.'

'I suppose Doug was quite good-looking,' admitted Amanda, cutting Sophie some slack.

'And when I first met him he had a job! And a car! It was only after he met me that things went pear-shaped, and I couldn't dump him then, could I?'

'Well, you could have dumped him because you'd found out how self-obsessed and boring he was.'

46

'No! Not then!'

'And what about the drunken texting, begging you to take him back?'

That had been a real pain and still happened from time to time, but if she mentioned it, Amanda would go on lecturing her for ever. 'Listen! I have dumped him and he won't be able to reach me in New York, anyway.'

Amanda let her off the hook. 'Are you planning to do much shopping?'

'I don't think I'll be in the actual city for long, if at all. I'm being picked up by my family at the airport and being driven to where they live.' A wrinkle of anxiety crossed her brow. 'Supposing I don't get on with the children? It could be quite isolated.'

'Of course you'll get on with them! You're brilliant with kids! You'll be making Thanksgiving costumes for them before you've unpacked!' Amanda gave her a little shove to emphasise her point. 'They'll be all over you.'

Soothed by this enthusiasm Sophie said, 'I'm not sure they dress up for Thanksgiving. I think that's Halloween.'

'Same difference,' said Amanda. 'Have another drink.' She poured them both another glass of wine, topped up their water glasses and went on, 'So you won't get to spend much time with Milly?'

'Only if I get time off and a bit at the end, I hope. I gather her flat is tiny. Not that that would matter.'

'So where does your family live?'

'Maine. I'm hoping for a clapboard house with its letter box—'

'Mail box.'

'—on a stick, where the paperboy just flings the Sunday papers on to the lawn.'

'Oh, you're going to have such a good time,' said Amanda. 'I can feel it in my water!'

47

Sophie made a face. 'You haven't started drinking your own water, have you? When did that happen?'

'Oh you!' Then she frowned. 'I am going to miss you!'

'You and Doug both!'

Sophie's mother sat on her bed while she packed. 'We are going to miss you, darling,' she said, unknowingly echoing Amanda.

'Not really. You've all got busy lives.' Sophie wondered if she could ask her mother to transfer to the chair so she could spread out her things and make sure she had everything. 'Now where's my list?'

'I can't believe you're so organised!' Sophie's mother made it sound like a fault. 'When I was your age I just flung things into a bag and took off!'

'I'd do that too, only I don't want to take things I won't need, or forget anything.' Sophie found her list, consulted it, and put in the last couple of items.

Later, when her mother had drifted off to make them both a cup of tea, Sophie emptied her rucksack, put her dossier in the bottom, and repacked. When she got there she'd start looking at telephone directories for Cousin Rowena, and possibly ask her employers for help.

She had much more room in her rucksack the second time around, but thinking of future shopping opportunities, she didn't add anything, she just went downstairs to join her mother in the kitchen.

Finally it was time for her to set off on her adventure; she'd begun to see it as such. Amanda drove Sophie to the airport, her family being otherwise engaged as usual. As she had to get back she'd just dropped Sophie off but it was still lovely to have a lift. It was a treat not to have to get there by public transport.

Sophie liked flying. She liked the little packets in the meals, looking at the other people, and having time to read and doze. But it was a long flight, and when they'd finally arrived and she'd gone through security, which seemed to take for ever, involving having her fingerprints and a picture of her iris taken, and answering a lot of questions, she felt a bit battered. To add to her feeling of anticlimax there was no jolly family holding up a placard with her name on it.

She forced herself to relax. They could have been held up in traffic, got the time of her arrival wrong – anything. She'd just be patient and watch the world go by.

She waited for an hour and then burrowed in her rucksack for the bit of paper with the telephone number on. She tried several permutations of the number, with prefixes and without, before eventually she got through.

'Hi! This is Sophie, Sophie Apperly? I'm here!' she said, fighting a wave of fatigue that hit her just at the wrong moment.

There was a horrified silence at the end of the phone and then, 'Oh, Sophie, honey, didn't you get my email? I sent it yesterday.' The woman sounded just as nice as she'd seemed over their email correspondence – but not happy.

Sophie's spirits, already lowered by jet lag, descended further. 'I was offline yesterday, before I left.'

'Oh honey, that's a shame! We've had a family crisis here and we all have to go to California. We're packing up now.'

'Oh.'

'My mother is sick and I couldn't leave the kids with someone they don't know – I'm sure you understand. I emailed you the moment I found out just how sick Mom is. I even tried to call you.'

Sophie found herself about to apologise for not getting the message or picking up the email and then she

49

remembered it wasn't her fault. She stifled a sigh. She felt deflated. An hour ago she'd been so excited to be here at last and moreover able to fund her trip and now it had all been snatched from her. What on earth was she going to do?

'Of course we'll still pay for your return ticket and everything as we dragged you over here,' the woman went on. 'We have your bank details, we can just transfer the money.' She paused. 'Have you got somewhere else you can stay? If you need money for a hotel . . .'

'Yes. I mean I have got somewhere to stay. I don't need money for a hotel.' Milly would help her out, surely. 'I'll be fine. Don't worry. I'll go now.' What she really wanted to say was, 'Could you transfer the money right now?'

She had a choice. She could have a panic attack and then ring Milly for help, or she could just ring Milly for help. Although it was fairly scary being alone in a big airport in a strange country she did at least speak the language, sort of, and panic was not constructive. She rang Milly's mobile.

Milly cursed in quite an Anglo-Saxon way when she heard Sophie's news but she didn't prevaricate. 'Get a taxi to my apartment. Don't pay more than forty dollars.' She paused. 'Have you got forty dollars?'

'Yes.'

'OK, but you'll need to tip him. It'll take you about an hour. I'll be waiting, but then I'll have to come back here. I'm at work.'

'But it's nearly ten o'clock at night! And it's Saturday!' Sophie felt another surge of panic.

'I know, but we've got our preview tomorrow and there's loads to do. I think I told you.'

Sophie remembered. Milly had a dream job, working for an artist who was not only famous for the amount of money his work sold for and his generous wages, but for the lavish parties he gave. But his employees worked hard for their money. 'Oh yes, you did.'

It was only when she was in the taxi she realised that not for a second had she thought about going straight home. How would she have faced her family? How could she have got so near to Milly and not even seen her, and how could she waste an air fare to New York? Besides, she had a mission, and now she'd have more time to pursue it.

Sure she was doing the right thing, Sophie's spirits began to lift. She was in New York, about to see her friend, and just being here was practically the same as being Sarah Jessica Parker!

She looked out of the window eager to spot landmarks and famous sights, but then she realised that the airport was quite a way away from the city itself and so she sat back and closed her eyes. She wanted to open them again and actually be in Manhattan.

The blaring of a horn wakened her from her doze. She sat up and looked out of the window, amazed at how familiar everything seemed and how different. Streetlights and billboards glittered and flashed, pulsating with life. Every song lyric or scrap of dialogue about New York she'd ever heard floated through her head, mostly in the voice of Frank Sinatra: 'The city that never sleeps'; 'So good they named it twice'; 'I like to be in America'.

She loved the Americanness of everything: the traffic lights suspended over the multilane highway; the yellow taxis; the bustle. As a child she'd spent quite a lot of time watching her older sister's video tapes and DVDs and sometimes she felt that she lived her life through the movies. Now she was actually here and it felt just like being in a film, not just being an observer.

What surprised her most was that the streets were wide,

and although the buildings were immensely tall, they didn't loom over narrow streets in the way they seemed to do in films. 'Too much *Superman*,' Sophie muttered to herself, excitement replacing jet lag and anxiety about having no job.

Even the buildings that weren't skyscrapers seemed much taller than similar buildings would have been in London.

How wonderful it would be to live here, she thought, or be like Milly and work here.

Milly's so jammy to have such an interesting job so young, she decided. She's only a couple of years older than me but she's got all that responsibility, working in a brilliant place at a job she loves, and look at me. Can't even get a job as a nanny!

Then she reflected that she'd been a very successful nanny and her lack of a job now was nothing to do with her shortcomings. And while it was a complete pain that her employers had pulled out like that, they were going to pay her air fare, and even if they didn't – especially if they didn't, in a way – she couldn't waste it. She had to make the most of every minute, follow her quest, track down her ancient relation and go home victorious. And even if it didn't make anyone a millionaire it would be something to have found out more about it. Uncle Eric would be impressed, anyway.

The taxi drew up outside Milly's building. They were in what Milly described as the Upper West Side, near Central Park, in a quieter street, and the building was 'a brownstone' (just like Carrie's in *Sex and the City*, Milly had told Sophie and Amanda when she first got her apartment). There was a long flight of steps up to the door and Sophie could see fire escapes marching diagonally down nearby properties; even at night, the place felt full of promise.

Sophie handed over some of her precious dollars, dragged her rucksack up the steps behind her and pressed the bell next to Milly's name. While she waited she looked up at the layers of red bricks divided by lines of white. The whole building seemed like the background for a film or television drama. Milly had told her that people quite often lived over their offices so residential and commercial properties were more mixed up than they were in most towns in England.

A few moments after she'd pressed the bell they were sharing an ecstatic hug, jumping up and down and screaming with excitement. 'Welcome to New York!' said Milly, and Sophie felt they were the most exciting words she'd ever heard.

Milly insisted on carrying Sophie's bag up the several flights of stairs to her apartment. 'I do warn you, it's tiny, but you can have it to yourself for a bit. I'm afraid I do have to go back to work. There's still loads to do before the show tomorrow. Here we are!'

She flung open the door on to what amounted to a bedsit with a small kitchen area up one end. There was a sofabed, a little table with two chairs and a row of bright raffia baskets full of clothes. 'It is a bit small,' said Milly, seeing it through Sophie's eyes.

'It's sweet,' said Sophie automatically, thinking that while it *was* tiny, far smaller than any of those in the television programmes, it would be so much fun to be with Milly. 'Size doesn't matter,' she said, and meant it. 'But it's so late! Do you really have to go back to work?' Sophie's spirits, made volatile by long-distance travel, took a dive. Suddenly she felt desperately tired – it was about five o'clock in the morning for her and the prospect of being abandoned so soon after her arrival was a bit depressing.

'I know, but it's the opening tomorrow,' Milly repeated

before carrying on with the guided tour. 'This is where it all happens: eating, sleeping, watching TV,' she said, 'and here's the kitchen.' She indicated an area of the room with a microwave, sink and fridge in it. 'Here is the bathroom. Only a shower, I'm afraid, but it works OK. Now, I've got to rush. Help yourself to anything you want.' She kissed Sophie again and opened the door to leave. Then she wheeled round. 'Oh, the bed's the settee. You have to pull it out. Can you manage?'

Sophie nodded.

'There's beer in the fridge,' said Milly, possibly picking up on Sophie's feeling of desolation. 'Help yourself. I'll sneak in when I come back, so as not to disturb you. You don't mind sharing a bed, do you? We did it hundreds of times when we were kids. We're going to have a great time!'

Sophie did feel a bit more cheerful once she'd been to the loo and washed her hands. Then she considered her options. Staying with Milly for more than the minimum amount of time didn't seem like one of them. Milly was right when she said they'd shared a bed, or rather a mattress on the floor, lots of times, but only ever for one night at a time. It wasn't going to work for more than a couple of days.

She found a beer and decided to drink it from the bottle. She needed to stretch out and sleep. She would work out how to turn the sofa into a bed and when she woke up, she'd make a plan. One thing she was absolutely certain of, she was not going to go back home to England without having achieved something worthwhile. If she did that, her family would never let her hear the end of it. Not only would she be a flibbertigibbet who'd spent a lot of money going after a job that didn't exist, but a gallivanting one as well. Her family were very fond of long words and liked to apply them to Sophie as often as possible.

As Milly set out for work again the following morning, having heaved a sleeping Sophie off the sofa and turned it into a bed in the early hours, she said, 'Why don't you come to the opening tonight? There'll be so many people no one would notice an extra bod.'

'I can't go to a posh gallery opening!' Sophie was shocked at the suggestion. She hadn't really got back to sleep after Milly got home and felt a wreck. 'People will think I'm a waitress and I'll develop a complex about it.'

Milly widened her eyes. 'Not if you don't dress like one! I'll lend you something. Now I've got to go. Have a nice day!'

Sophie waggled her fingers back at her friend, copying her ironic manner and wondering how to make the most of her time in New York. Job-hunting, she decided, she would leave until tomorrow. Today, she would explore.

Milly had given her a map, some instructions about the subway system that Sophie had forgotten, and pointed with her hand the way to the centre of town. Sophie decided to walk, especially as it was one of those glorious crisp-but-sunny autumn days.

Wrapped up against the chill, she managed to get herself to Central Park before she needed to get out the map. It seemed amazing to be in this huge, rural space, in which squirrels bounded about, people jogged and juggled, and yet still be within one of the biggest cities in the world. They had parks in London, of course, but for some reason that didn't seem so strange.

She had barely got her map unfolded when two separate people converged on her. 'Can I help? Are you lost?'

Sophie jumped. She'd been told, mostly by her family,

that New Yorkers were brusque and unfriendly, and in Central Park you were almost sure to get mugged. 'Not really lost – just checking—'

'Oh, you're English! What a cute accent! Where are you going? What are you planning to see?'

A second later she realised that neither of the two people, one a middle-aged woman, the other an older man in a suit, were in the least interested in mugging her and genuinely wanted to help.

'I just want to see as much of New York as I can, on foot,' explained Sophie.

'Shopping?' asked the woman.

'Window-shopping. I don't want to spend any money,' said Sophie firmly.

'Then I won't tell you where the discount stores are.'

'Let's get that map the right way up,' put in the man.

'You can have a great time in New York during the day, and not spend a cent,' said the woman.

'You can even go on a ferry ride,' the man agreed. 'The Staten Island ferry?'

'The one in *Working Girl*? Sorry, all my knowledge about New York is from films and television.'

'That's how I know about London,' agreed the woman, laughing. 'Never been there, but I know it well!'

By the time the pair of them had set Sophie on her way she no longer felt alone in a big city, she felt she was having an adventure; she loved it.

She had walked through the park and had arrived at the shops. She walked past the designer names, not daring to enter but just looking in the windows, wishing she was Carrie Bradshaw and could actually walk in heels that high, when she looked up and found she was outside Bloomingdale's. 'Bloomie's', home the of Little Brown Bag. With a little skip of excitement, she went in.

Almost instantly a beautiful young black woman stopped and asked her if she'd like to try some new perfume. Sophie hesitated and the young woman said, 'Would you like to come over to the counter? My colleague would be happy to help if there's something else you need.'

Sophie looked towards where the young woman was pointing. She saw an empty chair. She had walked a long way that morning. She went across.

'Hi!' said another beautiful woman, Hispanic this time. 'What can I help you with today?'

'Well, to be honest, I'm not going to be buying anything, but I'd love to—'

'Would you like me to put some make-up on you?' asked the woman. 'You have really lovely skin but I think we could bring out the colour of your eyes a little. Have a seat. Are you English?'

Half an hour later Sophie walked out of Bloomingdale's wearing twice as much make-up as she ever had before and with a clutch of samples that would keep her going for weeks. She had bought Milly a little something – a handbag-sized selection of make-up in a lovely purse – and herself some tights and was very happy to have two Little Brown Bags to swing. If she was careful the make-up would last until the opening that night.

The rest of the day was spent looking at New York. She found her way to the Empire State Building, went up in the 'elevator' with hundreds of other tourists and then discovered she really preferred the view with her back pressed against the building. Going down again she got chatting to a woman who told her she worked there, had done for years, and she didn't like heights either! She watched ice skaters at the Rockefeller Center, half wanting to join them, half glad to stop for a while.

She wanted to go everywhere on foot, partly to save

money and partly because the thought of a strange subway system was daunting on her first day. She got lost a few times and got her map out to find out where she was. Every time the same thing happened: people flocked to her, eager to help her on her way. She found Forty-Second Street and wanted to break into a tap dance, on Broadway she felt she ought to sing and, having got as far as Greenwich Village, she found the Magnolia Bakery, the shop where Carrie bought cupcakes. There was a queue of Japanese tourists outside it but she decided not to join them.

She had been absent-mindedly staring at what looked like a giant cake rack for cars, several layers of them, which was obviously a way of parking a great many cars in a small space, when she realised just how exhausted she was. Although it was extravagant, she hailed a taxi, deciding it was part of the New York experience and therefore a justifiable expense, and went back to Milly's. There she had a long nap, relishing having the bed to herself.

By the time Milly came home she was up for a party.

Chapter Five

❧

'It's a bit short,' Sophie said when she had put on Milly's dress and was inspecting herself in the mirror. It wasn't the first time she had borrowed Milly's clothes. Milly being that bit older than the other two, her wardrobe was more sophisticated than her friends', and Sophie and Amanda had always raided it.

Milly was inspecting her from behind. 'It's fine, as long as your tights haven't got ladders in them.'

'They're new,' said Sophie with her nose in the air, 'I bought them today, and they're called pantyhose.'

Milly laughed. 'Glad you're picking up the language. What about shoes?'

Sophie made a face. 'I haven't got anything smart. It's these old flat boots or trainers. On the whole, nannies don't need killer heels.'

Milly nodded. 'I'll lend you some heels. We're more or less the same size.' She burrowed in a box under the sofa.

'Those aren't shoes, Milly,' said Sophie when she saw the proffered footwear, 'those are stilts. I won't be able to walk.'

'But look how beautiful they are! Just put them on and quit moaning.'

Sophie fitted her feet into the shoes, unwilling to admit just how gorgeous they were. 'If you love them so much why aren't you wearing them?'

Milly looked quizzical. 'I could tell you it's because I

want you, my joint-best friend, to wear really heavenly shoes, Louboutin no less, to her first New York date.'

'But?' Sophie's mouth was twitching. She knew a better excuse was on its way.

'The truth is I'm working and you can't run around in those things. So I'll let you be the one to just stand about and admire your feet. Now, if you don't mind shifting yourself from in front of the mirror, I'd like to get my own slap on.'

Sophie went and perched on the sofa. 'While obviously New York is big enough for both of us,' she said, 'your flat really isn't. I'm going job-hunting tomorrow and I'll focus on the ones that say '"live in".'

Milly paused in her application of her second coat of mascara. 'Why don't you forget about trying to get a job, Soph? You can just stay with me and we'll have fun together. I know it's a bit cramped but I don't want you moving to the other end of town. That would be so dreary.'

'I'd feel bad just sponging off you. And you have to work. Besides, I'm on a bit of a mission. If I stayed with you I'd have to go home after a week – if I can change my ticket. I'll have run out of spending money, probably. Although if my air fare has been refunded directly into my account that would help.'

'There you are! No need to get a job or go home. We can just have fun together!'

'I must say it's just like when we were teenagers, getting ready to go out.'

'Yes,' agreed Milly. 'We just need Amanda to make it perfect.'

'Is it really going well for you in New York, Mills? Do you think you'll stay for ever?'

Milly shrugged. 'It's all just perfect now, of course:

lovely boyfriend, lovely job; but I think I'd miss England eventually.'

'Amanda's really settled too. It's just me who isn't.' She sighed.

'We're all too young to settle down really. Even me. Anyway, what mission? It sounds interesting,' said Milly, applying kohl under her lashes.

'It might be. When I was working for Uncle Eric I came across some papers that implied there are some drilling rights to some oil wells, left as shares to various members of my family . . .' She paused.

'Well, go on!' Milly said, reaching for her lipstick.

'It's such a long shot, but I'm going to see if I can track down everyone who's got shares and get them to join together so we can do something with the rights. Lease them out or something. Apparently some ancient relation was doing that before. She has an address in New York. If I could find out how far she got with the project, I could possibly carry on with it.'

'Mm, sounds fun – if a bit unlikely.' Milly made a doubtful face, obviously not wanting her friend to get too worked up about something that had such a slim chance of succeeding.

'I know, but I like a challenge, as you know.'

They exchanged glances in the mirror. 'Well, if anyone can pull something like that off, it's you. You're so resourceful.'

'Thank you. And think how my family would sit up and take notice of me if I was responsible for making them all rich.'

'They don't deserve to be rich! And they don't deserve you either. You're far too nice to them.' She paused and gave Sophie a little nudge with her elbow. 'Now, if you've put on your eyelashes, let's hit the town.'

Sophie gave a little skip and then wobbled precariously in Milly's high heels. 'I'm so excited to be going out in New York! Even if it is only going to a boring old art gallery.'

Sophie's philistine attitude to modern art was an old joke between them and Milly ignored this remark. 'Come on, you, and no putting off the buyers. If anyone asks you what you think of a painting, just say it's amazing.'

'Or bewildering.'

Reasonably confident that Sophie wouldn't deliberately do anything to embarrass her, Milly manoeuvred her friend out of the apartment door and locked it.

As they travelled through the streets of New York in a taxi (paid for by Milly's company) Sophie said, 'It's just like when we were at school, isn't it?'

'You were at school, I was at college. I didn't blag my way into pubs when I was underage. Just because you were tall you could get away with it.'

'I'm still tall,' said Sophie primly, 'and I still get ID'd.'

'You will here, too. You're not allowed to drink under twenty-one.'

'I know. Fortunately I have a passport. Oh look! Broadway's all lit up! This is so exciting! I can't believe I'm here! Now we're together it's even more like being in an episode of *Sex and the City*!'

Milly chuckled. 'You might not have had as much fun being a nanny. You wouldn't have been in the city, would you?'

'No, a little way outside, I think, but I would have had a roof over my head, and food. I could have got on with my mission.'

'Well, you still can.'

Sophie hesitated. 'I know. But I do need to find a job so I can stay here a bit longer than just a holiday. I need to earn some money to support myself.'

Milly bit her lip. 'I think finding work might be difficult.'

'Everything's difficult!' declared Sophie. 'But few things are impossible.'

'Huh!' said her friend. 'That sounds like the sort of slogan you'd find embroidered on a cushion.'

'It was on a little plaque actually,' said Sophie, chuckling.

Once at the gallery in Chelsea, Milly introduced Sophie to a few colleagues. Although they were friendly and welcoming, they were all busy and soon disappeared off. Sophie was left on her own.

She made her way through the crowds of people, none of whom seemed to be looking at the art, until she found herself within viewing distance of a picture. She examined it carefully, giving it the benefit of the doubt, but no, she didn't understand it, and she wasn't sure if she even liked it.

She tried a few more paintings, by different artists, but none of them moved her. She realised, sadly, that she really only liked paintings of things she could recognise.

Having just interpreted the signs to the bathrooms, and made her way to the corridor that led to them, she suddenly spotted an elderly lady. Something about her was wrong. Sophie stepped out of Milly's stilt-height shoes and ran.

As she rushed past the few people in the way to reach her, Sophie thought that if she was in a film, this scene would be shown in slow motion. Fortunately, in a sort of reverse rugby tackle, she reached the old lady just before she collapsed.

'Got you!' she said, skidding to a halt and catching her target. Then she lowered her gently to the ground, kneeling down with her to support her.

'Oh, my dear! How did you know I was feeling so faint?'

the old lady said after a few moments of panting and exclaiming, looking up at Sophie with gratitude.

'Something about you wasn't right. You just looked a bit tottery.'

The old lady shook her head as if still dazed. 'You have very quick reactions, and you're English!'

Sophie laughed. 'Yes, but I don't think the two things are necessarily related.'

'Well, maybe.'

The woman pulled down her skirt and patted her clothes back into place. She was wearing an elegant cream jersey suit and beautiful shoes and Sophie couldn't help noticing that the perfectly manicured hand supported a lot of flashing jewels. Sophie felt quite scruffy in comparison.

Other people came flocking up expressing concern. The old lady waved them away. 'This young woman will take care of me, thank you.'

Sophie sat down and stretched out her legs so as to be more comfortable. Now they were both sitting with their backs against the wall with their legs in front of them. 'Are you feeling better?'

'A little. Everything started to go black and I felt myself going.'

'That's what I must have spotted,' said Sophie. 'I've been looking after my great-uncle. It's sort of got my eye in for sudden wobbles.'

'I'm very grateful. If I'd fallen I might have broken something and been laid up for ages.'

'The trick is not to get up again too quickly. We'll just stay here until you feel completely better.' Her family sometimes complained that Sophie had no embarrassment gene. While she didn't think this was true, she was quite happy to sit there on the floor until it felt right to get the old lady up again.

'Just as well I'm too old to care about looking foolish,' said the old lady.

Sophie laughed. 'And I'm an English tourist and have no pride, so we can just sit and talk. But are you here on your own? Is there anyone I should find?'

'My grandson is in there somewhere. His girlfriend was meeting him here. He went off to look for her so I thought I'd go to the Ladies on my own.' She smiled up at Sophie with a twinkle. 'You see, I'm English too. Hearing your voice reminded me what we used to call things. Restrooms indeed, as if one would go in there for a little nap.' Then she frowned. 'Mind you, I was very young when I came over here, I am pretty well assimilated. I have tried to hang on to my accent.' To Sophie's ears she did sound American, but only slightly. 'I was a war bride,' the lady went on.

'Really? That's fascinating! Tell me about it!'

The two of them were happily chatting away, sitting on the floor of the art gallery, their legs being stepped over from time to time by women on their way to the bathroom, when a very tall and smartly dressed young man appeared, carrying Sophie's discarded shoes.

He was, Sophie decided, 'preppy'. He had a very neat haircut, a lovely suit, perfect shirt and very shiny shoes. His hair was dark blond and his eyes were probably green – she couldn't really see from where she was sitting. He didn't seem terribly amused to discover his grandmother sitting on the floor next to a young woman he had never seen before. There was a blonde woman hovering behind him wearing shoes Sophie realised she couldn't have even tried on without falling over. She didn't seem amused either.

'Are these yours?' The young man addressed Sophie, glancing down at her for a second before turning to the old lady. 'Grandmother, are you all right?' He crouched down. 'I heard you'd had an accident. Why didn't you call me?'

To his credit, Sophie decided, he seemed really concerned.

'Oh, don't fuss, dear. This lovely young woman has been looking after me. This is my grandson, Luke – Luke Winchester. Luke this is . . .'

'Sophie Apperly,' said Sophie.

'Oh!' said the old lady, turning sharply towards her. 'Is that a West Country name?'

'Yes, it is,' agreed Sophie.

This caused the old lady to give a nostalgic sigh. 'I came from the West Country!'

'Did you?' said Sophie. 'Which part?'

'You haven't put on your shoes,' broke in Luke Winchester, who didn't seem impressed by his grandmother's sentimental ecstasies about the Old Country.

'No.' Sophie could see his point. His grandmother could be ill; he wouldn't want to waste any time before getting her checked out. She took the offered shoes and put them on. 'They're too high for running in. When I saw your grandmother wobble, I just kicked them off and took off. I think she's OK.'

'Are you a doctor?' asked her grandson.

'No, but I do have—'

'I think my grandmother should see a doctor as soon as possible,' he went on.

'Absolutely,' agreed Sophie.

'Oh, don't fuss! I'm fine! It was just a little dizzy spell, but Sophie caught me before I could fall.' The old lady seemed to be thoroughly enjoying herself. 'And I'm Matilda Winchester, though my friends call me Mattie.' She patted Sophie's arm, as if conferring friendship.

'Are you going to sit there all night, Grandmother?' asked Luke.

66

Matilda twinkled up at Luke. 'Well, I am having a very nice time. Maybe I should!'

Something Sophie recognised as relief crossed Luke's rather stern features. 'If you feel well enough, I think you should get up. Besides, I've got someone I'd like you to meet.'

The blonde moved forward and took Matilda's other elbow as her grandson pulled her to her feet. Sophie, from the ground, pushed upwards on Matilda's bottom until she was safely upright. Then she clambered up herself.

'This is Tyler,' Luke was saying, 'Tyler Marin. Tyler, this is my grandmother, Mrs Winchester.'

Tyler put out her hand. 'I'm so pleased to meet you, Mrs Winchester. Luke talks about you all the time.'

'What an attractive characteristic you must find that,' said Matilda, looking up at the blonde intently.

Tyler laughed anxiously, not sure how to take this.

'Really, Grandmother, don't tease Tyler,' said Luke. 'I don't talk about you all the time, anyway.'

'Glad to hear it. It's one thing being a pillar of society but you don't have to be a crashing bore.'

Luke frowned. 'You've gotten very English all of a sudden.'

'I know!' His grandmother was unrepentant. 'It's meeting a fellow countrywoman. Now, dear – Sophie, was it? Come with us and have dinner. I want to get to know you better.'

The dismay on Luke's face almost made Sophie want to accept, had she been in a position to. 'I'd love to but I have plans – as they say here. I'm with my friend Milly and when she's finished here we're going out for dinner and then on to a club. It's to do with her work.'

'Oh, which club?' asked Tyler.

'Can't quite remember. Some animal name – with a number?'

'Bungalow Eight?' Tyler seemed impressed.

Luke, bored with this discussion, took action. 'Well, I hope you have a good time there, Miss . . .'

'Sophie, please,' said Sophie, sensing he really wanted to keep her at arm's length by calling her Miss but she got in quickly before he could add her surname.

At this moment Milly appeared. 'Sophie! What on earth are you up to? I heard there was some sort of commotion by the washrooms. I might have known you had something to do with it!'

'Oh, my dear, don't tell your friend off!' said Matilda. 'She saved me from falling on my – backside.' She gave her grandson a covert look. 'I want her to come and have dinner with us but she says she has a date. Is it with you?'

Milly nodded. 'Yes, I was just coming to collect her.'

'This is my friend, Milly,' Sophie announced, feeling that proper introductions would just go on too long.

'Good,' said Luke. 'I mean, it's great that Sophie won't be left on her own. We're leaving now. Thank you so much for looking after my grandmother.'

But Matilda wasn't going to be rushed. 'Now, Luke dear, I'm not going to let Sophie go without getting some contact details from her. Give her one of your cards; she can write her telephone number on the back for me.'

'It would be nice to see you again while I'm in New York,' said Sophie, taking the card and writing down her number.

'How long are you going to be here?' asked Luke, obviously not because he wanted to know but to be polite.

'It rather depends if I can get a job or not.' Sophie smiled and handed him the card. 'If not, I'll be here about another week.'

'Have you got a green card?' he asked.

'No,' said Sophie sharply.

'Then I'm afraid you'll find it very difficult.' He made this a statement, not an opinion.

'So everyone keeps telling me,' said Sophie, looking at Milly, 'but I'm afraid when people tell me things are very difficult, I just become more determined to do them.' As she said this she realised it wasn't necessarily a virtue.

Matilda obviously saw it as one. 'Good for you, my dear. A girl after my own heart. Luke, if you're not going to let me kidnap Sophie, take me to dinner!'

But although Luke would have done this with alacrity, Matilda wouldn't go without kissing Sophie, thanking her again and promising her that they'd be in touch. 'Oh and Luke, give her another of your cards, in case she needs to get in touch with me.'

'Grandmother, I had some very charming cards printed for you. Don't you have any with you?'

Matilda attempted to look apologetic, but not very successfully. 'I only have this silly clutch. The cards are in another purse.'

Luke handed over the card, his expression making it clear that he did not expect Sophie to use it.

Sophie looked at it and raised her eyebrows to express interest. She had no intention of getting in touch with him but she wanted him to worry that she might. What was it with him? Why was he so stuck up when his grandmother was so warm and friendly?

'Well, he was fit!' said Milly, holding Sophie's arm and leading her through the crowd.

'Yes.' Sophie was forced to concede this point, especially as she'd managed to establish that his eyes were in fact a sort of golden colour, with dark rings round the irises. 'But not friendly. His grandmother was lovely, though.'

'So how did you get involved?' Milly waved at the

growing group of her friends to indicate she and Sophie were on their way.

'I was staring into the middle distance—'

'As you do.'

'Well, as I do at art galleries, and I could tell she was about to faint or something, so I kicked off your shoes and ran to the rescue.'

'That was kind.' Milly sounded as if she were a little surprised by this act of mercy.

'Well, I couldn't let her fall, could I? She could have broken a hip.'

'But you don't know her. Someone else might have helped out.'

Sophie shrugged. 'I don't think so. Anyway, I sort of got into old people when I was looking after Uncle Eric. Everyone always assumes they're a real pain when lots of them are really fun.'

'Well, maybe I should drop you off at the old folks' home on our way to the club.'

'So, will we go to the top of the queue and give our names to the bouncer?' asked Sophie a little later. 'And when he sees we're on the guest list, he'll just let us in ahead of everyone?'

'No,' said a colleague of Milly's whose taxi they were sharing. 'He's booked an entire floor. We just go in.'

'Oh.' Sophie was obscurely disappointed. She wanted to have her name checked off against a list and feel like a celebrity.

Milly chuckled, understanding how Sophie felt. 'We can do that on another night if you like. Only of course we won't actually be on the guest list so we'll just be in the queue with everyone else.'

Sophie considered. 'Well, that would be fun in a rather different way.' Milly just rolled her eyes.

The next morning, Sophie, whose body clock was beginning to adjust to New York time but was still tired after an energetic night's clubbing, was dozing in front of the television, risking repetitive strain injury from pressing the remote control button. She was thinking about her job prospects, and slowly coming to the melancholy conclusion that everyone was right: it would be impossible, no matter how determined she was. Suddenly her phone rang. Still in awe of the fact that it worked so far away from home, she checked the number and realised she didn't know who it was. At home she didn't usually respond to numbers she didn't recognise but, thinking she was miles away from any stalker, or boy she didn't want to hear from, she answered it.

'Sophie, dear? Is that you? It's Matilda Winchester here. You saved my life at the art gallery yesterday.'

Sophie laughed with pleasure. 'I didn't exactly save your life—'

'Darling, you did – you may just not know how much.' There was a businesslike pause. 'Now, I'd like to see you again. How long are you going to be in New York?'

'Well, as I said, it really depends on whether or not I get a job.' Sophie sighed, she hoped silently. 'I do have some things I need to do before I go home anyway.'

'Well, let's not waste time! Have you seen the Frick?'

Sophie's mind whirled with possibilities as to what this dear woman might be talking about. Her family had conditioned her to scathing replies when she asked questions but she had to know. 'Sorry, what is the Frick?'

'Oh, I'm so sorry! Isn't it maddening when people just assume you know things when you have no *way* of knowing them? It's a perfectly delightful museum – art gallery – both, really.'

71

'Right. Um . . . although I was in an art gallery last night, I've decided I only really like paintings of things I can recognise,' Sophie replied cautiously.

'Then the Frick is for you! Let's meet there and then go for tea at this enchanting Austrian café nearby afterwards.'

Sophie was delighted at the prospect of seeing Matilda again, not only because she had really warmed to the old lady but because, with Milly out all day, she was quite lonely. However, she didn't want to spend a single unnecessary cent.

Matilda misinterpreted Sophie's silence and pressed on. 'Do you know where the Frick is? I'll meet you there at two. We can have a quick burst of culture and then have tea. The cakes at the café I have in mind are as good as anything you'll get in Vienna – or so people tell me. It's just next door to the Frick.'

Sophie couldn't help laughing. 'OK, that's a date. I'll meet you at two.'

Sophie showered and put on a bit of make-up, then she examined her wardrobe for appropriate museum-wear. Her flat boots were an absolute must, she decided, and built up her outfit from there. She ended up wearing a short denim skirt, opaque tights, and one of her customised cardigans and beads. It was a bit of a boho look, but it was comfortable and the best Sophie could do with the clothes she'd brought with her. She put on some lipstick, grabbed her coat and skipped out of the door.

The trouble with arranging to meet people 'at' places, Sophie decided, was that it was a bit vague. Was 'at' outside or inside? If she'd been meeting a friend they could have sorted out this problem in seconds with the aid of their mobile phones. Matilda may not have had a mobile phone. Sophie's only point of contact with her was her nephew Luke, with the dark blond hair and eyes to match.

As Matilda wasn't anywhere outside, Sophie decided to go in. Taking a deep breath, she climbed the shallow stone steps of the entrance.

Chapter Six

❧

Once inside the museum Sophie knew she'd made the right decision. The Frick, she decided, was like the ice cube in a glass of sparkling water, the stillness surrounded by the effervescence that was New York. She loved it.

'Oh, good you're here.'

Matilda's bright, nearly-English voice made Sophie turn round, smiling. She hadn't liked to wander far from the entrance and had been standing, drinking in the wonderful atmosphere. But she had been starting to wonder if she'd got the time or the place wrong, or if Matilda wasn't coming.

'I am sorry I'm late, my dear,' said Matilda, 'I was delayed.' She pursed her lips slightly and Sophie got the impression that the lateness wasn't Matilda's fault. The old lady paused slightly and then went on. 'My grandson Luke is insisting on joining us for tea. He seems to think . . .' She hesitated again. 'He seems to think I need protecting. He's unwilling to accept that you don't get to be my age without picking up a little bit about people.'

Sophie frowned slightly. 'Are you saying that your grandson thinks you're in danger from *me*?' She pointed at herself to make it clear whom they were talking about. 'But I rescued you! Without me you'd have ended up in a heap on the floor, possibly with a broken hip.'

'I know!' Matilda matched Sophie's indignation. 'Ridiculous, isn't it? But he is over-protective. When his father died, we became very close. His mother married again – rather quickly, he thought, and he's never really got on with his stepfather. Over the years the roles have reversed and he seems to think he has to watch out for me, instead of the other way round.' She paused and then exhaled and smiled as if shaking off the memory of a very unhappy time. 'But never mind, he can pay for tea. Let's go and look at some pictures. We're not due to meet him for an hour.' She chuckled. 'He had to get out of some meeting to join us, but he insisted.' Matilda took Sophie's arm, obviously determined to put her grandson's unreasonable behaviour out of her mind.

'Now, we can't see everything, darling.' Sophie's companion was firm, bordering on bossy. 'You never can, without getting artistic indigestion, so shall I take you to my favourites?'

Sophie was happy to go along with Matilda's wishes, still wondering why her grandson should worry about a woman who so obviously knew her own mind.

Matilda's favourites were the English paintings; they stopped in front of a canvas depicting Salisbury Cathedral. 'I come here when I'm feeling in need of a taste of home. Not that it's exactly the right part of England, but as England really is very tiny, Salisbury would be considered practically next door to Cheltenham to an American.' She glanced at Sophie. 'So where in the West Country do you come from?'

'I come from the Cotswolds – which is a pretty big area, really.'

'Me too!' said Matilda. 'Which is why when I heard your name I knew we were going to be friends. My grandparents came from Cornwall.'

They surveyed the two Constables. 'Wow,' said Sophie, 'they're really quite different from when you see them on birthday cards, aren't they?'

75

Possibly aware of the startled response of a couple of other visitors, Matilda drew her young friend along. 'There is something about seeing the real painting instead of a reproduction that is so different, like seeing the real sea and not just a postcard. Now, would you like to see some French artists? My grandson thinks they're rather vulgar but I like things to be pretty!'

'Is your grandson an art expert, then?'

'Oh, no, he's an attorney. Why would you think he was an expert?'

'Just because we met at that art show. I was there because my friend Milly works for the artist. You weren't considering buying anything, were you?'

'Goodness me, no! It was just a social thing. People don't go to those shows to look at the work, you know. At least, not many of them.'

Sophie chuckled. She may have been wearing clothes she'd bought from jumble sales and customised for probably half the price of one of Matilda's shoes, but they were having a conversation about art she could enjoy and take part in. Matilda didn't exclaim at her ignorance the way her family always did or dismiss her opinion outright.

Was it the fact that she was English that made Matilda so different from her handsome grandson? He seemed so buttoned up and tense, while she was so elegant and relaxed, wearing her wealth with nonchalant authority. It didn't stop her befriending a young woman who was obviously (although not too obviously, Sophie hoped) from a very different world.

They ambled through the girls on swings and ample women who didn't seem at all worried about their bums looking big in their bits of drapery and found their way to the Holbeins.

'You can really feel the softness of that fur, can't you?'

76

Sophie said, in front of a portrait of Sir Thomas More. 'It's all right,' she added, 'I know better than to touch. It's just so skilled though, isn't it? The paintings at the private view last night were just . . . well, different.'

'Thinking about art is like thinking about the sky,' declared Matilda. 'There are many sorts and they all have their fans.'

Sophie chuckled. 'I just like this sort best,' she said, indicating the perfect brush strokes they were looking at.

'So do I really,' agreed Matilda, 'but I do like to keep an open mind about art, otherwise one just keeps harking back to one's favourites and never learns anything. Talking of favourites, let's go and see the Vermeers, then we can have tea.'

In fact, they looked at far more paintings than they intended to and were late by the time they reached the café, which fortunately was very near. Sophie hated being late, but Matilda had no intention of hurrying, not even for her beloved grandson. Sophie tried to adopt her insouciant attitude.

Luke was already seated at a table and waved at them, which meant they could pass the small queue that was forming. As they moved between the tables to where Luke was sitting, Sophie noticed that the music was coming from a grand piano, and the dark panelled wood gave the impression of an earlier era. Huge carved coat stands reminded Sophie of stags' heads. It seemed to her to be like the Frick Museum, and unlike the rest of New York. Matilda had told her it was the nearest thing to Vienna outside Vienna.

On the table were two pots of tea and a selection of the most heavenly-looking pastries that Sophie had ever seen. Luke got up as they approached and kissed his grandmother fondly. He nodded to Sophie with cool formality, impeccably polite but somehow disapproving. She nodded back, wanting to laugh – he was so incredibly stuffy.

'I ordered because I am on a tight schedule,' he explained. 'Is Earl Grey tea good for you?' he asked Sophie.

'Oh yes, fine. I usually drink "builders'", but I like Earl Grey too.' Something in his expression told her that Indian tea wasn't usually described as 'builders'' in his circles. Being American, he probably didn't drink tea at all; he was drinking coffee now.

'I do hope this hasn't been sitting around for too long,' said Matilda, picking up a silver pot and turning to Sophie. 'You'll find it very hard to get a good cup of tea in America.'

'Considering you've been here since you were nineteen and tea was rationed in England when you left, I'm surprised you're such an expert,' said Luke.

'I have been to London a few times since, dear. You get lovely tea at Brown's,' said Matilda, taking this gentle tease for what it was. 'Have something to eat and don't be so grumpy. How's that lovely girlfriend of yours?'

'Still lovely, but no longer a girlfriend.'

'Why did you bother to introduce her to me if it wasn't going to last?'

Luke hesitated. 'I didn't know it wasn't going to last. And it's become known that getting to meet my grand-mother is very important for girls who go out with me.'

'Is it?' Matilda was bemused. 'Why?'

Luke shrugged. 'I guess people know you're important to me.'

Sophie couldn't help sensing there was something Luke wasn't saying. Was it to do with Matilda's vast wealth? Maybe Luke wasn't wealthy in his own right and any girl— She stopped her train of thought abruptly. It wasn't like her to be cynical. Why should women want Luke for his money or worry if he didn't have enough of it? He was seriously handsome. Sadly, far too preppy and conventional for her taste.

Matilda was looking pityingly at her grandson, who didn't seem at all sorry for himself. 'You do get through them! Poor Luke.' Matilda turned to Sophie. 'Girls are attracted to him by his enormous fortune and his good looks.' That answered that particular question.

'So why don't they stick around then?' asked Sophie. After all, if he was independently wealthy, what was putting them off? And then she realised it probably wasn't them dropping Luke, but the other way round.

'Maybe they sense when their presence is no longer welcome,' he said.

He looked at her coolly, possibly giving her a hint. Sophie looked back, her expression conveying that he really needn't worry, he wasn't her type.

Matilda frowned slightly and Sophie got the impression there was something she wanted to say but couldn't. Instead she picked up her pastry fork and studied the plate of cakes speculatively. 'New York is so full of lovely young women. The young metrosexual is spoilt for choice.'

Sophie and Luke both regarded her in amazement. 'Grandmother, where do you pick up these expressions?' asked Luke in astonishment.

Delighted by his reaction, she turned away from the pastries. 'Here and there. One does live in the modern world, after all.' She paused. 'And why don't you call me Granny any more, like you did when you were little? Grandmother is so matriarchal.'

'I just felt, now I'm an adult—'

'You have been for some time, dear. You're thirty-two.'

'That's not so very old,' put in Sophie, ten years younger. 'He's got plenty of useful life ahead of him.'

'I'm grateful you think so,' said Luke, giving her a look that implied only his grandmother was permitted to tease him.

Sophie twinkled at him. Anyone who knew her would recognise this was a sign that she might not conform.

'Let's concentrate,' said Matilda. 'This one, if I'm not mistaken, is chocolate and hazelnut, one of my favourites. And that one is . . . what's that one, darling?'

'Pistachio and chocolate,' said Luke. 'And that's a real Black Forest gateau.'

After some more chat about various family members and who should have which cake, still no cake decisions had been made. Matilda got up. 'I must find the restroom,' she said. 'Luke, can you get some more hot water, or maybe some fresh tea. Sophie, if you want to try a piece of genuine Black Forest gateau, this is your chance.'

'Would you like me to come with you to the Ladies?' Sophie asked, half rising.

'No thank you, dear. I feel perfectly well and I have no intention of fainting.'

As Matilda left, Sophie took another sip of tea. Over her cup she saw that Luke was fiddling with his cake fork nervously. She smiled encouragingly. She couldn't work out why this man of the world should be uncomfortable with her when in reality she was a penniless nobody and an acquaintance of his grandmother's, not his.

He cleared his throat. 'I want to talk to you!'

'Well, go ahead. I'm listening.'

'It's slightly awkward. My grandmother is a very warm-hearted and generous woman.'

'I know! She's lovely!' Sophie exclaimed, thinking how kind Matilda had been to her and how much fun they had had together.

'And you're very attractive.' He cleared his throat again

and went on quickly. 'I mean you're very appealing – to an elderly woman like my grandmother.'

'Oh. So you're taking back your compliment? You don't think I'm attractive, you just think your grandmother does?' While this was disappointing, it was also quite funny and she smiled.

'Yes – no – Why are you determined to wrong-foot me?' He scowled.

'Sorry!' She smiled again, but he didn't seem reassured.

'What I want to tell you, before my grandmother gets back, is that she intends to ask you to stay with her.' He sounded as if he was warning her about something potentially hazardous.

'Oh?' Sophie was surprised, but not daunted. 'How very kind of her.'

'And I want you to say no.'

'Why?'

'Because she's a vulnerable old woman! I don't want her preyed on by . . .' He paused. Sophie could tell that being caught out in quite appalling rudeness was not a comfortable situation for him.

'By "appealing"' – she made visible speech marks – 'young women from England?' Sophie liked to be helpful.

'Yes! I mean . . . That isn't to imply . . .'

'What you're saying is, you don't want to imply that I'm in any way a threat to your grandmother but you don't want to take the chance?'

'You're making this very difficult for me.'

'Not at all,' said Sophie calmly, sipping her tea. 'I'm making it very easy for you. I'm putting into words what you don't seem able to.'

'I really don't wish to be rude but I do have to look out for my grandmother.'

'Actually, I don't think you have to at all. She's very

bright and has got all her marbles. I think you're fussing unnecessarily.'

'I know she's bright, but . . . she does have strange flights of fancy. She befriends people – people who may not have her best interests at heart.'

'I see.' She felt sorry for Luke because she sympathised with his concern for his grandmother, but she couldn't help feeling that he was being over-protective. And, of course, impossibly smug. 'And you think I'm one of them?'

'No – maybe – I don't know! You are . . . different, and my grandmother is vulnerable . . .' He stopped.

'Yes?'

'And you're a young woman from her part of England. She's bound to be attracted to you.'

'You said.'

'And I don't want you to take advantage of her.'

Sophie frowned. She understood, admired even, Luke looking out for his grandmother but she wasn't going to be practically accused of being a confidence trickster. 'And I won't.'

'You would say that, wouldn't you?'

Now Sophie was cross. He was being impossibly rude, practically implying she was going to try and wheedle money or something out of his grandmother. 'Are you saying you don't trust me?' It was blatantly obvious that he didn't, but Sophie liked things spelt out.

'No! It's not you I don't trust! At least . . .' He smiled slightly and for a moment Sophie saw the grandson that Matilda loved so much and she forgave him, just a little. 'I don't trust either of you.'

Sophie inspected him, in his business suit, pale pink shirt and pink and grey striped tie and felt just a tiny bit sorry for him. He was obviously quite good at getting rid of his own unwanted girlfriends, but those of his grandmother he obviously found harder. She decided to put him out of his misery. 'But why not? I certainly have no intention of doing anything to harm her,' she began. 'In fact—'

She was just about to say that she had no intention of accepting her invitation to stay, should one be forthcoming, when Matilda reappeared.

'Did you order more tea, Luke?' she asked. 'The service here can be a bit slow.' She looked around for a waiter.

'The service is a bit Austrian,' said Luke, raising his hand in a commanding way.

'Why aren't you eating a cake?' asked Matilda, when she saw that Luke had attracted someone's attention. 'I left you ages ago. You should have made up your minds by now.'

'Luke and I were just chatting,' said Sophie, not wishing to worry her with the truth.

'Oh good!' Matilda almost clapped her hands in delight. 'I'm so glad you're getting on!'

Sophie caught Luke regarding his grandmother. Something in his expression hinted to Sophie that he was not convinced by her acceptance of Sophie's description about what had been going on, and that he thought her happiness was a little exaggerated.

Matilda was still inspecting the pastries. 'If you can't decide I'll narrow the choices for you. I'll have that one.'

Now Matilda was back, Sophie felt a bit more comfortable, but she still wasn't really in the mood for cake. Even a cream-and-black-cherry-filled dream like the gateau before her was less tempting with Luke's disapproving gaze on her. Why had he insisted on butting in on the tea party? She and Matilda could have had such a jolly time without him. And all that desire to protect his grandmother was excessive. She wasn't helpless and he should be a better judge of character and realise that she wasn't the sort of girl to inveigle wealthy old women out of their fortunes. Although, she admitted privately, he hadn't had a chance to really get to know her.

When they all had fresh cups of tea of the right strength and suitable enormous cakes on their plates, Luke said to Sophie, 'So, how's the job-hunting going?'

This seemed to be a loaded question. Was he about to accuse her of doing something illegal? Or was he suspecting her of being someone who didn't actually want to work and would rather get her money more easily?

'I think I've abandoned trying to get a job.'

'Oh?' Matilda leant forward. 'So why did you think of getting one before?'

'Because when I came, I thought I had one. As a nanny. But when I got to the airport and rang to find out where my family was, they told me they were going to California instead.'

'How awful for you!' Matilda put her hand on Sophie's. 'So now you're just going to stay for a holiday? Why don't you seem happier about that?'

Sophie wondered if it was wise to explain to two people she didn't really know about her mission, but then decided she had nothing to lose. 'I have something I want to do in New York and it might take a bit of time. I can't afford to stay just as a tourist, at least for more than about a fortnight.' She might make her money last that long if she was really careful.

'And what is it you want to do?' asked Matilda.

'I want to track down an ancient relative. I need to find something out from them.'

'Where do they live?' asked Luke.

'In New York.'

'But whereabouts?'

'I have the address here,' she said, rummaging in her bag. After a second or two she produced it.

84

'Why don't you sort it out for her, Luke?' Matilda said. 'You could track down this relative for her very easily.'

'No, it's OK!' Sophie really didn't want to be beholden to Luke. Although she held the paper near to her he leant over and tweaked it from her fingers.

'This address isn't in New York.'

'Yes it is! I copied it very carefully.'

'It's upstate New York, not the city.'

'Oh.' This was a bit of a downer and not just because visiting this relative – Cousin Rowena – would be more than just a matter of jumping in a cab and giving the address. It was giving Luke and his grandmother the impression that she didn't know New York was a huge state. She just hadn't looked at the address properly. She'd been so set on getting to the right side of the Atlantic, and since she'd arrived she'd been concerned with how she could stay. 'Well, I'll just have to get on a Greyhound bus or something,' she said brightly, trying not to think of old films in which people had done this and ended up not having a nice time, even if they were still alive. She often related her life to films, it came of having watched so many of them when she was little with her big sister.

'Are you sure they haven't passed on, dear?' asked Matilda. 'Not everyone is blessed with the good health I enjoy.'

'Well, no, I'm not.' Suddenly gloomy, Sophie gathered up some cream and cherry juice with the edge of her pastry fork.

'In which case,' said Matilda glibly, 'let Luke find out for you. No point in going all that way for nothing. And I don't like to think of a young girl like you alone on a Greyhound bus. I suppose I could send you with my driver . . .'

Sophie's gloom lifted as she saw the flash of horror cross

Luke's face. She was very tempted to accept this half-made offer, just to see what'd he do.

'But if Luke sorts that out for you, you can come and spend Thanksgiving with me. I mean at home, in Connecticut, not here.'

'Oh but you're being far too kind,' Sophie protested.

'Have you plans for Thanksgiving?' Matilda almost demanded.

'Um . . .' Sophie felt caught out. She and Milly had been discussing – arguing even – about this major American festival. Milly had insisted that her new boyfriend's family would be happy to include her in their plans but as the plan was that the family was flying in from Buffalo to stay in their son's tiny New York apartment, Sophie had refused. Thanksgiving was American, the day had no significance for her so sitting at home on her own would be fine. They hadn't resolved the argument before Milly had had to dash off for work.

'I don't think Sophie would really want to leave New York to stay in the country,' said Luke. 'She'll want to watch the parades, visit the sites, eat cupcakes from that little place in the Village, and all that sort of girly thing.'

'Not at Thanksgiving,' said Matilda firmly.

Until that moment Sophie had felt exactly like that. However much she liked Matilda she didn't know her all that well and she wanted to enjoy the city and continue playing at being Carrie Bradshaw, even if only for a short time. But hearing Matilda say Thanksgiving like that made her suddenly yearn to make biscuits (cookies even) in the shape of turkeys and not clatter about New York in stilt heels.

'Sophie?' Matilda's bright eyes were enquiring and a little imperious. 'What plans do you have?'

She hesitated just a moment too long.

'You see?' said Matilda triumphantly. 'She's alone in the city with no family, she must come to us.'

'I do have Milly,' Sophie protested.

'Who will have had her plans made ages since. Does Milly have a boyfriend?'

'Yes. He's a chef. His family are coming—'

'I'm sure they are good people who would make you feel welcome but you would be in the way, physically, I mean.'

Sophie mumbled something, half in protest, half in agreement.

'I would so love for you to join us for Thanksgiving,' said Matilda, putting her ring-encrusted hand on Sophie's. 'I'm planning a very big party, all the family, and I could do with a hand.'

'Granny!' Luke protested. 'You have about sixteen staff! You really don't need Sophie as well!'

'I want her. Need and want have very little to do with each other.'

Only a very rich woman could say things like that and mean them, thought Sophie, looking from one to the other as grandmother and grandson argued about her.

'You give parties all the time,' said Luke. 'Why would you want to involve Sophie?'

'It's going to be a large party, and I thought she might like to be part of a traditional American Thanksgiving,' said Matilda. 'Anyway, please don't interrogate me any more. You're putting me off my Klimt torte. And don't look so surprised I know what it's called. Luke dear, don't you have to be somewhere?'

Luke drained his cup and surveyed the two women in front of him. 'Well, I can tell I'm not wanted. Sophie, if you give me that address, I'll do some research for you and get back to you. May I have your cellphone number?'

Sophie gave it to him, feeling it was very unlikely that he'd use it.

*

She was recovering from too much sugar and cream back at Milly's apartment when he got in touch.

'You can't have found out about my antique relation already, can you?' she asked him when he announced who he was.

'Of course not. I haven't even started looking.'

'Oh. So why are you ringing?' said Sophie after a pause while she waited for him to tell her what he wanted.

'I wanted to invite you out for a drink this evening.'

Sophie nearly dropped her phone in surprise. 'Why?'

She heard a chuckle at the other end of the line. This surprised her, as did her instinctive reaction to it. 'Because I want to get to know you better?'

'Do you?' she asked suspiciously.

'You're a very questioning young woman. My grandmother has invited you to stay with her for Thanksgiving. I'd like to get to know you a little before that happens. It would be more comfortable for you too, if you knew me as well as my grandmother. It will be quite a big party.'

'Yes, I suppose you're right.' She wasn't entirely convinced.

'So? Are you free? Or do you have plans?'

The coward in Sophie, which was well suppressed, wanted to say: Yes, I have plans. But she was more curious than shy. 'Well, nothing that can't be changed.'

'Could you meet me at the Thursday House? It's a bar, not too far away from you.'

Sophie had heard of the Thursday House. It was, as her mother would have put it, '*le dernier cri du chic*' – in other words, drop-dead elegant. If Milly ever found out she'd been invited and not gone she'd be out on her ear. 'OK,' she said tentatively. 'What sort of time?'

She rang Milly at work the moment Luke had called off. 'Guess what? Preppy Luke has invited me for a drink at the Thursday House!'

'Ohmygod! That's amazing. He must fancy you!'

'No, really, I don't think so. I'm not getting that impression at all.'

'Well, if he doesn't fancy you why does he want to take you out, do you think? Are you sure he's not going downmarket, as a change from the model types he usually goes for?'

Sophie laughed. 'No! He says it's to get to know me better if I go to stay with his grandmother for Thanksgiving. Though I do think there's something else going on.'

'Well, we'll find out soon enough. Listen, borrow my dress again. And the shoes. Take a cab. And make notes, secretly of course; I want every detail!'

Chapter Seven

It would have been better if she'd had more clothes with her, thought Sophie, trying to disguise the outfit she wore for the private view with Milly's junk jewellery. Fortunately, she had a good selection of necklaces and Sophie selected three, one of which had a pair of matching earrings that Sophie also borrowed. One of the pieces had a fall of stones that drew discreet attention to her cleavage and, while only a hint of it was on show, it was a good look. Spraying on Milly's perfume added a final squirt of confidence. Putting her shoulders back and having a smile ready to produce at any moment finished off her preparations. Mixing with New York's high society was very hard work.

As Sophie wasn't sure how long it took to get anywhere in New York, getting a cab made her early. Had she not been wearing Milly's heels, she'd have walked up and down a bit so as not to arrive before her date, but she could only walk for very short distances before burning pain in the balls of her feet made her need to stop.

Several young men dressed in Armani suits were hovering round the entrance. Bouncers or doormen? Or were the two things the same? Sophie had no time to reach a conclusion before they'd flocked about her and ushered her into the building, opening the door, saying hello and wishing her a pleasant evening.

Once inside an equally stylish woman came up to her and asked if she could help.

Sure she was going to be either ushered out again or shown to the service area, Sophie said, 'Good evening, I'm meeting Luke Winchester?'

'Oh yes. Mr Winchester isn't here yet but if you follow Carla, she'll show you to his usual table.'

'Mr Winchester's usual table' was on the top floor, Sophie discovered, having joined Carla in a very fast lift, which got her there in seconds but left part of her on the ground floor.

Sophie tripped after Carla, wishing she'd practised walking, and followed her through a large area full of tables and chairs. As they made their way between them, Sophie spotted an open fireplace where what appeared to be real logs crackled merrily. She caught a glimpse of two pizza ovens and at least two bars before Carla stopped at a table that looked out over Central Park and the city beyond.

'Wow!' said Sophie. 'What an amazing view!' All of Manhattan seemed spread out before her. Everything sparkled; every building seemed outlined with light. It was magical.

'You can see why it's Mr Winchester's favourite spot,' Carla agreed. 'And you should see it when it's decorated for Christmas. The day after Thanksgiving, the lights go up and it's a fairy land.' She paused. 'Now, can I get you something to drink?'

Sophie was about to refuse but then said, 'A white-wine spritzer, please.' Drinking it would give her something to do with her hands. She was feeling a little nervous now she was here. She suspected Luke's wanting to 'get to know her' also meant checking her out.

A waiter appeared from nowhere and put a coaster, a napkin and a bowl of nuts on the table. She was about to sample the nuts when she remembered something she'd heard about beer nuts being tested and seven different samples of urine being found on them. This was caused by men not washing their hands after they'd been to the loo. Would this apply here? Would the clientele be properly brought up? Or would the Thursday House throw away any uneaten nuts? She sighed and decided to risk it.

She was just wishing she'd brought a book or magazine or something when a party of four young women came in: variations on a theme by Paris Hilton; tiny skirts, precipitous shoes and enough bling to furnish a medium-sized jeweller's. They seated themselves at the table behind Sophie so while she could no longer admire their flawless fake bakes or wonder if they'd had 'work' done to their ski-jump noses or self-supporting breasts, she could now eavesdrop without being noticed.

'So tell me, Kelly,' said one. 'Why have we chosen this particular table?'

There was amusement in her voice which had a tone and accent Sophie recognised from *Clueless* – one of her favourite films. Sophie stopped worrying about being bored. She sipped her drink and began to relax.

'You know quite well,' her friend replied, equally cool. 'It's for the view.'

'Oh,' said a third. 'It's not because a certain bachelor who must be due to come back on the market just about now sits here?'

'I'm not sure if you've been married, even if you're now divorced, you're ever described as a bachelor again.' There was a languorous sigh. 'Which is a shame.'

'It is a shame that Luke Winchester has been married before – it means his wealth has been diminished – but otherwise, honey, no one is perfect. If that's his only flaw—'

'You are shameless!'

Just then, a waiter appeared and while they were ordering drinks, Sophie was able to consider the fact that Luke had been married before. If he'd had to pay a very large divorce settlement it might make him wary of women, which could explain why he was so weird about her and Matilda. Now Sophie sighed. These young women were so cynical about marriage. They could only be about the same age as she was, but they seemed so world-weary. And although they were perfect to look at, they seemed older. She thought it likely they would go on looking the same for years until one year the age they looked would coincide with the age they were. At the moment they seemed twenty going on thirty-six, but definitely on purpose.

'Well, I can't believe we're stalking him,' drawled another, having taken a sip of a no-doubt highly sophisticated something. 'It is *so* childish.'

'But so fun! My mother will be thrilled if I meet him. She's been planning my wedding since I was six.'

'Since when did you care about what your mother wants?'

'Well, I suppose I've been kind of planning it too.' There was a tinkle of laughter, possibly indicating she was not alone in this.

'And Luke *is* the most eligible bachelor in New York,' said the one planning her wedding. 'I need a rich bridegroom. That is why we're here.'

'I'm not sure he's got enough money left after his divorce.'

'Does he have a Lear? I don't think he does.' It sounded as if this lack could knock him off that top spot for eligible men as far as this particular young woman was concerned. 'Commercial flights are so boring.'

'A Gulfstream, honey. A Lear is only for short hops.'

More laughter. Sophie sat there riveted, looking out at

Manhattan twinkling before her to disguise the fact that she was eavesdropping, although they clearly hadn't spotted the 'mystery' girl sitting at Luke Winchester's table. Since she was not quite up to their immaculate standards she was no doubt invisible to them.

'There's absolutely no evidence that the credit crunch has hit the Winchester empire,' said one.

'You're so obsessed with money,' complained another. 'Don't you want to marry Luke because he's so cute-looking?'

'He'll get all his grandmother's money when she dies,' went on the one who'd know what sort of jet the family had. 'She's really, like, old.'

Although young herself, Sophie didn't share the notion that anyone over thirty was facing death. Matilda didn't seem all that old. Anyone could have a funny turn, after all. She could go on for years. Cheered by this thought, she took another nut from the bowl in front of her.

'Do you think we should be thinking about marriage yet?' asked one of the girls, who seemed less comfortable with the conversation. 'I mean, there is more to life.'

There was a short silence while the group considered this revolutionary idea.

There was a sigh from one. 'You can't spend your whole life shopping and it kind of gets it over? You know? You're not having to constantly be on the lookout for eligible males, once you're married.'

'Although it didn't stop Luke's first wife . . .'

'Maybe Luke is boring in the sack.'

'Nah-huh.' This was denied by someone who obviously had inside information. 'He likes his women bright, apparently.'

'Which is why he'll like us. I'm very bright.'

'And very modest! Do you keep your SAT scores in your purse?'

This created more laughter. 'Not in this purse, sweetheart, they'd push it all out of shape.'

'Whatever, I think he'll be a tough one to hook. Apparently he's not keen on commitment. A girlfriend of my sister's went out with him. She had her dress designer all primed, silk ordered, but when he found out, he was off to LA in a second.'

'She should never have let him find that out!'

'Yeah, but weddings take so long to arrange! If you waited until the guy actually asked you to marry him, you'd never get it done in time!'

A gale of perfectly honed laughter greeted this. Sophie didn't know if she'd just heard a truth universally acknowledged in the world in which these girls lived, or a perfectly ridiculous statement.

'Are we going to get more drinks?'

Sophie could imagine French-manicured fingers waggling to get the attention of the waiter who must have been waiting for the call. She was just trying to work out if the cocktails they were ordering were alcoholic or 'innocent' when she saw someone approaching her table and realised it was Luke. She shot to her feet a second before she realised she should have stayed sitting down, cool and sophisticated.

'Good evening, Sophie,' he said, kissing her on both cheeks. 'You look lovely.' He sounded slightly surprised.

'Thank you. It's the dress I was wearing at the private view the other night.'

She wasn't quite sure why she said this but it may have been something to do with the young women sitting behind them, who were suspiciously silent now.

'Yes, I realise that.' Luke still seemed a little bewildered. 'I've never – I mean, I didn't know girls wore . . .'

'. . . dresses more than once?' The girls at the table behind her had given her a bit of valuable insight.

He nodded.

'Well, they do. At least I do.' Then Sophie realised he was waiting for her to sit down before he could and found herself wrong-footed by his good manners. None of her boyfriends in England would have even realised they were supposed to behave like this, let alone actually done it. She sat down and he took the chair opposite.

'What are you drinking?' He glanced down at her now empty glass. 'Would you like some champagne?'

'Oh yes,' said Sophie, thinking she needed more Dutch courage than another spritzer would supply. 'I definitely would.'

The party at the table behind them were still strangely quiet.

The waiter appeared without Luke actually doing anything to summon him and he placed the order.

'Are we celebrating anything?' asked Sophie after a bottle of champagne appeared, as if it had been waiting for the call, and the waiter poured it.

'Not particularly, but my grandmother said I was to be nice to you.'

'Oh. So if she hadn't . . . ?'

'Tap water.' He said it without even a flicker of a smile and it took Sophie several agonised seconds to realise he was joking. Nerves made her laugh more than the joke warranted; it wasn't very funny.

'Here's to your first visit to New York, Sophie,' said Luke a few seconds later and raised his glass.

'Thank you.' Sophie couldn't think of anything to toast in reply so just sipped her drink.

There was a long silence. The girls behind them were also silent, either unable to think of anything neutral to say, or anxious not to miss anything.

'This is a little awkward,' said Luke at last.

Sophie felt the same, only she'd have said 'very awkward'. This man had invited her for a drink, ostensibly to get to know her better, and now wasn't saying anything. 'Can I help? Make it less awkward?'

Luke sighed. 'Well, you could suddenly discover you had other plans for Thanksgiving, but my grandmother is determined you're to spend it with us. I'm resigned to it.'

'Why don't you want me to come? Matilda has plenty of room, surely?' He had tried to put her off at the café, now she was determined to get to the bottom of his reticence.

'Yes, she has plenty of room.'

'So what's the problem?'

'It's hard to explain.'

'Well, give it a go. You're a New York lawyer. According to films and television they're never short of a pithy explanation or snappy question.'

He smiled but still seemed discomforted. 'OK. My grandmother is a very wealthy woman and she has been preyed on before.'

'What do you mean?' Sophie bristled. Why was he using words like 'preyed on' in connection with her? Surely he didn't suspect her of ulterior motives still, did he?

He sighed. 'A young woman with a child came to stay with her. My grandmother gave the child some very expensive toys.'

'And that's bad?' Did this man want his grandmother to keep all her money so he could inherit more?

'It wasn't just that. My grandmother allowed this woman to stay in our place on the beach – just a little shack really, but she didn't leave for quite a while.'

Again, it didn't seem a major crime. 'She squatted, you mean?'

'She stayed there without permission. We had to have her evicted.'

'And you think I may do that? Well, let me reassure you, I'm English, I have a return ticket. I can't just stay in the country indefinitely. But if you prefer me not to come, that's fine, but you have to explain it to Matilda. I couldn't think of a way that wouldn't be incredibly rude.'

Sophie really hoped her indignation wasn't obvious but inside she was fuming. He really did suspect her of wanting to get something out of Matilda, of exploiting her good nature. She hadn't really believed it before. How dare he? It was insulting.

'If you want to stay, and promise not to do anything to hurt Granny, then you can. But if you do anything, anything at all, I'll have you deported before you have time to pack your toothbrush.'

Sophie took a breath. Throwing champagne over him and storming out was not an option, not even if she could walk properly. 'I appreciate you looking out for your grandmother but I really don't see why you see me as a threat. I haven't got a child, I'm on a tourist visa, I'm hardly going to camp out at your family's little shack on the beach, which probably has about three bathrooms.'

'Four, actually, and I'm sorry to seem neurotic but she's very dear to me. Since my father passed on I'm the only close relation Granny's got this side of the country.'

'Well, it's nice that you care about her. My family seem to think that elderly people are only good for—' She stopped, aware she shouldn't reveal her family's mercenary tendencies in case he thought it was a characteristic they all shared. 'What I'm trying to say is when my Uncle Eric – great-uncle really – needed someone to look after him for a little while, I was the only one who would go. But we had a lovely time.'

'Thank you for sharing,' he said, not sounding at all grateful. 'Can I have your undertaking that you won't stay with my grandmother for a prolonged time after the holiday?'

'You can have my undertaking that I would never, under any circumstances, do anything to harm her. You'll have to be satisfied with that.'

There was another pause. Sophie's fury was abating somewhat; she could see he probably meant well, but obviously had no idea how to get people to do what he wanted without bullying them. She tried to work out how long she would have to stay. Finishing her drink was not obligatory but she took another gulp anyway. The girls at the table behind them had started chatting about handbags but Sophie could tell they were just taking turns to make remarks so the others could over-hear what was going on at Luke's table. This cheered her up a bit. They must be desperately confused as to why Luke was with someone in a 'so-last-season' dress who looked completely ungroomed. Her English accent might explain some of her lack of style, of course. For their benefit, if she had an opportunity, Sophie thought she'd play on her 'Second-hand Rose' image to confuse them further. They wouldn't feel she was a challenge to their pampered beauty, of course, but they would wonder.

'So tell me about your life in England.'

'Is this part of the "getting-to-know-me" process?' Sophie tried to sound normal but she feared her indignation showed.

'Uh-huh. Have you a "significant other" back home?'

Although it was not in her nature to be suspicious of people, everything Luke said implied he really was checking her out. Normally she would have done everything she could to reassure him, but now she felt she wanted to make him worry more, not less. 'Not at the moment, no. I'm a free agent, and in New York. How great is that?'

'I'm sure it's wonderful if it's a new experience. More champagne?' He poured some into her glass, somehow making Sophie feel humiliated. His behaviour was making her feel like Holly Golightly; if she got up to go to the 'restroom' he would offer her money, 'a little powder-room change' and expect her to pocket it.

'Yes please,' she said, simply because she couldn't think of an exit strategy.

Luke sat back, visibly relaxing now the awkward part of the conversation was out of the way. 'So what have you done since you've been here?'

Sophie gave him an account of her sightseeing day, leaving out her fear of heights. She was relieved he had moved on to more neutral ground.

'If you should find yourself in the Village – Greenwich Village – you should try to find Bedford Street. Edna St Vincent Millay lived there. It's an incredibly narrow house – less than ten foot wide.'

'Really? How could anyone live in a house so narrow?'

'With difficulty, I suppose, but a number of famous people lived there. It has a very charming garden behind.'

'Well, if I'm down that way I'll have a look.'

'Do. My grandmother is very fond of Edna St Vincent Millay's poetry.'

'I'm not actually familiar with it, but you don't look as if you approve.'

He smiled. 'It's not a matter of approving or disapproving. But I think you might like it, if my grandmother does.'

Sophie put her head on one side. She felt herself relaxing too. 'Matilda and I get on very well. Maybe it's because we're both women, and English . . .'

Luke seemed a little rueful. 'Maybe it's because you're both a bit wayward.' As he spoke he smiled in a way that Sophie found intensely charming and she realised a second later that it was because it showed how much he loved his grandmother; he wasn't intending to charm her.

Sophie laughed. 'I've never thought of myself as wayward. I've always been a good girl, worked hard at school, helped out at home – that sort of thing.' She didn't mention Uncle Eric again. There was sticking up for yourself and there was boasting.

'But when you were doing those things, didn't you ever find yourself getting a bit distracted?'

She thought about this and remembered rushing through homework in the cloakroom just before the lesson, because she'd spent her evening study time finishing some sewing project. And the time she stuck up the hem of some curtains with Sellotape although she'd promised her mother she'd mend them, because hemming curtains was boring. The Sellotape was still there. 'Maybe,' she conceded.

'My grandmother gets distracted. She starts off doing something fairly sensible and ends up doing something quite different because she got bored. I just think you might encourage her.'

'I think that's unlikely,' said Sophie when she'd had a chance to consider. 'She's a very strong character.' Now she thought about it more she felt it was a very unfair suggestion. He was making assumptions again.

Maybe her expression betrayed her sense of injustice because Luke leant forward a little. 'Sophie, we seem to have got off on the wrong foot—'

'Borrowed shoes, bound to do that to you!'

He ignored this flippancy. 'But I assure you, as my grandmother's guest you will be treated with every kindness.'

Sophie put on a smile, feeling very uncertain.

'My grandmother asked me to give you this.' He produced a piece of paper from his wallet and handed it to her. 'It's an itinerary.'

'Oh my goodness!'

Luke ignored her dismay. 'And she asked me if you wanted her to send her driver to New York or if you'd be all right taking the train.'

'I'll take the train, of course! I'd never dream of—' Then, as she didn't want to overemphasise her point of never doing his grandmother any harm, she changed the subject slightly. 'Where is your grandmother now?'

'On her way home, if she's not home already. Her driver is devoted to her.'

'I can see why. She's very loveable.'

Luke didn't seem impressed by Sophie's pronouncement. Perhaps he still suspected her, although of what, she couldn't work out. What harm could she possibly do to Matilda?

She looked at the itinerary. 'So how long would Matilda like me to stay, do you think? I would really hate to outstay my welcome.'

Luke reverted to being the perfectly brought-up scion of an old and respected dynasty. 'Well, if you come down on Wednesday, then stay on for the weekend. There'll be a small family gathering on Wednesday evening – twenty or so – and then there's the main Thanksgiving dinner on Thursday; that's mostly family, too, but friends and neighbours come also.'

'Goodness me! How did you come to have so many relations?'

'I haven't that many really, but as you have already discovered, my grandmother's heart is far bigger than Texas and all sorts of hangers-on count as "family" to her.'

'Well, that's me put in my place.' She couldn't work Luke out. He seemed to want to ensure she felt welcome at his grandmother's home but at the same time he remained wary. And yet he could be quite charming when he wanted to be.

'I didn't mean to imply—'

'No, of course you didn't and I probably got you all wrong.' She smiled and suddenly found herself gazing into Luke's eyes. Their strange colour fascinated her. She wasn't 'interested' in him, but his irises were so weird she wanted to examine them. She pulled herself together. He would almost certainly misinterpret any look longer than normal. 'Anyway, I'll be delighted to come and stay with Matilda. And I'll do my best to help her in any way she needs.'

'She has staff, you know. You'd be staying as a guest not as a helper.'

Sophie smiled blandly, thinking that 'helper' was a politically correct way of saying 'servant'.

'What about dinner? I mean – I know it's short notice but if you're free . . .'

She'd jumped when she heard the word and now Luke seemed as surprised as she was. Perhaps he hadn't intended to extend the evening beyond just a drink.

Sophie and Milly had discussed the prospect of him asking her out to dinner. Sophie had felt it was highly unlikely; Milly had said if he did it would mean he fancied her. If he did he had a funny way of showing it. Now Sophie said, 'No thank you. My friend's boyfriend is making us dinner. He's a chef.'

Luke bowed politely. 'Then we'll meet again at my grandmother's house.'

The morning after an extremely jolly evening at Milly's boyfriend Franco's apartment the two girls surveyed the itinerary and all the clothes Sophie had with her. Milly had the day off and was giving her full attention to her friend's dilemma: how to turn clothes suitable for work as a nanny into something appropriate for a stay at a Connecticut mansion.

'OK, what have we got,' said Milly. 'Three pairs of jeans . . .'

'Which are new!' Sophie was already feeling defensive. 'I bought them just before I came!'

'Where from?'

The corner of Sophie's mouth twitched. 'A market stall.'

Milly grinned. 'Fine! If anyone asks just say they're an English brand.'

Relieved that her entire wardrobe wasn't going to be trashed, Sophie picked up a skirt for Milly's inspection.

'A tiny, sexy skirt,' said Milly. 'With the right top, perfectly suitable for a family dinner. You'll be sitting down after all. People will forget how short it is and Matilda is bound to have generous napkins to cover your thighs with.'

'Well, that's a relief, that's one down.'

'Not quite, we still need the right top.' Milly was making a list and writing notes on it.

'I can see now why you've got your high-powered job so young,' said Sophie.

Milly looked at her in a querying way.

'Oh, it was something my parents said when we were having the row about me coming over here,' Sophie explained.

Milly nodded and went back to her list. 'OK, you have a smart white blouse to go with the skirt. I can see why you're mistaken for a waitress.'

'It was only once and the person may have been drunk,' said Sophie sulkily. 'Presumably I can't wear that for the family party?'

'No. You need something prettier, clingy but not showing much cleavage.'

'I haven't got anything like that.' Sophie felt defensive again, wanting to rebel but knowing her friend had her best interests at heart.

'I've made a note. Now we need to think about the Thanksgiving party.'

'I want to look really glam!'

'Not like you, Soph. Why?'

Sophie sighed. 'It's Luke . . .'

'You do fancy him! Told you!'

'No, no, no, and no! I don't! But he makes me feel like Holly Golightly, you know, *Breakfast at Tiffany's*.'

Milly shook her head. 'Has it ever occurred to you that you spent far too much time watching your sister's old DVDs? You seem to use them as a yardstick for life.'

Aware this was true, Sophie felt admonished. Seeing this, Milly went on kindly, 'People really try to have breakfast at Tiffany's. They come to New York and expect scrambled eggs and bacon from a jewellery shop.'

Sophie smiled. 'I know. And the reason I don't fancy, couldn't ever possibly fancy him, is because he makes me feel like the poor relation, the hanger-on—'

'The girl who makes her money from handouts from rich men. I do understand, Soph.' She paused. 'So why are you so keen to look glam?'

'Because I don't want people thinking – him thinking, I suppose – that his grandmother has lost her marbles and picked up a waif from the street.'

'You picked *her* up!' said Milly, feigning indignation. 'Why are you so stressed? People will love your posh English accent, and if your clothes aren't exactly the same as theirs they'll put it down to English eccentricity. But you will look glam, I promise you.' She scribbled some more notes. 'What about my dress? Looks far better on you than it ever did on me.'

Sophie's flapping hands indicated she'd rather wear a black plastic bag. 'Luke's seen it twice and noticed! I can't possibly wear that.'

Milly shook her head. 'Then you need to get another. You must take one sexy dress.'

'Why? There's no occasion for a sexy dress. I want sophistication!'

'A girl should never travel without a sexy dress. Luke won't be the only man at these parties. You never know who you might meet. And it should be short.'

'Why?'

'You have great legs and short dresses are cheaper than longer ones.'

'Oh. Couldn't I just stretch a jumper?'

Milly laughed. 'Yes, but I'm sure you can do much better than that. You were brilliant about adapting clothes in England. I'm sure you haven't lost the skill. And if you can't get a good dress cheap in New York you don't deserve to be a girl.'

'Fair enough.'

'There's a wonderful shop that sells every sort of trimming.'

Sophie's eyes narrowed. 'Do you think it sells feathers?'

'I bet it does,' said Milly. 'Let's look up the address.'

While Milly was searching through the telephone directory, Sophie was searching through her friend's wardrobe. She pulled out a little black number. 'Do you want this?'

Milly looked up from her researches. 'I know what you're thinking. You're thinking if I gave you that dress that would save you some money.'

'You're reading my mind.'

'Well OK, you can have the dress but only . . .' She paused for emphasis. '. . . if you give it back when you've turned it into something sensational.'

'Deal! You don't mind if I slash it to the waist do you? Or make it backless?'

'As long as it's fabulous. And maybe not backless and slashed to the waist. I don't think even New York could cope with that and Connecticut certainly couldn't.'

'I'll try not to ruin it, but, Milly, you are coming shopping with me, aren't you?'

Milly winced. 'Oh, I'd love to but the reason I arranged to have this day off – ages ago – is so Franco and I could have some quality time.'

This was a bit of a blow. Sophie had been looking forward to a girly expedition, but she did understand. People seemed to work much harder in New York than they did in England and days off were extremely precious.

'OK, and she shops fastest who shops alone. Just give me a hint as to where the best charity shops are.'

Milly got out the map and put dots on it. 'And they're thrift stores here.'

'Thrift suits me just fine.'

Shops that sold second-hand clothes all tended to have a particular smell. It was one that Sophie was familiar with and she didn't let it put her off.

This particular shop had more vintage than thrift and was like a treasure trove to Sophie. It would undoubtedly be more expensive than shops she usually visited, but would be far more rewarding.

The floor was bare boards and the walls were covered in mirrors and advertisements from the fifties and sixties – possibly earlier. Jazz music played softly in the background and she felt that sense of excitement that retail therapy gave her. It wasn't about spending money for her, it was the thrill of the chase, the thought of what she might find in among the rows of unsuitable garments.

The woman in charge was doing some hand-sewing and after a moment's chat about Sophie's needs she went back to it, and let Sophie get on.

Sophie had a method; she went through every rail and rack so that she'd looked at everything. Some things could be dismissed instantly but many others had potential; these she returned to for a second look. She found a wonderful fifties poodle skirt which she could shorten from the top and wear with black leggings. She found a pair of dungarees which would be perfect for Milly and she found some fun jewellery she couldn't resist. But she didn't find anything that would be suitable for a very smart holiday in Connecticut.

Reluctantly she left the poodle skirt and just bought the dungarees. She couldn't afford to buy stuff just for fun. She was just paying for them and plotting where she was going to go next when she spotted a pair of shoes. They looked like her size and had beautiful scarlet heels. 'Oh, look at those!' she said excitedly.

The girl looked at them. 'I bought those in a sale but they don't fit. I thought I'd sell them here.'

'How much are they?' Sophie was pulling off one of her boots as she spoke.

'Well, as you're English you can have them for what I paid for them. They were real cheap.'

'That's so kind! I'm not going to argue with you giving me a bargain because I'm English – I'm just going to say thank you!'

Chapter Eight

❧

Sophie found the train and the right platform easily. The moment she opened her mouth to ask, thus revealing she was English, she was practically taken by the hand and lifted on to the train. She spent a happy journey talking to the woman who had helped her about that lady's grandchildren. She wasn't allowed to even think about missing her stop: she was warned in plenty of time for her to assemble her bits and pieces.

There was a smiling man in a chauffeur's uniform, including a peaked cap, waiting for Sophie when she got out at the station. He came towards her straight away and took hold of her rucksack. Matilda had obviously described her very accurately and she wished she had borrowed Milly's little case on wheels. There was something very hobo-ish about a rucksack. Had he ever collected anyone with one before?

'Miss Sophie Apperly?' he asked.

'That's me,' she confirmed.

'My name's Sam,' said the man. 'I've worked for Mrs Matilda for over twenty years.'

'Gosh,' said Sophie, and then wished she hadn't. Gosh was so English.

'Yes, miss. Now you come with me. I'll take you home.'

She smiled with pleasure as she recognised this kind man's obvious fondness for his place of work – and for Matilda.

When the huge iron gates swung open to let them through, Sophie suddenly understood Luke's doubts about stray young women being in close contact with his grandmother. She obviously wasn't just rich, she had to be absolutely loaded, and while with her Rottweiler grandson around she was perfectly safe, Sophie did begin to understand said Rottweiler's anxieties: Matilda's open and generous nature could possibly be preyed on by itinerant backpackers.

The contrast between this perfectly maintained mansion and her parent's rambling, slightly dilapidated home was startling. No leaf would settle in any gutter longer than a day or so and no incipient damp would be allowed to climb up the walls and grow mould.

She suddenly felt she'd been wrong to accept the invitation. Her motives were wrong. Although she did really like Matilda, she *had* wanted to visit her for her own reasons; she was determined to stay in America long enough to track down her relative. By the time they'd passed rolling lawns and turned down an avenue of maples and ended up in front of the house (which to Sophie's eyes looked one size down from Chatsworth), she had decided not to stay long, even if her mission failed. She'd be back on the train to New York first thing on Monday morning. She was just as much a sponger, sharing with Milly, but at least she and Milly could talk about it if necessary.

Matilda came out of the front door to greet her, seeming tiny in such a vast setting – tiny but completely appropriate. She embraced Sophie warmly.

'How lovely to see you! I can't tell you how much I've been looking forward to you getting here. I have so many little jobs for you.'

Sophie, who had returned the embrace with equal

warmth, said, 'I don't suppose you have any jobs for me. It's perfectly obvious that you have "staff".'

Matilda laughed delightedly. 'Well yes, of course I do, but there are some things you can only trust certain people with.' She winked and Sophie laughed.

'Very well, but I don't suppose it'll be anything like the jobs I did for Uncle Eric.' She thought of the sorting out, cleaning and gentle bullying that had gone on in her great-uncle's house.

'No, probably not, but possibly your Uncle Eric and I have different requirements. Anyway, come in and have some tea,' said Matilda, taking her arm.

Sophie really felt like a glass of wine but tea would do. Maybe there would be sherry later. Sophie liked Uncle Eric's Amontillado but she suspected Matilda would prefer something drier, which Sophie found hard to take. But beggars, or in her case, itinerant backpackers, couldn't be choosers.

'Would you like to freshen up before tea? Go to your room and change?' asked Matilda.

Sophie decided that Matilda should be under no illusions about the state of her wardrobe, or indeed anything about her. 'Um – no thank you. But I would like to wash the grime off my hands.'

A smiling woman in a uniform showed her into a downstairs bathroom the size of a swimming pool. She knew in America these people were referred to as 'house-keepers'. Uncle Eric would have called them maids.

Fortunately the housekeeper waited outside for her or Sophie would never have found her way to the conservatory where Matilda was presiding over a silver tea service, including a kettle on a spirit lamp and bone-china cups and saucers.

'Forgive me, my dear,' she said as Sophie approached. 'I

111

just love getting out all my old things and having an English visitor justifies it. My family think I'm mad to use things that need cleaning.' She gestured to the teapot, milk jug, sugar bowl and kettle. 'But Consuelo loves cleaning them.'

Consuelo smiled, indicating this was true. 'I put on my favourite television show and polish away. Now, Mrs Matilda, do you need me? If you don't, I'll get back to the kitchen. There's a whole lot of cooking going on there.'

'No thank you. Sophie will help me if I find the pot too heavy. How do you like your tea, dear?'

'Just with a dash of milk. Can you manage that pot?'

'No, actually. At least I could, if I were desperate, but as you're here . . .'

Sophie manipulated the teapot, enjoying the contrast with her usual tea-bag-in-a-mug method and loving the fine china, nearly transparent, painted with birds. Uncle Eric would approve.

'Have a cookie – biscuit,' said Matilda when the tea was dispensed. 'You'll notice that they're supposed to be turkeys.' Actually, Sophie hadn't been able to recognise them, but she supposed they were more or less bird-shaped. 'Tomorrow I wonder if you'd mind helping some of the younger children decorate them? They get so bored waiting for the meal.'

'Of course I wouldn't mind! That sounds brilliant fun. And I'm happy to help out in any way I can.'

'Luke told me I mustn't treat you as a servant.'

This was a bit of a surprise. 'Did he? I wonder why?'

Matilda shrugged. 'I think he just wants you to have a pleasant stay with us.'

Sophie felt this was unlikely. Although his manners had been impeccable, there'd been little warmth behind them. Then it occurred to her that he was probably worrying about her trying to wangle a proper job from Matilda and then somehow the coveted green card. He certainly wouldn't want his grandmother involved in sponsoring her or anything. God, the man was suspicious! Maybe it was being a lawyer that did it or maybe he just suspected anyone female and under sixty because of being taken to the cleaners by his ex-wife.

'Well, I love being with children. You know I was going to be a nanny, only the job fell through.'

Matilda frowned. 'You did tell me but I can't help feeling glad that it fell through. We may not have met if it hadn't and I know we're going to be great allies.'

'Allies? Against who? Whom?'

'No particular person,' said Matilda casually, picking up the teapot, lighter than it had been. 'More tea, dear?'

'Yes please.' Sophie watched as the tea, darker now, descended into the cup. Maybe she'd picked up Luke's suspicious habits but there was something about the way Matilda spoke which made her feel that she had an agenda.

'Would you like to see your room?' asked Matilda when the pot had been drunk dry and at least three turkey biscuits eaten.

'Mm, yes, please. But I'd better go to the bathroom again first.'

Matilda looked pained. 'My dear, your room has its own bathroom, and yours has a tub. Being English I thought you might not like to shower.'

'I can manage with a shower perfectly well, but if there is a bath, that will be lovely.'

Her room was palatial, bigger than the sitting room in her parents' house. It was on the ground floor and it had double doors opening on to the garden. In summer it would have been delightful to wander out into the sunshine and enjoy the paved Italian garden immediately outside. Now, Sophie just looked at it for a few moments before Consuelo drew the thick curtains enclosing Sophie in warmth and comfort. It must be difficult to adapt to a tiny New York apartment if you were used to living in such a huge space, thought Sophie, but then concluded that Matilda's apartment in New York was probably huge too.

Sophie smiled, declining Consuelo's offer to help her unpack. 'As you see, I haven't got very much and I really don't want you seeing my greying underwear.'

Consuelo laughed. 'Well, if there's anything you've forgotten, I'm sure we have it somewhere. We keep a stash of top-brand make-up if you need it.'

Sophie hesitated. She didn't wear much make-up usually and although she did have her samples, a drying mascara and a bit of lipstick retrievable only with the use of a lip brush, she did wonder if she'd need a bit more here. The samples were mainly eye-gel and things that didn't make much difference to someone of Sophie's age. 'You think I do?'

The housekeeper nodded. 'The girls who usually hang around Luke wear a ton of it. You don't need a ton – you have great skin – but you might want to add something.'

'Maybe if you could . . .'

'I'll bring it all along. You can have fun playing. Dinner is at seven, when the rest of the family are all ready. There's a gong. You'll hear it. But if you're ready before then, Mrs Matilda always has a glass of sherry at half past six. She'd be pleased if you joined her.'

At half past six precisely, Sophie tottered out of her room, grateful she didn't have to negotiate stairs, clutching the truffles she'd made at Milly's apartment. She hoped the home-made thing would make them seem special and not just cost-cutting. The wonderful shoes with scarlet heels she'd bought at the vintage shop were slightly too big but she'd bought them anyway because they were so gorgeous and it would have been rude not to. Milly had said they were a bit transsexual in style but Sophie felt willing to take the risk of being mistaken for a man in drag.

Her skirt was her trademark mini, again a bargain unless you considered how much fabric you got with it, and on top she had a simple cashmere V-necked cardigan. She'd bought this in New York – one of her most satisfying charity-shop finds. Her tights, or pantyhose, had cost the most, but as Milly pointed out, there was more of them than anything else and went on to say 'as your legs are so fabulous they are cost-effective'.

She had put on, and taken off, quite a lot of the make-up Consuelo had brought her and had sprayed herself lavishly with the Guerlain scent provided in her bathroom. She'd felt fabulous in her bedroom but her confidence was diminishing with every step she took towards the drawing room. She could hear voices. She was soon going to have to present herself to Matilda's family, who would, she was certain, all be like Luke and see her as a sponger disguised as a tramp. Maybe the skirt was too short.

At least getting across the hall gave her plenty of walking practice, Sophie decided, determined to get over her nerves and enjoy herself. And Matilda was lovely: it was quite possible that her relations would be too. Luke could be a throwback to a stuffier branch of the family.

There was a moment's silence as Sophie stood on the threshold of the largest room she had ever seen in private hands. At the far end of it a castle-sized fireplace crackled with tree-sized logs.

Although they were far away, the group of people who stood by it had obviously been watching for her. They looked at her appraisingly. Matilda, who'd been talking in a low voice to a man of about her own age, became aware of Sophie's appearance and set off towards her.

'Sophie, my dear, do come and join us,' she said as she reached Sophie and kissed her cheek.

'Hello,' said Sophie, kissing her back. 'I've brought you a little something. Nothing much, just some truffles I made.' She was aware of how much more comfortable she'd have felt if she'd been waitressing at this gathering, and not a guest.

'How lovely of you! But that wasn't necessary, you just had to bring yourself!'

'I know, but I'd have felt bad if I'd come empty-handed.'

'Well, I'm sure they're delicious.' She handed them to a uniformed butler with a tray who had silently appeared at her elbow. 'Have a glass of sherry. Unless you'd prefer something else?'

'Sherry would be lovely,' said Sophie. Actually a strong cocktail would have helped but while she was sure the butler could have produced the perfect Manhattan or Old-Fashioned, Sophie wasn't sure what these tasted like. Besides, she didn't want to add 'lush' to the list of complaints Matilda's family doubtless had about her.

'Come and meet the family,' said Matilda, once a glass had been put into Sophie's hand. 'You won't remember everyone's names, I don't suppose. We Americans have a little trick whereby we say the name of the person we're introduced to. That helps.'

A woman a little older than Sophie's own mother stepped forward, laughing. 'So you're American today, Mother. Usually, you're proud to be a Brit. Hi, Sophie, I'm Susannah, one of Matilda's daughters. I live in California. I'm Luke's aunt.' The woman sent a teasing glance towards Luke, who had his nose in a tumbler. He was standing next

116

to a very pretty girl with long blonde hair dressed in pink. Sophie instantly felt dowdy in her predominately black outfit, and desperately 'thrift store'.

'Luke, why don't you introduce Bobbie to Sophie first,' said Matilda.

Luke smiled. 'Sophie, this is Bobbie, she's the daughter of very old friends of the family.'

A woman laughed. 'We're not that old, sweetie.'

Bobbie stepped forward and made as if to kiss Sophie, which came as something of a surprise. Bobbie hadn't looked that friendly. 'Hi, Sophie! Come and meet my parents!'

She had exactly the same accent and intonation as the girls at the club. Sophie wondered if they knew each other. Bobbie, who must have been about the same age as she was, made Sophie feel very old.

The rest of the introductions were made and, on the whole, Sophie was made to feel welcome. But she did feel poor. The pre-dinner conversation flitted from private jets to the credit crisis (which didn't seem to have affected anyone present) via how impossible it was to get a good organic gardener these days. Sophie nearly put up her hand and said that she was quite good at gardening, and so get herself a job, but Luke's eye was on her, so she didn't. She didn't want to embarrass Matilda either. She restricted herself to fielding questions about England, many of which she couldn't answer: she had no idea of the population of her home town.

Luke led her into dinner: a casual family affair that required the butler, several housekeepers, including Consuelo, who winked at Sophie, and a lot of what Milly would have described as 'tra-la'.

Sophie was seated next to Matilda's old friend on one side and Luke on the other. Bobbie was on his other side, and seemed happy to talk to Sophie across him. Initially,

Sophie had to focus quite hard to follow her conversation but after a couple of sentences, she tuned into the speech pattern and was able to follow the words at least. The world she talked about made Sophie feel she was watching a very glitzy film: fascinating but nothing to do with her.

The food was superb. First, a tiny cup of soup, mostly froth, but underneath was the most delicious taste of fresh peas. Sophie asked Luke, 'Do you think this is where the word *soupçon* came from?'

The corners of his eyes crinkled, making him look quite different for a moment. 'Possibly,' he said before Bobbie captured Sophie's attention again.

'We must sooo spend some time together tomorrow!' she said excitedly.

Oh, we sooo mustn't! thought Sophie, wondering why on earth Bobbie had suggested it and how she could refuse.

'I think Grandmother has a job for Sophie, if Sophie doesn't mind,' Luke said, with a smile that was almost charming.

'Yes! I'd forgotten,' said Sophie. 'I'm helping the younger ones decorate biscuits – I mean cookies, which are in the shape of turkeys.'

Bobbie wrinkled her nose. 'Sounds sticky, even if kind of fun.'

'Well, do join me! I don't know how many children will be involved and how good they are with icing.'

'Frosting,' said Luke.

'Frosting,' echoed Sophie, and then said, 'Maybe the British and the Americans are truly two nations divided by a common language.' She'd heard her father say this often enough, maybe he was right.

'How do you mean?' asked Bobbie, her perfect brow slightly wrinkled.

'I think Sophie means, "You like 'tomayto' and I like

'tomahto'",' Luke explained.

'Yes, only that doesn't work for "potato", does it?' said Sophie.

'No. Why would anyone say "potarto"?' asked Bobbie. 'It sounds kind of silly.'

'Absolutely,' agreed Sophie, 'and the funny thing is, if I were in a restaurant and ordering "tomarto" it would sound silly if I said "tomayto" – even if I was over here.'

'I don't understand!' said Bobbie.

'Because it wouldn't sound like me. It would be as if I was putting on an American accent.'

'You mean instead of a British one?' said Luke, his head slightly on one side.

'I don't have an accent,' said Sophie primly. 'It's you colonialists that have the accent.'

Bobbie's eyes widened in confusion and Luke pursed his lips and shook his head. 'Now, don't you go patronising us. The Winchesters came over on the *Speedwell*, I'll have you know. It travelled more or less at the same time as the *Mayflower*.'

Sophie thought she could detect a twinkle in the corner of his eye. 'Very impressive. But it's still you who has the accent.'

Just for a moment their eyes met. Some sort of communication went on that Sophie couldn't have defined, but she liked it. 'If you say so,' he said.

Sophie's eyes widened. 'I can't believe you're conceding me a point!' she said.

'Just one,' he said.

Sophie turned away, confused. If that exchange had been with anyone other than Luke she'd have thought he was flirting.

'What are you going to wear tomorrow?' said Bobbie.

'Um, haven't decided,' said Sophie, wondering if Milly's

little black dress was going to be too eccentric for this gathering.

'Really?' Bobbie was astounded. 'I can't believe you don't know what to wear for Thanksgiving – the day before! If I hadn't decided by now I'd spend all tomorrow going through my closet, tossing things on to the bed. Nightmare!'

'You must remember that they don't have Thanksgiving in England,' said Luke.

'Oh really? But you do have Christmas, right?'

'Oh yes, all the other festivals, Easter, Whitsun . . .'

'But not the fourth of July?' Luke was definitely teasing now.

'We prefer to celebrate Bastille Day,' said Sophie. 'The weather is more reliable later in the month.'

Bobbie studied them for a few seconds before dipping out.

One perfect course followed another until Sophie was so full she felt she couldn't move. But before the dessert course Matilda clapped her hands. 'Gentlemen, if you'd all move two places to your left.'

It was only when Luke was about to be taken from her that she realised how much she'd been relying on him. He might be harbouring all sorts of suspicions about her, but at least he hadn't grilled her about Britain's economic growth, which the man on her other side had done.

'Well, hello,' said the elderly man who replaced him. 'What's a wild English rose doing in this neck of the woods?'

Sophie was prepared to be charmed and to treat this seemingly respectable gentleman rather as she had Uncle Eric. But with this compliment came a hand on her leg that squeezed in a way that made her wince.

She looked at Luke, hoping he could rescue her, but she could see his ear was being bent, probably on something

120

very technical and important, by another man, who was talking across the woman between them without seeming to notice her.

She moved her leg and did her best to smile. The man then went on to give her a detailed account of his exploits in Vietnam, all the while hunting for her knee. She draped her napkin over her lap and sat on it, so if he attacked her thigh he would only get napery. She looked around desperately for someone else who could help her. She could of course make a fuss about being sexually harassed but felt it would be rude. She might mention it to Matilda, if the opportunity came up, but she thought the man was doing it from habit rather than anything more threatening.

About a year later, or so it seemed to Sophie, Matilda got up.

'Well, my dears, I'm going to leave you to have coffee, tea and anything else you might like in the drawing room. I'm going to bed now.'

Sophie was on her feet so quickly her elderly dinner companion nearly fell off his chair as the absence of her leg made him lose his balance. She got to Matilda in seconds. 'Would you think I was terribly rude if I went too? I think I might still be suffering from jet lag.' She wasn't sure if she could still use this excuse, but she did feel extremely weary. It could just have been the strain of the evening. Whichever, she just wanted to leave the room.

'No, of course not, dear,' said Matilda. 'You must feel free to do exactly as you like. And old soldiers' tales do take it out of you,' she added with a wink.

'I'll go then.' Once certain that Matilda wouldn't think badly of her she didn't care about the others. A quick nod to her immediate neighbours and she set off across the vast acres of hall to her bedroom. She deliberately hadn't looked at Luke; she didn't want to see his disapproval.

121

She was wearing the robe Matilda had thoughtfully provided, having rinsed out her underwear in the washbasin, and was considering having the first bath she'd had in America when there was a knock on the door. Imagining it might be Consuelo offering to run the bath or do some other task that Sophie was perfectly capable of doing for herself, Sophie went back into the bedroom and called, 'Come in!'

As the door remained shut, she went and opened it. It was Luke, carrying her shoes. 'You left these behind.'

'Oh, so I did.' Instinctively she clutched at the neck of the robe although she'd shown much more flesh when she'd been fully dressed. She held out her other hand for the shoes.

'Do you always kick your shoes off before you run?' he asked, holding on to them.

'They're too big for me,' she explained. 'And I didn't run. I'd sort of lost them under the table.' She frowned a little. 'Why don't you come in?'

She felt embarrassed about entertaining Luke when she was only wearing a silk dressing gown but she didn't want to have the conversation she felt they needed to have with the door half open.

Luke stepped inside. 'Why did you rush off?' His curious-coloured eyes bored into her in interrogating-hostile-witnesses mode, she decided. Or possibly it was to avoid looking at her body, outlined by the gown, which adequately concealed her flesh but did nothing to disguise her shape.

'The man sitting next to me put his hand on my leg.'

Luke was appalled. 'That's outrageous! I'll go and speak to him now! He can't behave like that to my grandmother's guests!'

'He can't behave like that to anyone but now's not the time. It's late.'

122

'Not that late. You and Matilda have both retired early.'

Sophie chuckled. 'I haven't quite adjusted to the time difference. But he's old. I really don't want to make a big fuss about it. It would be so embarrassing for Matilda.'

He considered for several worrying seconds before tacitly agreeing to let the matter rest.

She held her hand out for her shoes. He didn't give them to her.

'Why do you buy shoes that are too big for you? Don't you try them on in the shop?'

Remembering that he'd had to bring her shoes back to her at the private view too she felt she'd better explain. 'Well, that first pair were Milly's; I'd borrowed them. They had terribly high heels. And those' – she gave them a longing look where they still dangled in his hand – 'those I bought because they were so lovely. Look at them! Scarlet heels! How could I not buy them?'

'Because they don't fit? Didn't they have them in your size?'

She considered for a tiny second before confronting Luke with the truth. 'Not at a thrift store, no. They don't have different sizes.'

'But they're huge!' He wasn't discomforted by the thrift-store reference.

Sophie nodded. 'I know. But so heavenly.' As he seemed to have loosened his grasp on them she gently removed them.

'Sophie,' he said.

'Mm?'

'I've a favour to ask you.'

'Really?'

'There's going to be a brunch. A big brunch, on Saturday. We'll all be going. I want you there as my date.'

'Do you? Why?' She was astounded. 'There must be girls queuing up for the privilege of being your date at a brunch.'

She frowned slightly. 'Although I've never been to a brunch. They don't really have them in England, unless you count having a late breakfast and not bothering with lunch. At least not in the circles I mix in.'

'Sophie!' He sounded impatient. 'I know I have girls queuing up to be my date at a brunch! Being very wealthy—'

'And quite cute-looking . . .'

He smiled briefly as if to concede how arrogant he sounded. 'Whatever. It makes me eligible. Too eligible. And round here, on my home turf, so to speak, any girl I took to—'

'A brunch!' Sophie couldn't take it seriously.

He ploughed on. '—would be assumed to be my chosen one. It would make us practically engaged. I don't know if you know, but I'm divorced and for some reason any girl I go anywhere with is considered to be the replacement wife. It puts any new friendship I may have under huge pressure.' He paused, considering how to continue with this sensitive subject.

Sophie decided to help him out. The overheard conversation in the bar made it all very clear to her. 'But if you took a thrift-store girl from England to the brunch, no one would think there was anything in it?'

Rueful agreement made Luke smile. 'I would never have put it like that,' he said.

'No, but being American, you don't have the British way with words. It's what you meant.'

'No it isn't!' He walked across to the window bay where there was a small sofa, an armchair and a desk. He sat on the chair. Sophie followed him over and perched on the sofa, making sure her knees didn't escape from the robe.

'You're a very lovely girl. No one will be at all surprised to see you on my arm. But no one would expect me to marry out of my family's circle of friends, not when there's so much money and so many lovely girls to choose from.'

'Uh-huh,' said Sophie, to encourage him. Wickedly, she was enjoying seeing him struggle to say what he felt without being rude.

'So would you very kindly come with me? If I go with Bobbie, for example, the local gossip magazine will have us honeymooning in Mauritius in seconds flat.'

'I'm sure if you discussed it with her Bobbie would agree to honeymoon somewhere you'd like better. Kayaking in New Zealand or something.'

Luke's exasperation was beginning to show. 'I'm sure she would but that's not the point! I don't want to marry Bobbie, and I don't want to take her to the brunch.'

'She's going anyway.'

'Exactly. So I can't take her, can I?'

'I don't see why not.'

Luke frowned. There was something rather sexy about men being stern, Sophie acknowledged. 'I said, I don't want to.'

'Then go alone, you're a big boy now.'

Luke took a breath, obviously wondering how best to get his point across having failed so miserably up to now. 'If I go alone every single woman in the place will either be thrust at me by their mothers, or hit on me in packs.'

She raised an eyebrow in mock-scepticism. She knew what he said was true, going on what those girls in the club had said, but she didn't think he should say those things unchallenged. It was very bad for his inflated ego. 'Really?'

He sighed, not yet aware she was teasing. 'It's not because I'm "cute"' – his eyes flickered, acknowledging that he remembered her saying that he was – 'or a good lawyer, but because I come from an old family and they couldn't bear to see all that money go out of the group.'

'I see. It's a clan thing.'

'That's it. Keep the wealth in the circle; that way we all just get richer and richer.'

'So you want me for protection, so I can beat off the single women for you.'

'No—' Then he stopped. 'Sophie, you're maddening sometimes.'

'Luke, I thought you considered me maddening all the time.'

The corner of his mouth lifted. 'I do, but I still want you to come to the brunch with me.'

She shook her head. 'I hate to be unhelpful, but I'm afraid I can't.'

'Why on earth not? You're not going until Monday morning – this brunch is on Saturday.'

She considered just refusing to go but then she thought she owed him the truth. 'I will be here but I can't go.' She got up. 'Come with me.' He followed her across the room to an antique wardrobe. It would presumably have struggled to accommodate half Bobbie's collection of summer skirts but to Sophie, it was huge. She opened the door. 'There. There is the sum total of my clothes. When I came here, I didn't plan for brunch. I'm awfully sorry.'

Luke regarded Sophie's clothes, huddled up into one end of the wardrobe. They took up three hangers. Her boots, underneath the hangers, had flopped over and suddenly seemed very tatty. He didn't immediately say, 'Why can't you wear that? Or that?' He just looked at her clothes and then back to her. He thought for a moment before clearing his throat.

'Sophie, I'm going to say something you're bound to find offensive. It is not intended to sound offensive or be offensive, or, in fact, be anything apart from a way to make it possible for you to help me out.'

'What?' Sophie frowned.

'I want you to come shopping with me and buy an outfit for brunch. If you do this for me, I'll expedite the search for your relative.'

'But, Luke! I thought you hated spongers. I thought that was why you didn't want Matilda to be friends with me, in case I tried to get something from her!'

'I know, but that's my grandmother, this is me. I can afford it.'

'In spite of your very expensive divorce?'

'Yes. Please. Do this for me.'

Sophie fought with Holly Golightly. Holly won. Holly would not have objected to having an outfit bought for her by a very rich young man so she could do him a favour.

She smiled. 'OK. Can I send it back if I don't spill brunch on it?'

He smiled back. 'You're almost bound to spill brunch on it, Sophie.'

Sophie went to bed thinking very hard about Luke. He really wasn't quite the same as she'd thought him. He was preppy; he was quite stuck up and impossibly rich; he was arrogant, and possibly a bit pleased with himself; but he had a sense of humour, and he could be kind. And he did have really interestingly coloured eyes . . .

Chapter Nine

❧❧❧

Consuelo brought Sophie breakfast in her room at seven. Had Sophie been asleep she wouldn't have heard her don't-want-to-wake-you knock, but she'd been reading for a while, luxuriating in the most delicious sheets she had ever slept in, hoping she wouldn't mind going back to the ordinary kind.

'You didn't need to bring me breakfast in bed!' she said, having opened the door. 'I would have got up. I just didn't know what time.'

'It's fine, honey. Mrs Matilda thought you might appreciate breakfast in bed. She wants you to be thoroughly spoiled.' She put down the tray on the bedside table so Sophie could smooth the bedcovers ready for it. 'Luke has gone for a run as usual and it's not late but we figured you might be awake now.'

'You're psychic. I'm starving.'

'Well, I hope I got your choices right. You have scrambled eggs, bacon, mushroom, croissants, orange juice, coffee and boiling water and a tea bag.' She paused as she adjusted the tray. 'Oh, and some toast. You English like it cold, right?'

'I like it anyhow, thank you so much!' Sophie sighed with happiness as she looked at the food. 'It all looks delicious!'

'Well, eat it up while it's hot. I'll take you to see Mrs Matilda in about an hour and a half. Is that enough time?'

Sophie nodded, retrieving a knife and fork from the napkin.

'You want cereal?' asked Consuelo, spotting a gap in the breakfast menu.

Sophie was eating a strip of the crispest, most delicious bacon she had ever tasted. She shook her head. 'I'll struggle to eat all this.'

Consuelo shook her head, smiling, and left the room. Sophie, alone with her breakfast, tucked in. As she ate her eggs and bacon and nibbled croissant and toast she contemplated what the day might bring. Could she really go to a brunch with Luke as his date? Well possibly, if Matilda was in favour, but could she let him buy her clothes? Surely not.

She tried to see it from his point of view. He needed her for a task. If she didn't have the right clothes she couldn't perform the task. He could easily afford to buy her the clothes; there really was no moral reason why she shouldn't accept. But it was the Holly Golightly thing – having clothes bought for her made her feel just a little bit like a kept woman. In the cold light of day, she couldn't do it.

'Was everything all right for you, darling?' asked Matilda when Sophie joined her in her room later.

'It was perfect! And luxurious, breakfast in my room!'

'We thought you might be hungry. You didn't eat very much last night.

'I thought—'

'Anyway, enough about that. Luke tells me he's taking you shopping?'

Sophie shook her head. 'I can't go. It makes me feel cheap. I'm having this lovely holiday with you, I can't accept clothes from Luke. It's just not right!'

'If Luke wanted you to go skiing with him, for his own reasons, and you didn't have the right clothes, would you let him buy you ski clothes?'

'It's not the same!'

'It is from his point of view. You need the tools for the job. Let him buy you them.'

Sophie considered this analogy but still shook her head.

Matilda put her hand on Sophie's. 'He's asked you a big favour, he wants you to get something out of it. Being generous works both ways – giving and receiving. You're a giver, be a receiver too.'

Sophie bit back a smile. 'That sounds kind of illegal. As if it involved drugs or something.'

Matilda laughed. 'Well, it doesn't. Luke is very law-abiding.'

'The trouble is, I'm not sure I really understand why he wants me to go. Why is it so useful for him?' Although Luke had actually laid his argument out quite clearly, she wanted reassurance from Matilda that it was vital she helped Luke out.

Matilda sighed and considered. 'In New York Luke can go out with whom he likes, more or less. Although I do wish he'd stop choosing stick-thin blondes with high-maintenance hair just because they look pretty on his arm, but it's really none of my business.' Matilda paused for breath and Sophie wondered if she had been about to add something but she continued: 'But if you bring a girl to a regular event – as this brunch is regular – it's significant.'

'You mean it's like inviting your boyfriend for Christmas? You don't do it unless you're serious? Well, I get that part, but why doesn't he go alone?'

'Because he'll be swamped. And word will get around that he doesn't currently have a girlfriend and every single woman in New England will – how do you say it these days? – hit on him.'

Sophie giggled at Matilda's use of language. 'But if I

go with him I'll protect him from the harpies, but it won't be "significant" because I'm English, and otherwise unsuitable?'

'You're completely suitable, but that's about it.'

'OK,' said Sophie, deciding to give in gracefully. If Matilda said she should go then go she would. 'So what do I wear for a brunch?'

'Let Luke and the advisor in the shop guide you. You don't need to worry about it. Now I suggest you relax, explore the grounds, do what you like until lunchtime. And then after lunch the children will be over for the cookie-decorating.'

'Oh. Who are the children? Family? Or friends? I didn't spot any last night.'

'The neighbours' children. They come and decorate cookies for the big party tonight. It's a tradition I started years ago and I can't seem to give it up. The staff hate it because they're so busy. If you supervise, they won't have to.'

Luke was nowhere around – probably working, Sophie decided, although she knew that Thanksgiving was a national holiday and no one worked. But she enjoyed walking in the gardens, curious to see how English – or how Italianate – the gardens were. They were extensive. There was also a wood to wander through and by the time she got back, she felt energised by the exercise and ready for lunch.

After lunch, which was just her and Matilda, she was ushered to the kitchen. It was a dream kitchen, as she told Matilda. It had every modern appliance but also a huge dresser covered with copper jelly moulds, pans and utensils, huge old majolica platters adding brightness and colour, and faded English willow pattern and other traditional patterned plates.

131

'Oh, it's delightful!' said Sophie, looking at the dresser in particular. 'I love it!'

'It's mostly for decoration,' Matilda explained. 'But when we have big parties in the summer, it's fun to get out all the pretty things. Now, I'm going to leave you with Consuelo. Everything is ready for you, I think. The children will be here soon.'

'Everything' consisted of quite a lot of premade cookies in the shapes of turkeys, horns of plenty and pumpkins, a large supply of disposable icing bags, each with a writing-nozzle, and tubs and tubs of decorations. There were the silver dragées that Sophie was familiar with but all sorts of other things: gold sugar, edible bugle beads in jewel colours, some wonderful things that looked like drops of water only edible, sugar stars, flowers and shapes, in fact every possible thing you could imagine except actual diamonds. Edible glitter was in shakers and there were pens you could write directly on to the icing with.

'This is amazing!' Sophie said. 'I can't wait to get started.'

The children filed in. There were five of them, three girls and two boys. They were between seven and five, Sophie guessed. The prime age for enthusiasm and mess. But they were not dressed for cookie-frosting – they were dressed for a visit to the Big House. This surprised her as she thought America was free from such things.

'Hello, I'm Sophie,' she said. 'I'm from England and we're going to frost cookies together. Consuelo? Do we have some pinnies – aprons for these children? They'll ruin their smart clothes otherwise.'

Conseulo produced a basket piled with old shirts, skirts with ties and other garments suitable for messy play. 'Mrs Winchester got these together years ago to save the children from the frosting. It gets messy!' She handed

132

the basket to Sophie and, with a 'Call me if you need me,' she left Sophie in charge.

'OK,' Sophie addressed her mini audience, 'now you know my name but I don't know yours. Why don't you tell me your names and then pick something to cover your clothes?'

The first little girl came forward. 'My name is Lola.'

'Hello, Lola, pick a pinny.'

One by one they came forward and chose coverings. They were still very shy.

'OK! Now gather round the table. Have a turkey and a bag of frosting and get going! I'm going to put spots on mine.'

'Turkeys don't have spots,' said a little girl who was called Crystal.

'They do, sort of, if they've got feathers on. But you don't have to make the turkeys look real, just pretty! There! That's lovely! Now do one of these.'

As the children stopped being shy they became more imaginative and used every product provided on every sort of cookie. Sophie had been told that they would be collected at four o'clock. It was only half past two. All the biscuits had been used. She cast around for some other way of keeping them entertained and spotted a tall glass jar. It was full of cookie cutters. Sophie decided they had to be used.

'OK! Let's make more cookies, only we'll use these different shapes, to make it more fun. There are still lots of different sparkly things left. We've run out of edible glitter though.'

'Can I eat a cookie?' said a little boy.

'Of course,' said Sophie, aware the child's parents might have issues with him and sugar but feeling that it wasn't human to expect a child to decorate cookies and not sample them.

133

All the children, and Sophie, picked a cookie and ate it. They were good, but not as good as the ones Sophie used to make. 'I think I'll use my recipe for the next batch.'

As she mixed up her standard biscuit dough in a corner of the kitchen she did feel perhaps she was being what Luke would describe as wayward, but she was sure Matilda would understand. The children were thrilled, especially when they discovered a cutter that created a *Mayflower* shape. Sophie cut those out as the sails and rigging made them very complicated.

She let them run wild with the other cutters though. Matilda had them for every festival there was and a whole lot more besides. There were the usual bells, Christmas trees and holly, as well as reindeer, shooting stars and Santas. But there were shamrocks, eagles and Native American headdresses too. They had a cookie-cutter orgy that meant each child had his or her initial to decorate. It had got a little wild at the end when the children felt they wanted to make hair slides with the leftover icing and apply them directly to their hair but once Sophie was wise to this she managed to stop them.

By the time the children were taken away, bearing baskets of cookies and looking more or less the same as they had done when they arrived, apart from their hair and faces, Sophie felt so sticky herself she walked carefully through the house, trying not to touch anything until she got to her own bathroom and could have a bath.

'I wouldn't actually eat that, if I were you.' Luke leant across the table to Sophie as Consuelo held out a bowl for her.

'What is it?'

'It's a traditional Thanksgiving dish. My grandfather

134

loved it and so my grandmother has them make it every year.'

'But what is it? It looks like green beans cooked in soup.'

'That's exactly what it is,' said Luke. 'With those onion things on top.'

'I think I'll pass,' she said.

Thanksgiving dinner was going well, she felt. Matilda's family were friendly and welcoming, obviously used to odd people being present at the occasion. She felt much more relaxed with Luke now even though he had caught her out with cookie-dough in her hair; she'd had to get dressed in rather a hurry. But at least she felt she looked OK in Milly's dress transformed with fringes and feathers the evening before she came to Connecticut.

The biggest turkey Sophie had ever seen had been placed in front of one of the men, who had taken on the carving with enthusiasm.

Just before its appearance, all the children, including the grown-up ones, had sung a psalm of thanksgiving, and after that, everyone round the table had had to say what they were thankful for. Sophie, who had to go first, said she was thankful that she'd met Matilda, and therefore the rest of this wonderful family, which went down well.

Now that plates of turkey were in front of everyone, the vegetables were being passed round.

Sophie passed on the green beans but took a tiny helping of everything else. Her plate was still laden.

'The trouble is,' she said to her neighbour, who was some cousin or other, 'it all looks so delicious and I don't want to miss out on anything.'

'Matilda always has very good cooks. Her husband was a great gourmet. So, honey, remind me how you and Matilda met?'

Sophie had answered this question several times and the

story sounded more ridiculous every time she told it. 'It was so random!' she said. 'I just happened to see Matilda nearly collapse at a private view at an art gallery, where my friend works.' She paused. 'We bonded, sitting on the floor outside the Ladies – restroom. I don't really feel I should be here, but when Matilda heard that I didn't have plans for Thanksgiving, she insisted.'

'Don't worry about it, Sophie, honey,' said the woman, 'that sounds just like Matilda. She always was a soft touch.' Although she smiled, this made Sophie feel awkward. Seeing this, the woman went on, 'Matilda doesn't feel that Thanksgiving is right without someone from the outside present. And I hear you helped with the cookie-frosting? My little girl told me all about you.'

Grateful to be able to stop feeling like a hanger-on and more like a helpful older child, Sophie went into a description of the cookie-frosting that had her neighbour hysterical with laugher and appalled at the same time.

The meal went on; the wine flowed. Matilda's guests were friendly and interested in her as a person. She nearly found herself explaining her mission to find her relative, but thought better of it. It was such a long shot, after all. And anyone willing to cross the Atlantic on the off chance there might be money in it would seem rather odd.

After the turkey and vegetables came the pies. There were dozens of them. Pumpkin pie, apple pie, fruit pies, pecan pies and various others. Some had lattice tops, some were open and some had double crusts. With them there was pouring cream, whipped cream, ice cream and something in a jug that was brought to Sophie first.

'It's Bird's Custard, darling,' explained Matilda loudly. 'I thought it might make you feel at home.'

'But you don't have to have it if you'd rather not,' said

Luke. 'Matilda always produces it for English guests but no one ever eats it.'

'Well, I'd love some,' said Sophie instantly, although she was so full. 'I haven't had custard for ages.'

If anyone suspected this was because she didn't really like it, they didn't mention it.

After the party she fell into bed thinking what a happy day she'd had. She'd had a brilliant time with the children and she'd had tea with Matilda. Luke had joined them and they'd been very cosy in Matilda's sitting room, chatting until it was time to get ready for dinner. And Luke had been surprisingly nice. And he had continued to be friendly all through the meal.

She woke up in the middle of the night aware that she'd dreamt about Luke. The warm, fuzzy feeling she woke to didn't seem to connect with the buttoned-up lawyer she'd first met. She'd started to wonder which one was the real Luke before she went back to sleep again.

Reasonably satisfied that it was OK for her to accept generous gifts of clothing from a very rich man, and as smart as she could be given her limited wardrobe, Sophie got into Luke's car the next morning to go shopping. She wished she recognised what sort of car it was – people loved that kind of detail – but apart from the fact that it was long and low and silver-grey, nothing else about it meant anything to her and she didn't want to ask him. But she was going to enjoy speeding along in Luke's lovely car seeing the tree-covered hills of New England from the window.

Now Matilda had persuaded her she wasn't behaving badly by accepting his largesse, she found herself quite excited. 'So, where are we going? The mall?' Sophie kind of hoped it was 'the mall'. Although they'd had them in

England for years and years American ones seemed more exciting, somehow, at least in films.

'My grandmother told me about some exclusive stores in the village while you were getting ready.'

Sophie groaned. 'They sound terribly grand. The sort of shop you can't get out of without buying anything.'

'I suspect my grandmother will have called ahead. They'll have clothes set aside. They'll be expecting us.'

Sophie squirmed in her leather seat. 'I do most of my shopping in charity shops – or Primark.'

Luke gave her a curious glance. 'I've never come across a girl so reluctant to shop.'

'I'm not at all reluctant to shop! I love shopping! But only when I can afford the clothes.' He would never understand.

'Well, I can afford the clothes. That will have to do you.'

Sophie laughed. 'It's a first for me, I can tell you, being with someone who has more money than I have.'

Luke took his eyes off the road to look at her sharply. 'Really? I had the impression you had very little money and so almost anyone would have more money than you.'

'Golly, Luke, that's a bit blunt, isn't it? We Brits never talk about money.'

'Fortunately I'm not a Brit, but am I right?'

Sophie shrugged. 'You are right really, although I hate to admit it. I think what I meant was that my previous boyfriends have been broke but also quite mean with money. They care more about the planet than about their girlfriends having a good time.' She bit her lip. 'Obviously the planet *is* a lot more important . . .'

'But you can occasionally treat a girl without damaging the ozone layer?'

Sophie laughed. 'Exactly! You've hit the nail on the head.'

'We Yanks can do that sometimes.'

He was looking straight ahead but Sophie thought she detected a twitch at the corner of his mouth.

'I can't believe all the place names are English!' she said a little later.

'Well, it's only natural to want to bring something of home with you.'

'Imagine leaving your country, knowing you'll never go back. Just going all that way on such a tiny ship must have taken huge courage.'

'Homesick, Sophie?'

She shook her head. 'No, I'm having a brilliant time.' She smiled at him, aware it was partly he that was making it so brilliant. 'Thank you!'

'My pleasure,' he replied, and for a moment they were in perfect harmony. Soon they reached a town that could have been in one of the wealthier parts of the UK. 'Now let's hurry right along. I gather I have to have you back for more cookie-frosting.'

'There were a couple of girls who couldn't come yesterday but who heard about it.'

'And that's at three so we'd better hurry.'

'It's only half past ten. How long do you think it's all going to take?' Luke sent her another bewildered look, which made her feel like a creature from another planet all over again. She was getting used to it.

She went on feeling like one when they got into the shop, which, as she had feared, was desperately intimidating. In her room at Matilda's house she had felt dressed down but respectable. Here she just felt scruffy. Yet her jeans were fairly new, her sweater was a good label (bought at high discount) and she'd cleaned her boots before she left Milly's flat. It was her parka that really let her down.

The owner of the shop swam towards them with her hand held out. She was the most perfectly groomed woman

Sophie had ever seen; as she got closer, Sophie realised this woman had probably had 'work' done. Probably in her mid fifties, she had enough lines to give her face character but no sagging jawline or hooded eyes. Her immaculate pink, knee-length two-piece – possibly vintage Chanel – showed off her perfect legs ending in medium-heel shoes that would have paid for ten of everything Sophie was wearing and have change. The highlights in her hair could have been put into individual hairs, and her make-up was flawless. Sophie felt herself shrinking towards Luke for protection.

But the moment the woman smiled, revealing small, straight, very white teeth, Sophie felt herself relax a little. This woman may have been perfect but she was good at her job too; she knew better than to intimidate her customers. She grasped Sophie's hand from where it had been clinging to the bottom of her coat.

'You must be Sophie. I'm Heidi. Mrs Winchester said you'd be a joy to dress and I can see exactly what she means. A model figure, dimples, great hair! I recognised you from her description the moment you walked in.'

'Oh.' Sophie couldn't decide if this made her feel better or worse.

'And you must be Mrs Winchester's grandson.' She shook Luke's hand too and Sophie had time to be grateful she didn't appear to know him personally; he hadn't brought other young women here to buy clothes.

She now had Sophie's hand in both of hers. 'Honey, would you like your gorgeous boyfriend to help you choose something? Or will we get on better on our own?'

Sophie felt slightly panicked. Should she say that Luke wasn't her boyfriend – and where had Heidi got that idea from? Would having him there make the whole experience better or worse?

He made the decision for her. There was a pile of

magazines on a table in front of a little sofa. 'I'll buy a newspaper and read, then I'm here if you need a masculine opinion.'

Heidi was obviously delighted. 'Honey, we gals always want a masculine opinion but not until we're clear in our own minds what that opinion should be and whether we'll listen or not.'

It took Sophie a moment to work this out and then she nodded.

'And would you like a glass of champagne or a cup of coffee while you catch up on the news?' asked Heidi, taking Luke's topcoat and ushering him on to the sofa.

'No thank you. I'll let you two get on.'

Heidi handed the coat to the minion who'd materialised, just as well groomed but younger than her boss.

'Thank you, honey,' said Heidi, getting Sophie's parka off her back without Sophie noticing how she did it. 'Now!' Her professional gaze raked Sophie from the top of her rather tangled top knot to her slightly scuffed toes. 'We have work to do!'

She ushered Sophie into a changing room at the back of the shop rather as a nanny gets her charges up to bed: kindly, and by not acknowledging that anything else could happen. 'You take your top clothes off and I'll bring you things to try. A brunch, Mrs Winchester said?'

'That's right. I think it's quite smart.'

Heidi nodded. 'It's Mrs St Clare. Very smart.'

'How do you know?' This woman seemed omniscient.

'She has one every year and, besides, Mrs Winchester told me.'

Heidi fell silent, looking at Sophie, who still hadn't stripped off, reluctant to let this woman see her underwear. 'Honey? Would you mind if I suggested we started from the skin out?'

'Um . . .'

'Lingerie. It seems to me your lovely figure is not being well served by your foundation garments.'

Sophie hadn't thought of the greying bra and skimpy knickers as foundation garments before – perhaps for good reason. 'I'm not sure . . .' Luke was buying her an outfit so she'd pass as his girlfriend. Surely no one would notice her bra?

'Shall I check with Mr Winchester?'

'I don't know!' The thought of him buying her underwear as well as everything else was too much. 'We hardly know each other!'

Heidi smiled. 'That's not the impression I had from Mrs Winchester, but if you feel you don't want to make a big song and dance about it, I understand.' Heidi paused for thought, an activity not reflected in her facial expression. 'Take your clothes off. I'm going to bring you some things to try.'

The changing room was spacious. Like the shop it contained a small sofa and a pile of magazines. As Sophie took off her clothes and hung them on some hooks she decided it was easier not to argue with Heidi. If she wanted to think that she and Luke were a major item then let her. And, she realised, seating herself, it probably made it less weird him buying her clothes. Maybe Matilda had told Heidi they were practically engaged to make it seem more normal. She picked up American *Vogue*. She had exchanged it for *Cosmo* and was well into an article about hypnotherapy as an aid to weight loss when Heidi came back. On her arm was a selection of bras, all-in-one bra-and-pant sets and also pairs of knickers and thongs.

'I checked with him,' said Heidi, correctly interpreting Sophie's look of horror. 'He said you were to have everything. Now let's have that brassiere – if you can call it that.'

142

At least she wasn't required to try on the knickers, and the bra Heidi was finally happy with did make her look fabulous.

'Now the top layer.' Heidi disappeared out of the changing room to return seconds later with an armful of hangers and plastic bags. Her assistant had obviously been picking out garments while Heidi had been adjusting Sophie's bra straps.

'Brunches are usually smart-casual, the hardest look to achieve in my opinion. Try these pants. Oh and put on these heels. You won't be wearing flats.'

Sophie thought she probably would be wearing flats as she'd declared her beautiful stilts a health hazard. Then, as she drew on the wide, silky, palazzo pants, she realised that she'd have to take up the hems if she stuck to her own boots. When the trousers were done up, she slipped her feet into the court shoes offered to her by Heidi.

'Fabulous! Now the top!'

The clothes were fabulous, but Sophie didn't feel herself in them. They were too smart, too slick. Her style was bohemian, quirky and original. But maybe it didn't matter? She was acting as Luke's girlfriend. She didn't want to look like herself, she wanted to look like a New York heiress, old money, or even the descendant of an oil millionaire. This made her giggle. If she ever achieved her quest it might turn out that she was.

Eventually Heidi was satisfied with her appearance. She'd found shoes, a bag, a gilt belt and a scarf.

'Now,' she said, 'time to show Mr Winchester.' Heidi led her to where Luke had the financial papers spread out in front of him. 'Well! Isn't she just gorgeous?'

Luke looked up. First he looked disbelieving and then he frowned. 'Um, I'm sorry, but that outfit won't do.'

'Honey!' protested Heidi, disappointment breaking through her professional veneer. 'She's to die for!'

'She is,' agreed Luke, 'but my mother would wear those clothes, not my girlfriend.' He suddenly cleared his throat, aware that maybe he'd told Heidi that Sophie wasn't his girlfriend. 'I mean, I think she looks at her best in jeans and a top.'

'I have jeans and a top of my own!' said Sophie indignantly. 'Have you put me through—' Then she stopped. She didn't want to offend Heidi, who'd worked very hard on her behalf.

'You need designer jeans,' said Luke. 'Which is it? Chloé? And then something on top, and some boots.'

'I have boots!' Sophie protested again, but quieter this time. She knew he'd add 'that aren't scuffed' if she made too much fuss.

'But keep the bra and purse,' said Luke. 'They're perfect.'

Chapter Ten

‧✦‧❦‧✦‧

When Sophie left the shop she was holding bags of clothes that made her feel exactly like herself, only the five-star, high-end version. She had a new handbag over her shoulder that she thought was possibly the new love of her life.

'Thank you, Luke, for saving me from getting all the wrong clothes. And thank you so much for the bag as well.'

'The wrong purse would give the game away completely.'

'I know. It just seems too much! I feel like Julia Roberts in *Pretty Woman*.'

He laughed. 'Are you a fan of Julia Roberts's films?'

'Oh yes! Especially *Notting Hill*. I *loved* it.'

'Did you ever see *Mystic Pizza*? One of her earlier films, before she was really famous?'

'Mm! My sister had it on DVD. I'd always make pizzas and she'd drink red wine while we watched it.'

'So you do like pizza?'

'Oh yes.' Sophie was aware she sounded as if pizza was her favourite dish of all time and that she'd been deprived of it. What she was really missing was an ordinary meal in an ordinary restaurant.

'And you like the ocean?'

'Who doesn't?'

Luke laughed. 'I think you deserve a treat after that shopping trip. My grandmother meant well, sending you there, but she's not the most fashion-conscious person.'

'Well, why should she be?'

'And while you did look lovely in those wide pants, no one your age would wear them.'

'I'm very impressed that you knew that, Luke.' Sophie looked up at him, trying not to smile. 'Or are you in the habit of buying your girlfriends' clothes?'

'You'd be surprised,' he said.

'Oh, I don't think so,' said Sophie. 'I can imagine.' She put on a soft, sweet voice, with a hint of an American accent. 'Luke, honey, would you help me pick out an outfit? Oh, baby! I don't seem to have my credit card with me!'

He laughed. 'You've got that quite wrong. It's all a lot more subtle than that. Now come on. I'm taking you to Mystic!'

Sophie bounced up and down in her seat, barely able to stop herself hugging him for joy. 'What a wonderful treat! Thank you so much!'

Was he this nice to his trophy girlfriends, she wondered, the ones Matilda disapproved of? Or wouldn't they like being driven miles just to eat pizza? Just for a little while Sophie let herself imagine what it would be like. Pretty nice, she decided, and then firmly switched off the daydream. He was so not her type.

Sophie was glad that the shopping hadn't taken up too much time. It was further to Mystic than she'd been expecting. They joined the Interstate 95 – a motorway to Sophie – and passed through some urban sprawl, and then they got into some really beautiful countryside. There were no horizons here, not like in England with its endless vistas of farmland and gently rolling hills. The Connecticut shoreline had miles and miles of trees, dark green pine and fir, with an occasional scattering of yellow and scarlet

146

leaves among the now skeletal branches of oak and maple. And through the trees patches of water shone like polished steel in the sunshine.

After they'd crossed what Luke told her was the Connecticut River the scenery became even lovelier. And at last they arrived in Mystic.

It was delightful. Luke drove slowly along the seafront while Sophie exclaimed with pleasure at the clapboard houses, churches with pointed steeples and gingerbread decoration.

She was enchanted. 'This is so pretty! I love this place! I can't believe I'm really here! I can't wait to tell my sister – she'll be so jealous.'

'I'm glad. Now I'll park the car and find you a pizza.'

After he'd found a spot, which took some doing, Sophie couldn't help putting her arm through his as they walked along. He didn't seem to mind.

'I really love the seaside,' said Sophie. 'I love where I live and everything, but I really wish I was nearer the sea.'

'I know what you mean. At least in England you can't be too far from it, even in the middle.'

'It seems far,' said Sophie.

'Here's the place,' he said later. 'The very pizza restaurant they used for the movie.'

Sophie clapped her hands. 'I feel like I'm in one!'

When the waitress had taken their order she leant forward. 'This is all so American, somehow. I love it!'

Luke laughed. 'I have to confess it's refreshing to take out a girl who's so enthusiastic. It is only pizza.'

'That's what makes it special! I love pizza and I love being here. Thank you so much.' Her hand moved across the table on its own. Sophie stopped it just before it reached Luke's. She wasn't sure Luke would want his hand patted. He was being really nice; they were having a good time

147

together; but Sophie wasn't sure how much exuberant affection he could take. She wasn't sure trophy girlfriends went in for that sort of thing.

'Here you go, guys,' said the waitress, setting down enough pizza to feed two small families. She must have sensed Sophie's feelings. 'If you can't eat it all, we'll box it up for you and you can take it home. It comes from a proper wood pizza oven, you know.'

'It looks and smells amazing!' said Sophie, looking up at her.

'Oh, you're English! Cute!' she said, and left them to it.

'Eat your pizza, Cutie,' said Luke, laughing.

Sophie refused to rise to his bait, picked up a slice and took a bite. 'This is so good!' she said with her mouth full. 'What a shame we'll never eat it all.'

'It does always feel like that when the pizza first arrives but it's amazing how much of it you do manage.'

It was amazing. Sophie ate most of hers before declaring she would never eat again.

'Don't say that. There's a leftovers buffet tonight, although they make a lot of extra food as well. If you can still walk after you get up from the table, my grandmother and her entire staff will think they've failed. Now we'd better get back.'

The next morning, Sophie put on all her new clothes. She had intended not to wear the lovely slouchy boots so she could take them back and not cost Luke so much money, but they were so perfect with the jeans she just couldn't. She tried them on to check the look and couldn't bring herself to take them off again.

She was now in the hall, waiting for Luke, although she knew he wouldn't turn up for another ten minutes or so. She felt if she'd stayed in her room any longer, she might be tempted to take all her make-up off and put it on again, again – she was so nervous about the brunch.

Matilda found her there, sitting on a Louis Quinze sofa, flicking through the *New York Times*, frantically scanning it for future topics of conversation. She might be really put on the spot at the brunch and asked difficult questions.

'Good morning, Sophie!'

Sophie leapt up and went towards the old lady. 'Oh, Matilda! I don't think I said thank you properly for letting me share Thanksgiving with you. It was so wonderful!'

Matilda chuckled, kissing her cheek. 'You said thank you very prettily. I always prefer it if we have guests for Thanksgiving, it makes it more special. And I was so touched by what you said you were thankful for.'

'Of course I'm thankful for meeting you!' Sophie hadn't had to think hard when she was asked to start off the tradition.

'And you joined in with the psalm!'

'I remembered it from school. Psalm one hundred, "Rejoice in the Lord all ye lands."'

'Have you a moment?' Matilda suddenly looked a little mysterious.

Sophie glanced at her watch. 'Oh yes. Luke and I aren't meeting up for five minutes or so. I came out of my room before I could change my mind about my outfit.'

Matilda scrutinised the outfit for the first time. 'Is that what Heidi picked out for you?'

'No. It's what Luke picked out. Heidi picked out a lovely pair of palazzo pants and a top but I wasn't really happy in it, and Luke said it was something his mother would wear.' She paused. 'I'm wearing the bra she chose for me though.'

Matilda seemed amused. 'Well, I'm glad Heidi had something to do.'

149

'It was so sweet of you to phone ahead!' Sophie didn't want to seem ungrateful. 'She was lovely.'

'She is, but I do understand that maybe her taste is a little old for you. Now come with me. I have something to show you and I don't want Luke to know about it.'

'But why? He adores you!'

'I know, but I have a bit of a project and until I know there's some point to it, I'd rather just keep it between us.' She paused. 'I do have funny spells sometimes – the doctor says it's nothing to be concerned about, but Luke does worry.' She paused. 'Besides, I never think it's a good idea to tell men everything. They just take over.'

Sophie followed Matilda, who led her through her bedroom (which made Sophie's seem rather poky) and into what could only be described as a boudoir. It had a selection of antique chairs, a chaise longue upholstered in silk, and the most exquisite bureau, inlaid with mother of pearl and full, Sophie was certain, of secret compartments. It made Uncle Eric's desk seem positively utilitarian.

'What a lovely room! Look at all these beautiful antiques.'

'What? Oh yes, dear. I'm very lucky, I have lots of lovely things, but it's this I want to show you.'

She pointed to a picture in an alcove. It was of a house and although the painting was very pretty, it didn't seem to Sophie to be by the hand of an old master, rather a talented amateur. She went up closer and read the brass plaque underneath it. 'The Rectory', it said.

'It's delightful . . .' Sophie began, wondering why on earth Matilda should have something not notably special in her room when she could probably have had a Renoir or something.

'It's a house I visited as a child. I want to track it down.'

Sophie began to get an inkling of why she'd been invited into Matilda's inner sanctum. 'Where is it?'

'I'm not exactly sure, which is where you come in.'

'How do you mean?'

'I want you to find it for me. I want to know if it's still standing.'

'Well, who did it belong to?'

'I don't know,' said Matilda, a little abashed. 'I realise it is difficult. I do have a name though.'

'That's all right then. We could look it up on the internet. People search for their ancestors all the time online.'

'The trouble is, I'm not sure if this is a place name or a surname. Or exactly how it's spelt.'

Sophie took this in. 'That does make it a bit harder.'

'Yes.'

'Why don't you ask Luke?' suggested Sophie. 'He obviously has all the contacts for tracking people down. He's finding my relative for me, after all.'

'That's here, dear. He knows nothing about England, and where would he start?'

'Where would I start? I haven't even got a car!'

'I'll give you the details of how we got there. We went by train. It took us quite a long time, I remember. But Dr Beeching did away with all those little stations, didn't he?'

'Did he? Can you remember the name of the little station?'

Matilda shook her head. 'I remember making up words from the letters in it, but not the name itself.'

Sophie sighed. 'Well, was this person a relative? I'm sure if you give me your parents' names I could find out who your grandparents were and where they lived.'

'I don't know if we were related or not. I just remember having this magical time. I've dreamt about that house ever since. I feel I have to know what happened to it. But because I have so little information I don't want to bother Luke with it. But I know you'll understand.'

'Because I'm English and slightly eccentric?' Although no one had said as much she had picked up that that was the impression she gave.

Matilda chuckled. 'Something like that.'

Accepting Matilda's opinion of her calmly, Sophie asked, 'But couldn't you hire a private detective or something? I just don't feel I'm the best person to ask to do this.'

'You are the best person because you understand why I'm looking. If I start hiring detectives the whole family would find out about it and think I'm developing Alzheimer's. They worry about me as it is.' She gave Sophie a quizzical look. 'Have you a job at home?'

'Not at the moment; at least, not a full-time one. I mostly do several part-time jobs. I'm saving up to go on a course.'

'What course?'

'Well,' said Sophie, 'the thing is, I can't decide what's best. I'd really like to learn proper tailoring, so I could make anything, not just add bits of decoration or do simple alterations, but create clothes from scratch. And then there's soft furnishings. I can make curtains well enough but I'd love to be able to do proper upholstery. But possibly I should do a small business course, so if I did set up something I could actually make money. I need to be practical.'

'Goodness me, you sound very determined, I must say.'

'Well, my family are all academics, you see, except my mother, who paints. I need to be practical.' She frowned. 'One day, when I'm truly independent, I'll move to the seaside and run my business from my own home.'

'Really? Don't you want a husband and children?' Matilda seemed surprised.

'Well, yes, but I can't just decide to have those, can I? I might not meet anyone. But if I had a business I'd be mistress of my own destiny.' She chuckled. 'I rather like the sound of that!'

'And so do I!' said Matilda. 'Go to it!'

'I will, when I get home.' She stifled a sigh. Getting the money for all that would not be easy.

Matilda hesitated for a minute. 'Maybe before you set off on your life's goal, you might do this little thing for me? Only I don't suppose it is little, really.' She frowned. 'Maybe we should discuss it when you see how life is turning out in England. I don't want you to waste your time on my behalf.'

'Oh, I wouldn't be wasting my time! If you want me to do anything for you, I'd be more than happy. I've had such a brilliant time staying with you.'

'I just know you're the one to help me. You have plenty of imagination and yet are practical. I also think you understand having a dream.'

'I certainly understand that!' said Sophie, smiling.

'And you're very kind. I'll be in touch. I do email you know,' Matilda said proudly. 'Luke taught me. But I'm not on Facebook. Luke thought I'd let just anyone be my friend.'

Sophie laughed and hugged Matilda, ending with a kiss on her cheek. 'Maybe you should Twitter instead.'

Matilda looked perplexed and Sophie laughed again.

'Ask Luke, he'll tell you,' she said. 'Oh, here he is.'

Luke was looking incredibly preppy, thought Sophie, and stunningly good-looking. He was wearing jeans and a cashmere sweater and smelt of something very expensive. Sophie was very glad of her own designer outfit and the scent left for her in her bedroom. She suspected it was rather an old lady perfume, but it was better than nothing and no one had seemed to notice when she wore it before.

'Hello, Granny,' said Luke, hugging her. 'Hi, Sophie. Wow! Don't you look the picture.'

'In England we'd say "the bees' knees", or "the cat's pyjamas",' said Sophie seriously.

Luke ignored this. 'Granny, I was wondering if I could ask a favour?'

'Anything, my darling.'

'Could Sophie borrow a ring? I think this whole charade would work better if she was my fiancée. Having a girlfriend will only buy me peace for a very short time. A ring on her finger would give me at least a year.'

'Erm . . .' broke in Sophie, feeling very uncomfortable.

'My jewellery is so old-fashioned,' said Matilda to Luke. 'You need a large solitaire.'

'But Sophie is English, she might well like something old-fashioned.'

'Excuse me!' Sophie broke in again but they still took no notice.

'Come and let's have a look. I've only got my less valuable jewellery out of the bank but you might find something there. I do have a very pretty aquamarine surrounded by diamonds. No one would know it wasn't a pale sapphire.'

Luke and Matilda set off towards Matilda's dressing room. Sophie followed them.

Matilda opened a cupboard and brought out a jewellery box the size of a small chest. She set it on the dressing table and opened it.

'Granny, don't you keep it locked?' objected Luke.

'Why should I? Thieves could just take the whole thing.'

'But the staff . . .'

'. . . would never steal from me. Anyway, which ring would you like?'

'I'm sorry,' said Sophie, as firmly as she could with her jaw slackened by the sight of so much lovely jewellery not in the window of a shop, 'but I can't wear a ring. At least, not on my engagement finger.'

'Oh,' said Matilda, her fingers closing on the aquamarine surrounded by tiny diamonds. 'Are you superstitious?'

'Yes, I'm afraid I am. I've never put a ring on that finger. I do sometimes smooth out toffee wrappers and see what a wedding ring would look like, but I've never put a ring on.'

Luke took a breath, possibly irritated by such a ridiculous idea, but was silenced by his grandmother. 'Well, I perfectly understand that. Luke dear, it has to be enough that you have a girlfriend. She needn't be a fiancée.'

Luke frowned. 'The trouble is' – he looked uncomfortable – 'I didn't correct Heidi in the shop when she referred to Sophie as my fiancée while I was picking out clothes. She will have told people. You know how everyone gossips.'

'Will she be at the brunch?' asked Sophie.

'No, but she will have seen people who will be, and told them.'

'Well, that's OK. We can be engaged but just not have a ring yet.' Sophie relaxed, although part of her did rather yearn to try on some of the rocks Matilda didn't consider to be her expensive jewellery.

Luke shook his head. It was rather touching to see him embarrassed and feeling in the wrong. Sophie felt it probably didn't happen often. 'I sort of told her we were going to buy a ring.'

'What do you mean?' said Matilda.

'She asked me what we were doing next and then the phone went just as I said, "Going to Mystic." She got off the phone, all excited and fluttery, and kissed me. I didn't know why, and then she said, "But don't worry, I won't say a thing to Sophie." It was only just now I realised what had happened.'

'Well, what had happened?' demanded Matilda. 'Oh . . . I think I see what you mean.'

'What?' demanded Sophie. Luke was biting his lip and Matilda had a more-in-sorrow-than-in-anger expression on her face.

'There's a jewellery shop in town,' explained Matilda. 'It's called Mystical Jewels.'

'Yes,' said Luke. 'And they've just called me to ask why I didn't go in yesterday.'

'That's outrageous,' said Matilda. 'They had no right to do that.'

'No, but they've done it, and Heidi will have told everyone we'll be turning up at the brunch as an engaged couple.'

'And you couldn't just tell people that Heidi made a mistake?'

Matilda and Luke both shook their heads. 'No. It would make an even bigger fuss.'

They both regarded her. Luke, tall, handsome, used to getting his own way, seeming as if he really needed this favour. And Matilda, who seemed to want it too, whom Sophie loved and to whom she owed a lot of lovely hospitality and friendship.

'OK, that's it,' said Sophie after a moment or two. 'I'll wear a ring but it has to be the smallest, most discreet little thing you have in there.' She indicated the treasure chest.

'Brilliant!' said Matilda. 'That will make you look as if you have taste and discernment.'

'Which I have,' muttered Sophie.

'I know just the one,' said Matilda, lifting out the top two trays. 'It's in here. It's a bit like an eternity ring but it only goes halfway round. It's pretty, though isn't it? Sort of like a basket, with the stones in the spaces.'

When Sophie saw it she instantly wanted to own it. It had six rubies across the middle in lozenge-shaped settings. In the spaces above and below were tiny diamonds.

'Would you feel superstitious about wearing it?' asked Luke, possibly realising how much she liked it by the way she was cradling it in her hand.

'If it makes you feel any better about trying it on,' said Matilda, 'I should tell you I had three wedding rings. Only one husband but I got bored with the rings and wanted different ones. We were still very happily married.'

Sophie took the ring and slid it on to her ring finger. It looked as if it belonged there.

'Perfect,' breathed Matilda.

'All the Bergdorf Blondes will stop wanting rocks,' said Luke, amused, 'and want antique rings instead.'

'It is very pretty,' said Sophie, examining her hand from every angle. 'You will so owe me if I wear it.'

'I will,' he said. 'Now come on. We don't want to be late.' He leant down and kissed his grandmother on the cheek. 'We'll tell you all about it when we get back.'

'And you make a very convincing couple, so don't you worry, Sophie.'

Chapter Eleven

❧

Sophie slid into Luke's car, wondering if leather seats were like Matilda's sheets – so lovely she wouldn't want to go back to bobbly polycotton – or like plastic car upholstery that you stuck to in summer.

She gazed out of the window wondering if she had been spoilt for ever – all her economical ways tainted by luxury. She laughed.

'What's funny?' asked Luke.

She considered for a moment and then told him. 'My life is so different at home. I'm just wondering if I'll be able to go back to it.'

'I'm sure you will.'

She shot him a glance but she couldn't tell if he meant anything by this. Usually she was good at reading body language but she found Luke's very confusing. Although she was trying to get over it, she still worried that he might think she was a woman on the make.

'Are we nearly there yet?' she asked.

He laughed. 'Why, are you feeling ill or just impatient to get to the party?'

'No!' She was indignant. 'I just thought we ought to get our story straight.'

'Our story?'

'Yes! How we met and everything.'

'We don't need to go into details. We'll just say yes, we're engaged, but your family doesn't know yet and we're not planning to get married for a couple of years. Say until you've finished university. You're very young.'

'I know! People will say you're a cradle-snatcher.'

'No they won't.'

She realised he was right and sank back in her seat, looking out of the window. She was wondering if all Luke's and Matilda's friends lived in houses that would convert to hotels without having to be extended and then frowned. 'But I'm not at university.'

'OK, some kind of training then. You don't have to be specific. No one will ask.'

'Aren't you worried about your mother finding out? Won't she be worried to hear you're engaged to a woman she's never heard of?'

'Not really. She's very involved with her own life.'

'The gossip columns? They could have a field day!'

'That would be to my advantage. It would tell the world I'm off the market.'

Sophie didn't quite know how to respond to this and felt a bit deflated. It seemed so strange that she, an impoverished girl from England, should take Luke, sought-after man-about-town away from all the other lovely women who wanted him. She wasn't convinced.

'Did I tell you how very attractive you look?' Luke said, possibly feeling obliged to cheer her up.

'Do I? If you spend enough money it's not hard.'

He laughed. 'Oh yes it is! Believe me! And while the girls might all wonder why I picked you and not one of them, the men will all be completely convinced.'

Sophie realised she wasn't very good at accepting compliments. Maybe she should practise with the make-you-feel-better ones that Luke was paying her. 'Well, thank you, Luke. That's very kind.'

*

Luke parked his car outside a house easily as big as Matilda's. Had she not been on Luke's arm, wearing very expensive clothes, a heavenly handbag and an adorable ring, Sophie would have been daunted by the exhibition of wealth and beauty that greeted them. Then she realised that being with Luke gave her status it would have been hard for her to achieve on her own. Her first emotion was pleasure: she knew what it felt like to have made it. Her second was shame: she shouldn't want to be the centre of attention because of who she was with and how much money he had. Still, she'd play the part even if it killed her.

'Luke, honey!' A very tall, very blonde girl with nearly waist-length hair, who could have stepped straight off the cover of American *Vogue*, seemed to have been lying in wait. 'What's all this about you being engaged? To this lovely girl?'

There was enough irritation and surprise in her voice to make Sophie feel almost guilty; she'd taken their best unattached man and she didn't even look right. But the blonde's attitude stiffened Sophie's backbone. She decided to stop feeling like a fake and really throw herself into the part!

Luke kissed the offered cheek. 'Hi, Lulu, meet Sophie.'

As Lulu moved forward, Sophie realised she was expected to kiss her too. She did her best through the blonde curtain that was offered. 'Hello,' Sophie said.

'English! That explains why none of us have met you before!'

Sophie smiled and nodded. She didn't want to gush.

'Well, come on in and get a drink.'

A uniformed waiter appeared at their side. He had a tray of Bloody Marys sporting sticks of celery and what looked like Buck's Fizz. Sophie took a Buck's Fizz. She had no idea how strong the Bloody Marys were likely to be.

160

'Come and say hi to everyone,' Lulu said.

She took hold of Luke as if he might run away and Sophie followed, beginning to understand why he'd been so eager to have a partner for this particular party. She really hoped he wouldn't be wrenched away from her. The place seemed to be full of the sort of high-maintenance girls who had been in the New York club. Matilda's party had been more of a family affair. Everyone had been extremely wealthy and well groomed, but here it seemed more competitive. She was so glad that Heidi had insisted on her having the right bag. Without it, even in her new clothes she felt she wouldn't find anyone to talk to who didn't make her feel shabby.

A group of girls clustered round Luke, not exactly ignoring Sophie but paying all their attention to him.

'So have you known each other long?'

'Yes, Luke, you've kept Sophie quiet.'

'Who will our mothers plan for us to marry now?'

Luke's mouth narrowed a little, and then he looked down at Sophie, who smiled up at him adoringly, feeling genuinely sorry for him.

'So, tell us,' repeated the first girl, also a blonde, 'how long have you known each other?'

Sophie continued to look up at Luke, partly to keep up the adoring fiancée charade and partly because she wondered what he'd say. She suspected this girl was on to their pretence.

'Not long,' he said.

'So did you fall for each other straightaway?' persisted the blonde.

Luke couldn't put off answering any longer. 'She fell for my grandmother, actually. When I first met Sophie she and my grandmother were sitting on the floor together, with their legs stretched out in front of them.'

161

'Oh, that doesn't sound very romantic.' Lulu seemed encouraged by this.

'But it was. Sophie looked just like Bambi, all long legs and big eyes.'

'I never saw *Bambi*,' said Sophie, wondering if Luke was paying her a compliment by this description or was just colouring in the pretence of their engagement. 'I made a point of missing it when I heard his mother died.'

Everyone seemed to think she'd made a joke and laughed.

'You can tell why I fell in love with her, can't you?' said Luke.

By now thoroughly unnerved, Sophie said, 'I expect people are wondering why I fell in love with you.'

'Oh no, honey, we all know *exactly* why you fell in love with Luke,' drawled another girl, obviously speaking for them all.

A stab of something inspired Sophie to speak. 'You mean, because he's very rich and very good-looking? Well, I can assure you, it wasn't that that attracted me. At all. In fact it put me off a bit.'

A gasp of surprise whistled through the group. This girl may have looked like Bambi, but she wasn't dumb.

'Really?'

Sophie nodded. Luke, who had put his arm round her shoulders, gave her a little squeeze, possibly of approval, but possibly not.

'So what was it then?' asked a brunette.

'Well, it was partly because he is so sweet to his grandmother, who is the nicest person in the world, and partly because in spite of being rather spoilt, he can be very kind.'

There was a gasp of horror from the audience but Luke kissed her cheek. 'You're outrageous!' he said. 'Now come on, Sophie, there are people I want you to meet.' He released her shoulder and took her arm.

'Now do you see why I needed protection?' he said when they were out of earshot, making their way to another room full of people. 'I feel like a piece of meat hanging over a tank full of piranhas.'

'But I'm sure you'd have no bother getting rid of them.'

'I don't, but I hate the thought they're convinced one of them will eventually marry me. And if I'm too blunt their mothers will complain to my grandmother who will tell me I must be more tactful.'

'Are you worried that one of them will actually make it through?'

Luke's expression made her laugh. 'I think maybe I am.'

Luke could be extremely charming, she discovered, as he introduced her to people. They exclaimed over her ring, obviously feeling it was an unusual choice. The more people looked at it, the more she liked it.

'If I were engaged to you, Luke,' said Lulu, who'd caught up with them by the waffle station, 'I'd have a diamond the size of a pigeon's egg.'

'Maybe that's why I'm engaged to Sophie,' said Luke. 'She has more subtle tastes.'

'And she's not engaged to you because of the money, the private plane and the cute butt?'

'Well, I hope not, anyway.'

Sophie felt she should help Luke out. She could really see now how hard it would be for him to know if a girl was really interested in him as a person or if she was just after his money. It made his attitude to her in the beginning much more understandable. 'Those things aren't exactly disadvantages – especially the "cute butt" – but really I fell for Luke because he's a bit mysterious. I do like a bit of mystery.'

'And one of the reasons I fell for Sophie is that she reminded me a little of my grandmother,' said Luke, picking up the theme.

'What?' Sophie pretended to be offended that she was being likened to a woman who must be eighty.

'Yes. You're both very charming and just a bit . . . unpredictable.'

Everyone laughed, as they were supposed to. Sophie joined in, very glad she wasn't really engaged to Luke and wouldn't have to socialise often with skinny blondes the colour of honey with clothes that cost a hundred dollars per square inch.

A tall, slightly older woman, with short dark hair cut in a sophisticated way that was very different from the Bergdorf Blondes, put her hand on her arm. She had dark, arched eyebrows and her large, shapely mouth was painted scarlet. 'Poor Sophie. We must all seem very strange to you. I'm Ali. My mother was French so we're geographically close relations. Come over here and tell me all about yourself. But not before you've had some of those pancakes. American cuisine might be a little strange to Continental tastes but there are some things they do brilliantly.'

Sophie did as she was told, feeling she'd found a human being in Barbie Land. She took some pancakes and bacon, added maple syrup, and then followed Ali. Luke gave her an encouraging smile as she passed.

'Ali works with us. I think you and she will like each other. You talk to her while I catch up with some people.'

'Come with me,' said Ali. 'I know somewhere we can be comfortable.' Ali tucked her arm in Sophie's and drew her through the crowds. She was aware of people looking at them and felt pleased to be with someone who wasn't Luke – she wasn't just his hanger-on.

164

'Here's a table,' said Ali. 'We can eat like civilised human beings.'

Sophie ate, hoping it was in a civilised way, given that Americans did complicated things with their knives and forks.

'So,' said Ali when Sophie's mouth was full, 'how do you feel about Luke's first wife?'

Sophie forced herself to carry on chewing. The fact that Luke had been married before was really none of her business, but as he'd asked her to pose as his fiancée, she should have a view on this. It was important to look relaxed.

'Oh well, you know,' she said, shrugging. 'We all make mistakes.'

'We do, unless we're very careful. Luke just wasn't careful enough, in my opinion.' Ali put her plate down, indicating she'd finished although it was three-quarters full.

'Did you know her?' asked Sophie, pleased to have worked out a way to get information without revealing her own ignorance.

'Not really, she was pretty much off the scene before I came to work for Luke, but I did meet her once, when she came to pick up some papers from the office. Very, very beautiful girl. But young. Far too young to be married.' Ali regarded Sophie as if she were warning her. 'I don't think Luke . . . I mean . . . Well, never mind what I think!' Ali smiled to cover up the fact that she'd started a sentence she couldn't finish. 'But it was all very, very expensive, and it's not a mistake he's going to make again.' She paused. 'He does seem attracted to very young women.'

For a second Sophie felt warned off, as if she really were engaged to Luke. Ali was smiling warmly as if she had been talking about some foolish prank Luke had got up to and wouldn't do again, but there'd been power behind her words that Sophie couldn't ignore.

'As long as he's learnt his lesson,' said Sophie, aiming to sound light-hearted but, really, feeling defensive, as she might have done if her engagement to Luke had been genuine.

Ali put her hand on Sophie's. 'You're so funny!'

'Ali's a great girl, right?' said Luke when he came to find her a little later.

'Yes,' said Sophie.

'She's a refreshing change.'

Sophie instantly interpreted this to mean they'd gone out together. If so, was it for long? Why did they break up? Or had her imagination gone into overdrive? 'She asked me how I felt about the fact that you've been married before.'

'And what did you say?'

'I didn't really know what to say, but I realised I should have thought of an answer beforehand. If we were really engaged I would have feelings about it. Wouldn't I?'

He shrugged. 'I guess.'

'I was worried about being caught out.'

'Did Ali catch you out?'

'I don't know,' said Sophie after a moment's thought. 'I'm not sure.'

'Well, don't worry about it. Now let's find our hosts and say our goodbyes. We've done our duty here.'

Sophie couldn't decide if they left comparatively early for her sake or for Luke's. Perhaps he didn't like having her as a fiancée after all.

'Oh, by the way,' he said when they were nearly back at Matilda's, 'I put some people on to researching your relative. They should have news soon.'

'Thank you! That's so kind.'

Sophie was confused. One minute she thought Luke was really nice and the next he seemed to stiffen up; she couldn't read him. It was probably because she just wasn't used to men born with silver spoons in their mouths, or whatever the American equivalent was. However, she realised Matilda wasn't the only person she was going to miss when she went back to England. Despite Luke's chameleon-like behaviour he had been good company and she'd enjoyed spending time with him. And it was a treat to be properly looked after by a man for a change, even if it was only out of politeness. The old-fashioned part of her appreciated it.

Luke had to go back to the city the day after the brunch, as did most of the house party. At Matilda's insistence, and also because she wanted to, Sophie stayed on for a couple of days. Matilda was going to New York and would take Sophie with her. More importantly, she would send her driver to pick her up from Milly's and take her to the airport a couple of days after that.

The big house felt very different when it was only Matilda and Sophie there. They had cosy meals in a little conservatory instead of in the big dining room. They spent their time together walking in the garden if it was fine, chatting about England in the old days and playing cards. Sophie was allowed to look through Matilda's wardrobe and managed to alter a few outfits for her that Matilda loved but hadn't thought worth bothering with.

Sophie privately considered that there were disadvantages to having so much money you could just buy new clothes; your favourite items didn't get used to their full potential.

And all the time Matilda reminisced about the house.

Eventually Sophie said, 'Have you got any old photos? If

167

you want me to track it down, it would help if I had a picture.'

'Well, that would be fun! It's always fun getting out the photos. But I'll have the painting photocopied and sent to you too.'

The family shots took a very long time to go through, by the time Sophie had asked questions and Matilda explained who everyone was and what they were doing. Among them there was indeed one of the house, tiny and very faded sepia. It showed a big house covered in some sort of plant, but gave no hints as to its whereabouts.

'I thought there might have been a name on the back or something,' said Sophie.

'I had hoped there would be too.' Matilda paused. 'It would be easier if I'd gone back there after I grew up, but the people died and there was no reason to visit.'

'Was it near the seaside?'

'Yes! Not far. We used to have picnics on the beach.'

'I've always wanted to live by the sea!' said Sophie wistfully and then realised she'd told Matilda that before.

Matilda went on, 'I used to sleep in an attic bedroom. I loved it. I remember sitting on the window seat, staring out the window for hours.'

'I would have liked doing that too,' said Sophie.

'I know,' said Matilda. 'We have a lot in common.'

Sophie smiled. 'I feel that too. And now, Matilda, you must let me give you back the ring. I know I tried to before and you stopped me but now I'm going home, I feel I must.'

'And I say you mustn't. Really. I have more rings than I'll ever have time to wear and it looks so pretty on your young hands. I spoke to Luke about it and he said you should keep it too, if you liked it and I wanted you to have it.'

'Well, I do like it! Obviously! It's gorgeous.'

'And I do want you to have it. You were very good to go to that brunch with Luke. I know it wasn't easy for you and you did such a good job.'

'But Luke bought me those wonderful clothes . . .'

'And I'd like to give you the ring.'

Eventually Sophie felt she couldn't argue any more and Matilda patted her hand, pleased to have got her own way in the end.

When they finally said goodbye, Sophie felt she was saying goodbye to a favourite relation, not a recent acquaintance. They were both a little tearful.

'But now we know each other,' said Sophie, 'we can keep in touch.'

'Certainly,' said Matilda. 'I'll email you the picture and tell you what Luke is up to.'

'It isn't really any of my business what he gets up to. We're not really engaged.'

Matilda sighed. 'I know.'

Chapter Twelve

❧

Amanda was a very satisfactory listener, Sophie decided. She had responded instantly to Sophie's request for a debrief and had agreed to meet Sophie, who was jet-lagged but also a bit hyper and desperate to talk through her recent experiences. Milly had heard the story, but until both of her old friends had, Sophie felt she hadn't talked it all through sufficiently.

Amanda had bagged a table with a sofa at their favourite wine bar and had ordered Sophie a glass of Pinot Grigio and a bottle of sparkling water. She pushed the wine towards her friend. 'Tell me everything, starting with your farewell dinner with Mills.'

When Sophie had taken a large gulp of wine she said, 'It was so sad to leave her! We didn't see all that much of each other but we did have some brilliant times. Her boyfriend cooked a lovely meal and then we went out for drinks afterwards.' Sophie rummaged in her bag – she hoped Amanda wouldn't ask about it just yet, or assume she'd bought a knock-off from the street – and produced a parcel. 'This is for you! Only little, I'm afraid, but I thought you deserved a present from me that wasn't home-made for once.'

'Oh, cool!' said Amanda. 'Bobbi Brown! My favourite!'

'Make-up is cheaper over there. I hope I got the colour right.'

Amanda opened the lipstick. 'Perfect. You have such a

170

good eye for colour. Now, tell me all – did you go to the Magnolia Bakery and have cupcakes?'

'Uh-huh! And oh, Mands, you should see the Christmas decorations! It's like fairy land. And they have outdoor skating in Central Park and in Times Square.'

'They do that in London, too.'

'But it's more glittery in New York,' Sophie insisted.

'So tell me about Milly. Is her boyfriend nice?'

'Sweet, although him being a chef they don't see that much of each other. She works really hard too. People do seem to, over there.'

'So, what else?'

'Well, I met a *wonderful* old lady. She asked me to stay in her mansion – I am not exaggerating, *mansion* – in Connecticut. I met her my second night in New York when I went to an opening that Milly was working on.'

Amanda sat back and listened while Sophie embarked on a detailed, if slightly garbled, account of her trip to America, ending with her feelings of guilt about the new clothes Luke had bought her.

'I have to say,' Amanda said, looking at Sophie's extended leg, 'I wouldn't have been able to take those boots back either. Or the bag.'

'You don't think keeping them makes me a sort of tart?' Sophie took another fond look before replacing her leg under the table.

Amanda took a thoughtful sip from her glass. 'No. Why would I think that?'

Sophie sighed. 'The trouble is, when you mix with very rich people you feel sort of touchy, as if you want to prove that you're as good as they are—'

'And you are!'

'I know! And I don't value myself because of how much money I have – which is just as well – but they were so generous to me. Matilda treated me like a daughter – granddaughter.'

'She liked you. If she didn't she would have just said, "Thank you for stopping me falling on my arse—"'

'She wouldn't have said that!' The thought of Matilda using such language made Sophie clap her hand to her mouth.

'And carried on looking at pictures,' continued Amanda, unfazed by Sophie's reaction. 'Or whatever she was doing.'

Sophie subsided and then sighed. 'I know, but giving me the ring.' She stretched out her right hand where the ring now set off her nail varnish very nicely. 'It was so kind.'

There was a tiny pause before Amanda said, 'What did Luke say about you keeping it?'

'Oh, he was keen too! Apparently he said I'd worked very hard for it and if Matilda wanted to give it to me, I should have it.'

'And had you worked hard at the brunch?'

Sophie nodded. 'It was quite hard to begin with. I felt such a fraud. This woman called Ali, who Luke really liked, sort of – I don't know – warned me about his previous wife, saying how young she was, implying I was too young too.' She paused. 'Having the ring gave me credibility. Although . . .' She paused. 'Looking back I wonder if the ring did convince her? She'd be able to tell it wasn't all that valuable. Maybe she knew we were just pretending?'

'Well, not being there I can't really say, but it sounds like you did as good a job as you possibly could and so Luke thought you should be rewarded.' Amanda peered at the ring. 'It probably isn't worth a huge amount of money, by their standards, anyway.'

Sophie decided to put her faint doubts about Ali out of her mind. Either she'd been convinced or she hadn't. She turned her mind back to Luke and his presents. 'True. But he'd already bought me the clothes and the bag and the boots, not to mention taken me to Mystic to eat pizza – we must get that film out – and, well, been really nice.'

'So you quite like Luke, do you?'

Sophie made a face. 'You're such a romantic! Just because you're really happy with David, you want to pair everyone else up.'

Amanda chuckled. 'No! But you are talking about him rather a lot. It is a bit of a sign.'

'I didn't realise—'

'So? Do you like him? Or not? Maybe you just don't fancy him.'

Sophie struggled to explain feelings she didn't understand herself. She had found herself thinking about him quite a lot since her return but she put it down to the fact that he was so different to all the other men in her life, past and present. She'd quickly dismissed the adage that opposites could attract.

'Well,' she said now, 'I wouldn't kick him out of bed, but honestly, Mands, I'd be better off fancying Prince Harry. At least he's fairly normal and lives on the same side of the Atlantic.' She sipped her wine, which she'd turned into a spritzer. 'Luke is too grown up for me, somehow.'

'But he sounds lovely!' Amanda had been impressed when Sophie had first described him with his good suits, nice shirts and lovely cologne. 'And you'd be really going against type, too.'

Sophie tried not to smile. Amanda and Milly were always going on about her hippy boyfriends who never took her anywhere nice, always expected her to pay – and not just her half – and didn't wash often enough. The cheese to Luke's chalk, in fact. 'Well, that's true.' She paused. 'But he would never fancy me. You should see the girls he usually mixes with. Paris Hilton lookalikes!'

'Who he wanted you to protect him from. If he liked that sort of girl he wouldn't have got you in to help.'

'I was the only person available. It's not going to happen. I'm not his type, not his class, not his financial bracket. These things don't work in real life.'

'So why drag you along to a "brunch"' – something about the way she said this gave it inverted commas – 'posing as his fiancée?'

'Because he's America's most eligible bachelor! Didn't I tell you about the bar where I met him? There were these girls talking about him. He's the one they all want. Probably because he's not only loaded but young – ish – and straight. He can't go anywhere without being hounded by gorgeous women. He's been divorced. He probably just doesn't need the hassle. If people think he's taken, they won't bother him so much.'

'He sounds a bit arrogant to me. "Oh, I'm so gorgeous, I can't handle all these gorgeous women fancying me."'

'No, it wasn't like that,' Sophie defended. 'He can handle it perfectly well but he didn't want to be rude – and they'd see it as being rude – to the granddaughters of Matilda's old friends.'

'Fair enough. So he chose you because . . . ?'

Sophie chuckled ruefully. 'Because I was in his grandmother's house? Handy, like?'

Amanda dismissed this. 'If you'd been . . . well, to put it bluntly, a bit of a dog, he wouldn't have taken you! He did it because you're gorgeous, English, posh and different from what he's used to.'

'America is supposed to be a classless society.'

'But it isn't. It may be more to do with money but I don't think any society is classless.'

Sophie silently agreed. 'Whatever. Anyway the money thing would always be a barrier. But we don't need to worry because he lives in New York and I live here. Let's have another drink.'

When they both had full glasses and had ordered a pizza to share, Amanda went back to her task of wheedling every detail out of Sophie. Sophie, who had now told Amanda everything she thought she needed to know, wanted to talk about something else but it wasn't easy to divert Amanda when she was in full interrogation mode.

'So does Luke know about Matilda and the picture?'

'Don't think so. I think she felt he would think she was on too much of a wild-goose chase, trying to find a house she knew so little about.' Sophie sighed. 'It's a shame. I'd really love to help her find it but I don't even have a name. She thought she knew the name of the place or person who owned it but when it came to it she couldn't remember. She is quite old.'

'Ooh, it is rather little to go on, just a photocopy of a picture of a house that might not still be standing.'

They both laughed. 'Just a little!'

'But Matilda said the name would come back to her if she stopped thinking about it and she would email me when it did. And if she can do email she's still completely on the ball. Then I'll have to think how to proceed.'

'It sort of matches, doesn't it? You're helping Matilda to find her house and Luke is helping you find your long-lost relatives. Any news on that?'

'He is on the case.' She frowned. 'Or maybe Ali is. He left a message saying "We're on to it", meaning my project. And she does work for him.'

Amanda sipped thoughtfully. 'I think you might see him again, Soph.'

'I don't agree but let's not argue about it. I'm just going to snitch that paper from that table over there and start looking for a job. I'm determined to get on my course, just as soon as I've got enough money. Lucky it's nearly Christmas, there should be loads about.' She got the paper and flicked through to the jobs section for a few minutes before sighing. 'None of these seem very inspiring. Mostly care work, which I do like but it's not terribly well paid. Oh, look at this!' She shoved the paper under Amanda's nose.

'What? Which one are you looking at?'

'This one. "Can anyone remember Mr Henry Bowles . . ."' She read out the advertisement.

'Yes? But why are you interested?'

'I could put an ad in a Cornish paper when I get the name. I could say, "Does anyone remember a person or place called whatever, and if so, get in touch." It could narrow down the search quite a lot.'

'Well, you need the name first.'

'And a job,' Sophie agreed.

'They might take you here,' said Amanda, finally accepting Sophie wasn't going to tell her anything else interesting. 'Then we could see each other without waiting for you to have a night off.'

Sophie considered. 'They're not actually advertising, are they? I didn't see anything written on the board outside.'

'Just go and tell them you're available. They'll snap you up.'

After some lively discussion about the unlikeliness of this happening, Sophie did as she was told. And fortunately for Sophie, they did just as Amanda had foretold and snapped her up.

Sophie's family were very pleased to have her back. It was only when she wasn't there to do it that they noticed how much she did. They were thrilled to hear all about her meeting and staying with Matilda. Sophie didn't show them the ring; she felt it would require too much explanation. She wrote Uncle Eric a letter, telling him that while she hadn't found her, Cousin Rowena was being looked for and that he shouldn't get his hopes up. This was a little tease; he'd told her it was all hopeless right from the beginning. She knew he'd appreciate the joke.

The wine bar got used to Amanda coming in after work and to her and Sophie having a good chat, especially after Sophie pointed out that Amanda's cups of coffee were bought and paid for. 'I'm bringing the customers in,' she explained.

As Amanda wasn't the only customer Sophie brought in and she polished glasses while she chatted, this was accepted.

'I've had an email!' Sophie said when she next saw her friend.

'Exciting,' said Amanda, sliding on to a bar stool, looking tired. 'And did it offer to extend bits of you that you don't have?'

Sophie started making a cappuccino without asking if Amanda wanted it. Her friend needed caffeine. 'It was from Matilda. In Connecticut. She's remembered the name.'

'Oh, that's exciting!'

'Yes, although it still won't be easy finding a random house. I'm going to put my ad in. Apparently the paper I need is called the *West Briton*. It's the national Cornish paper.'

'How did you find that out?'

'A customer told me. I'll do it online, if I can.' She paused. 'Oh, and Luke's coming to London – some special project or other – to do with work, I think.'

'Wow! Did you know he was going to do this?'

'Not a clue. According to Matilda it was all a bit of a surprise.'

177

'Maybe he's doing it so he can see you again.'

Sophie found herself blushing. 'I really don't think so, but apparently he's coming a month early, just after Christmas, so he can help me find the house.'

'So she's told him about her quest then?'

Sophie nodded. 'I suppose so. Why else would he come over early? Although how he'll take to searching Cornwall for a house that might not be there any more, I'm really not sure.'

'Fun for him! Fun for you too!'

'I'll just place the advert. If anything turns up, he can go and check it out. He won't need me.'

Amanda brushed this notion away with a flick of her hand. 'Of course he will! He'll need a native guide – he's American – he doesn't speak the language!'

Sophie laughed, thinking how much fun it could be, exploring Cornwall with Luke. She could show him a bit of England as he had shown her part of America. Then practicality set in: it was highly unlikely he'd need her. 'Oh, here come the after-office crowd.' She frowned. 'It never used to be this busy when we came in here, did it? It must be because it's nearly Christmas that they're going for a drink after work every day.'

Sophie's boss, who had heard the group of men arrive, said, 'Oh yes, that must be it,' and chuckled.

Sophie started making Amanda another coffee although she hadn't ordered it. 'Len is always laughing to himself these days.'

'Can't imagine why,' said Amanda, who knew perfectly well what made the place busier these days, and it didn't have much to do with Christmas. 'So what are you doing for Christmas?'

'Same old, I expect. I'm making Florentines for all the men this year, although I may do brownies for Uncle Eric as he really likes them. I'm decorating a huge cylindrical cardboard container that I found in a skip for my mother as you just can't get big enough waste-paper baskets. My sister is getting a little evening bag I got the pattern for in the States.'

'Lovely,' said Amanda.

'And don't worry. I'll do you something to wear. Anything you particularly need?' Sophie's ability to turn a charity-shop bargain into something verging on designer was something her close friends depended on.

'Something to go over a little black dress would be good,' said Amanda. 'For the office party?'

'Ooh, I know just the thing,' said Sophie. In her mind she went back to New York when she'd been adapting clothes to take to Matilda's. 'Do you like fringes?'

'I expect so,' said Amanda, 'if you think I should.' She got out her purse. 'I won't have that coffee, if you don't mind. I'll never sleep if I do.'

In between getting ready for Christmas, decorating the house, and longing for the access to greenery that Matilda's household had, Sophie sent off her advertisement, spending quite a lot of money to do it. The trouble was, looking for a person or a name meant that the ad had to be quite long. She didn't have much time to think about it though. She was working double shifts at the wine bar and spending every spare minute cooking and sewing for Christmas; she was also getting up early, because for some reason she couldn't sleep past six o'clock.

Hence it was half past six when she booted up her laptop and saw Luke's name in her in-box in the week before Christmas. He must have got her email address from Matilda. She clicked on it, half excited, half nervous. It was lovely to hear from him, but what was he going to say?

Hi Sophie,

Just to let you know, if my grandmother hasn't already, that I'm coming to London. She's told me she's gotten you involved with finding some house in Cornwall. Personally I think it's a ridiculous idea – far better for her to keep her memories than to find the house was razed to the ground thirty years ago. Would you please tell her the same thing? She won't believe me.

I do hope we can meet up when I'm in London. And by the way, we're still looking for your relative.

All best wishes, Luke Winchester

Dear Luke, she replied.

How nice to hear from you. Yes, it would be fun to meet up sometime when you're in London. And thank you so much for carrying on the search.

I have already mentioned to Matilda that finding a house that may not still be standing without much information is rather a long shot – rather like me trying to track down my relative – but as you probably know, your grandmother is a very determined woman! Please send her lots of love from me.

Best, Sophie

She didn't say anything about her advertisement, which so far had not produced any results. Apart from this little sin of omission she was pleased with her mix of formal and firm. Sophie sent the email, disappointed that, given the time difference, it would be a while before Luke read it.

She was thrilled (although she tried not to be) to see a reply when she got home from work after the lunchtime shift. *Dear Sophie, Sorry, I should have realised you wouldn't have encouraged my grandmother in her crazy idea. I should have known you would have been sensible about it. I will make sure she thinks no more about it.*

Sophie found herself surprisingly disappointed. Supposing

she did get some replies to her rather rambling advertisement? She went on reading. *By the way, I have now traced your relative in New York. Sadly she has passed away. However, I did investigate her will and she left her entire estate to a cousin in England: a Mr Eric Kirkpatrick.*

'Uncle Eric!' shouted Sophie. 'You had what I needed all the time! But you probably didn't know that,' she added more quietly, hoping no one in the house had heard her talking to herself. Having resolved to telephone Uncle Eric and possibly search through his papers herself if necessary, she sat down to compose a reply to Luke. It was shaming, she decided, how much time she spent thinking about him. When she had finally pressed 'send' she got out her phone.

After what passed for pleasantries between Sophie and her great-uncle, Sophie came to the point. 'Uncle-Eric-dear, I've just heard that Cousin Rowena, in New York, died! And she left her shares to you! It must have happened ages ago.'

There was a rustling and rumbling which somehow conveyed embarrassment. 'Oh yes, well, I did find that out. I got Mrs Thing to get those boxes down from the attic. Found all sorts of stuff, including a solicitor's letter.' He paused. 'Sorry I caused you to go off on a trip to America when it wasn't necessary. Frightful bore for you.'

'Oh no, it wasn't a bore at all! I had a lovely time.'

'Hm. Never had much time for Yanks myself.'

Sophie chuckled. 'Well, some of them are charming.'

'Have to take your word for it.' He paused. 'Thinking of coming up to see me any time soon?'

'Well, maybe. It might be a good idea to investigate your papers, the ones you've just found.'

'And it would be nice to see you.'

'And you! I could bring your Christmas present – save me posting them.'

'Them?'

'A surprise! I'll see how it goes.'

Annoyingly, a flu bug was whistling through the staff at the wine bar and Sophie was the only one not to get it. Thus visiting Uncle Eric before Christmas wasn't possible. She posted off the brownies saying she'd come and see him as soon as possible and reminded him to make sure he'd had his flu jab.

One of the brightest spots in Sophie's Christmas, which had lost some of its sparkle in recent years, was Amanda's delight in the little fringed bolero Sophie had crafted for her out of a plain black shrug, some antique sequins and some of the fringing left over from the little black dress that Milly was now wearing with pride in New York.

Another plus was the pleasure that her mother took in her monster waste-paper basket, covered with scraps of material in her mother's favourite colours. The men had enjoyed their Florentines, too. The best part, though, was the amount of money she had earned by working so many extra hours. She'd replaced the money she'd spent in New York – aided by having her fare refunded – and was well on the way towards her target amount for her course. Soon she'd be able to start looking for them on the internet. She would definitely look for something that dealt with the business side as well as the creative side of tailoring. While upholstery was still tempting, she decided that she could make curtains without the course, and that there was probably more money in clothes than sofa covers.

She received a very grand Christmas card from Matilda.

My dear, I am so excited to think you and Luke might be able to trace my house for me. Did I tell you that it belonged to friends of my grandparents, who died before I knew them?

This is why it's so hard to track them down. It's not just a matter of a bit of genealogy. But I'm very optimistic. I plan to tell Luke my plans over Christmas.

I do hope you have a pleasant time with family and friends. We so enjoyed having you with us at Thanksgiving. Do come back and visit us sometime!

The chance would be a fine thing, thought Sophie, feeling suddenly sentimental about New England at Thanksgiving. It had been so beautiful. Driving through it in Luke's wonderful car, with Luke by her side, had been very special. She would think about it when she ended up married to a hippy, having babies in a yurt, and making tiny dungarees out of her husband's worn-out jeans.

Another email from Matilda arrived after New Year. It was cheering: up until now the New Year had just held more shifts at the wine bar until everyone was better and could take their turn, but seeing Matilda's name in bold in her in-box lifted Sophie's spirits.

Luke asked me to email. He is arriving in London tomorrow. His new apartment isn't ready but I know he would like to see you. I wrote your details down for him in case he doesn't still have them. Here is his cellphone number.

Just before she was shutting down her computer at midnight, after a shift at the wine bar, she saw an email from Luke.

Ordering her heart to stop beating so fast, she opened it. *Sophie, I had no idea my grandmother thought the two of us were going to find her house for her. Did you tell her? No, I guess not. I'll be in touch when I get settled in London. All best wishes, Luke.*

She suddenly felt a little flat. She'd really hoped that

Luke would want them to meet up quite soon. Now he seemed to want to wait until everything was sorted out, which could take ages.

Her phone rang while she was at work the next day. She slid into the storeroom to answer it.

'Is that Sophie?'

Luke sounded either cross or stressed or both. Sophie was so pleased to hear him she became flippant. 'Who else would it be? It's my phone you've rung.'

'Sophie, I'm at Heathrow and I had my wallet and phone stolen on the plane. I've borrowed someone's to make this call.'

He paused and Sophie instantly remembered how it had been for her arriving in New York to discover she had no job. She at least hadn't been robbed.

'What do you need me to do?' she demanded, falling instantly into rescuer mode. 'Shall I pick you up? Have you a hotel or something booked?'

'No, the apartment isn't ready yet—'

'Then come and stay with us. Do you need to be in London?'

'Not really, in fact I've got a little time—'

There was something in his voice Sophie couldn't quite interpret. She would have thought it was amusement if the circumstances hadn't been so dire for him. He was probably exhausted and it had affected his voice. 'I can be with you in two hours. Have you got enough money for some coffee or something? And where shall we meet?'

They arranged a rendezvous, then: 'Thank goodness I had your details, Sophie,' he said as he disconnected.

Fortunately Sophie's so-far perfect work record meant that Len was willing to let her go immediately. He wasn't as short-staffed now Christmas was over. He even gave her a lift to the train station so she could get the train to Reading and from there a bus to Heathrow.

All through the journey Sophie tried to beat down her excitement at the thought of seeing Luke again. He'd only rung her because he needed help. Against her direct instructions, her heart swelled at the thought of it.

'Hi! Luke! I feel I should have one of those cardboard signs. How are you?' She had to stop herself rushing into his arms.

'Sophie!' He looked very tired but he smiled when he saw her and hugged her briefly. 'It's good to see you.'

Her heart singing, Sophie took hold of his suitcase. It was huge and on wheels. It looked very, very expensive. He carried a laptop bag. 'I'm afraid I haven't got a car,' she explained. 'We have to take a bus and then a train.'

Luke exhaled, disguising a tired sigh as a breath. 'Fine.'

'You can sleep on the train,' she said reassuringly, wishing she had borrowed a car so she could have whisked him away without having to put him through more stress. But she didn't drive much and it would have taken her a long time to negotiate with her parents and subsequently with the road system round one of the world's biggest airports. 'Just a little bus ride first.'

To his credit, Luke didn't complain at all, but Sophie could tell he was more used to a uniformed chauffeur and a limousine than putting his suitcase into a cave-like area under a bus and then, later, having to get it on to a train.

Fortunately for her, he soon fell asleep so she could make a phone call.

'Mum? It's me, Soph.'

'Hello, darling,' said her mother.

'I'm bringing a guest home.'

'Are you? Aren't you at the wine bar?'

'No. I'm on a train from Heathrow. I've got the grandson of the woman I stayed with in Connecticut with me.'

'Yes?'

'I was just wondering if he could stay for a few days. He's had his wallet stolen.'

There was a pause. Sophie's mother was not inhospitable but it took a minute for this request to sink in. 'Fine,' she said. 'I'll bake a cake.'

Sophie would have been happier if her mother had said, 'I'll get the spare room ready,' as her cakes weren't that good on the whole (which was why Sophie had taken over making them when she was nine). But she was grateful that her mother was relaxed about having a complete stranger as a guest.

Although Sophie's family home was a bit chipped about the edges, it was spacious. There wasn't too much furniture but what there was included some antiques. It had a sort of arty stylishness that could look wonderful. There was even a guest room right next to the bathroom, which was the nearest thing to an en suite. What worried Sophie was the fact that the spare room was currently full of her mother's canvases and the cleaning lady who came about once a fortnight hadn't been for a while. Still, there was no point in worrying about that. She paid the taxi that took them back from the station and ushered Luke up the path to the front door.

Chapter Thirteen

❦

Sophie's mother stood in the hall, ready to welcome them. She was wearing a long V-necked fitted cardigan and at least two scarves draped round her neck and shoulders. Her hair was coiled up into a nest on her head secured by combs and several strings of beads made their way down her front. Her long skirt was one Sophie had made her, large triangles of brightly coloured velvet connected with feather stitching. She wore green woollen tights and suede shoes. She looked 'arty', believing that looking the part was halfway to becoming an artist.

'Hello!' she said as Luke preceded Sophie into the house. And then, when she'd had a chance to look at him properly, she said it once more, with feeling. 'Darling, who is this gorgeous man?'

Sophie blushed deeply. She almost wished she hadn't been so impulsive and invited Luke home. Looking at her mother now, Sophie was aware that she'd gulped down a quick glass of sherry – to give herself courage, no doubt. It was making her sound a bit like a female Lothario. She trusted Luke wouldn't notice either the smell or the slightly unhinged behaviour. She kissed her mother's cheek.

'That skirt looks lovely. Mum, this is Luke. He's the grandson of the wonderful woman I met in New York and went to stay with. Remember? Thanksgiving? House in Connecticut?'

One glass of sherry hadn't affected that particular memory. 'Oh, the mansion? Of course I remember now. Luke, I'm very glad to meet you.' Her mother took Luke's hand in hers and held on. 'You and your family were so kind to Sophie.'

Cringing with embarrassment, Sophie said hurriedly, 'Luke, this is my mother, Sonia Apperly.'

'Very pleased to meet you, Mrs Apperly,' said Luke, shaking the hand that was still clutching his.

'Oh, call me Sonia, do.' She stayed staring into Luke's eyes.

'Mum!' Sophie interrupted this reverie, which she knew was partly caused by Luke's eyes being such an unusual colour. 'Mum, why don't you take Luke through to the sitting room and see if he'd like a drink? Luke, I'll go and get your room ready.'

'I'm putting you to a lot of trouble, Sonia.'

'Not at all! It's a pleasure to have you. Sophie's boyfriends are usually quite different.' Sophie's mother had now slipped her hand through Luke's arm. 'Come on through. Are you interested in art? I think Sophie told me she met your grandmother in an art gallery? I'll get you a drink and then you can tell me what you think of my work. Of course, time doesn't allow me to . . .'

Sophie escaped to the kitchen. Looking at her mother's not very inspiring paintings and hearing her bang on about what a great artist she could have been if only she'd had the opportunity would be the very last thing Luke would feel like doing but he would have to put up with it – at least until she could rescue him. She filled the kettle in case he wanted coffee, not alcohol, and then went back to the sitting room.

Luke was standing in front of a very large landscape of a wood, full of thick dark paint and symbolism. He seemed to have got rid of his hostess's arm and had folded his own, possibly so she couldn't grab his hand again.

'Luke, you probably don't want tea but would you like some coffee?' She was a bit anxious about coffee. Americans were known to be picky about it and the only way she could make it was in a jug, like tea, only using tablespoons instead of teaspoons to measure it out.

'Coffee would be fine,' said Luke.

Sonia Apperly put her hand on Luke's sleeve. 'But wouldn't you rather have a drink? A glass of sherry? We have some whisky, I think.'

Sophie waited. Maybe Luke would welcome a stiff drink. He'd had a very long flight, his wallet stolen, an awkward journey and now her mother in entertaining mode. She'd want one herself.

'Um . . .' Luke hesitated.

'A drink,' said Sonia firmly. 'Sophie darling, could you bring a tray? I'll have sherry but I'm sure Luke would like whisky.'

Luke smiled. 'I'll have to learn to call it that. In the States we call it Scotch.'

'People do here too,' said Sophie and went back to the kitchen.

Another problem had presented itself to her. What had her mother planned for supper? Had she planned anything? Would it stretch to five? Sophie was to have been working that evening so she wouldn't have been catered for and no one had known about Luke. She opened the fridge door, praying her mother hadn't bought lamb chops for three. She sighed with relief when she saw some large chicken breasts. There'd be bits and pieces of vegetables and rice. She could make a stir-fry.

Having delivered the tray of drinks and poured for them both, hoping no one mentioned ice because she knew there wouldn't be any, she said to her mother, 'Shall I light a fire? Then I must get Luke's room ready. He must be desperate to freshen up.'

'I'll do the fire for you, Sonia,' said Luke, smiling charmingly at Sophie's mother. 'I was a boy scout. I can light fires.'

'How clever,' said Mrs Apperly, although she wouldn't have thought Sophie clever for doing it. 'What did you say you did for a living?'

As Sophie went upstairs to the spare room she prayed that her brother hadn't decided to shave that day and that the basin wouldn't be full of bits of hair. With her mother in that mood, sucking up to Luke, she didn't want to leave him alone with her for longer than she had to. Then she'd have to cook supper.

The sheets she found for the bed were a bit thin and bobbly but they were clean. She allowed a second's thought to the wonderful, glass-smooth Egyptian cotton sheets in Matilda's house and then let it go. Polycotton was fine, really. There was also a clean bath towel, which was a bit of a result. It was tiny compared to the bath sheets he was used to in Matilda's house, but this would go round his waist with no problem. He was very slim.

She stashed her mother's canvases and spare art materials under the bed. The bedside light worked, and she'd found him one good pillow that could go on top of the lumpy one. Getting the reading matter organised was a challenge. A quick look round and she transferred her energies to the bathroom.

This took a bit more to make tidy. But she used a large towel that smelt strongly of her brother to clean the bath and basin, gave the loo a quick scrub and (kindly) found a clean towel to replace the one she'd done the cleaning with. She found a new bar of soap that wasn't cracked and streaked with black and then she went back downstairs and into the sitting room. What would her mother be doing to Luke now?

'Luke, your room is ready,' she announced from the doorway of the sitting room. 'If you're happy here, I'll cook supper, otherwise I'll show you?'

Luke got up. 'I'd really like to invite you all out to a restaurant. I've arrived unexpectedly—'

'You have no money,' said Sophie, smiling but making her point bluntly. 'And no credit cards. Don't worry about it.' She smiled. 'Come up and I'll show you where you're sleeping.'

'Don't be bossy, darling,' said her mother. 'Men hate that.'

Dying inside, Sophie led Luke from the room.

She didn't speak as Luke followed her up the stairs, dragging his suitcase, its nifty wheels no use now. It was better not to try and explain her mother, she felt, even though she longed to. At least she was friendly. Her father was usually taciturn and her brother could be positively rude.

'I think your mother is charming,' said Luke when Sophie had opened the door to the spare room and indicated the bathroom next door.

'Yes,' said Sophie. 'Would you like a bath? We do have a shower but it's a bit . . . slow.'

'You mean you have to run around to catch the drips?'

She nodded. 'The bath is fine though and there's plenty of hot water.' She'd already checked this. 'It'll take me about an hour to cook supper. Are you starving? I could make you a quick sandwich if you'd like.'

'Sophie, calm down. I'm fine. I'm used to foreign travel, you know.'

191

Sophie raised an eyebrow, feigning offence. 'This is England, Luke! Hardly foreign!'

This said she swept down the stairs wishing his presence didn't make her feel so twitchy. All would be well as long as her father and brother didn't show her up. It was one thing adapting her behaviour to fit in with Matilda's grand household; it was unlikely her household would adapt to fit in with Luke. She had to hope he'd be able to cope with the vast differences. She had imagined their first meeting in England taking place in a bar in London, all sophistication and elegance. She'd just have to rise to the challenge.

Sophie was calmer by the time everyone sat down to dinner. Luke, looking pink and prosperous and smelling of something lovely, was placed at the opposite end of the table to her father. Her mother was sitting on one side of him and there was an empty place on his other side, obviously designated as Sophie's. Her brother Michael sat next to his father. They all looked expectantly at her as she brought in a steaming dish. Conversation seemed to have been flowing but everyone was very hungry. Although Sophie had worked as fast as she could, supper was a little late.

She was pleased to see that her father had produced a couple of bottles of his better wine and that everyone had a full glass. She just hoped someone would fill hers – she badly needed a drink.

'I'll just go and get the plates.'

'Can I help?' asked Luke, starting to get up.

'No, no,' said Sophie's mother, patting his hand. 'You stay there. You must be feeling jet-lagged. What time is it at home now?'

Sophie got the plates. Her brother showed no sign of moving to help. He'd been at work all day, after all. Sophie had just been flitting around, being Sophie, obviously.

Sophie doled out large portions of chicken stir-fry. She'd taken a lot of trouble with it. She'd garnished the pile with crisply fried onion rings and had fried the chicken in the bacon fat. She had added some toasted almonds, a handful of frozen peas for colour and tiny cubes of red pepper. She'd also added a little chilli. It looked lovely and it was full of flavour and she would have been proud of it if the memory of the Thanksgiving dinner, the brunch, and even the pizza at Mystic hadn't been so much in the forefront of her mind.

'This looks delicious!' said Luke.

'Do sit down, Sophie. I can't bear you hovering around,' said her father.

'Does anyone want water?' she asked, hoping her father wouldn't get too irritated with her.

'Stop fussing, darling,' said her mother. 'Everyone's fine. Do start, Luke.' She patted his hand again.

She knew her mother would love Luke. He was, after all, a mother-in-law's dream. Good-looking, rich, steady job, rich, well educated, rich. But approving of him wouldn't stop her being embarrassing.

'So, Luke,' said her father after a satisfying amount of 'mms' had been heard, 'what is it you do again?'

'I'm an attorney,' said Luke.

'Well, you're a great improvement on the unwashed scum Sophie usually hangs about with,' said her brother. 'Glad to see the girl's developing some taste at last.'

'I presume you earn decent money?' said her father. 'From what one reads, you do.'

'I certainly can't complain,' said Luke.

'So what are you doing this side of the pond? You're not just here to pursue Sophie, presumably?' her father went on. Sophie winced. Could it get any worse?

'No, I have a special project to oversee in London. I

wasn't going to do it originally but' – he gave Sophie a fleeting smile – 'it seemed a good idea to take a personal interest.'

Sophie was just working out if there was something behind this when her father said, 'Well, I'm pleased Sophie's brought home someone with a decent career. None of us earns a bean!' He seemed to imply this was a virtue. 'There's no money in academia' – he shot his wife a look – 'or art, come to that. A lawyer in the family would be a useful addition.'

Sophie's embarrassment fuse finally blew. 'Dad! Luke and I aren't going out or anything. He's staying here because he was robbed on the plane – not because he wants to be here!'

'But of course I'm delighted to be here,' Luke said hurriedly, sending Sophie a look which was supposed to be reassuring. Sophie was past reassurance. Her family had gone too far.

Luke went on, 'By the way, I noticed a book in the spare room. By Sloan Wilson? Is someone here a fan?'

'Oh yes,' said Sophie's father, to her huge relief. 'Very fond of Sloan Wilson. You don't often meet anyone young who's heard of him, but he was a bestseller in his time.'

Sophie relaxed. While her father was probably telling Luke things he knew perfectly well, at least he'd stopped making desperately embarrassing remarks; he was filling Luke's glass (forgetting to fill hers) and treating him like a friend.

Sophie's mother continued to be sycophantic but Luke didn't seem to mind. Michael seemed happy that there was good wine to be had for once. Sophie, reaching for the bottle and filling her own glass, felt she'd rather be anywhere in the world except her own home. Every so often, the subject of money would come up. To Sophie's

194

ears it made her family sound overly obsessed with the subject. Matilda and Luke and their family had shown her nothing but kindness. Now her family, while not unkind and definitely welcoming, seemed just a little too interested in Luke's potential wealth. Somehow, she would have to get him away from them.

She was up before her usual time the following morning, unsure if Luke would want to sleep late or not. She wanted to be ready for him if he woke up early. She made sure the kitchen was tidy and then made batter for drop scones. They weren't quite the same as American pancakes but they were better than stale toast and some very bitty muesli left by her other brother Stephen's wife Hermione for their children to eat. Not only was it fairly old, some of the bits looked like squashed cockroaches. As a New Yorker, Luke would find that very off-putting.

Luke found her washing the kitchen floor, on her knees, reversing backwards out of the room. Not a good angle, she realised as she got up.

'Hi! I thought you'd sleep later than this. You must still be jet-lagged.'

'Well, I feel tired but also hungry. I've been emailing about my cards and stuff. Ali – you remember her? From the brunch?'

Sophie paused for a tiny moment. 'Oh yes. She was charming.' Sophie washed her hands under the kitchen tap. She planned to smuggle her bucket of dirty water out to the loo when he wasn't looking. It was a bit sordid somehow.

'She's going to sort out all my cards for me. She's coming over soon to help me with the project.'

'Good idea!' said Sophie, wishing the spectre of Ali hadn't intruded on her time with Luke. He'd mentioned her a few times now. 'Things like that are much more fun with two doing it,' she said, trying to be brave.

Luke appeared slightly confused at the suggestion that fun was important but he nodded.

'So,' said Sophie. 'Would you like to try my pancakes for breakfast? We haven't any maple syrup but golden syrup is very nice. We have bacon and eggs. How hungry are you?'

'What I need most right now is a cup of good strong coffee.'

Sophie hid her sigh behind a smile. 'I'll do my best with the coffee but this isn't a coffee-drinking household on the whole. Sit down. I'll just get rid of this dirty water.'

She came back to find him not sitting, but staring out of the kitchen window.

'You have an amazing view from here. When we arrived last night I had no idea how pretty the scenery is.'

'It is lovely, isn't it? We're very lucky. People come here for holidays and days out but we actually live here.' She smiled. 'Very jammy.'

'Pardon me?'

'I mean lucky,' she said. 'Now do sit down.'

Luke picked up an abandoned newspaper and sat down at the big scarred old table. The kitchen was reasonably sized and pleasant in a scuffed, lived-in way, but Sophie wasn't sure Luke ever went into the kitchen at his grandmother's house – or his mother's house either, let alone his own. Still, he seemed to be coping and she carried on whipping up her batter.

Her mother drifted in wearing her dressing gown. 'Oh, Luke! Are you up already? Is Sophie getting you breakfast?'

'Yes thank you,' said Luke politely. 'She's been working extremely hard making me comfortable.'

Sophie put a plate of drop scones on the table and then produced butter, honey, golden syrup and anything else she could think of that might go with them.

Luke helped himself and took a bite. 'Delicious pancakes, Sophie,' he said.

'We call them drop scones,' said her mother, helping herself to a couple. 'Sophie is a very good little cook. I taught her all I know.'

Sophie dropped a tea bag into a mug. 'Mum, do you want tea? Or there's coffee.'

'Oh, coffee please, darling,' her mother said contrarily.

As her mother didn't get up to help herself Sophie took the hint and poured her a cup. She might as well, she was on her feet already.

'So what are you going to do today?' asked Sonia. 'Do you have to sort out getting some money and things?'

'Will that be difficult on a Saturday?' asked Sophie, who didn't want Luke whisked away on a cloud of money.

'I will have to make a few calls,' said Luke, 'but then it would be nice to see some of your part of England, Sophie.'

'Why don't you go for a walk?' suggested Sonia. 'You needn't go far. Just up to our local common?'

'Are you up for that, Luke?' asked Sophie.

'Oh yes.' He smiled. 'You may think of me as a city boy, but I like hiking.'

Sophie laughed. 'I don't know about hiking, but I'm glad you like exercise.'

After breakfast he helped her stack the dishwasher with their sticky plates and she realised he must be much better house-trained than she'd thought. She'd panicked, rather, she now realised. Just because she'd only seen him in the rarefied atmosphere of New England's high society, it didn't mean he couldn't behave like a normal person.

Then he went upstairs to find shoes suitable to walk in.

Sophie looked dubiously at what he produced. Leather and obviously hand-made, they were very shiny and very lovely. Quite how they'd look after they'd been for a walk up the hill she wasn't sure. Still, they could always be cleaned. She found an old coat of her brother's for him to cover up his casual cashmere sweater.

He was fit, she had to give him credit for that. He kept pace with her up the steep hill without panting or stopping to 'look at the view'. She was always panting fairly hard when she got to the top and genuinely looked at the view and she was used to hills, living where she did.

'There! You have a wonderful view from up here. Look, you can just about see the river snaking away in the distance,' said Sophie.

'It's amazing. I don't know what I was expecting but this is spectacular.'

Sophie stood next to him, thrilled that her home was so pleasing to him. 'We do have some lovely walks round here. I could borrow the car and take you on one – if you've got time.'

Luke looked down at her. 'I do have a little time before my apartment will be ready. If my wallet hadn't been stolen I'd have checked into a hotel.' He frowned. 'I could still have done, I suppose, but not having any credit cards or money is a little unsettling. I was very grateful for your offer of a place to stay.'

Sophie regarded him. 'I do realise it's not what you're used to.'

'But it's delightful.' He paused again. 'Are you very busy at the moment?'

'In what way?'

'Have you a job?'

'Yes! In a wine bar.' As she suspected he was going to say something else she added, 'Why do you ask?'

'It's just I came over early partly to look for my grand-mother's house – not that there's much chance of finding that – but also to see if you needed help looking for your relatives.'

'That's very kind! I did say I'd go and visit Uncle Eric soon. He told me he'd discovered another box of papers in the attic, when I told him he'd inherited Cousin Rowena's shares. I want to go through it.'

'But could you take a few days off from your job?'

Sophie considered. She was very conscientious usually but the chance to spend a few days with Luke was not to be passed up. She hadn't realised how much she wanted to until he suggested it. 'I'm sure I can arrange it.' If necessary she could hand in her notice.

They walked on for a while before finally heading for home. Sophie was wondering what to do about lunch. She should have checked the freezer for a joint. Not for the first time Sophie longed for a mother with a sense of social responsibility. Sonia could be extremely welcoming but she didn't think about the practicalities. It was probably why Sophie was so practical herself. It was born of necessity.

She was wondering if she should make a visit to a supermarket when Luke stopped and turned to her. 'I really don't like imposing on your parents like this,' he said.

'I imposed on yours – well, on your grandmother. It's only fair.'

He shook his head. 'No, it's not the same. My grand-mother wanted you for her own purposes, and I used you too. This is different.'

'It's really not a problem, but we could go to Uncle Eric tomorrow. It'll mean another trip on a train, I'm afraid. But some of the scenery is wonderful. It's a good way to see a country.'

He smiled and not for the first time she appreciated his even white teeth. Most of her boyfriends could use advice on the benefits of dental floss. 'Then let's do it.'

Explaining to the family that this prize catch – about the only thing Sophie had done that seemed worth anything – was going to be taken from them and given instead to Evil-Uncle-Eric was not easy. Sophie was forced to confess that there were papers they needed to look at because of the possibility of drilling rights. This fact was met with open derision.

'Typical Sophie!' said her father, who did at least seem to know about them. 'Chasing after rainbows. My father left his shares partly to me and partly to any offspring I may have, but I've never done anything about them. If there'd been any money attached to those rights we'd have had it by now. There's no earthly point!'

Sophie had of course been told this by Uncle Eric but by now she didn't care. She just wanted to get Luke away from her parents, to Uncle Eric, who at least liked her and didn't think she was stupid.

'I don't understand why you should drag Luke up there to see that horrid old man,' said her mother, who was the most put out. 'He'll hate it. His house isn't even clean!'

As her own house wasn't exactly an example of perfect hygiene, Sophie thought this was a bit rich. 'Uncle Eric – who's not evil by the way – has a live-in housekeeper. And I cleared a lot of stuff when I stayed with him.' Clean his house might be, but it would still be a candidate for a clutter consultant.

'But he's so miserable!' her mother went on. 'Always complaining! And mean as stink! He won't help you find those drilling rights or whatever they are because he doesn't need the money!'

There was an element of truth in this but Sophie refused to be downcast. 'He's very fond of me and I'm sure he'll like Luke. He won't mind us searching for things.'

'I think Luke should decide. You've been bossing him around since he first arrived in England.'

Luke didn't appear to notice Sophie's look of entreaty. He said, 'Sonia, I have to say it was my idea for us to visit Sophie's uncle. As an attorney I have a fascination for old documents and I love detective work.'

'The trains will be all to hell on a Sunday,' said Sophie's father.

'They'll be fine!' said Sophie. 'I'm going to get a few things together. Luke, if you want to put some overnight things in with mine, that'll be best. We don't want to take too much luggage.'

'Do you know what time the train is?' asked Sophie's father.

'I'll just have a quick look on the internet,' said Sophie. 'Luke, you go and pack.'

'There you go, bossing him about again. That's no way to keep a boyfriend.'

Sophie sighed and went into the study to research trains, leaving Luke to explain that he was not her boyfriend this time. She really didn't want to know how he played it.

They stood on the platform looking at each other. There was no one else around because they had missed their train. Sophie wasn't sure it was really her fault but she felt guilty anyway. It wasn't good that the man in the ticket office had told them that after Birmingham there might be some disruption to the service but if there was, there was almost sure to be a replacement bus.

'We could go home if you think this is a really bad idea,' said Sophie, when she had related all this to Luke.

'It was my idea. If I had my drivers' licence we could have hired a car.'

Sophie did have a driving licence but she wasn't all that keen on using it. She'd never been able to afford a car of her own and her parents made it difficult for her to borrow theirs.

'We'll give the train a go then, shall we?'

Luke nodded. 'England is a very interesting place to visit.'

'With some wonderful scenery,' said Sophie, in case he was being critical.

'Absolutely.'

'Did you pack anything to read?' she asked him.

'No. I was in a hurry.'

'Me too. Let's see if we can buy a paper.'

They couldn't.

Chapter Fourteen

The first part of their journey went smoothly enough. The train was nearly empty. They sat next to each other, looking at the hills speeding by, spotted rabbits in the fields and, as the area became more urban, saw canals, sometimes prettily done up, at other times gloomily filled with supermarket trolleys and polystyrene. They looked into people's back gardens, deciding which families used their garden to play in and which as a place to put things they didn't often use.

There were still fairy lights up everywhere. Sophie told Luke she felt that some of the houses had gone over the top with their Santas on the roof and choirs of snowmen singing round deflating sleighs. Luke told her that in many parts of the States these would have seemed paltry – hardly decorations at all. Sophie giggled. 'Although I love fairy lights, I think I prefer them white and on trees. I don't mind if they twinkle, though.'

Luke smiled down at her. 'My grandmother is the same. She has many, many sets of lights, but they're all white.' Then he frowned. 'Although maybe she has some chilli-pepper lights somewhere.'

'She and I have a lot in common,' said Sophie. 'I have a set of chilli peppers in my bedroom.'

Luke and she exchanged glances. She thought he was going to say something but just then they were plunged into the darkness of Birmingham station and the moment passed.

When they finally located the right platform for their onward journey, which was underground and dimly lit, they found it crowded, mostly with young men singing.

'Why are there so many people wanting this train?' Sophie asked a woman who, unlike most of the other people, wasn't drinking extra-strong lager out of a can.

'Some big match. Not everyone could get back last night. I think there was supposed to be a special train but it didn't happen so they're going to be crammed on to this one.'

'Football fans,' she reported back to Luke. 'Do they have them in the States?'

'Oh yes, but we call it soccer and they don't usually cause a problem on trains.' Luke frowned. 'At least, I don't think they do. I don't use the train very much.'

As more young men piled on to the platform she edged nearer him, feeling protective. He was wearing a long overcoat and under it his shirt was pink. His chinos were pressed and his shoes shiny. It may not have been obvious to people not examining him closely that his coat was cashmere but anyone who touched it would feel its softness. No one would mistake him for a football fan coming back from a big match. He was wearing his scarf the wrong way for a start.

'Did you bring trainers with you?' Sophie asked, wondering if there was anything he could do to stop himself looking so different.

'Pardon me?' he said, obviously not understanding. 'Why would I need those? I haven't worn diapers for a couple of years now.'

Sophie chuckled. 'Sorry. You'd call them sneakers, maybe.'

'Oh. But I didn't bring them with me. I thought your uncle might not appreciate a stranger turning up without proper shoes.' He frowned apologetically. 'I have an uncle who would have made a big fuss about a thing like that. I packed light.'

More people crowded on to the platform. She stood as close to Luke as she could without actually holding on to him. 'Uncle Eric wouldn't notice, frankly. He's not exactly gaga, but he is eccentric.'

'Your mother told me he's very wealthy.'

'Did she? I don't think she's right. And what is it to do with her anyway? He'll have to spend it all on care anyway, when he can't manage at home any more.'

'She also said that he'll – um – "pop his clogs" any minute now.'

Even through the shame, Sophie couldn't help laughing. 'She means she thinks he'll die. I don't think he will – at least, not for a few years. He's very healthy and I don't even think he's that old. No one knows how old he is, really.'

'I thought she meant that but the terminology was bewildering.'

By now they were pressed up against each other as more and more people came on to the platform and she was holding on to his arm. It felt lovely. She looked up at him. He seemed taller close to, somehow.

The train was already several minutes late when at last there was an announcement. It was to say there'd been a platform change.

Hoping she was more on the ball than most of the football supporters she said to Luke, 'You take the bag. Hold on to me and don't let us get separated.'

With Luke in tow, she wriggled her way through the crowd and got ahead as they started to stream up the stairs. She was sweating ferociously, and really hoped she wouldn't start to smell. She looked up and saw the right number platform and dragged Luke down another set of stairs.

'We just have to trust they won't let the train leave without us,' she said as they went down the steps.

'Or without all the other people who were waiting for it,' said Luke, panting slightly.

'To be honest, it would be a lot pleasanter if they did abandon them but I suppose that wouldn't be fair.'

They were among the first on the platform but the train was already fairly full. Sophie didn't let Luke get on straight away but shouted to him to follow her down to the end of the train where, with luck, it might be less busy and possible to get a seat.

It wasn't. She got on to the train to discover it was full of students. Going by the amount of dirt on the rucksacks that filled the luggage rack, they had probably been on a field trip, studying mud and bringing samples home on their clothes.

She was just going to get out again to fetch Luke when she felt the train start to move. Please, oh please let him be on the train, she prayed silently. Then she saw him up the other end of the carriage, surrounded by football fans all shouting and calling to each other as they tried to re-establish contact with the people they'd been travelling with.

She could only see Luke because he was tall. She was tall herself but there were hundreds of male bodies between her end of the carriage and his. She decided she couldn't leave him alone. Anything could happen. Someone could take against his shiny shoes or his overcoat and attack him.

Being slim and female was definitely helpful. She wriggled her way down the carriage, smiling and apologising until at last she got to the end. Luke had disappeared.

She was wondering if she could page him somehow, by getting the train manager to announce him lost, when she found him. He was in the space between two carriages, squatting down next to a group of students, chatting away.

'I was worried about you,' she said, annoyed to hear herself sounding reproachful.

'No need. There aren't any seats, are there?' he asked.

'There might be right up the other end of the train but I doubt it and I'm not going to go and look.'

'I could go!' Luke stood up.

'No, it's not worth it. It's quite comfortable here, isn't it?' She looked around. Three male students were looking at her. They all nodded.

'Would you like a drink?' One of them pulled a can of lager out of his pocket. 'Only got one spare, I'm afraid, but you could share.'

Before Sophie could even worry about Luke declining too politely, he'd said, 'Thanks, I'm really thirsty,' taken the can and pulled the ring cap. 'Here, Sophie, you go first.'

'This is very kind of you,' said Sophie, sounding terribly middle-class and English to her own critical ears. Then she belched. She handed Luke the can without looking at him, made a rueful face at the students and everyone laughed.

Luke and the students were comparing educational systems when Sophie realised she needed the loo. Even half a can of lager was enough to do this to her and she felt grateful she didn't have to fight her way past all those fans again. They were singing now and sounded very drunk. She fought her way into the cubicle convinced she'd made a terrible mistake. It wouldn't have been easy if they'd stayed at home but this journey was completely hellish. Luke would have a terrible impression of England and never come again. Sophie found this thought extremely sad.

At last they were on Uncle Eric's doorstep. Uncle Eric himself answered the door. 'Is that you, Sophie? Family thrown you out? And you've got a man with you. Eloping, what?'

Sophie kissed her uncle in a rush of love for him. In that instant she knew that if Luke didn't 'get' her great-uncle, she'd go right off him. 'No Uncle-Eric-dear, we're not eloping and the family haven't thrown me out. We're just escaping.' She paused. 'And I did ring and tell you we were coming.'

'So you did. Well, come on in, don't stand there letting the heat out. Are you going to introduce me? Or don't you know his name? He could just be some scruff you picked up in the road. I know what you're like.'

Luke laughed. 'I'm Luke Winchester, sir,' he said, 'and I met Sophie in New York, not on the road.'

'Yes,' Sophie explained, 'I met Luke's grandmother and then Luke.'

Uncle Eric frowned. 'Sophie, I don't like to mention it but is he – you know . . .' He cocked his head in Luke's direction. 'American?' he said in a stage whisper.

'Yes he is, but it's all right to mention it. No one will accuse you of being politically incorrect. It's not generally considered to be a handicap.'

'Humph. I've never taken much to Yanks,' said Uncle Eric, 'but if you're a friend of young Sophie's I'll give you house room.'

'I'm honoured,' said Luke and Sophie relaxed. Luke did understand Uncle Eric.

'Uncle Eric, do you mind if we stay for a couple of days? As I said on the phone, we'd really like to go through that box of papers you found. I'll make sure we don't make any work for Mrs Thing. I mean Mrs Brown.'

'She doesn't object to being called Mrs Thing,' said Uncle Eric. 'She knows I'm an old man and can't remember names.'

'Yes, but I'm not an old man,' said Sophie.

Uncle Eric made a wide gesture. 'Of course you can stay. Bags of room. Far too big a house for a single man – so they keep telling me.'

Sophie beamed at him. 'And what about something to eat? We've been travelling for four hours and we're starving.'

If he'd remembered to tell Mrs Brown they were coming she might have cooked something.

'Good God, then you must eat!'

He obviously hadn't remembered to tell her, or if he had, she hadn't taken the hint and left supper.

'Go and have a look at what's there,' he went on. 'There's always toast and that brown stuff—'

'Marmite,' supplied Sophie.

'— if all else fails.'

Sophie chewed her lip. 'I think maybe we've inflicted enough Englishness on Luke for one day without asking him to eat yeast extract. Shall I put the kettle on?'

'Or would you rather have a drink?' Uncle Eric asked Luke.

'Uncle!' She looked at her watch. 'It's only four thirty! Though it does feel later than that. It was a killer journey.'

Uncle Eric looked questioningly at Luke.

'I guess at home it's about eleven thirty so just about time for a pre-prandial snifter,' said Luke, apparently channelling Bertie Wooster.

'Good man!' said Uncle Eric. 'Sophie, you go in the kitchen and ferret out something to eat and then come and join us in the study. There's a good fire going. So,' he asked Luke, 'it sounds to me like you've got a good grasp of English.'

'I'm a P. G. Wodehouse fan,' Luke explained. 'And my grandmother is British.'

As she knew her great-uncle was also a P. G. Wodehouse fan, Sophie went into the kitchen happily, knowing they had something to talk about while she produced a snack. Luke was good at fitting in with new people. First of all he'd known of that American author her father and brother were fond of, and now he knew about Jeeves and Wooster. He was either extremely well mannered or extremely well read – possibly both.

The fridge was depressingly empty but she knew there was a shop nearby that would be open until five, even on a Sunday. Her wallet was depressingly empty, too. She went into the study where Luke and Uncle Eric clutched tumblers half filled with what seemed to be neat whisky.

'Uncle-Eric-dear,' she asked. 'Have you got any money?'

'Good God! I thought you were the only member of your family not after my money! Have you changed your spots since I last saw you?'

'The thing is,' said Sophie, feeling abashed in spite of her bold appearance, 'I'm terribly short of cash and I need to pop down to the shop before it closes. There's nothing to eat.'

Uncle Eric half rose out of his chair, feeling for his wallet in his back pocket. 'Take whatever you need then. Would have been half a crown in my day. Probably a tenner now.'

'A tenner would be plenty,' said Sophie. 'I'll bring you back the change.'

'I feel responsible for this,' said Luke. 'My wallet was stolen on the plane and I've been living off Sophie ever since. I could have arranged—'

'Shouldn't worry about it,' Uncle Eric interrupted. 'She works all the hours God sends. She's probably loaded.'

A glance at Luke told him that the irony of this statement was not lost on him.

She bought more bread, cheese, milk, eggs and bacon.

There was macaroni, which she knew was Uncle Eric's favourite. Quite what he'd have eaten if she hadn't appeared she had yet to find out. Probably toast and 'brown stuff'.

When she got back to the house she realised she should have bought tomatoes but it was too late now. She made some toast, buttered it liberally, and then put Marmite on some and jam on the others. She took it into the study.

'Not sure how this'll go with Scotch,' she said, 'but it'll stop you both dropping dead with hunger while I cook. Or getting drunk on neat whisky.'

'Aren't you hungry too?' asked Luke. 'You had the same hellish journey.'

'Oh, I'll have a bit of toast while I'm working. Luke, I'm making macaroni cheese. Basically, it's—'

'We have that in America. You don't have to explain.'

'Macaroni cheese!' exclaimed Uncle Eric. 'My absolute favourite! You're a good girl, Sophie, I don't care what they say about you.'

Sophie placed her macaroni cheese on the table in front of the men, who looked at it as lions look at a freshly killed carcass.

'My word, Sophie! You've done us proud! She'll make someone a nice little wife one of these days,' he said to Luke. 'You'd better get in there quick before she's snapped up by some other greedy bugger.'

'Luke and I aren't romantically involved,' said Sophie calmly. 'We're just thrown together by circumstance and a couple of joint projects.'

'Joint projects? What's that? Carpentry?'

Sophie shook her head in despair, as she was supposed to do. 'No, Uncle. Luke is helping me find the beneficiaries of the drilling rights. Remember? I found some papers in your desk. And we're going to investigate the box you found?'

'Oh yes. Some nonsense that took your fancy because you had time on your hands.' Her great-uncle finished his plate of macaroni.

'More?' asked Sophie, picking up the spoon. She loved to see Uncle Eric with such a healthy appetite.

'Mm, little bit, but feed Luke first. The way to a man's heart is through his stomach.'

Sophie sighed pointedly and helped them both to seconds.

'You're named as the beneficiary of the woman Sophie hoped to trace in New York,' said Luke, glancing at her.

He frowned. 'Yes, I discovered that, but Sophie had already hared off across the Atlantic. Couldn't tell her. Still, I don't suppose it amounts to much or the tax people would have been after it.'

'Well, we don't know. But maybe you wouldn't mind if I had a look to see if you've received the share certificates – or whatever proves she left her drilling rights to you,' said Luke. 'I am legally trained.'

'Wouldn't make any difference to me. Young Sophie had a look. Don't think she's trained for anything, are you?'

'No. I will be one day,' although not as a lawyer, obviously, she added silently. She picked up the spoon and started scraping at the crispy edges of the dish. One day I'll be a professional tailor, running my own business, living in a house by the seaside. 'Do either of you want these bits?' she said aloud.

The following morning, when Sophie had made her peace with Mrs Brown, who was slightly surprised but not entirely displeased to find her charge had eaten breakfast and that breakfast had been washed up, she showed Luke to Uncle Eric's desk, cleared by her just before she went to New York. By it was the cardboard box retrieved from the attic.

She couldn't help reflecting how much her life had changed in the couple of months since she'd dusted and polished the desk with love and then discovered the papers. She'd been to America, met Matilda and Luke, experienced the high life with them, eaten pizza in Mystic. She didn't let herself even think about falling in love. What she felt for Luke was just a bit of a crush, wasn't it?

'I'll leave you to it. I want to help Mrs Brown repair some curtains. Uncle Eric won't have new ones. He said he won't get value for money at his age.'

'He is very entertaining,' said Luke.

'He speaks very well of you too,' said Sophie. In fact he had said, 'Very sound chap, that Luke. I'll stand by you if your family cut up rough about him being – you know – American.'

'No problem there, Uncle, they think he's wonderful too. It's a shame we're just friends and look like staying that way.'

Uncle Eric had grunted in disbelief and the matter was dropped.

Now Sophie said, 'Shout if you want anything. I'll just be in the sitting room. I wish I'd brought my sewing machine with me.'

'Oh, that would have been fun, carrying a sewing machine on that train.' He smiled. 'I feel really out of touch not being able to catch up on emails.'

She hastened to reassure him. 'Don't worry. I'm sure we can find an internet café or something. There's one down the road that advertises having Wi-Fi.'

'But don't they expect you have your own computer?'

'We'll borrow one. Now you go and do your detective

work. I'm going to see if I can do sides to middle with these curtains.'

'I think I've found all the relevant documents,' said Luke, after a couple of hours and a cup of instant coffee.

'What do they say?' Sophie and Eric were in the study, drinking hot chocolate.

'Well, Eric has inherited the rights from Rowena Pendle – that's her married name – in New York. It appears that she managed to buy the rights from all the other interested parties, except Eric, your father, Sophie, and a certain Mr Mattingly. So they're all accounted for except his, but there's no address for him.'

Uncle Eric screwed up his face in thought. 'Mattingly. Think he died. Didn't know he'd have drilling rights though. Extraordinary – we were hardly related at all.'

Sophie sighed. 'So now we've got to find out who he left his shares to. This would be so much easier if we had a computer.'

'We don't need a computer!' said Uncle Eric. 'He probably left them to his widow, who married again.'

'Brilliant! Do you know who to?'

'Haven't a clue. But the wretched woman sends me a Christmas card every year with one of those letters in. Why do they think I care about their grandchildren's violin lessons?'

'Uncle-Eric-dear, if you can remember about the violin lessons, surely you can remember the name of her husband. We need to get in touch with her.'

'Why?'

'We need to get in touch with all the beneficiaries so they can decide how to maximise the rights,' Luke explained. 'No one will deal with an individual who owns half a dozen shares. But if everyone – which seems to be you and her now – bands together, we've got something to offer a drilling company.'

'And that would be good?'

'Yes!' said Sophie, failing to hide her exasperation. Uncle Eric had obviously forgotten he'd told her all this himself when she'd discovered the papers in the first place. 'Then we can all earn lots of money!' She pressed the point home.

'Money is the only thing your family ever cared about,' declared Eric.

'Huh! And there I've been, on my knees repairing curtains you're too mean to replace!'

'I didn't mean you, Sophie dear. You're a bossy little piece but there's no harm in you. And if you really want to get in touch with that woman you can find her Christmas card.'

'Really?' Sophie instantly regretted saying that her great-uncle was mean. 'How come?'

'Mrs Thing put them all together. She wanted to "recycle" them. Personally I think they've been cycled enough already.'

'Brilliant! Where are they? Oh, and any clues as to who we might be looking for?'

'Violins may be one,' suggested Luke, who seemed to be enjoying himself in a quiet way. 'But I suppose the letter may have got separated from the card.'

'Tell me where they are – oh, don't worry, I'll ask Mrs Brown,' said Sophie and galloped to the kitchen, hoping Mrs Brown hadn't gone home early, knowing Sophie would give Uncle Eric lunch.

She came back with a fat brown envelope. 'There aren't too many. We can just look through them all.'

She spread the Christmas cards out on the table. 'Apart from violins, what are we looking for? And did they put their address on the card?'

'Think they did. Think they live in Cornwall.'

'Cornwall? Fantastic!' said Sophie. 'We might have to go there anyway.'

'Why?' demanded Uncle Eric.

'Something to do with my grandmother,' said Luke. 'Wild-goose chase.'

'Might be more fun with two geese to chase,' said Sophie.

'It'll just be twice as impossible and twice as frustrating,' said Luke, no longer quite so amused.

Sophie went on leafing through the cards. 'Here's one from Cornwall. Do you have many Cornish friends?'

'No Cornish friends at all,' stated Uncle Eric. 'Just the one distant relation. They moved there for the milder climate. Thought it would keep them alive longer. Well, it didn't work for Mattingly! Look at me! Lived in this bloody freezing cold house for years and I'm fit as a flea.'

'So this must be it.' Sophie held up the card. 'Is this woman the last person we need to contact? I think it is!'

'Unless her husband bequeathed his shares to someone else – a grandchild maybe,' said Luke.

'Well, if they're still having violin lessons we should be able to coerce them into agreeing to do what we want,' said Sophie, encouraged.

'What do you want her to do?' asked Uncle Eric.

'If everyone signed a paper that meant Sophie could act for them, that would be helpful,' said Luke.

'Hang on,' said Sophie. 'I don't want to act for anybody. I was just going to get everyone together, find out where all the shares were.'

'Any company who might be interested would need to deal with an individual,' Luke repeated patiently.

'And that individual should be Sophie,' agreed Uncle Eric. 'Slip of a girl, of course, but with a good head on her

216

shoulders. I'll sign at once. She's a good cook too,' he added, looking at Luke.

'I'm not sure . . .' said Sophie. 'For a start I'd never get my family to agree to me doing it. They think of me as an idiot-child – no harm but no use either. Apart from domestic duties, of course.' She smiled to give the impression that she didn't mind.

'I'll persuade them,' said Luke firmly.

'So, if this is the right person, there's her name, address and telephone number on this card. We'd better ring her up.'

'Don't look at me,' said Uncle Eric. 'I never ring people up. Made it one of my rules. Never ring anyone if you can avoid it.'

'Oh, Uncle! If I ring it'll take me half an hour to explain who I am! They send you Christmas cards! They obviously love you dearly!'

'After my money, probably.'

'I don't think you've even got any money but you will have if we pull off this thing, won't we?'

'He will,' said Luke. 'We'd have to find someone interested in leasing the rights, of course, but there will be someone.'

'Oh all right, I'll telephone, but I'm only doing it for you, Sophie, because you're a good girl.'

Uncle Eric wanted to wait until after six, when calls were cheaper, but they persuaded him that wasn't worth the saving. Sophie would have offered the use of her mobile but she was running low on credit. Luke had to have some way for people to contact him and hers was the only number anyone knew.

'Hello?' Uncle Eric shouted. 'Is that m'cousin Mattingly's widow?'

Sophie cringed, wishing she'd made it easier for him by

writing down the name of the person he was calling. She should have remembered how bad he was with names.

'Eric here. Listen, I've got a young great-niece, name of Sophie, wants to come and visit you about some drilling rights. Would that be convenient?'

There was a long pause while 'Mattingly's widow' worked out who was calling her and then asked, presumably politely, what on earth her late husband's cousin was talking about.

'Can't be bothered to explain,' said Uncle Eric, 'but young Sophie will come and visit you. She's got a young man with her. A Yank, but decent enough. Goodbye!'

'Well, that's ensured us a warm welcome,' said Sophie, dryly. 'I'd better write down her details.'

Chapter Fifteen

❦

'I really need to catch up on my emails,' said Luke the next morning. 'And see how Ali is getting on sorting out my cards and my cell phone,' he added. 'I may need to go back to London right away if I can't get some money soon. I don't like sponging off you.'

Sophie smiled at him. 'I don't mind, really! But I need to get an internet connection too. I'd like to see if there have been any replies to my ads. If we do go to Cornwall to find "Mattingly's widow", we should find that out first.'

'I have at least a week before I need to be in London if I'm not needed there to get my affairs in order. Much as I love my grandmother, I can't just go to Cornwall on a whim – I need some evidence that this house is still standing.'

Sophie, who would quite happily have gone to Cornwall on a whim, said, 'OK, we need to find a computer. We'll try the library. I know where it is. I just don't know the opening hours.'

Sadly for them, Tuesday morning was not one of the ones the library was open. It would be open in the afternoon but neither Luke nor Sophie wanted to stay with Uncle Eric too much longer, and so didn't want to wait.

'There must be an internet café or something,' said Luke.

'Or a café with Wi-Fi.' Sophie felt this was slightly more likely in the town where Uncle Eric lived. 'There's a nice little place down here that might help us out,' she said. 'Uncle Eric and I had a snack here when I took him shopping once.'

There was a card in the window that declared it now had Wi-Fi and to ask for the password at the counter.

'No use without a computer,' said Luke.

'Don't be so negative.' Sophie opened the door and Luke followed her in.

The place was a bit of a shambles, thought Sophie. Almost every table was cluttered with dirty crockery. The man who appeared behind the counter as they approached it seemed harassed. Not the best time to ask anyone a big favour, Sophie realised. She smiled at him. 'Two pots of tea please.' She heard Luke rumble behind her, probably wanting coffee, and ignored him. 'You look as if you've been busy.'

'Yup. Coachload of sightseers – well, minibus full – all wanting coffee and cake. And I'm short-staffed. I'll clear you a table in just a moment.'

'Don't worry about that. Luke, I think we should have something to eat.' She prayed that he would hear the emphasis in her voice and not say, 'I'm not hungry.'

'I guess I'll get a chocolate muffin,' he said.

Sophie made a face. 'I don't like muffins. Inferior cake. I'll have a slice of lemon drizzle, please. Are all your staff off sick?'

'Flu bug. Damn nuisance.'

'It does seem to be everywhere.' Then Sophie got to the point. 'If you have a laptop we could borrow I'll work for you for two hours, for nothing. I'll clear the tables, wash up . . .' She noticed a plate with a solitary scone on it. 'And make you a fresh batch of scones or something.' A second later she wondered if society was ready to return to the bartering system.

The man frowned. 'Come again?' He began putting teapots on a tray and filling a jug with milk as he struggled to make sense of what Sophie had said.

'We really need to check our emails. We're staying with my uncle who hasn't got a computer. The library's shut and I just wondered whether, if you have a laptop or something, I could swap the use of it for some work. I'm very experienced in bar work and I'm a brilliant cook.' She crossed her fingers behind her back. She *was* a good cook but boasting went against the grain. However, necessity overcame her modesty.

'Oh. I see. Well, I don't know.'

'Pass me a tray and I'll sort us out a table.' She stacked a couple of tables' worth of dirty crockery on to the tray with a practised hand. 'Have you got a computer?' Sophie felt if the answer was yes, she could overcome any other obstacles.

'Upstairs in the office,' said the man doubtfully.

'I promise you, we only want to check our emails. If it's a laptop you could bring it down here so you don't need to worry about security. You'd be amazed at how much work I can do in two hours.' She put the loaded tray on to the counter for him to take.

He hesitated for a very short time. 'OK. I'm desperate. I'll bring it down. You finish those tables. There's an apron you can borrow on the back of the door in the kitchen.'

Just as he said this a crowd of women with shopping bags came in. 'If I don't get a cup of tea in one second I'm going to expire!'

Fortunately the fact that Sophie had worked in several cafés and wine bars meant she had no trouble finding her way round this one and was a very quick worker. There was no time to hang around. To Luke's considerable amazement, she had the tables clear in no time, loaded the dishwasher with the cups and was tipping flour into a huge food mixer while she waited for it do its job. He was

221

even more amazed when he realised the dishwashing cycle lasted only minutes and Sophie soon had it empty and was piling in plates and saucers.

Luckily for Sophie's nerves the man, whose name was Jack, came down from the office with his laptop before she made some hideous mistake, spoiling Luke's good impression of her for ever and getting them thrown out before they'd had a chance to connect with the internet.

Sophie felt strongly about giving good value, even if in this case it was not for money and she could have done with some. She had told Luke that she didn't mind him sponging off her and she really didn't, but she was aware he probably didn't know quite how little money she had. He was welcome to whatever she did have, but managing on so little would be a shock to him.

While Jack was setting everything up, she trained Luke to dry the cutlery and serve coffee and tea so when he had finished and she wanted to check her own emails, she needn't feel too guilty about dragging him into the maelstrom that was a busy café.

While he emailed Ali and other people in the office, she glazed the cheese scones she had made with milk and carefully stuck on grated cheese. She had just put them in the oven when Luke told her it was her turn.

'OK, If I'm more than ten minutes, tell me, and I'll check on those scones.' She hesitated. 'I don't suppose you'd like to . . .'

'No. I'm not taking responsibility for scones. What are scones?'

She laughed. 'You'll see.'

She nipped quickly through her emails. Two had Cornwall in the subject line. Her heart leapt with excitement. A response at last! Hooray!

She went and found Jack. 'Do you have a printer? I have

a couple of emails I really need to have a paper copy of. Any chance?'

Jack was delighted by how much Sophie had achieved in such a short time. 'It's as if you're on speed!' he said.

Sophie laughed. 'Luke said I had ants in my pants, but there's a lot to do and you're doing us a big favour. I want to make it worth it for you.'

'Well, you're doing that all right.'

'Luke, you go with Jack to sort out the laptop while I get on here.'

She checked the scones, decided they needed a few more minutes, looked at her watch and then served a couple of customers. Next she nipped upstairs to the office to see if the men were in print mode yet. She got down just in time to take the scones out of the oven, glad her inner cooking timer hadn't let her down.

'Sophie, are you sure you don't want to come and work for me?' said Jack as they left. 'I'd pay double whatever anyone is paying you now.'

'If I lived here I'd love to,' said Sophie, 'but sadly, I don't. We're just staying with my Uncle Eric.'

'And you won't let me give you any money for all the work you've done?'

Sophie could have done with the tenner he was offering her but she'd made her bargain, she wouldn't go back on it. 'No, no, two hours' work for the use of your computer – and printer. We're cool, thank you.'

'You are a piece of work, Sophie Apperly!' said Luke when they had left the café. 'Amazing!'

Blushing at this praise, Sophie brushed it off. 'It's what I do – for work, anyway. When I'm not being a nanny I work in cafés and bars – have done since I was still at school. Not the bars though, obviously.'

223

'Don't put yourself down! You're a great girl, even if most of your family don't seem to appreciate you.'

Sophie shrugged, still blushing. 'Well, you know what families are like.' Then, wanting to change the subject, she said, 'But what about the emails? Two different leads for Matilda's house!'

'Yes, that is good.' He was less enthusiastic.

'You don't seem pleased?'

'It's not that I'm not pleased, but my cards are proving hard to replace. I can't transfer money into your account apparently, although why not, in this electronic age, I do not understand.'

'You don't need to transfer money into my account.'

'Yes I do. I am not used to being paid for by . . .'

'A girl?'

He grinned sheepishly. 'That's about it.'

'It's good for you,' said Sophie firmly, but she was a bit anxious about how long her money would last them. If she found a bank she would check her balance.

'So, are we going to Cornwall then?' asked Luke.

'Are you up for it?' Sophie was delighted.

'Sure am.'

'Well, let's find out about trains and then we need to get you some different clothes. I'm not going round Cornwall with you in that long cashmere overcoat. It'll make you look like a tourist.'

'Sophie, you can't afford to buy me new clothes!' Luke was concerned.

'I can at the shops I shop at. Follow me. I know where all the charity shops are in this town.'

'Thrift stores, you mean?'

'Yup!'

'I have never—'

She took his arm before he could finish his sentence. 'I

224

know, Luke dear, I know. The station is this way.'

'I can't believe it's so expensive!' said Sophie through the glass at the man. 'We could buy a small car for that!'

The man shrugged. 'Buy one then.'

Just for a second, Sophie processed the idea: finding a car, getting the money, insuring it, and then actually driving it all the way to Cornwall.

'Or', the man went on, 'try the coach. I don't think you have to change so often either.'

'A coach! Brilliant idea!' said Sophie. 'Would you mind directing us to the coach station?'

Luke, being Luke, wrote down the directions. It was a very long walk.

The coach was far cheaper and, Sophie pointed out encouragingly, meant only one change. She knew Luke wouldn't enjoy a coach journey of nearly seven hours, she wasn't going to either, but she was used to long inconvenient journeys. He was used to first-class flights – if he wasn't using the executive jet he was reputed to have, chauffeur-driven cars, or trains with trolley service. It was going to be a shock, but it would be good for him to see how the other half lived.

'Come on,' she said when she had paid for the tickets. 'Let's get you something less townie to wear. Although that coat is lovely,' she added, giving it a surreptitious stroke, hoping that one day she'd be able to work with beautiful fabrics for a living.

When Luke was kitted out with jeans, a battered leather jacket and a pair of 'sneakers', which mercifully were brand new (Sophie knew she'd never get him into second-hand shoes), she felt he looked a little more suitably dressed for a spell in the country.

'Think of it as the same as you buying me clothes suitable for that brunch,' she said when he protested. 'It's a matter of fitting in.'

In the back of her mind was the thought that they might need to hitchhike round the Cornish lanes. She hadn't done it herself for years but if they had to, they had to. Doing it with Luke looking so much like a New York banker would be hugely embarrassing.

When they arrived back at Uncle Eric's house she collapsed into a chair beside Luke and accepted the huge glass of whisky Uncle Eric put into her hand. It had been a long day.

'I know,' said Uncle Eric, 'why don't we have fish and chips?'

Sophie looked at Luke and chuckled.

'Haven't had them for years. Used to eat them out of newspaper in my day. I think the newsprint added something to the flavour,' Uncle Eric persisted.

'Now they serve them in polystyrene containers with little wooden forks,' said Sophie.

'I must say, I would love to try fish and chips,' said Luke.

'Uncle?' said Sophie.

'Yes?'

'Can you stand us the fish and chips? I promise you, when we've sorted out these drilling rights I'll pay you back for everything.'

'Make sure you do, you minx.' He found his wallet and pulled out a twenty-pound note and handed it to Sophie. 'You'd better get him some mushy peas while you're about it. And maybe a pickled egg. Young man in his position' – he looked at Sophie – 'needs to keep his strength up.'

'You're a naughty old devil,' said Sophie, kissing him. 'But I think maybe Luke has suffered enough.'

*

Walking back through the winter streets, with tightly wrapped parcels smelling faintly of vinegar, Sophie felt she wanted to put her arm through Luke's and pretend they were the item everyone seemed to think they were. A girl could dream. He'd come with her, to get the 'whole fish-and-chip experience', as he'd put it, and he'd put his own clothes back on. His overcoat and shiny shoes were in some ways incongruous, but he was still very attractive.

'I really like to eat fish and chips out of the paper as I walk along, but it's terribly bad form to eat on the street,' said Sophie wistfully.

'I didn't think you cared about things like that. You seem very much a free spirit to me,' said Luke, a little surprised.

'I know. I am a free spirit and if it wasn't for Uncle Eric waiting at home for his, I probably would suggest we opened them and sat on a bench and ate them. It's best when you've got them really fresh and burn your fingers and your mouth.' She paused. 'My mother would be appalled.'

'You are a bit of a changeling, aren't you?'

She chuckled. 'Maybe. But I look too much like my mother to have been swapped at the hospital.'

'Your mother is a very handsome woman,' said Luke.

'Well, thank you! I'll take that to mean that when I'm my mother's age, I'll be handsome too.'

'And before that, very attractive.'

Sophie was blushing again. 'And you're very attractive too.'

He laughed and she realised that this wasn't the sort of remark the women who usually surrounded him would make, however much they thought it.

'Would Matilda eat fish and chips in the street, do you think?' she said to move the conversation on from compliments.

227

'I'm not sure about my grandmother. I never know what she's likely to do next. Like finding this house. Why hasn't she thought of it before?'

Suspecting he was going to blame her again for his grandmother's flight of fancy, she said quickly, 'I don't know but I do hope we can find it for her. How thrilled she'd be!'

Luke just shook his head slightly, smiling.

'These chips are very soggy,' complained Luke, watching Sophie divide them on to plates she had just taken out of the oven.

'They're supposed to be,' said Sophie. 'Or at any rate, that's how they always are. The sogginess somehow makes them even more of a guilty pleasure because you know they've absorbed more fat.'

'Used to fry 'em in beef dripping in the good old days,' said Uncle Eric.

Sophie was surprised. 'I wouldn't have thought you knew so much about fish and chips, Uncle Eric!'

'You'd be surprised what I know, young lady.'

'You do seem to have a very eclectic knowledge,' said Luke, looking dubiously at his plate.

'Let me make you a real treat.'

Sophie buttered the end of the new loaf and then cut off the slice and buttered another bit. Then she laid a few chips on to the soft, white bread and handed it to Luke. 'Eat that and tell me it's not delicious.'

'What is it?' Luke regarded it as if it might bite.

'A chip butty. You can put Tommy-K on it if you want to. It does have cancer-preventative properties,' said Sophie. 'Want one, Uncle Eric?'

'And what is "Tommy-K"?' her great-uncle asked.

'Tomato ketchup,' said Sophie. 'How's your butty, Luke?'

'Surprisingly nice.'

'See! Told ya!'

It was evening when they arrived in Truro the following day. They'd hardly slept on the coach and they were both exhausted.

'But I did get to see a lot of the country,' said Luke gallantly.

'And we had that cute little loo on the bus. That helped,' said Sophie.

'I wouldn't describe it as cute, but it had its uses.'

'When we've stopped having the Pollyanna competition, I think we need to find a bed and breakfast. Two rooms,' she added, wistfully.

'One room would be cheaper,' said Luke.

'Yes,' said Sophie, 'but they might give us a double bed and then where would we be?'

Luke laughed. 'I think we know where we'd be. In bed together.'

'I think I should tell you, Luke, that I never sleep with anyone on the first date,' she said, matching his teasing tone.

'I'm glad to hear that, Sophie, but I should point out that this must be at least our fifth date, one way or another.'

Sophie eyed him firmly. 'They haven't really been dates and we're still not sharing a room.'

Luke shrugged. 'You're in charge!'

Sophie decided that being in charge was not all it was cracked up to be.

Finding a bed and breakfast that was open in January was a bit of a struggle, but they managed to do so, and it had at least two rooms.

'So, are you just friends?' asked the man who showed them the rooms, curious about surprise visitors in winter.

'I'm gay,' said Luke blandly. 'We prefer not to share.'

Sophie suppressed a giggle. Lack of sleep was making Luke frivolous – she loved it!

The man nodded. 'We get all sorts here. No problem. What time would you like breakfast?'

'Eight o'clock,' said Sophie. 'Is that OK for you, Luke?'

'It's fine if we can go to bed really early. I need to stretch out or my muscles will forget how to do it.'

'What about something to eat?'

'There's a great little restaurant round the corner,' said the man.

Sophie gulped. She wasn't at all sure they could afford a 'great little restaurant'.

Fortunately Luke seemed to realise this. 'I'm too tired to eat,' he said to the man. 'Jet lag.'

'Oh, right. I understand,' said the man.

'Me too,' said Sophie, knowing that thanks to Uncle Eric, there were sandwiches left in the bag.

'Can you get "coach lag"?' asked Sophie when they had met up in her room to eat the sandwiches and drink tea.

'Definitely.' Luke stretched out on one of the single beds. 'I definitely have coach lag.'

Sophie chuckled. 'Well, brace up and let's get these sandwiches out.'

Uncle Eric had insisted that she made them sandwiches because they were going 'on a journey'. He explained that during the war you never knew when you were going to get fed again. Sophie had felt it easier to make 'sangers' as he called them than discuss whether or not England was at war and if the fact there was no rationing made any difference. It would definitely save her money.

'The Marmite ones have held up best,' she said, having unwrapped a foil package. 'Just as well you like it.'

Luke took the offered sandwich. 'Mm, although I'm not

230

sure the trip in your bag has really added much to the flavour.'

Sophie nodded, eating a horribly soggy cheese and salad sandwich. 'I know, but better than nothing.'

'Definitely better than nothing,' agreed Luke. 'Now, what about the tea?'

Amused that Luke had become so fond of tea during his trip to England, Sophie got off the bed and made it.

'So that was the "Full Cornish",' said Luke when they had paid their dues and left the bed and breakfast the next morning.

'Yup, almost indistinguishable from the Full English.'

'But Cornwall is in England, isn't it?' Luke seemed confused.

'It depends on who you talk to. It does have its own language.' Her phone rang. 'Oh, it's for you!'

Luke took her phone away and talked on it for some time. While she was on her own, Sophie got out her wallet and counted her money. Then she looked at the statement she'd got when she had last been to the cash machine. She had fifty pounds left in her account. She still had her savings, but she couldn't easily get at them. It was worrying.

Luke hurried back to her, looked pleased. 'Hey! We have money!'

'Do we?'

'Yup! Ali has arranged for money to be left in the bank here.'

'Which bank?'

He named it. 'I can withdraw it all in cash. It'll stop me being utterly dependent on you.'

'Brilliant!' Actually Sophie didn't know how she felt about this. Apart from the worry about not having enough, she'd quite enjoyed Luke being financially dependent on her.

'We can hire a car,' Luke went on, jubilant. 'No more public transportation!'

'Have you got your driving licence with you?' asked Sophie.

'Er, nope. But you have.'

'Mm,' Sophie admitted, unwilling to confess she wasn't a very experienced driver. 'Don't worry, I'll hire the car and then you can drive.'

He shook his head. 'I'm an attorney. It means I have to obey the law. But I have to confess, I'm not a good passenger.'

'Great,' said Sophie quietly. Still, what better way to get driving practice than driving a millionaire through Cornish lanes?

Hiring a car took until way past Sophie's lunchtime, but eventually they were ushered into a nice little Renault Clio. Sophie was at the wheel; Luke folded his long legs into the passenger seat. Luke took hold of the maps that came with the car.

'We might need to buy an Ordnance Survey map,' said Sophie, 'if we're going to find the place suggested in that email. It's tiny.' Sophie had had two leads emailed to her, both in roughly the same area. They had decided the simplest thing to do would be to start with the one nearest Truro.

Luke folded the map back perfectly and almost instantly. Sophie looked at him. No one who could do that was properly human, in her eyes. He was probably from another planet; she'd always suspected it.

'OK, let's drive to a shop where they can sell us one of those maps.' He might not like being a passenger, but having a car and money obviously made Luke feel in control.

'Do you happen to know what direction that might be?' Sophie asked.

'Nope. Try the centre of town. There's bound to be somewhere there.'

Sophie fiddled about with the gears until she knew where they all were and set off sedately.

'I'd forgotten about the stick shift,' said Luke. 'Why didn't we hire an automatic?'

'It would have been more expensive,' said Sophie, who had had to get the cheapest of everything all her life. 'How much money have you got?'

'Five hundred pounds,' said Luke. 'The car was about sixty for three days. We'll have this sorted in three days. Britain is a small country.'

'Yes, but distances are long,' said Sophie, aware she probably wasn't making sense. 'The roads can be quite slow in the country.' Luke hadn't really seen Cornwall yet, she thought. She didn't know it well herself but she had been there on holiday. She knew about the narrow lanes bounded by high walls and hedges and how confusing they could be.

'Three days is all the time I can spend on this project,' he said. 'My cards and apartment and everything will be waiting for me in London by then. I will have to go back.'

'Well, keep back a couple of hundred pounds for your train fare then,' said Sophie, a bit hurt that he seemed so keen to get away from her now he had the means to do so, and that their time together was just a 'project' to him. She'd thought they'd been having fun.

'Really? That much?'

'Probably. But don't worry, the coach would be cheaper.'

'I'm never going on a coach again,' he said firmly. 'And, Sophie, it's not that I want to rush back but once we've found your relatives and I can, hand on heart, tell my

233

grandmother that her house is no more, I do have to get back to real life.'

'I knew that,' she said and plunged into the thick of the traffic, looking for a car park. The sooner they got the map, found where they were supposed to be heading and got out of the town, the happier she would be. If they only had a short time left together she didn't want to spend it trying to work out a one-way system.

Chapter Sixteen

❦

'Don't give me that women-can't-read-maps crap,' said Sophie irritably. 'I'm an excellent map-reader, I'm just not brilliant at left and right. I just went the "other left".'

'Which is right,' stated Luke.

'OK!'

They were lost. Luke, the map on his knee, no longer neatly folded, was being patient but with gritted teeth. 'Maybe if you're so good at navigating I should take my chance with the stick shift.'

'That's not necessary. Now just tell me where I should go now.'

Sophie was trying hard to make Luke feel better. She knew he hated not being in control of the vehicle. She was a perfectly competent driver so he had no reason to feel unsafe, but he clearly needed the wheel between his hands to feel comfortable.

Luke stared down at the map but didn't speak. Eventually Sophie took it from him, making a huge effort not to snatch. 'I think we should head on to this road, which we can join here. Can you see?'

'Yes!'

But he was obviously struggling with the map. 'Maybe you need reading glasses?' suggested Sophie. 'You are a bit older than me.'

'That's it. Pull over. I'm driving.'

Aware his patience had expired, Sophie slowed down

and prepared to pull over so they could have this discussion in safety – just in case it became a bit more than a discussion. She found a lay-by and turned into it.

'OK, Luke, currently you have no driving licence.'

'I have one, just not with me. And Ali is arranging a duplicate. It'll be in my hands in days.'

Sophie thought better of exclaiming at how quickly this was being organised; she didn't believe it was possible.

'I'm not sure you're insured . . .'

'I'll take my chance with that too.'

'You're a lawyer. It's your duty to obey the law.'

'Ali will hire me an attorney who'll have me out of jail in seconds.'

Sophie sighed. Ali again – the solution to all his problems, just as she longed to be.

'Ali can't do anything about the stick shift,' she said, grumpily. This should have been a lovely adventure for them to have together and now, because he couldn't read a map or be a passenger, the all-powerful Ali had intruded into it.

'I can handle the stick shift on my own. Now take the map and point me in the right direction!'

Annoyingly, Luke, much happier once he was driving, got the hang of driving on the left and the gears very quickly, and, because Sophie really was good at navigating, they were soon on their way towards Falmouth. She could do left and right if she had time to think about it. Matilda's ring, now on her right hand, was helpful. Her mind went back to when Matilda had given it to her before they had gone to the brunch, where she had met Ali. She, Sophie, had been the saviour then. Now that role had been usurped by charming, efficient, sophisticated Ali. An unsettling thought suddenly occurred to her but she'd have to pick her moment to pursue it.

They drove pretty much in silence apart from a few directions from Sophie. When they were on the main road she had time to have a private fume about the unfairness of men being better at spatial awareness and mechanical things.

'We're meeting our contact in a pub,' said Sophie after she'd swallowed her indignation at this essential truth.

'Why doesn't that surprise me? Just don't ask me to drink British beer. I'm sure it's very authentic but I don't like it.'

'I wouldn't dream of asking you to drink anything,' said Sophie, offended, although she didn't like traditional bitter either. 'You can have what you like in a pub. Coffee even. In fact, if you're driving, you'd better stick to soft drinks. Left at the next crossroads.' She gestured firmly with her hand to prove it was left she meant.

'So how much further is this place?' asked Luke after they had negotiated high-banked Cornish lanes for half an hour or so. 'We saw the sign for it ages ago and I'm getting hungry.'

'Me too. I don't think it can be too much further. Another couple of miles and we should be in the village,' she said. 'It's near the river.' She paused. That unsettling thought would not go away. 'Luke?'

'Yes?'

'Does Ali still think we're engaged?'

It took him a moment to realise what she was talking about. 'Oh no,' he said easily. 'I explained all about that to her. It wasn't fair to keep her in the dark.'

Why not? Sophie longed to ask. Why wasn't it fair?

'It was just to keep the Blonde Bimbos off me,' he explained.

'You could have used a big stick,' said Sophie. 'That would have worked. Pretending you were engaged to me cost you loads and Matilda a very nice ring.'

237

'Worth it, I assure you. Down here?'

'Yup,' said Sophie. 'Oh, isn't this pretty?' The sudden view through a gateway distracted her from this little niggle. 'And it feels like spring down here.'

'When I left home, we were under a couple of feet of snow,' said Luke.

'I love snow!' said Sophie. 'Proper thick snow though, not the stuff that turns to slush the moment it hits the ground.'

'You might not like it if you had to live with it,' said Luke.

'I'm sure I would. Now let's not argue. Golly, the road has got terribly steep.'

Slowly they wound down and down until they saw the river at the bottom. The road seemed to lead straight into it. Fortunately, just as they seemed on the point of getting their wheels wet the road widened and they saw a large pub. 'Oh goody,' said Sophie. 'They'll definitely do food.'

'And we have money to pay for it,' said Luke, equally enthusiastic. 'I'm not used to having to watch every cent.'

'Watching every cent – or even every penny – is character building,' said Sophie. 'Consequently my character is like the Great Wall of China.'

Luke gave her a glance that made her wonder. It was amused, indulgent and something else. Could it possibly be attraction? The thought made her blush.

They weren't due to meet Sophie's contact, Jacca Tregorran, until two, so they had an hour to enjoy their lunch. The pub was delightful, full of small, dark-beamed rooms, interesting artefacts, comfortable chairs and tables and a couple of crackling log fires. They found a table right next to one and examined the menu.

'We should have fish,' said Sophie. 'It'll be brilliant down here.'

'And they have chips on the menu,' said Luke. 'Will they be soggy?'

'I hope not. It's only chips in fish-and-chip shops that are like that. And then not always.' She really wanted Luke to have a good culinary experience. She didn't want him to think badly of Cornish food; she knew that it could be amazing.

Cornwall, as represented by this particular establishment, didn't let Sophie down. The soup came promptly, smelling delicious with crusty bread that seemed to be just out of the oven. The crab cakes were tasty and fresh and the chips were fabulous: crisp and golden on the outside and soft and yielding on the in. They went extremely well with the home-made mayonnaise.

They shared a bottle of mineral water, having decided that either of them might need to drive.

'This is great food,' said Luke. 'Is it always this good in Cornwall?'

'I hope so,' said Sophie, trusting that it was. 'Have another chip.'

'Mm.' Luke carried on eating hungrily. 'It's the best meal I've eaten that you haven't cooked since I've been in the UK,' he said.

Sophie blushed and looked away, inordinately pleased. He hadn't had to add the bit about the meals she'd cooked; he must really have liked them. 'Thank you.' To reward him she added, 'I'll drive next if you like. You should look at the scenery. It's so beautiful. No wonder Matilda is nostalgic about Cornwall.'

'I do understand better now why she's so keen to find her old house. I think as you get older you want to gather up your memories and have them safe around you so you know where they are.'

'Luke!' said Sophie. 'That was almost poetic.'

'I do have a spiritual side, you know.'

'You just keep it hidden most of the time, under your smart suits and crisply ironed shirts.'

'You have no idea what goes on under my suits and my shirts, young lady,' he said sternly.

Sophie smiled, scooping up the last of the mayonnaise with a chip. 'Are we going to have pudding?'

'Dessert? I think so. We don't know when we'll eat again, after all.'

Sophie laughed. 'I think we'll know roughly what time we'll eat, it's where that's the mystery. That and where we're going to lay our heads. I quite like this gypsy lifestyle. Do you?'

'Hm. I suppose it is fun. My life is very ordered, usually. Meeting you has changed all that.' His gaze lingered on her and she couldn't quite read his expression. He was almost frowning. Was he annoyed with her?

'Don't blame me for this! This is all because of Matilda!' Then she remembered 'the Mattingly widow'. 'Well, mostly.'

'OK, I'll rephrase that. You and Matilda meeting has changed my life.'

'For the better?' Sophie said this as if she didn't care about the answer but she desperately wanted him to say yes. She'd put him through a lot of slightly strange experiences since he'd been in England. She didn't want him to have hated every moment of it.

'Well, you've opened my eyes to a whole different sort of life and that's always a good thing.' He paused. 'Sophie—'

Just then a large man with a handlebar moustache and matching personality came into the bar. 'Aha! You must be Sophie Apperly!' he declared. 'Jacca Tregorran.' Sophie's hand disappeared for a moment and re-emerged slightly crumpled.

Jacca Tregorran was a character. Sophie decided that he probably worked on it. His large frame, loud voice and expansive personality would mean he was recognised by the locals and admired by the tourists as a genuine Cornishman wheeled out for their entertainment.

'Hello,' she said, reeling back slightly from the force of his personality. 'Let me introduce you to Luke Winchester. It's his grandmother who's looking for the house.'

Luke's hand was similarly crushed. 'What are you drinking? Water? That won't do.'

'I'm driving!' said Sophie quickly. 'And I'll just pop to the Ladies.'

When she came back Luke and Jacca had stretched out their legs in front of the fire and were clutching pint mugs of cloudy amber liquid.

'Luke!' she said, surprised. 'I thought you weren't going to drink? Not that it's anything to do with me, really,' she added hurriedly, before Jacca could accuse her of being a nag.

'This is cider,' explained Luke. 'That's not alcoholic.' He took a huge long gulp and then choked.

'Not quite what you were expecting?' asked Jacca, amused.

'No,' said Luke. 'In America cider is more like apple juice.'

'Here – the genuine kind anyway – is quite like vinegar, in my opinion,' said Sophie. 'I only like the fizzy stuff.'

'Ooh, you don't want to drink that gassy rubbish! You want the genuine thing. Good Cornish cider . . .' Jacca Tregorran expounded on the topic for some time, implying that what Sophie had said was sacrilege, that good honest cider would never do you any harm, and that there was no truth in the rumour that they put dead rats into the mix – or if they did it was a perfectly harmless practice.

'So, about the house?' asked Sophie quickly, hoping Luke hadn't been able to follow Jacca's broad accent. It appeared he hadn't, because he took another long draught, presumably enjoying it.

'Well now,' said Jacca. 'About the house.' He paused to get the level of liquid in his glass down to that in Luke's, not wanting to be left behind. 'I don't think the house is still standing, but there was a big house just near here. Thought of it straight away when I saw your ad in the paper. Got in touch.'

Sophie rummaged in her rucksack and pulled out her now very crumpled picture. 'Did it look like this?'

Jacca took the paper. 'No, my lover, it didn't look like that at all.'

Luke and Sophie exchanged glances. Luke drank some more cider.

'So the house you had in mind isn't there any more?' asked Sophie.

'That's right, my bird.'

'But it didn't look like this house, so this house maybe *is* still there?'

Jacca scratched his head. 'I don't know. You've got me confused now.'

'Me too!' said Sophie. 'But I hope it's in a good way!'

'But we can have another pint though?' Jacca didn't seem to think that having discovered his lead was the wrong house was any reason to stop socialising.

Luke got up. 'My shout,' he said. 'Sophie? More water?'

She shook her head. 'I'm awash.'

'Did you want dessert?' Luke went on. 'We were going to have it.'

Sophie shook her head. Now that she'd started to digest her first course she discovered she was full. She didn't want to waste time, either. 'I think when you and Jacca have had another drink we should go. We have a house to find and it's getting late.'

'Ooh, my dear, the chances of you finding that house are slim,' said Jacca, shaking his head in a way appropriate for one breaking bad news. 'You didn't know much about it, did you?'

'No,' Sophie agreed brightly. 'That was why I put the advertisement in the paper. It's a long shot but I'm going to do my best. We've got one more lead to follow up.'

Luke put down one pint mug and a half-pint. He handed the pint to Jacca.

'I hope that won't put you over the limit, Jacca,' said Sophie, who was annoyed with him for pointing out the truth about the likelihood of them finding the house.

He winked at her with a deep sideways nod. 'We be a bit more lenient about these things in these parts, my dear.'

She pursed her lips, half expecting a fake parrot to appear on his shoulder and for him to call her Jim, lad.

'This stuff isn't very alcoholic, Sophie,' said Luke reassuringly, sounding perfectly sober.

'I think it goes to your legs,' said Sophie, fighting a losing battle. 'So I've heard.'

'Ooh, you don't want to believe everything you hear, my dear,' said Jacca. 'Another couple of pints here, barman, please!'

Sophie sighed and looked at her nails. It was fun to see Luke so unbuttoned but it was also a bit worrying. They had to find somewhere to stay and it would be dark soon. The Cornish lanes would be even harder to negotiate then.

Half an hour later Luke walked unsteadily to the car and tried to get in the driver's side, not, he assured Sophie, because he thought he was going to drive, but because he forgot for a moment that he was in England.

Once he was buckled in she took the map from him and then compared it to the napkin on which Jacca had attempted to draw his own map of the way to the village suggested in their second lead. It wasn't too far away. Neither seemed to make much sense, but she knew her way back to the main road. Luke fell asleep and snored gently. She glanced across at him, loving the vulnerability revealed by his lashes against his cheek and his slightly open mouth. She wondered longingly what it would be like to wake up and see his head on the pillow next to her. Adorable, she imagined, then shook her head.

She set off hoping she wouldn't have to wake him to get him to navigate.

She realised she should have woken him when the lane she was on started growing grass up the middle. She was on some tiny track that was so narrow she couldn't turn round so she just had to plough on, hoping for a turning space. She'd done quite well to begin with, keeping going in the right direction, passing signs and place names she was expecting.

Then suddenly there stopped being signs to the village she was after, as if it had been removed from the planet just as she approached it. She slowed down, checking the occasional farm gate to see if she could turn. She didn't want to risk getting stuck in a ditch.

She crossed a shallow ford, and was trying to remember if Matilda had mentioned crossing one when she'd talked abut the house when the road took a sharp right. And then she saw it, on a little rise: Matilda's house, not in the village at all, but quite a way outside it.

Noting with relief that she could also turn and so wouldn't have to reverse for several miles, she drove up to it, parked the car and got out, closing her door as quietly as she could so as not to disturb Luke.

The house was beautiful, even in the gloaming. Large, with two sections making a U shape so that the two windows on either side of the front door gave views into the other room. There were French doors on both sides and diamond panes added to the charm. It obviously hadn't been lived in for some time. Some sort of creeper covered the walls and most of the windows. The roof looked higgledy-piggledy, some of the diamond panes were missing and one of the chimney stacks leaned slightly. But in spite of this air of neglect and abandonment, Sophie instantly recognised why Matilda had loved it so much – she felt exactly the same.

She set off round the house to see if there was a way in that didn't involve major breaking and entering. It was hard to get round at the back. Outbuildings sprawled from the house, odd walls had fallen down and elder trees grew wherever they could find a foothold. Eventually she found a coal shed or something that had a door on both sides. She fought her way through cobwebs and dust to the far door and escaped into the dusk.

The house was just as lovely from the back. There was a stable block, what could have been pigsties and, through a gate, a walled garden with glasshouses, many of the panes broken, abutting the walls.

Feeling just a little bit spooked, Sophie went back to the main house. She felt safe near that as if the ghosts were kept away by the happy atmosphere. Or maybe it was the presence of Luke that reassured her. He might be asleep, but he was still there if she needed someone to scream to.

There was a window that was partly open. Inside were drifts of autumn leaves, blown and dried by possibly years of Cornish winds. She opened it a bit more and hopped inside.

She was about to explore further when she realised that

she'd do better with a torch and, she was forced to admit, Luke. There was a tiny torch on her key ring. If she went back and got that Luke might wake up. Then they could explore the interior together.

Luke wasn't in the car when she got back to it. It gave her a bit of a shock, but then she decided he had probably gone for a pee or something and would reappear soon. He hadn't locked the car so she was able to retrieve her bag and find her torch.

She went and stood in front of the house, waiting for Luke. When he came up behind her she jumped, although she knew it was him.

'Did I startle you?' He sounded apologetic.

'No, not really. I knew it was you.' She paused. 'This is the house, isn't it?'

'There's not much doubt about it. How clever of you to find it, without a navigator too.' He was impressed. Then he went on: 'I should have believed you when you told me that cider was alcoholic.'

She smiled at him. 'Yes, you should!'

'You see at home —'

'I know, cider is like apple juice in America. Scrumpy in Cornwall is quite different.'

'I won't make that mistake again. Although I enjoyed it at the time.'

She made a face. 'I hope you don't get a hangover.'

'If I do, I deserve it. So how did you find it?' His eyes crinkled at the corners in a way she hadn't noticed before. Perhaps it was because she hadn't seen him so relaxed before.

She wanted to say, 'You see, you don't need to know the difference between left and right to get to where you want to go,' but she didn't. 'Actually, I got completely lost and found it by accident.'

He chuckled and came nearer to her, putting his hand on her arm. 'Shall we see if we can get in?'

'We can!' said Sophie. 'And I've got a torch now.'

It wasn't easy but they found their way round most of the ground floor. They didn't go upstairs. Sophie was frightened of ghosts and Luke said the floorboards might not be sound and it would be dangerous.

'I wonder why it's been empty for so long,' said Sophie. 'It's such a beautiful house in a beautiful situation. I just love it!'

He was amused by her enthusiasm. 'I suspect it was left to several members of a family and they couldn't agree about what to do with it,' he said. 'It happens all the time.'

'Hm,' said Sophie. 'Bet they're kicking themselves that they missed the property boom. This would have made a lovely project.'

'Don't say that to my grandmother.'

'What do you mean?'

'It's just the sort of thing she would say. It would be crazy.'

'I don't see why.' The thought of some other property developer getting hold of it was like a cold hand on her heart. 'If it's for sale, why shouldn't she buy it?'

Luke shook his head. 'Because she lives in New England? She could come visit, and see it. That would be OK, but buying it?' He sucked his teeth.

'She could afford to just buy it and keep it as a pet,' said Sophie, determined now that Matilda *should* buy it, if only because at that moment she wanted it so much herself.

Luke shrugged. 'She could. But I imagine if she did, she'd want to do something good with it – maybe turn it into a centre for disadvantaged children to have holidays in. Although it would be a little small. She wouldn't want it lying empty, I don't think.'

247

Sophie was pensive. 'That's a very specific use for it. Has she talked about it to you?'

'No, but she donated a lot of money to a centre like that back home. It's something she's keen on.'

'It could be a brilliant place!' Sophie put a firm clamp on her own unexpected desire for the house. 'But we really need to see it in daylight.'

'Yes. Let's go find somewhere to stay nearby and come back in the morning. I won't be able to hang around for long though, I need to get to London soon.'

The reminder that their adventure together wasn't going to continue for much longer made Sophie suddenly sad. There was something magical yet poignant about them being together, in the quickly gathering darkness, outside the house where Matilda had been so happy as a child. She didn't want to leave, although she did accept they couldn't stay. They had to rejoin the real world.

'OK. Are you feeling all right now?'

'I think so. I don't want to drive though.'

'It's all right, I'll drive. When I was coming down here I was just grateful to see there was somewhere I could turn. I thought I might have to reverse all the way back to the main road.' She gave him a stern look. 'My brother is convinced that women can't reverse.'

'I wouldn't dream of saying anything of the kind,' said Luke, his hands held up in a gesture of peace.

Sophie chuckled. 'I'm not very good at reversing actually, but my three-point turns are amazing!'

'Your what?'

'Oh, you'll see.'

Chapter Seventeen

❧

It was pitch dark by the time they set off again. Sophie located all the lights on the car and realised that she felt completely safe with Luke sitting beside her. Had she been alone she'd have been nervous about breaking down, getting lost or landing in a ditch while she tried to pass something. With him there she knew he'd help deal with it. She drove back across the ford and up the long, steep lane to the main road and they turned left. The road to the village involved another descent until they were by the water and just as they reached it the moon came out from behind a cloud.

'Amazing!' said Sophie, seeing how it danced across the water. 'It's like one of the scraperboard kits we had as children. Did you have them? You have a little tool and create moonscapes.'

Luke didn't reply immediately and they just sat in the car and looked at the moonlight reflecting off all the little yachts that were moored along the harbour. 'Is that the ocean or a river?' asked Luke eventually.

'The ocean,' said Sophie when she'd shaken herself out of her reverie and had time to think about it. 'Can you look out for somewhere to park? Oh, over there. I wonder if we have to pay as it's out of season?'

'I have money! I can pay!'

'Don't let it go to your head, Rich Boy. You'll have lots of things to spend your money on. But it won't be much,' she added.

249

The car parked, she said, 'OK, let's see if any of these cottages do bed and breakfast.'

They were just wondering which of the two little streets they should try first when they saw a woman walking her dog. Sophie ran over and asked.

'Oh yes,' said the woman. 'Moira does B & B. She lives in that little thatched cottage over there. Lovely woman. Great cook. I think she opens out of season.'

'When you go back to the States you can tell people that you've slept in a thatched cottage,' said Sophie, and then listened to herself and realised how silly that sounded and chuckled. 'I'm sure they'll be very impressed down at the country club.'

Luke laughed. 'Well, my half-brothers and sisters in California will be impressed anyway. And my grandmother.'

'That's the most important thing. Right, here we are.'

They walked up the little path to the front door, in Sophie's case revelling in the quaintness of the house. There was no bell, only a knocker in the shape of an anchor. She banged it hard.

They waited in silence. Then Sophie said, 'You can sort of tell when there's no one in, can't you?'

'Mm. The clue is no one answers the door,' said Luke.

'I didn't mean that! But how annoying! How sad! I so wanted to stay here.'

'Well, why don't we put a note through the door with your cellphone number on it and we can go for a walk or something? Then if this Moira comes back within an hour or so and is open for business, she can ring us. If not we'll probably have to find a larger town with a hotel.'

'You want a hotel really, don't you? A decent shower, Egyptian cotton sheets, big towels . . .'

He looked down at her, his eyes narrowed, but she

couldn't read his expression. 'I want what you want, Sophie.'

As this totally confused her she didn't reply, just burrowed in her bag for some paper and a pen. Surely he didn't really want what she wanted? He wouldn't even know what that was – and she wasn't going to tell him.

'It's just beautiful here! So peaceful!' said Sophie for about the third time. They were looking at all the yachts bobbing up and down on their moorings, the halyards tinkling against the metal masts. 'Look at the lights over there on the hillside. Imagine all the people snuggled in for the night. I'd so love to live nearer the sea. Where I live is lovely – you've seen it – but this is more special, somehow.'

'It is,' agreed Luke. 'But I'm getting cold. Let's walk along a bit. There's a church there.'

'Good plan. I love churchyards, although I do always find them terribly sad. Especially old ones that have children in them.' She paused. 'I'm just warning you, in case I cry.'

To Sophie's relief, Luke didn't seem too put out by this admission. Maybe he was getting used to her.

'Would you rather not go? I'd hate to make you cry,' he said.

'Oh no, I want to. Exploring the graveyard means we can put off making the decision whether we should give up on staying here and find a town.'

Luke put his arm round Sophie's shoulders and hugged her to him. 'You are funny, Sophie.'

'I'll take that as a compliment,' said Sophie doubtfully.

They opened the gate and went in. Sophie had her torch and set off on the tiny, narrow path between the graves. 'It's really quite large for such a small village, isn't it?'

'It seems to go right up the hill,' Luke agreed, following

her. 'Still, if it's an old village, lots of people would have lived here over the years.'

'They seem really packed in.' She shone her torch at some of the graves so they could read the inscriptions. 'Look how old they are. And how sad! Look – there's been space left on this one for other family members but they obviously got buried somewhere else.'

'Here's a sad one: "In Memory of Alan, who died doing what he loved best: sailing."'

'I wonder how I'd feel if my husband loved sailing more than me,' said Sophie.

Luke seemed amused. 'I'm sure no one would love sailing more than you, Sophie – especially if they were your husband. But sailing was his favourite activity.'

Was he flirting or teasing? Or both? The thought made her heart flutter. They'd shared some mad, quite intimate times together since he'd arrived in England and she'd got to know him far better. But she still couldn't really read him in the way she usually could other men. The uncertainty intensified her growing feelings for him and about him. She accepted now she found him very attractive, but did he feel the same about her?

The path was too narrow for them to walk side by side. As they got to the top of the hill the graves were a little newer.

Sophie had just decided that churchyards weren't sad places and instead terribly romantic when she spotted a grave which held a mother's entire family, who had died, one after the other, a few weeks apart, in some dreadful epidemic. Luke touched her arm and her hand stole up and held on to his coat. Luke's arm instantly wrapped around her. 'Are you OK?'

'Mm. Just sentimental.' She stayed there, half suffocated by aged leather until she got herself under control. She knew it was partly because all her senses were heightened by the moonlight, Luke, and finding the house, and she should just get a grasp on reality. 'I'm fine now,' she said, having cleared her throat.

'Well, come over here. Look at this. I want to show you something.'

It was a fairly plain headstone and almost covered in ivy and lichen and Sophie didn't know why Luke had drawn her attention to it.

'Look!' he said. 'The names!'

'They don't mean anything to me.'

'I'm fairly sure that Pencavel was the name of Matilda's family. Can you read the date?'

Sophie produced her tiny torch and directed it towards the gravestone. 'Well, the husband was born in 1860 and died in 1930 and the wife was born in 1865 and also died in 1930. Maybe she died of grief.'

Luke did some calculations. 'These must be her grandparents – my great-grandparents. They lived here. Look, there's the name of the farm where they must have lived.'

'So they would have known the owners of the house. I wonder if they're here too. Oh, Luke! It's like going back to the past. Your past!'

She paused and breathed deeply, hoping the rush of emotion she had just experienced wouldn't make her cry. It was foolish to cry about people she'd never met, who'd died a long time ago and had enjoyed, going by the dates, long and happy lives. But she couldn't help thinking of their bones lying under the stone. As she shone her torch away from the main names she saw a child's name. She really hoped that Luke would be too taken up with reading the headstone to notice her reaction.

He wasn't. 'Sophie, honey,' he breathed and took her

into his arms. 'No need to be sad!' he whispered. And then he kissed her.

For a second his lips touched hers in comfort but soon it became a proper kiss. They clung to each other, their mouths at first pressed together, and then parting so their tongues could explore each other.

When they finally separated they were both breathing heavily.

'Sophie,' Luke began when a sound, familiar yet alien, intruded upon them. 'Your cell.'

'Oh yes.' Sophie groped for it and caught it just before it went to voicemail. It was Moira.

'Is that Sophie? I've just got back and got your note. I've got a lovely room and can give you supper if you'd like that. There's nowhere else to eat around here.'

'That would be great,' said Sophie. 'We'll come right away.'

'She's got a room,' she said to Luke when she'd disconnected.

'Good,' said Luke.

'And she can give us supper.'

'It sounds perfect.' Then he kissed her again, for quite a long time.

They walked back in silence, neither of them mentioning the fact that only one room seemed to be on offer. From Sophie's point of view, this was not a problem and, judging by his recent behaviour, Luke would be perfectly happy with this situation too.

It was a lovely room: white walls and plain furniture and an enormous bed covered with a patchwork quilt.

'What a beautiful quilt!' said Sophie immediately she saw it.

'Yes, it was left to me by an old lady who died before she

254

could finish it,' said Moira, who was checking the bedside lights worked.

'How sad!' said Sophie.

'Not really,' said her hostess matter-of-factly. 'She always had a quilt on the go. It was inevitable that she'd die before she finished one of them. This has got my school dresses in it, and my sister's. Now, your bathroom is just across the hall. I'll find you some towels.'

'I'd love a shower!' said Sophie, thinking she wanted to be extra clean and buffed for Luke.

'Me too,' said Luke. 'You go first.'

'When you've finished, come downstairs and I'll find you a glass of wine and something to eat,' said Moira. 'There's plenty of hot water.'

She went out of the room and opened a cupboard and produced two large, warm towels from it. She handed one to Sophie. 'Use any of the products you want. They're there for guests.'

'Lovely!' said Sophie, buzzing with happy anticipation. After the shower and the meal she and Luke would have that huge bed. Life just couldn't get better.

'Before you disappear in there, can I borrow your cell?' asked Luke. 'I should check in.'

'Help yourself!' Sophie practically skipped into the bathroom.

There was a good fire going in Moira's sitting room, half of which was used as an eating area. There were candles on the mantelpiece and on the table and some classical music emanated from somewhere. Luke was sitting by the fire reading the paper when Sophie came down.

'Is it my turn?'

She nodded, wondering if he'd notice she was wearing the one skirt she'd brought with her and had put on make-up. The anticipation was almost the best bit, she decided, now pretty certain she'd spend the night in Luke's arms. Even she couldn't have misread the signs this time.

Unable to settle to reading the newspaper, Sophie went and found Moira in the kitchen chopping cabbage. Like the other rooms, the kitchen was very much to Sophie's taste. The furniture probably wasn't antique but it was old and serviceable and simple.

'Can I do anything to help?'

Moira, an attractive woman in her forties, smiled. 'If you like. It's not professional to let guests help, but I'm not very professional. I just take in the odd guest when they happen to pass by. I'm an acupuncturist really.'

'How interesting!' said Sophie, taking over the chopping. 'Do you get many clients in this area?'

'Oh yes. I'm very busy. I started doing the B & B when my husband left me. It makes the house pay for itself. Now,' she said, 'I've got a casserole and I thought I'd do mashed potatoes and cabbage – maybe some cauli? That sound all right?'

'Delicious! It smells amazing.'

Moira nodded. 'I'm not a bad cook, although I say it myself as shouldn't. Now, pudding? I've got some bananas and some rum and of course, clotted cream. I think I could make something fairly edible with that.'

'I'm sure you could!' Sophie agreed, laughing.

'Let's get the wine open. Your young man will be down soon.'

Luke had been referred to as such, in various ways, since he'd been in England but for the first time Sophie didn't take offence. For tonight at least, he was her young man. The thought of it made her catch her breath. She hoped Moira wouldn't guess they weren't an established couple. She didn't want embarrassment to spoil the wonderfulness of it all.

Luke appeared, looking damp and fresh with his hair wet. Moira handed him a bottle and a corkscrew. 'Here, fight your way into that.'

'Do bed and breakfasts usually give you wine?' he asked.

Moira laughed. 'No, but it's out of season, there's nowhere to eat and what's a good meal without a bottle of wine?' She looked at Luke. 'I'll put it all on the bill, don't worry. Now pour yourselves both a glass and go and sit by the fire. This won't take long.'

Sophie and Luke sat opposite each other, by the fire, glasses of wine in their hands. They didn't talk and didn't feel the need to. They just relaxed and gazed into the gently flickering flames. Sophie was thinking over their day and looking forward to the night ahead. Judging by the little smile at the corner of Luke's mouth, he might well have been sharing her thoughts. Sophie took another sip of her wine.

Moira set the table with a candle and when she was happy with it she summoned them to it.

'I haven't got a starter for you, but there's plenty of casserole if you want seconds.'

Two plates of stew steamed gently in the candlelight. Beside them were dishes of vegetables, including cauliflower cheese.

'My favourite!' said Sophie.

'Cornish cauliflowers – can't beat them,' said Moira. 'Bon appétit!'

They were both hungry and they tucked in eagerly. Eventually Luke said, 'Moira's such a good cook, I'm surprised she isn't married.'

Knowing he was teasing, Sophie said, 'Luke! That's just the sort of thing Uncle Eric would have said!'

'Uncle Eric is a jolly good chap,' replied Luke.

'"Jolly good chap"! Luke! If you talk like that you won't be allowed back into America!'

'Not for a while maybe, but that's fine by me.'

Sophie sighed, hoping he wouldn't notice. The thought that he was going to be in England for a little while, albeit in London, was quite wonderful.

Pudding was as delicious as Moira had made it sound. Bananas fried in butter with brown sugar and rum, with lots of clotted cream stirred in, was delivered in little bowls. Another bowl of cream was put there on the table 'just in case'.

'What is this?' asked Luke, picking up the cream and examining it.

'Clotted cream,' said Moira. 'A Cornish speciality, although I think they make it in Devon too. You collect the cream from several days' milk and gently scald it. Then you leave it for a while before skimming off the top and it thickens up.'

'It seems like a heart attack in a bowl,' said Luke, wondering at Sophie as she forced her spoon into the cream and levered some on to her plate.

'If you take lots of exercise you're fine,' said Moira.

Sophie giggled and had to take a sip of wine to disguise it. She couldn't help connecting exercise with what she and Luke would be doing quite soon.

'I'll leave you to it,' said Moira, satisfied her guests had everything they wanted.

They didn't finish the flambéed bananas. Their eyes met over their half-eaten puddings and Luke took hold of Sophie's hand and led her up the stairs.

The bed had been turned down and the beautiful quilt taken off and folded on a chair. A tiny fireplace that Sophie had assumed was for decoration now had a fire in it. Tea lights were dotted about creating a truly romantic atmosphere.

'I think Moira thinks we're on our honeymoon,' said Luke.

'Something like that,' Sophie agreed.

'It's very pretty,' said Luke, 'but I couldn't want you more if we had to make love in a barn.'

Sophie felt herself glow with desire and happiness. 'A bed is a lot more comfo—' She stopped as Luke took her in his arms, kissing her and fumbling with her clothes.

Jumpers, tights, her camisole and skirt were wrenched from her, while she fought through buttons, his shirt and an undershirt until she got to his trousers and he took over. 'I always thought you were buttoned up,' she said breathlessly.

'Well, I'm not now,' he said, stepping out of his jeans and taking her into his arms. They both fell on to the bed, panting and laughing and naked.

They slept in each other's arms, their limbs tangled. Neither of them seemed able to detach themselves from the other, the skin-to-skin contact was too heady, too sensual.

Sophie woke first. Her arm had gone to sleep and she withdrew it from under Luke as gently as she could, half wanting him to wake up so they could make love again. Not that she could complain of being neglected, she thought, smiling as she tried to remember just how many times they had done so.

She lay there, listening to him breathe, savouring her memories and enjoying the sheer bliss of waking up with the man she loved. She could admit it to herself now. She did love him; it wasn't just a crush. Then, unable to drop off again and realising that Luke, snoring gently, was deeply asleep, she slipped out of bed and went over to the window to get enough light to see her watch. Half past seven. A perfectly reasonable time to get up, in fact.

She managed to get washed and dressed without disturbing Luke and went downstairs. There was no sign of Moira either although there was a note on the table: *If you're up before I'm back, help yourself to tea etc. Breakfast when I get back from seeing to my neighbour's hens!*

Sophie decided not to bother with tea. She wanted to go out herself, to revel in her new state of happiness.

The shore was as appealing as it had been last evening, only today she saw birds running along the water's edge, their bills dipping in and out of the surf. Last night it had been magical and moonlit and serene, today it was a bustling strand supporting birds and fish and insects. The yachts were bobbing up and down more and the sound of the halyards on the masts was brisker, more businesslike. Sophie found it just as appealing if in a different way.

But it was the churchyard that drew her. It was almost as if she wanted to tell Matilda's grandparents about what had happened, how happy she was. She smiled as she thought this: Matilda's grandparents would be horrified at the thought of a young unmarried couple spending the night together.

Sophie hadn't been a virgin when Luke made love to her so passionately but he was only her second lover. For Sophie sex was only possible if she was truly in love and while she knew from experience that 'in love' didn't necessarily last for ever, she knew that she did love Luke. And if he didn't love her as much, or if it didn't last for ever, she had gone into it true to her own standards of behaviour.

She found the grave and stood over it, feeling awash with emotion and the afterglow of wonderful sex. After breakfast they could go back to the house, explore it in daylight and take pictures with her phone – it had been far too dark the day before. Sophie wasn't someone who was constantly snapping away but Matilda would love pictures. Even if the house was run-down it was still there. So many big houses had been pulled down over the years and Matilda would be thrilled to discover this one had survived.

Sophie spent time exploring the rest of the graveyard, reading all the inscriptions on the graves that were legible, until her stomach rumbled and she decided to go back. Even if Luke wasn't awake yet, she needed food!

There was a car parked in front of the house; Sophie could see it from a little way away. It must be Moira's, she thought. She probably parked it somewhere else usually, but had to deliver something to the house. But it didn't feel right. It was the wrong sort of car.

As she got nearer the front door opened and Luke came out with a woman, not Moira, and she had her arm linked through his. The pair reminded Sophie of a just-married couple, about to go on honeymoon in a shower of confetti.

She tried to hurry, to dispel the picture that was like a dream but real, and all wrong. She recognised the woman now, it was Ali, and she was looking up at Luke as if she adored him.

Sophie felt dizzy suddenly. How had that woman magicked her way here? Wasn't it enough that she was sorting out Luke's life for him from afar? And what right had she to be looking at Luke like that? Well, maybe she did adore him, but Luke was hers!

He was talking on a mobile phone, wearing a suit that looked crumpled. He hadn't packed a suit. Ali must have brought it for him. His tie wasn't straight. Why was he wearing a tie? What had happened to the world? What could possibly have happened to make it all go so horribly wrong, so quickly?

'Hello!' she said when she was near enough to be heard. 'What's going on?'

They both turned to her, away from Moira who was standing in the doorway behind them.

'Oh hi, Sophie!' said Ali briskly. 'I've come to take Luke back to London. There's an emergency.' She spoke as if she was airlifting him out of a war zone, or at the very least getting him out of prison, or boarding school – not the very floor of heaven.

'Oh!' Sophie's voice was high. 'Has someone died?'

'No, no. Nothing like that,' went on Ali, 'but no one except Luke can sort it out. Not even me.' She gave him another loving look. 'Although I did try, we can't manage without Luke.' Luke was still on the phone. 'We can give you a ride back to the station if you like, Sophie. We won't abandon you down here.' Ali was apparently unable to believe that anyone could be happy this far away from a major metropolis.

Luke put the phone into his pocket. 'There's a crisis at the office,' said Luke. 'I have to go back immediately.'

Ali was still clutching on to him. 'And I tracked you down! Wasn't that clever of me? I feel so proud of myself,' she said. 'I knew you were in Cornwall but it was only when Luke called me last night that I knew where. These lanes are a nightmare!'

'What sort of crisis?' asked Sophie. 'I didn't think you'd even set up the office yet.'

Ali gave Sophie a look which indicated Sophie would never understand even if she did have time to explain. 'Luke's needed ASAP, honey, and I'm going to drive him to the airport and we'll fly up. Are you sure you don't want a ride?' Ali said this as if she was now certain the answer would be no.

'No thank you,' said Sophie. 'I have commitments down here, not to mention a hire car.'

'You could just leave that, Sophie,' said Luke. 'We could get someone to take it back for you.' He glanced at Moira before going on, 'We can come back to see your relatives.'

262

'Why would you want to see Sophie's relatives?' Ali said wonderingly, as if this was the weirdest thing she'd ever heard.

'No, there's no reason why Luke should see them,' said Sophie carefully, aware that their idyll had been shattered and interested to find that she could still walk and talk in a fairly normal way.

Luke turned to Ali. 'I need to speak to Sophie.'

'Honey, there's no time for long goodbyes.' She clutched at his sleeve. 'Really, this is urgent!'

'It's all right,' said Sophie, 'Luke doesn't need to speak to me. We can say goodbye now.'

Luke seemed momentarily torn. 'It really is an emergency, Sophie.'

'She knows that,' said Ali. 'I explained.'

Sophie almost told her that she hadn't explained anything but she didn't think there was any point.

'I must give you some money,' said Luke. He reached into his inside pocket and withdrew a wad of notes. He held them out to her and she stepped back as if he'd offered her a snake.

'I don't need money!'

'You do, Sophie. You know you do.' He continued to hold out the money.

'No, really, I don't.'

She felt to take money from him would confirm her as cheap – the girl he was happy to spend the night with, have sex with, but just as happy to leave in the morning. Being honourable, he had to pay her, of course. She couldn't have felt more humiliated if he'd hit her. She stepped back a few more steps to stop him thrusting it into her hands.

Luke, accepting defeat, turned and put the money into Moira's hands instead. She took it without thinking.

Ali marched over to the boot of the car, and put into it the overnight bag – Sophie's overnight bag. Presumably Sophie's clothes had been tipped out on the bed? She looked at her watch. 'Come on, Luke.'

Just for a moment Luke held Sophie's gaze but she looked away. She didn't want his unspoken apology, she just wanted him to go, before she embarrassed herself by crying or something. 'Sophie—'

'Oh, just go! You'll miss your flight.'

Then she turned and stomped into the house.

Chapter Eighteen

'They've gone,' said Moira.

Sophie was still in the hall, not knowing quite what to do.

'Come into the kitchen.' Moira took her arm so Sophie had no choice but to follow. 'I'll make you some tea. And you haven't had breakfast. You'll feel better after something to eat.'

'I don't know what happened just there,' said Sophie.

'It was all very fast. That woman marched in with a suit bag over her arm, asking for Luke. I told her he was upstairs and asked if she wanted to wait but she just went straight up. Luke was in the shower. Not long afterwards they came down. He was wearing the suit.'

Sophie pulled out a chair and sat down. Her knees were shaking and she thought she must be suffering from shock.

'Then what?'

'Luke came in here and put your phone on the table and said, "Make sure Sophie gets this." And the woman said, "I think there's a message for her."'

Sophie took the phone. There was no message indicated but she flicked through to 'received messages' and saw a number she recognised. 'Oh no,' she said, and opened it. *Saw Mandy. Still miss you, Soph. Come back to me?*

'What?' said Moira.

'It's from an old boyfriend. He sometimes texts me when he's drunk.' Sophie considered. 'I can't decide if I want it to have been Luke who read it, because we were sharing the phone and he sort of had the right – or Ali.' She made a face. 'That woman is called Ali.'

'Well, one of them did,' said Moira briskly. 'What about breakfast?'

'No thank you.' There was some sort of obstruction in her throat and chest and she didn't think she'd get any food past it.

'You need to eat,' said Moira. 'If every woman who was ever walked out on by a man gave up eating there'd be no women left in the world.'

'I was left, wasn't I? I just feel very confused. One minute Luke and I were . . .' She blushed. 'And the next he was taken away. It's hard to take in.'

'I'm sure you'll find out why soon. It was a bit odd and melodramatic though.' Moira put down a mug. 'Do you want sugar? No? They say you should have it for shock but I think it's a myth. I'm going to make you a bacon sandwich. I've cooked the bacon so we might as well eat it. White bread, lots of butter. Cures everything.' She paused. 'Well, some things.'

'I don't want to eat.'

'Come on, to please me. I can't have one if you don't and I'm starving.'

Sophie watched as Moira took a large white loaf and buttered the cut side, sliced it off and then repeated the process. 'There!' She put a plate down in front of Sophie. 'I'll just make mine.'

Moira continued to give a running commentary on everything she was doing until at last she was sitting opposite Sophie with a bacon sandwich in front of her. 'Do you want to talk about it?'

Sophie shook her head. 'I knew he'd have to go to London soon. It's probably fine. I just wasn't expecting him to . . .'

'Be airlifted out?'

In spite of everything a tiny smile lifted the corner of Sophie's mouth. 'It was like that, wasn't it? Ali should have been wearing a leather flying suit and come down on a rope to scoop him up.'

'She did, practically,' said Moira.

Cheered very slightly by this image, Sophie took a bite of her sandwich to show willing, but she couldn't taste it. She chewed and chewed but it just stayed in her mouth, not seeming to get any smaller. Swallowing seemed impossible. With a huge effort she got the first mouthful down and took a sip of tea.

'You seemed such a lovely couple,' said Moira, eating her own sandwich with more enthusiasm.

'We were . . . I mean – Maybe we weren't. We haven't been a couple long. In fact yesterday was the first time he'd even kissed me.'

'Oh? You seemed so welded together I would have thought it was longer than that.' She frowned. 'Or maybe not. How did you meet?'

'It's complicated.'

'It's good to talk,' said Moira. 'Have another bite and some tea and then tell me everything. It'll help. Not sure why but it does.'

'OK, well, we met in New York. Through his grand-mother really.'

Sophie did find it helpful to talk. Somehow it organised things in her mind and while they were still horribly painful she could check that it wasn't anything she'd done that made him run off like that. It also gave her hope that things weren't actually over but had simply been interrupted.

When she got to the bit about finding Matilda's grand-parents' grave her voice did crack a bit and Moira handed her a tissue from a box she then put on the table.

'I just wish there'd been time to say goodbye properly.'

'That would have helped. But he did give you money!' said Moira, suddenly remembering. She put her hand into her apron pocket where she'd stashed it. 'Quite a lot of money! These are fifties!'

'Fifty-pound notes? I've hardly ever seen one!' Just for a moment Sophie was distracted.

'Well, there are lots of them.' Moira laid them on the table. 'Eight, to be precise.'

'I can't take it,' said Sophie.

'Why not? Didn't you say you'd paid for everything when he'd had his wallet stolen and you were running out of money?'

'Yes! But I did that because . . . well, I had to help him, didn't I? I was paying him back for everything he and Matilda had done for me in New York. Oh dear.'

'What?'

'My ring. Do I have to give it back?'

'No! It's not an engagement ring.' Sophie had told Moira how she came to own it. 'And he may call you in a minute, explain what's going on.'

Something about Ali and her proprietorial behaviour towards Luke had given Sophie the impression that this was an optimistic notion. She took the ring off, turning it round and round in her fingers. 'He may not.'

'I'm sure he will!' But in spite of trying, even brightly optimistic Moira didn't sound convinced. 'And you do have to take the money.'

'No! It makes me feel like a prostitute, as if he's paying me for sex. Buying me off.' All her feelings of being like Holly Golightly, which she'd forgotten, came rushing back to her.

'You do need the money. You've got expenses. Besides, I can't keep it, can I?'

Sophie shrugged, still not willing to touch the pile of notes on the table.

Moira put the last of her sandwich into her mouth and brushed the crumbs off her hands. 'What were you going to do today?' she asked when she'd finished. 'If he hadn't been dragged off by a harpy?'

Sophie smiled bleakly. 'We were going to go back to the house and take photos. Then we were going to see those distant relations of mine to try and persuade them to let me take control of their drilling rights so I can do something with them.' She'd filled Moira in on her mission in between telling her about how she'd met Luke and why they'd come down here in the first place.

'Then you must still do that.' Moira paused. 'If you could do with company, I'd love to see the house and I'm quite a good photographer. If we used my camera I could help you email them to Matilda. Unless you've got a digital one?'

'No, I've only got my phone,' said Sophie, 'and although I'm sure it is possible, I've never worked out how to get the pictures on to a computer.'

'Well, use mine then.'

Sophie hesitated. 'I'm not sure I want to communicate with Matilda when I don't know . . . I mean . . .'

'When you don't know how things stand between you and Luke? You don't have to mention him and she was the reason you came down here in the first place, wasn't she?'

'I suppose so.' A wave of anguish swept over Sophie, catching her by surprise. She looked at Moira. 'He shouldn't have just left me like that without telling me what was going on.'

'You've got to trust he'll be in touch soon. Keep the avenues of communication open.'

'That sounds like something you've read,' said Sophie with a reluctant chuckle.

'Mm. Yes. I worked on my marriage for quite a long time before I finally gave up. Now, you go and have a quick bath while I tidy up and then we'll go.'

When Sophie got back into the bedroom she found that Moira had made the bed and put back the quilt so Sophie could dress without the disturbing sight of a bed that has been thoroughly made love in. It helped.

'Oh, it is a lovely house,' said Moira. 'I don't know why I didn't know about it, but then I haven't lived here all that long and it is quite hidden away.'

They were standing in front of the old building. In some ways the daylight made it seem more dilapidated but also a lot less spooky.

'It's more lovely now we can see it, although it was very romantic in the dusk,' said Sophie wistfully.

Determined to keep Sophie occupied, Moira kept focused on the task at hand and got out her camera. 'Come on,' she said briskly. 'I'll take loads of pictures and then we can go through them at home and send Matilda the best ones.'

Sophie sighed, glad that Matilda didn't know she and Luke had been to bed together. If only he'd phone and she could stop feeling he'd just abandoned her.

They spent a happy morning taking photographs and then Moira guided them to a jolly pub. While they stood at the bar reading the board for what was on offer for lunch, Moira produced a fifty-pound note. 'This is on Luke!'

Once the first fifty-pound note had been broken into and had bought soup and salad and crusty bread for them both, Sophie felt a bit better about spending it.

'You don't have to spend all of it anyway,' said Moira. 'You can give what's left back to him.'

Sophie was silent for a few seconds. 'He hasn't phoned. I don't think he's going to.'

Moira hesitated in a way that made Sophie felt she agreed with her. 'You don't know that.'

'No, I know. But I just feel—'

'There could be any number of reasons why he hasn't phoned. No signal for one.'

Sophie instantly got out her phone to see if she had coverage. She had.

'Well, he might not have coverage.'

'True.'

'He's bound to get in touch about your quest, apart from anything else. He was helping you with that, wasn't he?'

'Yes, but he's helped loads already, and it was in exchange for me helping Matilda. We're quits, really. There's no real reason why he should get in touch. I mean – no practical reason.'

This sounded so cold and businesslike after what they'd shared that Sophie found her throat closing as if she was going to cry. She swallowed a spoonful of soup too quickly. It was hot and she had to follow it with water. But the time she'd done all this she was back in control again, superficially at least.

'So you don't think all is lost then?' she asked Moira, when they'd moved on to salad, and were sharing a bowl of chips.

'What? With Luke? No. I agree it didn't look good but there could have been lots of reasons why he didn't kiss you goodbye passionately. Apart from catching a plane, I mean.'

'OK,' said Sophie. 'Let's think of some.'

The two women exchanged glances for a moment or two before going back to eating.

'All right,' said Moira, 'supposing he thought you'd gone out for a walk because you were so horrified to find yourself in bed with him. Maybe he felt you'd left him?'

Sophie considered. 'Good, but not perfect. He can't have thought I'd left him when I'd been so – well – loving, just a few hours earlier.'

'You don't know that. Men are funny! Maybe he was suffering from empty-bed syndrome.'

'It's what women get, usually.'

'No reason why men can't have it too! After all, they're supposed to get the menopause.'

Sophie sighed. 'It's all very well to joke about it, but why *do* you think he just left like that?'

Moira shook her head. 'I still don't know, but I do genuinely think there may be an explanation and I think you should see your relatives, do all the things you would have done, without him. Then if he does turn out to be a love-rat you haven't wasted your time as well as your love – and money – on him.'

Sophie nodded. 'OK. And it would be wonderful if I could achieve everything without his help. Who needs preppy rich boys?'

'I'm taking that as a rhetorical question,' said Moira, 'but as the rich boy is paying, shall we have pudding?'

A little while later, they got back to Moira's house and she led Sophie through to the sitting room. There was a laptop on the table.

'Now let's see what we've got.'

'Let's send the ones with the house looking good,' said Sophie. 'I'll tell her about it being quite run-down, but it would be nice for her to see it at its best.'

'OK,' said Moira. 'What about this one?'

'Yes. And that one from the back. You can see there are

some tiles missing but Matilda might not be looking at the pictures too closely.'

'Here's a nice one.'

When at last they were pleased with their choices, Moira attached them and Sophie wrote her email.

Dear Matilda, We found the house! Sadly, it's not lived in and is in a fairly bad state as far as one can tell. She was pleased with that 'one'. She didn't want to say 'we' or 'I'.

I'm sending these pictures as Luke had to go back to London suddenly, with Ali. Apparently there was some emergency at work.

I'm going to look up some of my relatives and then go home.
I hope you are well and not missing Luke too much.
Lots of love, Sophie

Sophie pressed 'send' and then worked out that it would be roughly ten in the morning for Matilda. Then she went upstairs and lay on the bed, trying not to cry. She really, really did want to leave Moira's immediately, but going home without finishing her mission would just be pathetic. And the bed was a real impediment to her return to normal.

She went downstairs to find Moira, who put the kettle on the minute she appeared. 'Is it all right if I stay another night? I'll go and see these relations tomorrow and then go.'

'Will you drive home?'

Sophie shook her head. 'No, we hired the car down here. I'll take it back and then catch the train.'

Moira looked as if she wanted to say something but couldn't quite decide what. In the end she said, 'Why don't you check your emails after tea? Matilda may have replied.'

'Oh yes, I will.'

273

There *was* an email from Matilda. She was delighted with the photographs but less delighted to hear that Luke had gone to London. *Although he had helped you track down the house, as I asked him, and with everything going on in London, I suppose he hasn't got time to go into it all further.*

Sophie wrote back agreeing, adding, *Cornwall is so lovely – even at this time of year.*

She checked again later while Moira was cooking supper. There was another email.

Darling . . . Sophie could tell when Matilda was being imperious, even via email.

I've been in touch with Luke and, as I thought, he hasn't got time to find out who owns the house just now. As you're down there already, on business of your own, could you stay with your nice bed and breakfast lady and make some enquiries? I'd like to know if the house is for sale.

Sophie told Moira straight away. 'Well, I'd love it if you stayed a few more days,' Moira said.

'I'd like it too,' said Sophie. 'I don't want to go home just yet. Everyone will ask me about Luke and that will be awful. And I can pay you, Rich Boy left me the means!'

'I really hope you two get back together. It would be a shame to let such a catch slip through your fingers. Money and looks don't often go together, in my experience.'

'Oh, you should go to New York, or high-end Connecticut!' said Sophie. 'Loads of very rich, very beautiful people!'

'I'm sure you fitted right in!' said Moira, laughing.

'Yeah, right,' said Sophie.

'I wasn't joking, actually. Now let's find something nice to watch while dinner cooks. We've got about an hour before we can eat.'

'So how am I going to find out about the house?' Sophie asked later, as they were eating. 'I'm not a private detective.'

'You know, that's a job I've always fancied. Why don't I see what I can pick up while you visit your relatives,' said Moira. Sophie had rung and arranged to meet them the following day.

'Have you really always fancied being a private detective?' Sophie asked.

'Mm. Don't know why. I just like the puzzle aspect of it, I suppose. So what do *you* want to do with your life – apart from the get-married-have-kids thing?'

'I want to run my own business, making clothes out of old clothes. "Designer Shabby Chic", if you can work that out. I just love making and mending.'

'So what's stopping you?'

'Money, really. I'd need capital, and I also want to train properly. Doing it by guess and by God is all very well, but it probably takes me far longer than it needs to. You can't make money if you're too slow.'

'You sound very talented.' Moira sounded genuinely impressed. 'I mean you're very young to have worked out what you want to do with your life.'

'I've always liked making and mending. In fact, if you've got anything in your wardrobe that doesn't quite work for you as it is, I'll have a go at it and prove how talented I am.'

Thus the two women spent a jolly evening sewing, watching television and, in Moira's case, going through her wardrobe looking for things for Sophie to transform.

The following morning Sophie set off for her relations. She felt a lot better than she had yesterday: still heartbroken, but functioning, which was a big step forward.

With Moira's help and her computer and maps, Sophie had planned a very detailed route and set off up the hill, away from the sea, towards the main road.

Apart from her feeling of total loss about Luke, she found she liked being on her own in the car. There was no one to comment if she crashed a gear; no one to notice if she had to go round a roundabout a couple of times to find the right exit.

When her relations' village was in sight, she realised she was going to be far too early, having factored in lots of getting-lost time, and so she found somewhere to park and went for a walk. She was suddenly feeling anxious about wishing herself on people she didn't know and asking them a rather obscure question. She'd have felt much more confident with Luke by her side, she realised. But he wasn't by her side and she'd just have to get on without him. In fact it would be better if she never thought about him again. She wouldn't get over him if she kept him in the forefront of her mind the whole time. The trouble was, when you're in love with someone they are in the forefront of your mind the whole time and there isn't a whole lot you can do about it. It kind of defines being in love.

At last she had used up enough time, and Sophie set off on foot to their house. It was up a hill and she started to worry that she'd be panting and sweaty when she arrived. In fact she began to get so nervous that a trip to the dentist seemed preferable. At least at the dentist they are kind to you even if you end up in agony.

The house didn't look promising. It was a bungalow with a dormer and the garden was steeply sloping and mostly stones – with gnomes.

Sophie wasn't a gardening snob; she was capable of appreciating gnomes, but seeing them dotted around such

276

an arid landscape was faintly chilling. Gnomes should make you laugh, not make you feel nervous, and she was sure they needed to live amongst grass and little tiny flowers. Maybe flowers in January was asking too much but the potential for some would help.

The bell 'ding-donged' and Sophie could see movement behind the frosted glass of the front door. A woman opened it and Sophie smiled her very best smile.

'Hello! I'm Sophie! You must be Mavis? Mrs Littlejohn?'

'That's right. You'd better come in.'

Mrs Littlejohn didn't actually smile but stood back so Sophie could enter. The moment she got across the threshold, a vile smell hit Sophie, almost making her gag.

'Turkey giblets,' explained Mrs Littlejohn, who obviously wasn't the sort of person who liked to be called by her Christian name by a complete stranger, even if they were related. 'We can't afford to waste good food in these hard times.'

As Sophie's times had always been hard she nodded and followed her hostess to the living room, trying not to breathe through her nose.

What should have been a spectacular view was obscured by waterfalls of heavily frilled net curtain. The two inches between the bottom layer and the window sill was obscured by a large collection of china 'ladies' in period costume, almost certainly individually numbered and bought for several large instalments from the back of a magazine.

The actual curtains were covered in cabbage roses and were the same fabric as the three-piece suite enjoyed. The carpet was also rosy, but its roses were a slightly different colour. There was a sideboard covered with more ornaments and a 'whatnot' in the corner. Looking more closely, Sophie saw that 'Joan the Wad' featured in several different guises.

'I've made coffee,' said Mrs Littlejohn, 'I'll just bring it through.'

Sophie would have preferred tea but felt she'd rather endure coffee than disrupt this woman's careful plans.

'Do sit down, dear,' said Mrs Littlejohn.

Sophie perched on the edge of the sofa, being careful not to dislodge the cushions that stood on their points and so would be prone to toppling.

Sophie did not have a good feeling about this. Mrs Littlejohn was friendly in a formal sort of way but her bungalow and manner didn't indicate a great spirit of adventure or a person willing to take risks.

A trolley laden with cups, saucers, plates, a jug of coffee, a jug of milk, biscuits, sugar, and napkins was rattled into the room. Serving the coffee took some time.

Sophie had been going to refuse a biscuit but then succumbed to a Nice. She might need the sugar hit.

Mrs Littlejohn didn't speak once she'd served coffee, leaving it to Sophie to explain her errand.

'Did my great-uncle make it clear why I'm here?' she started tentatively, aware that Uncle Eric hadn't said much that was useful.

'Not really, dear.'

Sophie smiled briefly. 'Then I'll try and explain. It is a bit complicated.'

'Then maybe we'd better wait until my husband is here. He deals with all the financial matters. He's just gone down to the council offices to complain about the recycling.'

'Right. Well, it's not really financial – at least not yet. Do you remember inheriting some drilling rights from your late husband?'

'I inherited everything from him. I can't remember the details.'

'I suppose you wouldn't. I don't suppose you have a

copy of his will, have you? Handy, I mean?'

Mrs Littlejohn felt she was having her privacy invaded, Sophie could tell. 'I'd rather wait for my husband to come home.'

'But you don't need him really. This is to your advantage. You don't have—'

'I'd rather wait. I'm not one of those women who do things without their husband knowing.'

'Oh, I'm not suggesting anything like that! In fact you don't have to do anything.'

'Shall we just have our coffee and wait for my husband?'

Sophie nodded and took a sip. It was terribly strong and quite bitter. 'I wouldn't ask,' Sophie went on, fired up by the coffee, 'but . . .'

Just then a key could be heard turning in the lock and Mrs Littlejohn got to her feet with relief. 'This will be my husband. He'll sort everything out.'

Mr Littlejohn opened the door. 'Don't sign anything!'

Chapter Nineteen

❧

Mr Littlejohn's accusing glare as he came in made Sophie jump in her seat so the cushion behind her fell over. She realised at that moment that whatever career prospects she might have they didn't include door-to-door selling. Just seeing him glare at her made her feel instantly guilty.

'Don't let this young woman talk you into anything!' he went on. He clearly assumed his wife was under threat.

Obviously feeling safer now her husband was with her, Mrs Littlejohn soothed, 'Don't worry, dear, I'm not going to sign a thing!'

'Really,' Sophie protested, 'I'm not asking you to do anything!'

Mrs Littlejohn's ill-supported bosom heaved. 'And I'm not going to do anything. I'm not sure why you've come and I know you're a relative of Cousin Eric's but I'm not signing anything over to you.'

'But it's to your advantage!' said Sophie. 'Other members of the family own these rights but we can't do anything with them unless we band together and act as one.'

In her head that had sounded rousing and 'let's-all-pull-together', but in that cluttered room it was a bit pathetic.

'What's she trying to get you to do?' demanded her husband, looking at Sophie as if she'd put her foot in the door and forced herself into the house.

'Really, I'm not trying . . . Look, what it is . . .'

'Have a cup of coffee, dear,' said Mrs Littlejohn, attempting to get to her feet but hampered by the depths of her chair.

'I'll get it!' said Sophie, leaping to her feet. 'Once a waitress always a waitress!' As she poured him a cup, glad that his wife had already loaded the trolley with enough crockery, she realised that she had acted completely out of turn, not to mention oddly. These people would never trust her now. Chastened, she handed Mr Littlejohn the biscuits.

Mr Littlejohn subsided into a chair. Mrs Littlejohn looked annoyed. Sophie looked apologetic. 'Sorry,' she murmured. 'Just trying to be helpful.'

Somewhat pacified, Mr Littlejohn took a sip and seemed to relax. Sophie found herself wondering what sort of job he'd had before he retired and then realised she was shying away from the business at hand and forced herself to focus.

'I'm not here to make you do anything you're not happy with,' she said, 'but if you did agree to let me act for you with regard to these drilling rights, it could be to your advantage.'

'How?' demanded Mr Littlejohn. 'Why would we want to do anything with them?'

'Because, potentially, they could earn money, possibly a lot of money.' She smiled and then realised that made her look as if she was trying to promote pyramid-selling.

'I don't see how,' said Mrs Littlejohn.

'Well,' Sophie took a breath. 'The drilling rights that we inherited could be valuable, but only if they're all put together.'

'Why should putting them together make a difference?' Mrs Littlejohn folded her hands and her lips in the manner of a headmistress asking her girls why they thought rolling up the waistband of their skirts was a good idea.

Sophie took another breath and smiled and then wished

smiling wasn't so habitual with her. It was in danger of making these people think her both deranged and dishonest. 'We none of us own enough to make it worth any oil company's while to drill. But if we put our rights together we *have* got a package big enough.'

'Why has no one done it before then? My late husband inherited those shares when he was a small boy.'

'Because the shares relate to a piece of land from which it's hard to extract oil – or it *was* hard. Drilling equipment has got so much better, more sophisticated. And oil is much scarcer now.' Sophie wished that she had Luke with her and cursed Ali for taking him away. If only she'd boned up a bit on the oil industry before coming.

'The price of oil has gone down recently,' said Mr Littlejohn. 'I don't see your argument at all.'

'Of course it fluctuates,' said Sophie fluently. She was fairly certain she'd never used that word in conversation before. 'But fossil fuels are in short supply these days.'

'They've just discovered oil in Siberia. I don't believe they're scarce at all,' said Mr Littlejohn. 'It's a con put about by the "Greenies".' Here he waggled his fingers in the air to indicate inverted commas. Then he drained his cup decisively and set it down on a small table, making it wobble.

'And what would it cost?' asked Mrs Littlejohn. 'We can't afford to go shelling out on wild business schemes.'

'It wouldn't cost anything!' said Sophie, immediately realising that it probably *would* cost something – possibly quite a lot. They'd have to hire an American lawyer or someone to negotiate for them.

'There's no such thing as a free lunch,' said Mr Littlejohn, tapping the side of his nose knowingly.

'I know but they're wasted, just sitting there. They could make us all a lot of money!'

'I don't think we'd want the upheaval,' said Mrs Littlejohn.

'There wouldn't *be* any upheaval,' said Sophie, briefly wondering if this woman thought she'd have to go out to the oil wells herself, wearing a hard hat and carrying a pick. 'It would just be a cheque in the post.'

Both Mr and Mrs Littlejohn shook their heads in unison and Sophie gave up. She didn't say anything, she just slumped a little and another cushion toppled. Maybe if she hadn't been broken-hearted she'd have persevered, but she didn't have the energy.

'The thing is, young lady,' Mr Littlejohn persisted, sensing he'd won the battle and was now going to make sure of the war. 'We don't know you from Adam—'

'I do have my driving licence,' she muttered, 'and I am quite obviously female.' But she didn't expect to be heard. Mr Littlejohn was delivering a lecture and nothing was going to stop him.

'You come into our house talking about drilling rights, wanting to take my wife's shares—'

'I wasn't going to take them! I just wanted—'

'—so you could do what you liked with them. Well it's not on.'

Wanting nothing more than to run away, Sophie located a place for her cup and saucer and put them carefully down. Then she stood up. 'I do understand. It's not a problem. It is a bit of a shame for the other members of the family, some of whom really, really need the money, but if that's the way you feel . . .'

'You're just a slip of a girl,' said Mrs Littlejohn, magnanimous in victory. 'How could we be expected to trust you?'

'Would you have trusted me if I'd been a man?' she asked, buttoning up the jacket she'd never taken off.

'An older man, yes,' said Mrs Littlejohn, following Sophie into the hall, obviously keen to get her out of the house.

'I'm sorry to have troubled you,' said Sophie. 'Goodbye.' And she opened the front door and let herself out to freedom and fresh air.

As she drove back to Moira's she realised she'd have to go back to her family a complete failure. This jaunt to Cornwall had achieved nothing – for her family anyway. She'd hit a dead end with the drilling rights; she had no job; she'd have to explain where Luke was and why she wasn't ever going to see him again. It was a disaster. The only comforting thought was that Moira would understand.

'You don't look as if you've cheered up at all,' said Moira when she'd opened the door to Sophie.

'I haven't. I failed in my mission.'

'Well, come in. I'll put the kettle on.'

'Tea would help. They had the nastiest sort of coffee: strong but tasteless. Oh and the house! If I never see another frilled settee or matching curtains, covers and carpet – that didn't actually match – it'll be too soon.'

Moira laughed. 'Talking of houses, I've got news!'

'About the house? Already? That was quick.'

'They say it's not what you know, it's who you know, and I do know some useful people.'

'Well, tell me then! I need something positive to think about.'

'Come and sit down. Did you have lunch? I'll make you a sandwich. I'd have made soup but I've been out.'

'Do you feed everyone like you do me?' asked Sophie, slipping into her chair at the table. It felt like home now.

'Pretty much. I get a lot of satisfaction from making people feel better. It goes with the acupuncture. Do you like mustard?'

'No thank you.'

'Nor me! I just don't get it! I don't like wasabi either. But you do like ham?'

'Yes please.'

Very few minutes later a sandwich containing ham, salad and just a smear of mayonnaise was put in front of Sophie.

'Right, now tell me about the house,' said Sophie, once she'd taken a couple of bites and Moira was satisfied that she really was eating.

'Well, it's owned by an old lady who's gone into a nursing home. Apparently her relations – pretty distant – aren't sure what to do with it.'

'Oh?' Sophie took another bite. Food definitely helped. She'd managed not to think about Luke for – well – a couple of seconds at least. Except that's exactly what Luke had said, so he was back in her head again. She sighed and took another bite.

'Yup. It needs so much doing to it. They can't decide if they should do it up and sell it, or just sell it. Or divide it into flats.'

'You did find out a lot! If you get fed up with acupuncture you could become an interrogator.'

Moira ignored this. 'The thing to do is buy it from the old lady. If you wait until she dies it'll take for ever, what with the will and all, and it'll get in a worse state.'

'I'm not buying it!'

'Didn't you say Matilda might want to?'

Sophie nodded.

'Well, if she does, she'll have to move fast. The old lady could die at any time and then it could take years before it was properly on the market.'

'The trouble is, I don't know if Matilda *really* wants to buy it.'

'Well, I think you should email her and tell her what you know,' said Moira. 'After all, she wanted you to find out if it was for sale. You have. If you explain the situation to her the matter is out of your hands.'

'Yes . . .' Suddenly Sophie wasn't sure she wanted it out of her hands. 'She might put Luke on to it.'

'She might.'

'Then I wouldn't have to do anything.'

'True.'

'Which would be good. I have enough to do with this drilling-rights business.' Just for a moment she wondered if this were true. She shook her head, trying to rid herself of negative thoughts. 'Although how I'm going to get round those wretched people, I don't know. Did I tell you their bungalow stank of turkey giblets? And they had gnomes in their garden but not a single blade of grass?'

'No! That's cruel!' Moira understood what a serious matter this was.

'That's what I thought!' said Sophie and they both laughed. 'We could start a society. "Green Homes for Gnomes" or something.'

Moira shook her head. 'No. We have lives.'

'Well, you do,' said Sophie. Hers had nothing much worthwhile in it any more.

Moira was not having this. 'So do you! You're young, you're lovely, and you're talented!'

'And broken-hearted.'

'Are you?'

Sophie nodded. 'There's no way in the world that Luke could not have got a signal or a moment to ring me by now if he was going to. He's not going to. He's gone back to his real life and realises I have no place in it. I would never fit in.' She paused. 'He probably thinks it's kinder this way.'

Moira didn't speak and Sophie was grateful that she

didn't call Luke vile names or rain abuse on the heads of all men. She put her hand on one of Sophie's, which was clenched in her lap.

'You won't feel like this for ever,' she said eventually. 'Either you'll find out why Luke hasn't been in touch or – ' and she obviously felt this was the more likely scenario '– you'll fall in love with a lovely Cornishman!' She squeezed Sophie's hand. 'It is absolute hell, what you're going through, but you will get over it. Everyone does. Very few people go on loving people who've behaved badly to them for ever.'

'It just feels like for ever,' said Sophie, to whom this had never happened before. 'Probably.'

Moira nodded. 'It can drag on a bit but it does fade away. Eventually you can't think what you ever saw in the person.'

'You're talking from personal experience.'

Moira nodded. 'My ex-husband. My sun rose and set with him. When he left I thought I'd never be happy again. Now I really can't remember why I liked him in the first place. He was dreadfully grumpy and didn't have much sense of humour.'

'Luke has a sense of humour but he doesn't let it out often.'

'That's why you'd . . .' Moira cleared her throat. 'Come and stay down here and I'll find you a lovely man who'll make you laugh all the time.'

'I do like the sound of that,' said Sophie, 'but I don't fall in love often. Some people seem to do it all the time but I can't. Shame really.'

They sat in silence for a couple of moments and then Moira said, 'Well, let's go and see what Matilda has to say.'

'I wish I knew what her plans were. If it was just she wanted to see it, well, she's had photographs.' She thought for a minute. 'What would be rather lovely would be to take a whole lot more pictures, Photoshop them a bit, and then send them to her so she could get them printed and framed.'

'What a lovely idea!'

'And if it's frightfully expensive we could get Luke to do it.' She paused. 'You could contact Luke and suggest it.'

Moira sighed softly. 'Come on, let's tell Matilda what we've discovered.'

Sophie glanced at her watch. 'It's still only nine o'clock in Connecticut.'

'Elderly people get up early.'

Sophie sent an email, explaining about the old lady and her indecisive relatives and carefully not mentioning Luke, and then Moira rang up a builder friend of hers and arranged to meet him at the house. 'I think it would be good if you could give Matilda some idea of how much she's going to need to spend on it if she is thinking about buying it,' said Moira.

'But will your builder friend come and look? We're in no position to offer him the work.'

Moira smiled very slightly. 'He'll come if I ask him.'

Sophie nodded in comprehension. 'Well, that's good. It'll be lovely to have something positive to do in connection with a beautiful house. That way I've got something to think about apart from a . . .' She tried to think of an epithet for Luke that fitted and failed. '. . . man, and a project that seems to have reached a full stop.'

'I'm glad to hear you're being positive already,' said Moira. 'And your project hasn't come to a full stop, more a semi-colon. You'll find a way to bring your giblet-boiling relatives round somehow.'

Sophie shrugged, trying to look convinced.

*

288

Moira and Sophie were in the walled garden discussing if it should have a swimming pool in it or be returned to growing vegetables. Sophie kept changing her mind. Suddenly Sophie noticed Moira's expression change. She turned to see why and saw Luke.

Her heart responded, making her gasp for breath with pleasure, while all the time her brain was saying, No, don't be pleased to see him. He's not yours. She forced some moisture into her mouth in case she had to speak. With luck Moira would say something. She did.

'Oh, hello! Where did you spring from?'

'I came as soon as I could.' He was wearing a business suit and polished shoes; his voice was very tight as if he was keeping himself under control.

Despair swamped Sophie, making her sway a little. When he'd left her, and she hadn't heard from him, a tiny part of her had hoped there was some reason for it, some silly excuse she hadn't thought of, and things might really be all right between them. At his tone the hope died like a spark from a fire that won't light, leaving nothing.

He directed his attention to Sophie. It was as if she were being spoken to by a statue carved from ice. 'What have you been telling my grandmother? Giving her ideas about buying this place? Actually buying it? I couldn't believe it when I heard!'

Sophie searched for some words, any words, but her brain had disconnected, leaving her with only emotion.

Moira glanced at her quickly. 'I don't think Sophie's done anything—'

'Who's that man?' demanded Luke.

'He's a builder friend of mine,' said Moira. 'He's only here to—' She stopped as Ali appeared, also looking angry.

'It seems things have gone quite a long way,' said Ali. 'They've engaged a builder who's crawling all over the house – oh, hello, Sophie.' Her previously friendly manner had disappeared.

'I'd better go and see what's going on,' said Luke, and strode off towards the front of the house, obviously looking for the builder.

'We are – well, I am; I can't speak for Luke, of course – a little disappointed in you.'

'Why?' asked Moira, when she realised Sophie couldn't ask for herself.

'Because she seemed such a nice girl! Mat— Luke's grandmother was so fond of her. She helped Luke out with a tricky problem at home.'

'Did I?' For a moment Sophie couldn't think what Ali was talking about.

'Of course you did!' Ali was softening at the memory. 'Pretending to be Luke's fiancée? I'd have done it myself only there's an anti-fraternisation policy and it could have got me into trouble at work. But it was never real, you did know that.' She frowned again. 'So it is sad to see you're obviously not the girl we thought you were.'

'I don't understand what you're talking about.' Sophie felt she was a long way away from the walled garden at the house – either that or she was speaking from behind a screen, observing rather than being actually present. She was quite surprised her voice was audible.

'Oh, Sophie!' Ali was magnanimous now. 'We know you're very fond of Luke's grandmother but is it really kind or sensible to encourage an old woman in her delusions?'

'Matilda doesn't suffer from delusions.'

'She's an old woman.' Sophie knew Ali wouldn't have been talking about Matilda like that if Luke had been present. 'What does she want with a house so far away from her home that obviously needs a great deal of money spending on it?'

290

'It's not for me to say,' said Sophie, annoyance at the way Ali was talking about Matilda giving her some backbone.

'But when you knew she was thinking of buying it, instead of telling her exactly what it is like – a complete wreck – you got a builder in! And how do you know he's not going to rip Mat— Mrs Winchester off?'

'We didn't know she was definitely thinking of buying it, and he's only here to have a look round – to give a rough estimate on how much the house needs spending on it,' said Moira, chipping in on behalf of her friend. 'He came as a favour to me!'

Ali regarded Moira and recognised a worthy opponent. 'Well, I'm sure you meant well but you may not fully comprehend the situation. Sophie had no authority to instigate anything like this.'

'Sophie didn't instigate anything. It was my idea to get my builder friend in,' said Moira. Her hands were now on her hips.

'Well, it's just as well we arrived in time to stop things before they went too far!' Ali wasn't remotely intimidated by Moira's somewhat aggressive stance.

'What I don't understand,' said Sophie, 'is what any of this has to do with you, Ali? If Matilda wants to buy this house and do it up, for whatever reason, why do you care?'

Just for a moment Ali seemed put out but then she made a little fluttery gesture and became suddenly coy. 'I care about what Luke cares about, naturally. He and I—'

'I wasn't aware there was a "he and I" between you,' said Sophie quietly.

'Didn't you? Well, there was no reason Luke should tell you.' Ali was back on track now. 'You do have a boyfriend, Sophie, and Luke and I go way back.'

'I have a boyfriend?'

Ali nodded. 'I – we saw the message on your phone. It

was hardly prying, you and Luke were sharing it.' She did have the grace to look embarrassed.

'You looked at my phone? You opened a text message?' Sophie was outraged, but she was beginning to understand. The last message she'd received on her phone had been that drunken text from her ex-boyfriend Doug. If she hadn't been obsessively checking for messages for Luke she would have forgotten all about it by now.

'As I said, you and Luke *were* sharing the phone.'

'I didn't realise that meant I was sharing it with you too!'

Ali sighed and shook her head as if tired of arguing with an unreasonable teenager. 'Oh, don't be childish, Sophie! It's no big deal.'

Sophie was trying to decide if Ali and Luke seeing that text really made any difference when Luke reappeared.

'Tell me, Sophie, what exactly have you been telling my grandmother?'

For a second Sophie pictured him in court, demanding answers from a hostile witness, and then felt maybe she was mixing up lawyers with barristers. She didn't appreciate his tone though. 'I told her it belonged to an old lady who was about to die.'

'I know that part,' he said. 'What did you tell her about the house?'

'We sent photographs,' said Sophie. 'And of course we sent the best ones, that made the house look nice, but that was because I didn't want to make her sad to think how badly the house she'd loved had deteriorated.' She'd picked up the long-word habit from somewhere, it seemed, and she was glad. It made her feel less like a victim of playground bullying. 'We weren't trying to pretend the house was fit to live in or anything.'

'Well, she got the impression that a lick of paint and a few roof tiles would do the job,' said Luke. 'She also gave me the impression she had authorised you to act on her behalf.'

Sophie frowned. 'But even if I had the money in used, non-sequential notes, it takes longer than a few hours to buy a house in England. I don't know how it happens in America. How could you possibly think I could act for her?'

'You could get things so far along the way it would be hard for her to back out,' said Luke. 'This is a big project; you should have made it clear to her it would only ever be a dream.'

'But why should it only be a dream? Why are you so against her buying the house?' She hoped he would remember how they'd talked about it when they first saw it.

'Oh, for goodness' sake,' broke in Ali. 'It would be crazy to buy a house in England! What would she do with it? She lives thousands of miles away! It would be a millstone round her neck.'

'That's her decision, surely?' said Sophie. 'She knows how far away it is.'

'Ali's right,' said Luke. 'It's just a dream, totally impractical. You shouldn't have encouraged her.'

'I didn't! I really didn't! I love Matilda and would never do anything to hurt her. Now if you don't mind I've got things to do.'

'What things?' demanded Luke.

'Just things!' She needed to get away. In a minute she'd think of a reasonable excuse.

'Sophie, wait!'

She knew she should have just kept on walking but she stopped.

'How did you get on with those relatives? The drilling rights?'

Sophie shook her head and bit her lip.

'They said no,' said Moira. 'Turned her down flat.'

'Then I'll go and visit them with you,' said Luke. 'I might be able to help.' He was so polite, so businesslike it hurt.

'Are you talking about the drilling rights you had a conference call about yesterday?' asked Ali, cutting in. 'Yes,' she said to Sophie, 'it's important to get them sorted.' She managed to make Sophie feel it was all her fault they hadn't been dealt with years ago. 'We'll all go.'

Unless she could locate a cliff and could thus drive them all off it, Sophie was not having this. She was not going to be cooped up in a small hire car with Luke and Ali.

'I'd have to ring first,' she said. 'Going on spec will just annoy them. They lead very structured lives.'

'Do that,' said Luke. 'I'm not happy with the way you've dealt with the house, but I have a duty to make sure those drilling rights get sorted.'

Sophie sent Moira a pleading look that said, please wave a magic wand and stop this happening!

Moira rose to the challenge. 'Um, are you sure you've got time for this?' she said to Ali and Luke. 'You probably have other things to do.'

'It's fine,' snapped Luke. 'We're not going back until tomorrow.'

'But have you arranged somewhere to stay? In the off season it's not always easy—'

'Oh, we found a darling little hotel near Newquay,' said Ali. 'I booked it online.'

Sophie bit her lip hard, her pang of jealousy needing a strong counter-irritant. She didn't want to know if they'd only booked one room but would have dearly loved to hear they'd booked two.

'Oh, that's OK then,' said Moira, her attempt to save Sophie having failed. 'And you'll eat there?'

'Of course,' said Ali. 'We have a table booked.'

Seeing there was no escape Sophie capitulated. 'I'll ring them.' After all, if Luke was able to talk them round she'd be able to go back home with something positive to say about her life. In fact, it was a very big positive.

'Come in the car with us,' ordered Ali. 'Then you can guide us back to where you're staying. Perhaps you' – she looked enquiringly, and commandingly, at Moira – 'would take Sophie's car back?' She waved a hand vaguely in the direction of the parked hire car.

Moira glanced from Ali to Sophie and nodded. She obviously couldn't think of a good reason why not. 'I'll just tell my friend that we're leaving,' she said, and disappeared round to the front of the house.

Ali watched her go. 'Is that woman your landlady? She seems cool, if a little eccentric. But then she's English, so that would explain it.'

'She might describe herself as Cornish,' said Sophie, not knowing if Moira was a native Cornishwoman or had just become one because she lived there. She just wanted to contradict Ali if she possibly could. And who was Ali to describe Moira as 'eccentric'? Moira seemed perfectly normal to her.

As she couldn't find a reasonable excuse not to travel with Luke and Ali, Sophie folded herself into the back of their hire car. Why had Luke hired such a basic model? Surely he could have afforded one with four doors? Although to be fair – Sophie found, to her chagrin, where Luke was concerned she found it all too easy to be fair – he probably hadn't thought he'd have passengers.

They all arrived at Moira's house at much the same time. 'Did you two have lunch?' Moira asked before Sophie had finished extracting herself from the car, which took a certain amount of flexibility. 'Maybe Sophie could . . .'

Sophie guessed that Moira was feeling guilty about abandoning her and was now having another go at extracting her from Luke and Ali's clutches.

'We're fine,' said Ali. 'I wouldn't want to put you to any trouble.'

'We ate when we arrived, thank you,' said Luke. 'Moira is a wonderful cook,' he added to Ali.

'I'm sure she is,' said Ali with a smile warmed to perfection. 'Now, Sophie, honey, if you would just ring your people, then we can get on.'

As Sophie found the number and pressed 'call' she wondered if she should warn Luke and Ali about the smell of boiling giblets.

Chapter Twenty

❧

Sophie would have preferred not to eavesdrop while Ali talked to the Littlejohns. She was sure to hear something to her own detriment and her self-esteem was low enough; it didn't need any more hammering into the ground. But Ali grabbed hold of her arm. 'In case I can't understand their accents,' she said. 'I might need you to interpret.'

Ali didn't give Sophie a chance to explain that her relations spoke with a pretty standard English accent and not the rich and rolling Cornish burr Sophie had come to love.

'Hello? Am I speaking with Mr Littlejohn? Good afternoon. You don't know me, but I'm speaking on behalf of Winchester, Ambrose and Partners. We're dealing with the drilling rights Sophie Apperly came to see you about this morning?'

Sophie could imagine if not actually hear the harrumphings and grumblings that were going on at the other end.

'Mr Littlejohn, I do understand how you and you wife must feel about this but I don't think matters were explained properly. This is a highly complex issue and if all the details weren't gone into sufficiently, it's hardly surprising you weren't willing to sign.'

She went on in this vein for some length, making Sophie feel as if she'd gone there and talked double Dutch while looking shiftily at the family silver in case there was anything she could pinch. She looked at Luke questioningly. Was Ali saying the company was acting for her just to make the Littlejohns take notice, or had they really undertaken all that?

Luke had his hands in his pockets and was staring down at his shoes as if he were distancing himself from what was going on. He seemed to have reverted to the distant New York lawyer she had first met, looking down his nose at her with his strange-coloured eyes. It was as if none of the other, wonderful things had ever happened.

She went into the kitchen to talk to Moira.

'I'm not sure I can cope.'

As expected, Moira became firm. 'Yes you can. It won't be easy going there with them, and it may not work, but if it does, it'll be worth it. Think of the money!'

'I've never believed that money is all that important. I've got this far without it. Anyway, there might not *be* any money in all this.'

'Well, if there is, money would give you independence. You could do your course, set up your business, follow your dream.'

Sophie sighed. 'I'm not sure that's true.'

'Not your romantic dream, obviously, but your real dream, the one that's for you and doesn't involve anyone else. Don't be dependent on another person for your happiness, Sophie. It isn't fair on anyone.'

'So you think Ali and Luke are together too?'

Moira hesitated. 'I don't know. But I must admit it looks like it. All their body language says they're a couple – and an established one.' She paused. 'I don't necessarily think they're a happy couple though.'

'OK. That's what I thought but I wondered if I was just being silly about it, jumping to conclusions because of my own feelings.'

Moira bit her lip and shook her head. 'Now go out there, and knock 'em dead!'

As it was supposed to, this caused a reluctant smile. 'Honestly! It's not a theatrical performance!'

'Oh yes it is,' said Moira. 'Break a leg!'

'Maybe Sophie should sit in front,' said Luke as the three of them climbed back into the car, 'and then she can map-read.'

'Are you suggesting I'm no good at it?' Ali laughed and pushed Luke's arm in a playful way. 'Really, you men! Constantly making assumptions about us girls!'

'I just meant Sophie has been there before,' said Luke.

Sophie didn't argue, or even comment, she just got in the back. Having Moira confirm what she had instantly felt was a blow; she'd been hoping her feelings for Luke had affected her ability to interpret body language. She also didn't want to explain to Luke that the fact she had been somewhere before wasn't an absolute guarantee she'd be able to find it again. It was all going to be hard enough as it was.

Ali directed them to the Littlejohns' house without difficulty. In spite of the girly front she put up sometimes she was as super-efficient as Sophie had always suspected. Perfect for Luke. Why wouldn't he prefer Ali to her? She was highly intelligent, beautiful, and knew what was what in the world. They were in the same financial bracket – or at least a lot nearer the same one than Sophie was, with her charity-shop clothes and eco-nomical recipes.

Sophie's only advantage was that she loved him, but even if he knew that, it probably wouldn't change anything. He probably didn't consider love an issue; you chose a woman who was suitable and would be a good mother for your children. Romantic love was just silly. She couldn't bear to think that he might actually love Ali.

'That's the house,' said Sophie. 'Bungalow, rather.'

'But it has a window on the second floor,' said Ali.

'That's a dormer, and in England that's the first floor,' said Sophie. 'It's still technically a bungalow. Shall we go in?'

They climbed the steps to the front door in silence. While they were waiting to be admitted, Sophie turned and looked at the view, hoping that once inside the memory of it would sustain her. She also took a gulp of fresh air. She hadn't warned Ali and Luke to do the same.

Apart from some involuntary twitching of the nostrils when he first went in, Luke was impressive, and so was Ali. A lordly double act, they used charm, long words and a patronising attitude to such good effect that in no time the Littlejohns were looking at them like hungry birds, waiting for the next tasty morsel. Ali and Luke refused coffee. Sophie wasn't offered it.

'So have you got the papers there?' asked Mr Littlejohn.

Papers? thought Sophie. What papers? She didn't know about any. But she wasn't going to ask about them in front of the Littlejohns – they had to present a united front. She remembered what Moira had said about it being a performance and continued to play her part – a spear carrier obviously – who could watch the action without any lines to worry about.

Mr Littlejohn seemed torn between hanging on this golden couple's every word and actually wanting them to leave quite quickly. Sophie could sympathise; they were rather like angels, swooping down on innocent people and making a momentous announcement that would change their lives for ever. In a good way, of course, but still very scary.

'Before we sign anything,' said Luke, who had let Ali do most of the talking up to this point, 'I think I should explain what very good hands you are putting your affairs into when you agree to let Sophie be your representative.'

Sophie felt herself blush so violently she wondered if she was ill. What was Luke saying about her?

'Sophie is a very able young woman. It was entirely her initiative that anything useful is being done with these drilling rights. Without her they would all still be languishing in old files, no one benefiting from any of it. But now many of your relations, distant I know, but still your family, will be able to realise this asset.'

Sophie felt she had to use all her energy to keep her expression neutral. Mr and Mrs Littlejohn, who had been so dismissive of her earlier, were now giving her looks of admiration, as if Luke had made her a Dame of the British Empire or something. Ali, she noticed, was looking as if either the smell, or something else, was getting to her.

'So,' Luke concluded, 'are you ready to sign the affidavit I have here giving Sophie the power to act for you? I don't think you should do so if you're not entirely happy, but I should point out that several thousands of pounds – possibly several tens of thousands – would be your share of the money forthcoming. Although of course it may take some time to arrive. There is a lot that has to be done before money will change hands.'

If she was blushing before, Sophie's face now drained of all colour. Thousands of pounds? What was Luke talking about?

'I think you should sign, dear!' said Mr Littlejohn, who had made a grab for a pen before he remembered it was his wife who had the power, not him.

'And you're a solicitor?' Mrs Littlejohn asked Luke, still tentative.

'I am.' He smiled down at her in a way that made Sophie's heart clench. He could be so lovely to older people. He was a good man, he just didn't love her.

Mrs Littlejohn looked up at him and took the pen.

'You won't know anything about this,' said Ali, 'but before we came away from London, Luke was able to put in place a very lucrative deal with a major oil company.'

'Why didn't you ring and tell me?' asked Sophie indignantly from where she sat in the back seat with her knees very near her chin. She was relieved to be able to ask him why he hadn't called without it being in connection with their relationship.

'I don't have your number, Sophie,' said Luke gently. 'I have a new cell, but not my SIM card.'

Sophie took this in and then said, 'Hang on! You had my number when you rang me from the airport!'

'That's my fault, honey,' said Ali. 'Naturally I sent all his clothes to the dry cleaner and the note must have been in one of the pockets.' She paused. 'They were very strange clothes – Luke told me they came from a thrift store.'

Sophie let out a breath. That was one mystery solved. So horrified by the thought of Luke in charity-shop clothes, Ali had had them all dry-cleaned. She probably wanted to have them fumigated. 'You could have rung Moira, she'd have given me a message.'

'I didn't have Moira's number either. Nor could I remember her surname or her address so I couldn't look her up on the internet.'

'What about Matil—'

'I think you're being very ungrateful,' said Ali interrupting. 'Luke has been working extremely hard on your behalf – many of us in the office have been too. And all to make you a rich woman.' She paused. 'Of course it's all relative, but you should get a good amount. It'll make a big difference to a girl like you.'

Sophie hated that Ali should know so much about her personal circumstances. Did Luke tell her that he'd had to buy her clothes to go to that brunch in?

'Of course I'm grateful, but I'm sure Luke didn't do it for nothing. I know how expensive American lawyers are. I do expect to receive a bill.'

'There will be no bill,' said Luke – from between clenched teeth, judging on how the words came out.

'Of course I won't be in a position to pay it until the money actually comes through.' This was a shame, but not unreasonable. Payment by results sort of thing.

'I said: there will be no fee,' Luke repeated, just as tightly.

'Honey! There's no reason why Sophie shouldn't pay. She could get the money from the other parties – we've all worked hard for this project!'

Ali wasn't short for 'altruistic', obviously, Sophie thought. 'I will pay, Ali, don't worry,' she said. 'I really don't want to be beholden. To anyone.'

'That's good,' said Ali. She didn't sound particularly thrilled.

'But, Luke,' Sophie went on, 'I want to know why you didn't tell me about this deal. Would you have said anything about it if I hadn't told you the Littlejohns refused to sign?'

'Of course we would have told you,' said Ali, speaking for him. 'But when the deal was completely through. No point in getting your hopes up if it was going to come to nothing.'

'So it's not through yet? And it's all right to get the Littlejohns' hopes up, but not mine!'

'Sophie, honey, you're not quite getting this . . .' began Ali.

'No, I'm not. Maybe you'd care to explain? Luke?'

'Let me handle this, honey,' said Ali, obviously determined not to let Luke get a word in edgewise. 'It's all coming together beautifully. There aren't going to be any problems. Luke called in every favour he could, contacted everyone he knew in the oil business and put the deal together. He wouldn't have told you that part, which is why I am.' She turned towards Luke somewhat defiantly.

'Whether it's done and dusted or not, you should have kept me informed. Matilda has my number if every other bit of technology failed you.'

'My grandmother was not at home when I called and didn't have your number with her. So she said,' Luke snapped.

'Oh.' But Sophie wasn't satisfied. 'I still don't see how you and Luke found it perfectly possible to find me – get in touch with me – when it was to do with Matilda's house, but it's "Oh! How could we contact you?" when it's my business?' She paused. 'And anyway, you didn't have to come down in person, you could have sent a message in some other way!'

'How?' asked Ali, maddeningly reasonable.

'I don't know. There must be some method.'

'We did try to handle it from London,' Ali explained, 'but it was proving impossible, so Luke said he'd jump in a car and come down before you went home. Obviously I came with him.'

'It is fairly obvious you're here, yes!' said Sophie, knowing she was being childish but unable to help herself.

'Turn left now,' she said a few moments later, when Luke hesitated at a crossroads.

The moment Sophie was out of the car she headed off down the road towards the beach. She needed to process her feelings in private, with no one to try and rationalise things, or say, 'There, there.' Her emotions were so confused it was like having a thunderstorm in her diaphragm, churning away, desperately needing to escape. She'd made such a mess of everything – falling in love with Luke had been so stupid! Not even the most idiotic teenager would have done such a foolish thing.

Fortunately there were no dog-walkers and the shingle beach was empty. Spray stung her face and it started to rain. Sophie felt she needed a jolly good cry, to get rid of the knot caused by tension, heartache and anger that had been building all day. But the tears would not come. Instead the knot inside her just got bigger and tighter and more destructive. She hated Luke, she hated Ali, she hated everyone. She even hated herself. She was so silly, so naïve, so utterly idiotic. No wonder Luke wanted nothing to do with her.

Sophie went into the churchyard, hoping to find some peace, or even the trigger to make her have a good old howl. Even when she was feeling perfectly happy, cemeteries were likely to make her weep, and this one had very special significance for her, but nothing happened this time. She headed back to Moira's house, still angry and confused and heartbroken.

She saw Ali and Luke standing by the car from some way away. The ghastly déjà vu of the situation made her turn sharply behind a hedge of hydrangeas. Was there a back way in to Moira's? she wondered. There must be, she thought, although it might involve climbing over a fence or something.

When she saw them turn back towards the house she wondered why she'd bothered to sneak around – they could probably see her.

'I can't go without saying goodbye again,' Luke was saying. 'I felt bad enough about it last time.'

'Lukey, it's the best way and she won't mind. You found out for yourself – she has a boyfriend! You were just a little fling for her in the same way she was for you. And we've agreed to put it all behind us.' Sophie couldn't see Ali put her hand on Luke's arm from her position behind the hydrangeas, but she knew she was doing it. 'Girls of that age don't stay in love for more than five minutes, you know that. It'll be out of sight, out of mind for her, especially if there's no long-drawn-out farewell scene.'

Sophie didn't wait to hear what 'Lukey' thought about this, she decided to see for herself. 'Hello! Are you off?'

'Sophie!' Luke spun round. He looked pale and anxious.

'Are you OK, Luke?' Sophie asked. She sounded admirably controlled, she thought.

'Of course. I was just a bit worried about you.'

'Why? There's no need! I'm going to be rich! I'll have money to do whatever I want!' She wasn't as convinced by her performance this time and so she forced a smile to reinforce it.

'Yes,' agreed Ali. 'And it's down to you, Luke. I'm sure Sophie's very grateful.'

'Oh yes,' agreed Sophie. 'Very grateful indeed.'

'So there's no need for us to hang around. We'll be in touch.' Ali made as if to kiss Sophie's cheek but she dodged.

'How will you be in touch?' asked Sophie with a touch of asperity she was proud of.

'Give me your cellphone number,' demanded Ali. She produced a business card from her bag with a flick of a well-manicured hand, like a conjuror. A gold pen followed and soon Sophie was writing her number on the back of the engraved card. 'Here!' Ali handed Sophie another card. 'Now you have my details. Come on, Luke.'

Luke didn't move. 'Sophie, are you sure you're OK?'

'Of course! I'm going to be fine. I'm going to have enough money to do my course and set up a business. How could I not be fine? Now do get on. Long-drawn-out goodbyes are so tedious, aren't they?' She looked at Ali who turned slightly pink. She may have realised Sophie had overheard their previous conversation.

'Absolutely. We've said goodbye to Moira,' she breezed. 'Goodbye, Sophie! We'll be in touch!'

'You know something?' Sophie said to Moira when she was back in the kitchen. 'I don't even want to cry any more! I've so had it with that man. He's spineless and pathetic. I don't know why I fancied him even for a second. Plenty more – far better – fish in the sea than him!'

'Good girl!' said Moira, relieved. She banged the kettle down on the hotplate in triumph. 'So now what are you going to do?'

'Well,' said Sophie after a couple of moments' thought. 'As soon as the money comes through I'll go on my course. There may be enough to set up a business. It's a bit annoying that we don't know how much we're due to get. My share is tiny, it might be only tuppence. But it's something good to look forward to.'

'You're very young to set up on your own,' commented Moira, handing Sophie a mug of tea.

'I'm fed up with being young! Or rather I'm not really fed up with being young, but why is it, because I'm only in my early twenties, people think I must be an idiot? Or incapable of having feelings for someone for more than five minutes?'

Sophie's indignation made Moira smile and shake her head. 'I do know what you mean, Sophie, but I promise you, being young is a huge advantage. And you have much better skin than Ali.'

Sophie bit her lip. She'd been so proud of her I-don't-care act and yet it hadn't fooled Moira, not for a minute.

'I know. I have a huge advantage.' Then she frowned. 'How long do you reckon it takes to get over a man, usually?'

Moira shook her head. 'Hard to say. But work on it. Don't spend every second thinking about him.'

'Fine, I won't!' declared Sophie, failing to follow this very good advice in the very next instant.

Sophie spent a few more days with Moira, visiting the house and taking more photographs. This time, however, she didn't send them to Matilda; she had a feeling that Luke had fallen out with his grandmother over the house and she didn't want to make matters worse.

Then she took the car back to where they'd hired it and got on the train home.

'Well,' she said as the family sat round the dinner table. 'Don't you want to know how I got on?'

'Of course, dear. How did you get on?' asked her mother, who did at least seem to have missed her.

'Very well! We found the last member of the family who had shares and—'

'Who's we?' asked Michael who liked details.

'Me and Luke,' said Sophie, deciding not to mention Ali. It would involve far too much painful explanation.

'And where's Luke now, darling?' asked her mother, loading mashed potatoes on to Sophie's plate as a gesture of affection.

'In London. He has to work now. He only had a few days before he had to go back.'

'I liked Luke. A change for you to have a boyfriend with a brain,' said her father.

'And a bank balance,' added Michael.

308

Sophie exhaled silently and dug her fork into the potato. 'Luke isn't my boyfriend, and never was, and I do wish you'd all just let me finish my story and not keep banging on about him.'

'Sorree!' said her brother, mockingly. 'Touched a sore spot, have we?'

'No! It's just I have news – and Luke isn't part of it!'

Her father and brother put down their knives and forks in an exaggerated gesture of paying Sophie attention.

'We got Mrs Littlejohn's – she's Uncle Eric's cousin's widow – to sign an affidavit making it possible for me to act for her. Luke is tying up a deal that will mean the drilling rights are leased and we should all get some money. Not quite sure how long it'll take but it shouldn't be too long.' Sophie added this bit of optimism to disguise the fact that she was kicking herself for telling her family before it was all finalised. 'So that's good, isn't it?'

Her mother was smiling and nodded, chewing away happily, but her father and brother were looking at her in horror. 'Sorry, did I hear that right?' said her father. 'Did you say she signed something so *you* could act for her? Why you? You're the youngest member of the family and you've very few shares. Why are you going to act for them?'

'Yes! It should be me, as the eldest,' said Michael.

His father gave him a look. 'Me, actually. I'm the previous generation. It shouldn't be any of you lot.'

Sophie considered. Should she point out that if it hadn't been for her none of this would have been happening? Or that Uncle Eric was a generation older than her father even, and if that was how it should be decided, it should be he who acted for them?

'Well,' she said after a moment or two while people fumed and exclaimed, 'it's me. End of.' She hadn't actually signed anything yet but her name was on the papers Luke had drawn up. 'Sorry if you don't like it.' She paused. 'I'm sure Luke would have put someone else down but as I was the one who started searching for everyone, I think he thought it should be my name on the deal. It simply means that you all have to sign an affidavit giving me power to act on your behalf. Uncle Eric's happy to do it. That won't be a problem, will it?' she finished defiantly.

Michael was dumbstruck. Her father blinked. He'd never heard Sophie being so decisive. 'It's very irregular,' he said eventually. 'I'm not at all happy.'

'Yes,' her brother, recovering his voice, chipped in to support his father. 'How can a girl like you possibly take responsibility? It's mad!'

'It's not mad, it's fine,' said Sophie firmly. 'It'll all be very straightforward. I'll ask if I need help,' she added, suddenly anxious in case she did need assistance.

'Well,' said her father, 'if it's your name on the deal with the oil company, we'll have to accept it. But it's very irregular.'

'No "Well done, Sophie, for potentially making us all rich?"' said Sophie quietly. 'No? Thought not.'

Sophie had been home long enough to tell Amanda the entire story and send Milly a series of emails bringing her up to speed. Both girls were very supportive and Sophie was beginning to feel, if not better, at least accustomed to feeling a little bit sad, when she had a phone call from Uncle Eric.

'Can you come and see me, m'dear?' he asked.

As he was not a man who was free with his endearments, Sophie instantly worried. 'Are you all right? Does Mrs Brown want some time off?'

'I expect she does. She's always wanting time off to visit her grandchildren.'

'I thought her grandchildren were in Australia!' said Sophie, thinking Mrs Brown must be paid much more than she thought if she could keep visiting them.

'Not those grandchildren! The ones in Rugby! Do try and keep up!'

Sophie chuckled, thinking how soothing Uncle Eric's acerbic manner was. 'Thought you might want to see me!' He sounded reproachful.

'Of course I want to see you!' said Sophie instantly. 'I'll come up tomorrow.'

Chapter Twenty-One

❧

Sophie went to Uncle Eric's on the train, trying not to think about the time she went there with Luke; trying not to think about him, however, guaranteed that she thought about him with every bump and jerk and all the bits in between for the entire journey. But arriving at Uncle Eric's house, her rucksack on her back, made her feel better. He would be on her side, whatever happened.

He opened the door to her. 'Well, don't just stand there. Come in.'

'Lovely to see you too, Uncle-Eric-dear,' she said and kissed his cheek.

'You're letting all the warm air out.'

Later, when Sophie had settled in to what she thought of as her room, Uncle Eric joined her in the kitchen while she made supper. She made him sit at the kitchen table; it was an unfamiliar place for him but better for her than having him wander about, wondering about things.

'So, you got Mattingly's widow to do the decent thing eventually.'

'Yup. But it took Luke and his – ' she swallowed ' – girlfriend to convince her. I told you in my letter.'

'So you did.' He paused. 'Pity about the Yank. I liked him. Thought he was decent.'

'He is decent, he's just not my boyfriend.'

'Thought you'd have made a match of it.'

Sophie put down her wooden spoon and turned to her

great-uncle, unsure if she wanted to laugh or cry. 'You sound like someone out of Georgette Heyer! And I admit, I would have liked us to get together, but I'm not really suitable. It probably wouldn't have worked.'

'Hmph.' Having expressed his opinion on that subject he reverted to their original topic of conversation. 'I gather it might be a while before the money actually turns up from the oil thing?'

'Oh yes. These things always take time.' She tossed her spoon into the sink and then put the macaroni cheese into the oven. 'Even macaroni cheese – although that'll only take half an hour or so. Would you like a cup of tea or something while we're waiting?'

'No, I fancy something stronger. Come into the study.' With relief, Uncle Eric left the strange and arcane room that was the kitchen and led Sophie to his study.

'I think we should have a glass of port,' he said. 'It'll never get drunk otherwise and I hate waste.'

'Port? Not what I'd usually have, but if you fancy it, I'll find a glass.'

'Ought to be sherry, of course, before dinner, but haven't got any. And I want you to have some too. Something I want to discuss with you.'

'That sounds very ominous. You're not ill, are you?' Sophie kept her tone light but a pang of dread touched her. Uncle Eric was very elderly and although she hadn't really known him all that long the thought of him dying was awful.

'No iller than I've ever been, thank you very much. Now get the port, there's a good girl.'

Sophie found glasses and the bottle of port in the cupboard he waved at, still worried. Then she filled the glasses and waited.

'Are you sure about the Yank?' said Uncle Eric, having taken a sip.

'Oh yes! He's got a much better girlfriend.'

'Sure about that too? You're a damn good cook, Sophie, and handy about the house.'

Sophie couldn't help laughing at the thought of Ali being handy about the house in the way she was. 'Oh yes. She's ideal for him. They work in the same office. She's bright, attractive, nearer the same age. Tailor-made, practically.' She tried to sound pleased about this, as if she was happy that Luke had such a nice girlfriend, which in a way she was; she still wanted the best for him.

Her great-uncle took a thoughtful sip of port. 'Think you may be wrong. I thought he was a decent chap, Yank or not. But still, he's neither here nor there, really.'

'Half right, said Sophie, falsely bright. 'He's not here, but he's probably there.'

She didn't know where he was. He'd been vague about how long the project at work would take. He might still be in London. The thought of him there with Ali gave her a cold feeling. She could imagine them living in a smart flat in Canary Wharf, surrounded by glittering high-rise buildings, working together, leading a smart and glittering life, which she could never have been part of, even if he had loved her.

Maybe he had loved her in Cornwall, in the way that you can have a lovely holiday somewhere without wanting to live there. She was his Cornish, away-from-home romance. Ali was the woman he'd marry and spend the rest of his life with.

'Well, never mind about that,' said Uncle Eric. 'What I want to tell you is, I'm planning to give you some money. In fact, if you rummage around in my desk – which I know you like doing – you'll find a cheque. No, don't go all sentimental on me. It's my money and I'll do what I like with it!'

314

He did sound sufficiently cross for Sophie to go to the desk, find the cheque and bring it to him.

'Well, I don't want it!' he declared. 'It's for you. I know you want to do some course or other – although education is wasted on women, if you want my opinion – and if you have to wait for this oil money to transpire, well, you'll be too old to learn.'

Sophie couldn't help laughing. 'Uncle Eric! You mustn't say things like that! And I don't want to take it. It's not right.'

'Why isn't it right? If I want to give you money I will!'

'But I'm going to get all this money from the drilling rights. We all are. Even you!'

'But you said it was going to take time to get the actual cash – as if I didn't know – and that's why I'm giving you the money now. Planning to leave you everything when I die but even if I drop dead tomorrow, it'll be years before you get your hands on the boodle.'

'Uncle Eric!'

'Got to leave it to someone,' he went on. 'Not so fond of cats I want to leave it to a cats' home or whatever charity it is that muddled old people are supposed to leave their money to. Might as well be you!'

'But—'

'Do stop banging on, child,' he said. 'Take the cheque and give me the satisfaction of doing something with my money when I'm still alive and can see it do some good.'

Chastened, Sophie looked at the cheque. It was for twenty thousand pounds. 'Uncle Eric!' she squeaked. 'You can't give me all this!'

'Why not? It's mine. I can do what I damn well like with my money! Mind you, if I peg out before seven years are up – and I well might – you might have to pay tax on it. But still.'

'But it's such a lot of money!' Sophie was staring at the figures, wondering how long it would have taken her to earn that much in the normal course of events.

'Not particularly. You couldn't buy a house with it, although I suppose it would be a deposit.'

'I don't want to buy a house with it.'

'Apart from your course, what do you want to do with it then?'

Sophie considered. 'I could spend some of it on a trip to New York; take Amanda, so we could see Milly. Have I told you about my friends from school?'

He nodded, making it clear he hadn't found them that fascinating. 'And I could pay for the course and have enough left to support me through it. It's brilliant!' Then her bubble of enthusiasm collapsed. 'But I still feel it's wrong to take your money. You might need it.'

'I think that's very mean-spirited of you. I'm an old man, I don't have many pleasures left in life, and you'd deprive me of those still available to me. And I won't need it. I've made provision for the rest home when the time comes. That's spare.'

Sophie got up and put her arms round him. 'Then I'm very, very grateful, darling Uncle Eric. Thank you so, so much. This means I can get on with my life and not have to work in bars and run up debts. It's brilliant. Thank you!'

He patted her arm, indicating he'd been hugged quite enough, thank you. 'Does that mean you can stay a few days?'

She chuckled. 'Oh yes. The course I want to go on doesn't start until September.' She'd been doing some research and found the perfect course for her. It could have been designed specially for her.

'Good. You cook better than Mrs Thing.'

But in bed that night Sophie realised one of the things

316

she ought to do with the money was to pay Luke for the legal work to do with the drilling rights. But how much should that be? She didn't want to give him too much or too little but what was the right amount, approximately?

As she had no real idea of even how to find out she decided to grit her teeth and get in touch with Ali. She had her card with her email address on it.

The following day, having arranged to spend a few more days with Uncle Eric and paid in her cheque, she set off to the café where she knew she could borrow a computer – even if it did mean she had to do a bit of clearing up, or cake-making, or even a whole shift, in exchange.

Jack, the owner of the café, was happy to see her and agreed she could use his computer in exchange for the occasional shift.

'I'll have to check with Uncle Eric, but I'm sure he doesn't want me underfoot all the time.'

'I'd pay you, of course,' said Jack.

Sophie hesitated.

'If you work, you get paid. It's not a lot, but you'll earn it.'

As Sophie didn't know if every penny Uncle Eric had given her would have to go to Winchester, Ambrose and Partners, she accepted thankfully.

After her first session, which involved making scones, pizzas and a couple of quiches, Sophie was let into Jack's office and offered the laptop.

'This is terribly kind.'

'It's fine. Now I must press on.'

After she had logged on to Hotmail, Sophie got out Ali's card and composed her email. *Dear Ali, Circumstances have made it possible for me to pay Luke and his firm for the work they did for me regarding the drilling rights. Would you kindly let me have a bill, and I'll arrange to pay it forthwith.*

She realised it was staying with Uncle Eric that had made her say 'forthwith' and not 'immediately' but she was glad she had; she didn't know how long Uncle Eric's cheque would take to clear. And if the bill was for the entire twenty thousand pounds (or the equivalent in dollars) could she morally keep back a bit for her course? After all, that was why Uncle Eric had given her the money.

The next day she went to the café there was a reply: *Dear Sophie, Thank you for your email. This firm charges $400 an hour. I'm currently searching for records of how many hours have been spent on this and I'll let you know the exact figure as soon as I can but I imagine it'll be about ten hours, possibly more.*

Sophie sucked her teeth at the amount, tempted to write a cheque immediately so she need never think about it again. But maybe it would be better to wait for an accurate figure?

Eventually, she wrote a cheque and enclosed it with a letter. *Dear Ali, I have pleasure in enclosing a cheque for the equivalent of four thousand dollars on account. Please let me know if I owe any further money.*

There was a great deal of satisfaction in paying her dues, she realised, although contrarily she felt a bit guilty about it. Luke had been so adamant in the car that he didn't want paying. Still, he might not find out. He might not trouble himself with the accounts department.

She stayed with Uncle Eric for a week before reluctantly deciding she should go home. She needed a proper job, to go back to saving money. Although she now had a sizeable nest egg, she didn't want to mooch about spending it and a job would give her less time to think about Luke, for in spite of all her instructions to herself she still couldn't stop doing so.

Back home she returned to her job at the bar, had regular meetings with Amanda and was taken out a couple of times in the hope she might meet someone else, because Amanda said watching your friend mooning over a man was no fun.

Dressing up to go out and meet men who were as unlike the man in her head and in her heart as was possible, given that they were male, wasn't a lot of fun either, but Sophie didn't say so. She tried hard to appear as if she was enjoying herself.

She heard nothing more from Ali. Either that was the exact amount owed or she'd forgotten about it.

February had finally come to an end, and March was halfway through, when Matilda, via email, asked Sophie to do something for her. She and Matilda had been exchanging emails regularly and, so far, Matilda hadn't mentioned Luke. This was a little strange, Sophie felt, because she mentioned other family members frequently. What Sophie always dreaded, until she'd scanned down the email, to make sure it wasn't there, was the news that Luke and Ali were getting married. She didn't even know if Luke and Ali were still in England and she didn't care – just as long as they didn't marry each other. Matilda had gone ahead and bought the house from the old lady, with Luke's blessing Sophie assumed – or perhaps not? Matilda kept her regularly up to date. Moira too – she had kept in touch with her Cornish friend and saviour.

Matilda's email went straight to the point: *Darling, is there any chance you could go down to Cornwall to look at the house? I want to make sure the builders are doing their job?*

Sophie wrote back to say that Moira would do that for her if Matilda felt it was necessary, but as the builder was a friend of Moira's, he was probably very reliable.

The next day Matilda was more insistent. *Colour schemes, darling. You must agree you can't rely on a builder to do that! Please go down for me; I'll be happy to pay your expenses. I just want you to go! You could take a little break from your job, couldn't you?*

Sophie was even more happy to tell Matilda that she didn't have to pay her expenses. *My lovely great-uncle has given me a huge cheque. I'm a rich woman! And of course I can take a break from my job and I'll go and see about colour schemes if that's what you want.*

Sophie rang Moira and arranged to stay, found a good deal on a ticket for the train and set off for Cornwall on 1 April. Although thoughts of Luke still made her desperately sad, she was excited to think she'd be seeing the house again and she loved Cornwall dearly. She felt it was her spiritual home and hugged to herself the thought that soon she'd be spending loads of time down there: she'd applied for the perfect course in Falmouth and had been accepted.

She hired a car from Truro and set off for Moira's, concluding as she drove down roads she had driven with Luke that melancholy could be a liveable-with condition. Heartbreak was harder, but she'd get over that soon, surely? She hadn't seen Luke for nearly three months.

As she left the town her spirits rose a little. Spring had definitely arrived and the lanes that had enchanted her in January were even more delightful now, dotted with primroses, celandines, violets and daisies; life without Luke might be bleak, but she could still take pleasure in the beauties of nature.

Moira opened the door wide with her usual welcoming smile. 'Sophie, darling, how lovely. It's been doing nothing but rain for days and days and you've brought the sunshine with you. Come on in.'

In spite of this cheery greeting Sophie felt Moira was not her usual self. Something wasn't right. 'What's up?' Sophie kissed her friend. 'There's something the matter. Are you OK?'

'I'm fine! Really, it's just . . .'

'What? Isn't it convenient for me to stay? You could have said.'

'Come into the kitchen. You need a glass of wine. Trust me.'

Sophie followed Moira into the kitchen, feeling instantly embraced by the warmth and the homely surroundings, even though the last time she had been there, over two months ago, she'd thought she would never smile again.

Moira poured a glass of wine. 'I'll make you tea in a minute if you'd prefer. Sit down.'

Sophie pulled out a chair and sat. 'Don't tell me, Matilda's house has burnt to the ground.'

'No, of course it hasn't! Don't be so melodramatic!'

'It's your fault! You're filling me with doom and gloom and giving me wine when . . .' She glanced at her watch. '. . . it's only five o'clock.'

'Don't you know? Five is the new six.' Moira poured a glass of wine for herself and took a bracing sip. 'The thing is . . . Luke. He's coming.'

'Luke?' Sophie stiffened. She'd spent so much time and energy striving to forget him, she really didn't want him brought up in conversation the moment she got through Moira's door. 'I thought he might have gone back to New York by now.'

'I don't know where he's coming from but he's arriving tomorrow. I've put him in the single.'

Sophie felt sick; butterflies swirled in her stomach and she was glad she was sitting down because she suddenly felt boneless. 'Oh God, I'm not sure – I don't think—' She stopped trying to talk and bit her lip instead.

'I realise this must be really hard for you. I didn't know

what to do when I heard from him. I thought of ringing you but I really wanted to see you.' She paused. 'I had to put him up here as there isn't anywhere else to stay. My friend who does B & B is away.'

'But it's only him?'

Moira nodded. 'He didn't say anything about Ali coming too.'

This was a huge relief. 'But why? Why is he coming?'

'The same reason as you. That's what he said on the phone anyway: that he'd been asked to come by Matilda to check on the builders. Who do not need checking on, by the way.'

Sophie put her elbows on the table and her head in her hands. 'I don't understand. Is Matilda trying to get us together or some mad thing? She's never mentioned Luke in her emails, never given me a hint that she'd like us to get together. Thinking back, she did a bit in America, but not since Luke came over to England. But why else would she get us both down here? It can't need two of us to check on the builders – even if they did need checking on. And Luke was against it all the last time we saw him. She asked me to think about colour schemes.'

'Colour schemes?'

'Yes. She said you can't expect builders to deal with them, which is fair enough.'

'I know, but Matilda asked me to hire an interior designer! They do colour schemes!'

'So why the hell does she want me here?'

Moira considered for a while and then shook her head, obviously having failed to find a reasonable explanation. 'I wonder if Luke knows you're going to be here?'

Sophie shrugged. 'He might be so horrified he goes back to London the moment he sees me. Which would be the best thing, really.'

Moira opened her mouth as if to question this and then shut it again.

'But he's definitely not bringing Ali?'

'He certainly didn't mention her and they'll have to find a hotel if he does. That single bed is only three feet wide.'

The thought that a three-foot bed would have been quite wide enough for them, that one spectacular night, flashed into Sophie's mind. She forced the thought out again.

'I'm not sure I can do it, Moira. I've tried so hard to get him out of my mind; I'm not sure I can cope with seeing him again.'

Moira regarded her sympathetically. 'The trouble is, you haven't got a choice. And it might be good! You might think: What a dork! He might not even be good-looking any more, although I suppose he will still have those amazing colour eyes.'

Sophie exhaled hard. 'OK. It's like you said before, it's a performance. I can do it. Drama was one of the things I was good at at school. I just have to pretend I'm fine. Which I am!' She went on. 'Did you find one – an interior designer?'

Moira nodded.

'Friend of yours?'

Moira nodded again. 'Friend of a friend. And it's a she. She wants to make a mood board.'

Sophie put on a scowl. 'I can give her a mood, no problem,' she growled.

Moira laughed, as she was meant to. 'Don't be like that. She's lovely. She's got some wonderful ideas. The trouble is, she doesn't know what the house is for.'

'What do you mean? Houses are for living in!'

'I know but Becky, that's the designer, says she doesn't know if it's going to be a family home or for holiday lets, or what. Matilda hasn't told her.'

'Don't the builders know? They must have had instructions.'

'They're doing the roof, replacing anything rotten – just stopping it from falling down, basically. Becky's there to say if they're to knock walls down, put on a conservatory, put in a Jacuzzi – stuff like that.'

Sophie's nostrils wrinkled. 'Not keen on that idea. But I don't know what Matilda wants it for either, so I don't see how I can help. Luke may know, of course. In fact she's probably told him everything.' She sighed. 'But why get me involved?'

'Your general taste and discernment?'

Sophie acknowledged this gentle tease. 'I do understand why Matilda bought it. She's got the money and she couldn't bear the thought of it falling down. But now what? She's getting on a bit. She's not going to want to be popping down to Cornwall for weekends from Connecticut.'

'Well, as you say, maybe Luke knows. Do you want more wine?'

'Actually, I'd kill for a cup of tea. And then I must tell you about my course. I've found one down here! Uncle Eric gave me some money. Isn't that sweet of him? My family are furious, of course – they thought giving money to me was a complete waste. But we'll all get loads of money eventually, so I don't see why they're making such a fuss.'

Chapter Twenty-Two

❧

Sophie went over to the house really early the following morning. It had rained a lot in the night and the day had that just-washed feeling that made it especially beautiful. She wanted to see the house before anyone else got there, so she could have it all to herself. She wanted to think about Matilda being there as a little girl, to imagine what she might want from the house now. She also wanted to have her own daydreams.

She thought she'd be fine seeing Luke again. She hadn't slept well and whenever she woke up she rationalised her feelings, practised her first words, rehearsed how she would behave. When she finally got up she thought she had it all worked out.

There was a faint mist in the valleys: a promise of a beautiful day ahead. Birds sang and the hedgerows were dotted with flowers. Sunlight caught spiders' webs so they shone like fairy cloth. As a little girl, Sophie had believed in fairies; there were moments when she still did. Sunlight on dewdrops creating a prism counted as seeing one and that was always a good omen. Sophie didn't believe in bad omens, only good ones, and had she not been trying to get over Luke – not very successfully – she'd have been feeling very positive.

Now, with nature going about its business so urgently and vocally, she couldn't decide if it all made everything sadder by throwing her own melancholy into relief, or if she felt comforted that life went on in its relentless, optimistic way.

She arrived at the house glad to be able to see it without the noise and bustle that would soon envelop it.

It had been a lovely house when she and Luke first discovered it in winter when it was sad and neglected. Now it was beginning to look cared for and in good condition. It sat on its little hill proudly surveying the countryside. Not for the first time Sophie speculated on how lovely the views must be. You might be able to see the sea from the top of the house.

The roof had largely been replaced, as had the eaves and many of the window frames and doors. The climbing plant that twisted its way over the house was still there. Although she couldn't identify it, Sophie was glad it had been left. The house would have looked undressed without it.

Sophie began to inspect the house in more detail. Peering in through one of the windows she could see new floorboards in the downstairs rooms. The garden had been cleared but not landscaped; the cement mixer and generator made it look like a work in progress but there was an air of promise about it, an expectation of being once again beautiful.

Luke was due at about midday, so until he came Sophie could enjoy the house without the tension his presence would cause. She rambled about, investigating, and speculating, until eventually hunger became pressing and she drove back to Moira's for breakfast.

'Do you want eggs and bacon?' Moira asked. 'You didn't eat much last night and all this fresh air and exercise would justify it.'

Sophie shook her head. 'Not sure I could face that.'

'OK, sit down and I'll heat up a croissant. I've got some in the freezer.'

Sophie pulled out a chair. 'Do you think I actually have to be here?'

'What do you mean? You are here!'

'Yes, but I could go home again. I just don't think I'm going to be that useful, and . . .'

'You can't face seeing Luke?' Moira put the warm croissant in front of Sophie.

'No! I just think with the interior designer, the builder and Luke, I'm surplus to requirements.' She reached for the jam. 'OK, I can't face seeing Luke.'

'You wouldn't want him to think you were too cut up to see him, would you?'

'No.'

'Well,' Moira pressed on, 'if you're here and fine he won't think he broke your heart. And you don't want to let Matilda down. What would she think if she found out you came all the way down here and then just went away again?'

Sophie shrugged. 'She should know better than to matchmake.'

'Are you sure that's what she's doing?'

'I don't know. Perhaps for some sentimental reason – probably to do with her being English – she wants to see us together. But Ali is perfect for him. They're the same age, same nationality, same culture. Luke and I have nothing in common at all. When I think of the things I put him through – fish and chips, Marmite, trains on a Sunday . . .' He had coped well, she remembered. He hadn't moaned or compared England unfavourably to America, he'd just gone with the flow and experienced being hard up without complaint.

Moira said, 'He did seem a good sort of man. Good-looking, wealthy, all that, but not a snob.'

'No, well.' Sophie licked her finger and collected her croissant crumbs. 'If I've got to stay . . .'

'You've got to stay,' Moira confirmed.

'I think I'll go and sort myself out. If I'm going to see Luke I want to be looking my best – or as "best" as I can manage.'

After breakfast, Sophie went upstairs, brushed her teeth and redid her hair, but she didn't put on make-up. She didn't often wear it and she didn't want Luke thinking she'd put it on for his benefit. Then she compromised with some mascara and a tiny bit of lip-gloss. Then she wiped off the lip-gloss. She had a kohl pencil in her hand when she heard him arrive.

She felt almost physically sick – with anxiety, excitement, indecision and, cruelly, desire. She wanted the man who had caused her so much pain. She pushed her fists into her stomach in an attempt to quell the butterflies, and then she took a couple of deep breaths and opened the bedroom door. She went downstairs before she could talk herself out of doing it.

Luke was in the kitchen with Moira. The shock of seeing him, even though she was fully prepared, was almost physical. He was so good-looking and she fancied him so much she almost cried.

He turned as she came into the room but didn't smile.

'Luke!' she said.

'Sophie.' He sounded bleak. His eyes bored into her as if he was trying to see into her soul.

Frantically thinking of something to say, she said the last thing she wanted to say. 'You haven't got Ali with you?'

He frowned slightly. 'Ali? No – no, she's gone back to the States.'

'Oh.' This was something. Not exactly good news but not bad, either.

'I'll be going back there myself soon.'

'Oh.' This was definitely bad news. In fact she felt tears

328

prick her lashes. She thought she'd been so utterly bereft already. She wasn't prepared to be even more so.

'Yes. My grandmother wanted me – and you, obviously – to sort out the house before I go back.'

'I see. I don't know why it needed two of us.'

He shrugged. 'Good to have a woman's eye on things, I guess.'

Moira broke the silence. 'Would you like coffee or anything? I'll be making soup and salad for lunch a bit later, but if you'd like something now I could easily—'

'No thank you,' said Luke. 'I had a cup of coffee while I waited for my hire car to be ready.' He looked at Sophie. 'Shall we go to the house now?'

Sophie opened her mouth to refuse but Moira said, 'Yes, do go. Becky said she'd be there at half past twelve. She's joining us for lunch here.'

'Come on, Sophie,' said Luke. He moved round the kitchen table to where she stood. 'And by the way, how are you?'

'I'm absolutely fine,' she said crisply, still fighting tears. 'How are you?'

'I'm good too,' he said. 'Come on.'

He led them to his car in the car park; she didn't argue or insist they travelled separately or in hers. She wasn't going to show him she cared; she was going to keep her feelings hidden whatever happened.

'I was surprised that Matilda wanted me to help decide on paint colours and things,' she said after they had set off. 'Especially as she's hired an interior designer. A friend of a friend of Moira's.'

'I think Moira must know an example of every kind of tradesman there is,' said Luke.

'Yes, she is that sort of person. I love her,' she added, in case Luke thought she was being critical.

'She's a great woman,' Luke agreed.

'Talking of great women, your grandmother—' Sophie stopped, suddenly aware that she was about to be critical of someone very dear to Luke.

'Yes? What about her?'

'I think she might be up to something,' said Sophie.

'What do you mean?'

Sophie looked out of the window. If Luke didn't suspect that his grandmother wanted him and Sophie to be together, she wasn't going to mention it, and she was probably wrong anyway. 'Oh, I don't know. You don't mind that she bought the house?'

He shook his head. 'I did think it was foolish and whimsical at first but her heart was set on it.'

'But why involve us?' She wanted to say 'me' but didn't want to make it too personal.

He shrugged. 'She needs us to tell the designer and the builders, if necessary, what we think should be done with the house.'

'But we don't know what she wants the house for, do we? Has she told you?'

'No. She said we were to look at it and think how best it could be used.'

'It could be converted into holiday flats,' said Sophie, hating the idea. 'That would make the most money, I should think.'

'I don't think my grandmother is interested in making money out of it.'

'Oh. So what does she want done with it, do you think? It's a pity she can't come over herself and see it. I mean, what is the point in buying it if she doesn't come and see it? It's crazy.'

'Well, at last we agree on something.'

A couple of young men were mixing cement. The

machine was whirling away, fuelled by the generator. Sophie was terribly grateful she had seen it in silence, in the beauty of the morning.

'They seem to be doing a great job!' said Luke over the noise of the machinery.

'They've replaced the roof, quite a lot of the woodwork and the floors,' she shouted back. 'Let's go inside.'

They said hello to the builders and explained who they were, and then went inside, where it was quiet. Sunshine poured in through the big windows. They walked through the house in silence, taking in the space.

The old kitchen had high windows you couldn't see out of, a huge range and a built-in dresser.

'I can't decide if I like this kitchen or not,' said Sophie. 'I do love the period features but it's not very cosy, is it?'

'Does it need to be cosy?' asked Luke, inspecting the bell indicator above the door.

'Oh yes. Kitchens have to be cosy. Think of Moira's.'

'But only if this was a family home,' said Luke.

'Yes.' The thought of this house being converted into flats was suddenly depressing. It should be full of children, running through it, making a noise and banging into chairs. 'I wonder if they'd let you lower the windowsills, and maybe put on a sunroom. Then you could have a huge, live-in kitchen with an open fire and a sofa. I've always wanted a kitchen with an open fire and a sofa.'

'Have you?'

The bleakness Sophie was aware of when she first saw Luke seemed more pronounced. She so wanted to make him smile, make him happy, she almost ran to him so she could hug him. But whilst they were conversing quite easily there was still an air of formality between them. He was so polite.

Fortunately her sense of self-preservation made her

prattle instead. 'Oh yes! Think of being curled up on a sofa by the fire – or a woodburner – while someone else is cooking, chatting away. And if it was a sunroom as well, that would be bliss. You could have big double doors that you'd open in summer. You could have some solar heating panels.'

'You seem to have very definite ideas,' said Luke. 'I thought you didn't know what the house needed.'

'Oh, I know what I'd like if it was my house, but it isn't. It's Matilda's.' Her joy in her daydream faded along with it. Her mind was no longer full of chubby, barefoot children running in from the garden to show her something as she made nourishing soup, and she was back to being the girl who was never going to be part of Matilda's family.

'Shall we look upstairs?' said Luke.

There were five big bedrooms on the first floor. A family bathroom still had an exceptionally long bath in it, with claw feet. There was a lavatory with a wooden seat and an overhead flush.

'So is that period detail or something you'd change?' asked Luke.

'I'm not sure. It's fun but, like the kitchen, not exactly cosy. Although of course you could fit a lot of children in that bath.'

'Would you like to have a lot of children, Sophie?'

Something about the way he said her name made her want to weep. For the first time there was a gentleness to his tone, a flicker of warmth, but perhaps she had imagined it. 'Yes,' she said huskily. 'Let's go up to the attic. I want to find the bedroom Matilda slept in when she was little. And I want to see if you can see the sea.'

They found what must have been the room. It hadn't been touched. There was a narrow metal bed, a rag rug on the floor and a blanket box. Sophie went straight to the window.

'Look! The sea!'

Luke came up behind her. She could hear his breathing, smell his cologne. It was only too easy to imagine leaning back against him. 'Oh yes,' he said. 'There's the sea.'

They stayed looking at the view for a few moments and then it became too much for Sophie. If he wasn't hers, she didn't want to be near him. He didn't seem the same Luke now. He was so cut off, reserved, it was as if he didn't have feelings any more. Or if he had them, no one but he was going to know about them.

'Let's see what there is in the other attic room. The builders don't seem to have been up here at all.'

'Oh, there's a double bed in here, and a mattress,' she said. 'No priceless antiques though.' She went to the window and looked out to see if the view was different.

Just then a car drew up.

'I think the designer is here.'

'I'll go down and let her in,' said Luke.

Sophie stood looking down as Becky parked her car and Luke greeted her, and then she went down a flight of stairs to the first floor so she could get a quick look at the master bedroom. She was just turning away so she could join them downstairs when a huge black car came through the gate.

She watched, transfixed, as Luke and Becky turned to see it. It pulled up and a woman got out of the back seat and then waited as an elderly lady got out.

'Matilda!' said Sophie and started to head for the stairs. Then she hesitated. Let Luke greet Matilda first, let him introduce her to Becky.

She watched Luke cross to his grandmother in two strides. He lifted her off her feet to hug her before gently setting her down again.

Sophie couldn't hear what was said but there was laughter and then silence as Matilda stood and looked at the house she'd been searching for so long.

After a few moments Sophie could bear the suspense no longer. She had to find out what Matilda thought. She took a last look out of the window and suddenly noticed that the creeper was just coming into flower. It was a wisteria.

Chapter Twenty-Three

❧

'Sophie! Honey! How lovely to see you! You look – well!'

Sophie hugged Matilda almost as hard as Luke had done. 'Matilda! Why didn't you say you were coming?'

'Well, to be honest, I didn't know myself. Then I thought of you being here, and Luke being here, looking at my house together, and I thought: Why aren't I there too? So I arranged for April and me to come over. I just thought we should all be together at this time.'

Sophie wanted to ask 'What time?' as there seemed nothing special to celebrate but didn't. Matilda was quite elderly and had just endured an Atlantic crossing. Instead she said, 'I'm sure you came first class and have been chauffeur-driven but it's still some journey! Was the traffic awful from London?'

Matilda shook her head, ever so slightly pitying. 'No, dear, we just came from the airport. Only about forty minutes or so.'

'Granny came from Newquay,' Luke explained. 'Private jet.'

'Oh.' Sophie had assumed she'd got used to being around rich people but the thought of taking a private jet across the Atlantic just seemed like a fantasy, or a film.

'And April looked after me,' said Matilda. 'April? Come and meet Sophie.'

April appeared. She was a pleasant, middle-aged woman who seemed a little surprised to find herself in

Cornwall surrounded by strange people. 'If you don't mind,' she said, having greeted everyone politely, 'I'll go and sit in the car and rest. I don't sleep well on planes.'

'So how did you find the house?' asked Sophie, remembering how difficult it had been for her and Luke to track it down.

'Our driver put in the postcode and brought us straight here,' said Matilda.

Of course he did. What a boringly practical answer.

'It seems funny – and sort of wrong – for the house to have a postcode,' said Sophie, to herself, really.

'I know,' said Luke, to Sophie's surprise. 'It seems too modern a concept for this place.'

Just for a moment their eyes met and Sophie wondered if the house meant as much to him as it did to her. But it didn't seem possible – not the Luke he was now. Before he'd been whisked back into the real world by Ali, she would have believed that, but things had changed. She knew where he really belonged.

'Now, let me see the house,' said Matilda. 'Becky and Sophie, come with me.' She hooked her arm through Sophie's and seemed to sink into reminiscence. 'I'm not sure how old I was when I first came here, but we were collected from the station in a horse and trap. I do remember that. The horse was a giant! He probably was pretty big, but to me, about two feet tall, well, I barely came up to his knee. It took a long time to get here from the station and when we'd gone through the ford my grandmother – I think it was my grandmother – one of the two old ladies, anyway, said: "Not long to go now." I slept in that little room . . . Hey! I have my camera! I promised them back home that I'd take pictures.'

Matilda wandered from room to room finding a memory in each one and taking photos. Becky and Luke went with her up to her little bedroom, but Sophie stayed behind. The stairs were too narrow and the space too small for everyone. Thinking that Matilda would be getting tired, she gathered together the chairs that the builders used for their breaks and arranged them in the sitting room, where it was sunny. The wind was getting up a bit and she didn't want Matilda getting cold. She wished they had a flask or something, so Matilda could have a drink.

But Matilda still seemed full of energy when she led the others to where Sophie had arranged the chairs. 'My little room is just the same! The bed, the blanket box and the rag rug. All those years!' She frowned. 'It may not be the same rag rug, of course, but it's very like it.'

'That's amazing,' said Sophie. 'Now why don't you have a bit of a rest?'

Although she seemed to have coped with the journey amazingly well Matilda obligingly sat down and so did everyone else.

'So, Becky, honey, what are your thoughts?' she asked when they were all seated.

'The thing is, Mrs Winchester,' said Becky, 'unless I know what you want to do with the house, I really can't help. Is it going to be a family home? Are you going to rent it out? Or you could divide it into holiday flats?'

'Let's think of it as a family holiday home,' said Matilda, having glanced at Sophie and Luke. She might have been seeking an opinion, but she didn't get one.

'OK,' said Becky. 'Let's think of the big picture. What room is the most important?'

'The kitchen,' said Sophie, forgetting it wasn't really her business. 'And currently, I don't like it.'

'It's very traditional. Change it and you might lose period features,' said Becky. 'Fortunately it's not listed so you can do what you like, but you should think of the integrity of the building.'

'You can't see out of the windows,' said Sophie. 'It reminds me of old schools where the windows are high to let in light but you can't see out. I expect they were like that here for the same reason, so the skivvies could go on skivvying without distraction.'

'Oh!' said Becky, who seemed surprised Sophie was so vehement.

Sophie was a bit surprised too. 'But if you put a big conservatory on the side of the house and took out that wall, you could have the fireplace, sunshine and loads of space.'

'It is an outside wall,' said Becky, making notes, 'but we could put in a steel or something to prop it up. It would be expensive though,' she added.

'Let's not worry about cost now,' said Matilda.

'And we need more bathrooms,' said Luke.

Becky nodded. 'Fortunately the rooms are large and we could put in en suites without having to lose bedrooms. I had a good look when I came the other day,' she added to Matilda, explaining her knowledge of the building.

'Would you want a formal dining room, if you expanded the kitchen so much?' asked Sophie warming to the theme. 'If not, what would you do with that room? It's huge.'

'A family room would be a good idea,' said Matilda. 'A place where the younger folks can hang out.'

'Hang out, Grandmother?' said Luke, smiling.

'You know what I mean, dear,' said Matilda.

'What sort of budget are you looking at?' asked Becky. Luke and Matilda both looked at her blankly. 'How much money is there to spend? It helps if I know how much you want to spend before I start planning on gold taps in all the bathrooms.'

'That's faucets to you,' said Sophie to Luke.

'We don't need to worry about expense,' said Matilda. 'We just want quality.'

'Fine,' said Becky, scribbling madly.

Matilda got up, 'Sophie dear, would you take me upstairs again? I want to go into the attic to take a picture of my little bedroom, I forgot earlier.'

'Of course!' Sophie went behind Matilda, ready to catch her on the twisting attic stairs if she fell, but Matilda went up sure-footedly and crossed to the window.

'Isn't it wonderful? Those views!' said Sophie 'This must have been the perfect room for a little girl.'

Matilda took pictures before they went into the other room together. 'This is bigger,' said Matilda. 'You could possibly knock through and make a master suite up here.'

'You should tell Becky, if that's what you want,' said Sophie. 'It would be amazing.'

'Well, would you like that?'

Sophie frowned. 'Well, actually, if it was my house, and I had children, I wouldn't want to be so far away from them.'

'Do you want children, Sophie?' It was the second time that day that someone had asked her that question.

'Oh yes. Always have. Not until I've got the right man, of course, but I've always wanted a big family.' She paused. 'There's no guarantee I'll have one though.' She sighed, wondering if she'd ever fall in love again or if Luke would always be the man who stayed in her dreams when her real life was with someone quite different.

Matilda patted her arm. 'There are wonderful techniques for those with fertility problems these days.'

In spite of her wistful mood Sophie chuckled. She hadn't actually been worrying about her fertility, more the father of her children. 'Have you seen enough? You must be getting tired.'

'I am a little,' Matilda confided. 'But don't tell Luke. He's still a little cross with me for buying this house but I have my reasons and I think it's going to be great fun setting it all in order.'

'And I suppose if you have a private jet you can pop over and visit whenever you like.'

'Yes, dear,' said Matilda and set off down the stairs.

Becky had a clipboard and had been making sketches. 'I just need to find out a bit more about your tastes, what colours and fabrics you like, Mrs Winchester,' she said as Sophie and she appeared again. 'It's such a gift of a project! I'll make you up a mood board.'

Matilda smiled. 'Well, dear, I think you should talk about it with Sophie. My ideas might be rather behind the times.'

Sophie laughed. 'I don't think so! You suggested making the attic into a master suite! That's a very "now" sort of idea.'

'Mm, Sophie didn't care for it, so we won't do that.'

'Don't go on what I want, it's your house! I was just saying what I felt—' Suddenly aware of Luke's gaze upon her Sophie stopped. She didn't want to share her dreams of children with him!

'So, Mrs Winchester. . .' said Becky. She was probably finding her client a little difficult to pin down. 'What do you like? Are your tastes contemporary, as Sophie suggests? Or do you like something a bit more in keeping with the house?'

'In keeping with the house, I suggest,' said Luke. Everyone turned to him.

Matilda inclined her head. 'That sounds right to me? What do you think, Sophie?'

'I don't know! I don't like those houses you see in television programmes where everything is exactly in period but you wonder how comfortable they'd be. I think you need a middle way between traditional and modern.'

'Your instincts are perfect,' said Becky, scribbling away. 'Now I should have a look round the outside of the house.'

'Luke and Sophie, do go with Becky. I think I'll rest a while.'

Sophie shivered as they got outside and Becky fetched her coat from her car. The beautiful morning was changing and now dark clouds were crossing the sky, reminding the world that it was still only April, it was not summer yet.

While they walked up to the walled garden and Luke and Becky discussed the virtues of swimming pools – covered and heated with solar panels – versus a vegetable garden, Sophie wondered if she should stay. With Matilda here herself, she wasn't really needed. And was being near Luke but not with him a pleasure or a pain? It was lovely hearing his voice and seeing him; watching him with Matilda, so fond and protective, she couldn't help remembering when he'd been like that with her. But then Ali had come, forcing reality on to them – her, anyway. Luke had probably always known it was only a transient thing that never could have survived the real world.

She wandered down from the walled garden to the back of the house, where nothing had been changed for years and years, and rejoined Becky, Luke and Matilda.

'Sophie, honey,' said Matilda, who seemed full of energy again after her rest. 'What colours would you like in your kitchen?'

'In this kitchen, do you mean? Well, obviously, it would be up to the owner, but I like warm yellows and reds. Maybe a pale biscuit colour. What do you think, Becky?'

'If you had some pretty curtains, you could pick up a shade from them,' said Becky. 'And if you had a sofa, you could pick up another shade, unless you find something old that you just leave – for the shabby-chic look.'

'Shabby chic?' Matilda looked at Luke and they both looked at Sophie, who was laughing.

'That may be a foreign concept to you,' Sophie said. 'It's probably a British thing.'

'Not at all,' said Luke. 'We have it in the States too.'

'So what sort of fabrics do you like?' Matilda asked, moving on, obviously not keen on things that were tatty.

'I don't know really,' said Sophie. 'I've never actually chosen fabric for anything. I always make do with what's available. I think the thought of having too much choice would be rather daunting.'

'Becky, honey, why don't you put together some samples and let Sophie choose from those,' suggested Matilda.

'I don't understand! Why are you going with my choices?' asked Sophie. 'Matilda, it should be what *you* like. Can you remember what sort of fabrics were here when you were little?'

'Not really. I was very small, although I do remember birds,' said Matilda.

'Oh, William Morris!' said Becky. 'It would be about right for the house. I'll source some samples.'

Matilda yawned and Luke was instantly by her side. 'You're tired, Granny. Let me go with you to your hotel. Where are you staying?'

'We don't have anything booked. We thought we'd just find something when we got here,' Matilda said.

'The nearest decent hotel is in Truro,' said Becky. 'There's nothing nearer.'

'Where are you staying, honey?' Matilda asked Luke.

'We're staying in a bed and breakfast—' he began.

'With a lovely woman called Moira,' interrupted Sophie, seeing a way to leave without appearing to be running away. 'You could have my room, Matilda. It's very quaint

342

and comfortable.' She was about to say, 'Isn't it, Luke?' but managed to stop herself in time.

He didn't seem to care so much about discretion. 'Yes, it is a nice room, even if it is much smaller than you're used to.'

'It's a double!' said Sophie indignantly and then remembered that Matilda's suite at her home in Connecticut probably exceeded the square footage of Moira's entire house.

'And there is another room for April,' said Luke.

The realisation that Luke might have been seeking reasons to leave too suddenly felt like an affront, even though life would be so much easier without him. It was, she decided, because she didn't want to be left again, she wanted to be the one to leave this time.

'I'm sure Moira will know of another bed and breakfast where you two could stay,' said Becky.

'We need two rooms,' said Sophie, in case Becky didn't understand.

'You could have as many rooms as you like.' Becky didn't understand why Sophie needed to make a point of it.

'Anyway, let's all go back to Moira's,' said Luke. 'We can sort out sleeping arrangements then.'

'Do you think we should call ahead?' said Sophie to Becky. 'Having Matilda might seem a bit like receiving royalty.'

'I don't know Moira that well, but I'm sure she'll cope.'

Sophie made sure she got there first, although it meant driving faster than she usually did and parking her car outside Moira's house, partially blocking the road, instead of in the car park.

'Moira! Matilda – that's Luke's grandmother – is here from America, with a companion. They'll need your rooms. Is there anywhere Luke and I can stay? Or shall I just go home?'

'Calm down, you're gabbling,' said Moira. 'How many people do I have to find room for?'

'Four, but don't worry, I know you can't. I'll just go and park the car. The others will be here in a minute.'

Although it was now raining quite hard, she took her time walking back. She wanted to allow Luke time to do introductions and explanations, and also to give herself an opportunity to plan a short speech of farewell, using the lack of accommodation as an excuse for her having to hurry back home.

She took off her wet coat and was ushered into the kitchen where the others were drinking tea and eating cake. She opened her mouth to explain about why she should leave immediately, when Matilda said, 'It's fine, honey. Moira has a friend with rooms. You and Luke can go and stay there. I still need you to be around.'

'I should be going back to London,' said Luke. 'I have a meeting.'

'Not till the afternoon,' said Matilda, 'you said. And you can take the plane. I need you here to help Becky with decisions.'

Sophie sipped her tea, reflecting that Matilda could be quite imperious when she needed to be. It would be very foolish to dismiss her as a sweet old lady. Old and sweet she may be, but she had a strong will and seemed to have no trouble getting people to do what she wanted them to.

'We don't have to decide anything yet,' said Becky. 'I'll put together a mood board, based on what we've talked about. That should give you enough to say if you hate anything.' She said this to the kitchen table, laden with mugs and plates and cake, obviously not sure who her client really was.

'You could send Matilda pictures, couldn't you?' said Sophie. 'Then she can show her family the house and your ideas.'

'Of course I could,' said Becky. 'Just as soon as I've got some thoughts together, I'll do that.'

'Pictures!' said Matilda. 'I've just realised, I don't seem to have my camera with me. April, honey? Did I give it to you?'

'I was napping in the car,' said April. 'Did you give it to Mr Winchester?'

Luke shook his head.

'You definitely had it in your old bedroom,' said Sophie. 'You took loads of pictures. You've probably left it there.' She got up. 'I should have checked you had it. I'll go back and get it.'

'But it's raining!' said Matilda.

'I know! I won't dissolve!' said Sophie gaily, glad of an excuse to leave the crowded kitchen, which seemed full of confusion and misunderstanding, not to mention Luke.

'Really,' said Moira, 'I wouldn't go unless it's really urgent. What with this wind and all the streams being full—'

'I'll be back before you know it!' said Sophie, pushing her chair back under the table.

'Well, you shouldn't go alone, obviously,' said Luke, frowning.

'There's no obviously about it. Just have the kettle on when I get back home.'

The wind did whip her with icy rain and her coat was still damp from before, but Sophie didn't regret her decision to go back to the house for Matilda's camera. Luke's protest that she shouldn't go on her own was pleasing. In a small way she was proving she could get along without him, and while he had been immensely helpful with her drilling-rights project, emotionally she could do just fine on her own.

Suddenly there was water everywhere and she realised that the hills must be riddled with little streams which were now turning into bigger streams, and the excess water was escaping down the road. She drove carefully, and felt perfectly in control. She was a practised driver now and, with her brand-new hire car, had confidence she could get to the house and back without mishap. She wondered what Moira would do about feeding everyone and felt a bit guilty about leaving her to start without help. But she'd be there in time to peel potatoes if any needed peeling, Moira knew that.

The little ford did look rather full and Sophie stopped to consider its depth. Had there been anywhere to turn round she might well have done that and gone back to Moira's. But there wasn't and so the best thing seemed to be to go slowly on.

The car stopped in the middle and she realised she'd drowned it. Fear, belated but strong, overtook her. She'd have to get out and walk. She opened the door, with some difficulty, and water rushed into the car. She just managed to grab her handbag before it was soaked too, and her mobile phone fell out.

Just for a second she watched it disappear and then realised she had no time to waste. She must get out of the car and out of the flood before it got any worse – while she still could.

Fortunately she could cling on to the car for support. She went onwards, knowing she couldn't go back. The house was not far ahead. She could break in there and find shelter.

When she had to let go of the car she was almost washed off her feet but she managed to grab hold of a branch and

346

haul herself out of the ford and on to the road. She stood there, breathless and shaking slightly. It was from relief, she realised. She was out of the stream. She hadn't drowned. The journey to the house, although it took twenty minutes, seemed like nothing.

She went to the back door straight away, hoping no one had locked it. To her relief, they hadn't and she let herself in.

Once out of the rain she burrowed in her bag for her torch, praying it hadn't been got at by the water. By a miracle, it hadn't. When she switched it on, the first thing she saw was a pile of wood shavings on the floor. She was in a pantry, she discovered, where the builders had swept up some rubbish to make the main house look tidy. Thank goodness they hadn't been tidy enough to sweep it into a plastic bag and actually throw it away. If she could find some way of lighting it, she could get a fire going if the emergency services took too long to get to her.

Her brain knew that she was perfectly safe, but the shock of being nearly swept away by the stream, and being on her own in an empty house, in the dark, was beginning to make her panic slightly. She didn't like the dark.

What she needed was something practical to do.

Her torch wouldn't last long so she turned it off and tried to get accustomed to the semi-dark as she gathered shavings, discarded newspaper, cigarette packets and other flammable items and took them into the dining room. It had a fireplace that she really hoped would work, and was smaller than the sitting room, so would warm up quicker.

She had to use the torch more than she wanted to and the thought of being alone in the empty house in the dark and cold pressed on her. She was frozen even though she was moving around. She couldn't keep moving all night to stave off the cold.

A combination of desperation and hope sent her to the back regions beyond the kitchen and pantry. It was an old house, there must be something she could get a light from, a stub of candle or a lamp with some oil still in it, maybe some meths she could get to start the fire.

The first two rooms she tried were empty and she became more frantic. Surely to goodness in this whole huge house there must be something she could use to help her.

In the last little room there was a shelf. It was obviously where the household had kept unconsidered trifles, jam jars full of rusty nails, old balls of gardening string, raffia for tying up plants and anonymous cardboard boxes. Sophie knew there would be spiders. There was no way she could go near that shelf without disturbing some monsters.

It was the thought of those spiders that sapped her spirit. She'd escaped a flood; she'd walked through the pouring rain; she was so wet even her knickers were soaking and she was so cold she was shivering convulsively. There on the shelf there could well be matches, a candle, oil, anything, and those humble household items might save her from freezing. Yet the thought of the eight-legged creatures who would run over her hand or flee from her fingers was stopping her from seeking her salvation.

'OK,' she said aloud, and immediately wished she hadn't; her voice sounded scary in the dark. 'In a minute, I'll just sweep everything off the shelf and see what lands.'

Then she realised she might break something that might be really useful and make warmth and light an even more impossible dream. There was nothing else for it, she'd have to face the spiders. She'd have to reach up and feel along, discerning by touch what might be of use and what wouldn't. She'd do it. In a minute.

She crouched down with her back against the wall, her soaking clothes squelching slightly as she did so, and closed her eyes. She was shivering violently. It will all be all right in the end, she told herself, very soon this will become a funny story to tell my friends. She imagined describing the awful spideriness of this cell-like little room, and everyone laughing as she described how utterly horrible it was. It would be all right, she knew – was certain. But when?

She wasn't sure how long she'd been there, crouched on the floor, willing herself to either go back into the main house or look for some matches – however slim her chances of finding some were – when she heard a noise. She screamed.

Chapter Twenty-Four

❦

Her brain knew it was not a mugger, a burglar, or even a ghost. She knew it was the police, the fire brigade, or someone sent to find her. But she couldn't stop adrenalin surging through her in violent waves making her body panic. Her scream echoing in the dark added to her terror.

There was a loud, confused mixture of swearing and exclamation and someone fell over her foot, landing on the floor. The swearing increased and Sophie detected an American accent.

'Luke?'

'For fuck's sake! Sophie! What the hell are you doing in here? I thought you were drowned!'

'Sorry to disappoint you.'

There was a roar, more swearing and then Sophie felt Luke's hands on her shoulders. They were gripping so tight it hurt. 'I thought you were dead, and you make jokes! What is wrong with you?'

'Sorry! I was scared out of my wits! What are you doing here? And why did you think I was dead!'

'Because you went out in a flood and you didn't answer your phone. People drown in flash floods, you know!'

'But I didn't drown, I'm fine!' Although she spoke bracingly she did feel a bit ashamed.

'You don't deserve to be fine.'

Under the distinct impression that she wouldn't stay fine long unless she was very careful, Sophie cleared her throat.

'But why did you look for me here? Not in the main house?'

'I searched the main house and you weren't there!' Luke was still roaring. 'What the hell are you doing in this hellhole?'

'I thought there might be something useful in here. I was looking for matches – something I could make a light with.' Sophie was aware she was gabbling. It would have helped if she could stop shaking.

The grip on her shoulders relaxed a little. 'I did wonder if that was what you were doing. If you weren't here, it would have meant you'd been swept away.'

'But I wasn't!'

'You didn't answer your phone!'

'Oh. That *was* swept away. It fell out of the car door when I opened the door.'

'It could have been you! Do you realise how much danger you were in? Moira said, just after you left, that if there's a lot of rain the streams get clogged up and then if the blockage gives way the water rushes down and floods happen in minutes!'

'Do they?' She didn't shout back because she felt incredibly stupid and ashamed.

'And you risked your life for a fucking camera!'

Sophie's sense of shame immediately diminished; she didn't respond positively to shouting and he was still holding on to her shoulders, giving her a little shake with every sentence. 'I didn't know about the flooding. Moira didn't tell me.'

'She did tell you!' He was shouting again. 'You just didn't listen! You're so headstrong!'

'I'm sorry. I didn't know—'

'You could have been drowned. I could have been drowned.'

351

'You didn't have to come! You could have just called for the fire brigade or the police or whatever!'

There was a pause. He let go of her shoulders. 'It's a wild night. They'll have had hundreds of calls. They might not have gotten to you before morning.'

As he became calmer she found her own anger. 'I'd have been fine! There was no need for you to risk your life to get me! I didn't ask you to!'

'Moira's going to see if she can round up someone with a vehicle – a tractor or something – to help.'

'I don't think I want to be responsible for anyone else getting soaked or risking their lives.'

'Oh, don't be bloody ridiculous!'

'I'm not being ridiculous! You could ring Moira and cancel the rescue vehicle!'

'No I can't!'

'Why?'

He sighed in exasperation. 'Because I left my cell in the car, on charge.'

'Where is your car?'

'On some higher ground. I walked quite a way.'

'Oh.'

'I came across your car and used it to help me cross the ford – which is now a river.'

Sophie slumped shivering back into her dark corner. She felt utterly miserable. She was soaking wet, freezing cold and Luke despised her. She despised herself. They could both of them have lost their lives.

'So,' he said after a few moments, 'did you find anything useful?' He sounded calm, but not friendly.

'Not yet. It's hard to find anything in the pitch dark.' She didn't add that her efforts had been hampered by her inability to engage with spiders.

'Let's go back to the main house,' said Luke. He leant

down and caught her elbow and then her wrist, pulling her up. 'You're freezing!'

She couldn't speak, her teeth were chattering too much. She knew it was shock as much as cold.

'Come on.' He hooked his arm round her shoulders and held on, half pushing her along back into the main part of the house. Once there she calmed down a bit and shook herself free from his arm. She pushed back wet strings of hair and felt she'd never be warm again. Although it was dark outside some light came through the windows. She could see Luke rummaging in a bag.

He pulled something out. 'Here's the flashlight.' The torch being on somehow made the room seem darker. 'Hold it.'

Luke handed the torch to her and she aimed it at the bag while Luke sorted through it. 'Here.' He pulled out a bag and handed it to Sophie. 'It's a sweater. The rest is food, a couple of candles and some matches.'

'That's amazing.' She took the jumper out of its wrapping and pulled it on over her wet clothes. 'There wouldn't be a towel in there, would there?'

'No!'

He still sounded incredibly cross; although it could just be that he was so cold. 'Never mind,' said Sophie, trying to sound positive, 'we can make a fire and have a picnic. Warm ourselves up.'

'How will we make a fire?'

'There are wood shavings and all sorts in the old pantry. I expect we could find logs in one of the outhouses. You brought the matches. I don't suppose Moira put any fire lighters in her emergency pack, did she?'

'No. She was in a hurry. We thought you might drown or be so wet and cold you'd die of hypothermia. We hoped you'd get to the house but we couldn't be sure you would.'

Sophie swallowed, taking in how much danger she'd been in. 'I'm sorry.'

She was freezing and she also wanted to do something to make Luke stop despising her so much. She had to. 'I'll get going on the fire. Do something to keep us warm.'

'I don't think much of your chances. But you'll need these.' He tossed the box of matches at her and they landed on the floor.

'Thanks.' She spoke warily. 'Perhaps you could look for some logs?'

Taking the torch, he stormed out of the room. She found her little key-ring torch and made her way to the pantry into which the builders had swept all the rubbish. Why was Luke still so furious? She could understand relief at finding her alive could translate into anger; that was normal. But to go on being angry was unreasonable. She was the injured party here – if anyone, it should be her being angry with him!

Fortunately there was a bucket there and quite a lot of timber offcuts as well as shavings. She soon filled the bucket with good flammable stuff. Maybe if she got a fire going, and he felt warmer, his mood would improve.

She knew that people didn't usually get that cross with someone they were indifferent to. Was this true in Luke's case? She squashed the tiny stirring of hope immediately she recognised it; Luke didn't want her, he had Ali.

She started building a fire. A copy of the *Sunday Sport* was rolled into balls and placed in the grate. Wood shavings were placed on top. Then splinters of timber and, finally, a couple of the larger offcuts.

Smoke billowed out and the fire suddenly seemed a very bad idea, but it could just be because the chimney was cold. It could also be, Sophie knew perfectly well, because the chimney was blocked. This wasn't good. If Luke had been

354

ready to throttle her before, how would he be with her now the room was uninhabitable? They could always go somewhere else but Sophie wanted the warmth and comfort of a fire, not to sit in the freezing cold with a hostile man.

She opened a window and let some of the smoke out. With luck the worst would have gone by the time Luke came back and she could put it down to a cold chimney and not a completely dysfunctional one. The house had been lived in by an old lady; surely she would have had real fires, as in the old days?

The smoke began to clear and, when no more came, Sophie shut the window, trading fresh air for warmth. Then she drew up two chairs left by the builders to the fire and peered inside the bag.

It produced several plastic boxes. One contained fruit cake, another cheese. There were oatcakes and a bottle of brandy, half full. There were some metal beakers and a bottle of water and a couple of candles. These she lit and stuck with wax on to the mantelpiece, trusting that the woodwork would be stripped or painted or something and she wouldn't be doing permanent damage.

Luke was being ages, she realised. Why was he taking so long? He had the torch. What could have happened to him? Now worry about Luke added to her general misery. She sat as close to the fire as she could get, her hands practically in it, but it had no warmth yet, and she was as cold as ever.

She decided to rearrange her soaking clothes. She took off Moira's jumper that she'd put on over her coat, took off the coat and then put the jumper back on. Her jeans were clinging to her horribly and after a moment's consideration she took off first her boots, which were completely ruined, and then her jeans. At the moment they were just making sure her legs stayed wet and cold.

The wettest clothes she draped over the back of one of the chairs and put it at the side of the fire. If they got up a really good blaze some of them might get slightly less damp.

She had only just made herself decent when she heard Luke. 'What took you so long?' she demanded, startled. 'I was really worried!'

It was the wrong thing to say. 'I found logs,' he said, depositing a huge basket of them down with a thump. 'But they needed splitting. Fortunately there was also an axe.' His heavy breathing indicated this had been hard work.

'Oh, can you do that?' went on Sophie, partly to cover her self-consciousness about being only half dressed.

'Yes I can do that! I don't know what sort of an idiot you think I am but I can split logs!'

'I just thought—'

Luke threw two big logs on to Sophie's fire, causing sparks to fly up the chimney. 'I don't think you think much at all!'

Sophie wished she'd kept her clothes on. She felt very vulnerable with bare feet. 'Yes I do.' She didn't sound very convinced.

'You didn't have to go out in this weather – fetching Matilda's camera is hardly a life-saving activity! It wasn't just your life you put at risk, you know.'

'Actually, you know, I think I've apologised enough! I made an error of judgement; I didn't know that floods came up so quickly here but no one has died. We're fine. When will you stop being so angry about it?'

A log fell and suddenly there was more light. She could see his expression but she couldn't understand it.

'I had faith in you, Sophie. I thought you were a nice girl, talented, with integrity. But I was wrong.'

'Really?' She didn't know if she was questioning his first opinion of her, or his second.

356

'Yes! I discovered that, actually, you had your eye on the main chance all along.'

'I'm still not getting it.'

'You made friends with my grandmother—'

'She made friends with *me*.'

'She trusted you! You helped her, although it was in a mad scheme—'

'You helped her too!'

'Not to sink a fortune into a wreck.'

Sophie shrugged. 'I didn't do that. She's a very determined person. She does what she likes.'

'She would never have done it if it wasn't for you! She almost said as much.'

'Did she? Well, that's not my responsibility.'

'I think it is, and I think you should *take* responsibility!'

'No! You knew she wanted to buy the house. You're her grandson, she would have listened to you.'

'Well, she didn't – because of you!'

Her control gave way. She'd tried so hard to be reasonable, and understanding, but the unfairness of this fused all Sophie's adrenalin, discomfort and anxiety into a rage that matched Luke's and then some.

'*How dare you!* You pompous, overbearing idiot, blaming me for what Matilda has done!'

'Ali said . . .' He paused.

'What? What did Ali say? And what has what Ali says to do with the price of fish?'

'She told me that you and your boyfriend were probably planning to get something out of my grandmother – possibly the house!'

'Oh did she? Well, for a start I haven't got a boyfriend—'

'Yes you have!'

'No I haven't! I wasn't the one who—' But she couldn't finish the sentence out loud, that she wasn't the one who'd

357

had amazing sex with a person who was actually committed elsewhere.

'You have a boyfriend,' Luke stated. 'There was the text. Ali read it. It was quite clear.'

'We won't go into the matter of Ali reading texts on my phone but if she assumed that about my life, I assure you . . .' She paused. 'Did you read the text yourself?'

'No.'

'Well, that's a shame because I think it would prove that while this particular person, who I did go out with for a short time, is in the habit of texting me when he's drunk and lonely, we are no longer together and hadn't been for months when I met you.' She paused for breath, no longer worrying about keeping her feelings for him hidden. 'You, on the other hand, you preppy millionaire rich boy, took me for a high old ride! Will you pretend to be my fiancée so the girls won't pester me? Will you take me in when I'm penniless in England? Will you have sex with me almost the whole night through because *my girlfriend*' – she spat out the word – 'isn't available and I get a headache if I don't have sex!'

'It wasn't like that!'

'And don't think the fact that you helped me with my drilling rights makes it any better. I paid you for your time!'

'You what?' Suddenly it was Luke who was the most angry again. 'You did what?'

'You heard me! You're not deaf! I paid you for your time out of money Uncle Eric gave me.'

'Oh, so you've got him giving you handouts, have you? Why doesn't that surprise me?'

'How dare you say that! I love Uncle Eric and he gave me that money so I could do my course without having to wait for the oil money to come through. I spent some of it on paying for your time.'

'I didn't know that,' he said stiffly.

'Too up ourselves to check the accounts, are we? Well, Ali told me how much I owed and I paid it. And no, I didn't get a receipt!'

'You were not meant to pay me. I gave my time pro bono. For nothing.'

'I know what it means, thank you! And nobody likes a smart-arse!'

'Sophie!'

Luke sounded shocked, whether because of her language or something else, Sophie couldn't tell, but she suddenly found herself wanting to giggle. She tried to hide it but she couldn't. The more she knew it was the wrong thing to do, the more she giggled.

'Are you laughing at me?' He didn't wait for an answer. He strode towards her, knocking over the torch, and took hold of her shoulders so hard it hurt. He growled, 'I don't know what to do with you! Murder seems a good choice.'

Sophie was frightened but she wasn't going to show it. She licked her lips and cleared her throat.

'No so fast with the smart replies now, are you?'

Sophie knew she had to make him laugh too, if she possibly could. It was a high-risk strategy but she had to try. 'If this were a film you'd call me a silly little fool and kiss me passionately.'

'Oh would I? Well, we'll see how you like it!'

The pressure of his mouth was such that Sophie tasted blood as their teeth clashed. His hold on her was punishing, as was his kiss, but she responded to him as petrol responds to flame.

They swayed and fought in the firelight, neither willing to let go, both wanting to inflict damage with their passion. Tongues, lips, fingers bit and clung until at last Luke broke away.

'Jesus Christ, Sophie. My life would be so much easier if I didn't want you so much.'

Sophie couldn't speak. Even fighting her way out of the swollen river hadn't taken so much out of her. She closed her eyes and tried to get her breath back.

'Here,' said Luke after a few moments. 'Drink this.' He handed her a metal beaker. 'Brandy. I think you need it. I think we both do.'

She took a large sip, coughed and then felt a bit better. 'You're a good kisser, Luke Winchester. I'll say that for you.'

'Why, you little—'

There was a banging on the front door that made them both jump.

'That'll be the cavalry,' said Luke, looking down into Sophie's eyes. 'Just in time. Before I have my preppy-millionaire-rich-boy way with you again.'

Sophie was laughing, hiding her desperate disappointment under her sense of the ridiculous. 'You'd better let them in. I'll make myself decent.'

Sophie forced her legs into her wet jeans, thinking there was nothing more unpleasant and wishing and wishing that the cavalry had not arrived and she and Luke could have shared another night of passion, even if it did mean spending it on splintery floorboards. She would have felt terribly guilty – she knew now that Luke was taken – but she would have done it.

'Well, my bewdy, what you been up to then?' A couple of burly Cornish farmers came into the room. 'Should have known better than to come out on a night like this!'

'I'm terribly sorry to have caused so much trouble,' said Sophie. 'Where I come from floods don't happen quite so quickly.'

'How did you get here?' asked Luke. 'If the road is flooded and blocked with Sophie's car?'

'Back way up the fields,' said the farmer. 'Young Moira told me where you were. Had to come and get you, didn't we?'

'We're terribly grateful,' said Sophie. 'It would have been dreadful to have to spend the night here.'

'Looks like you've made yourselves quite cosy,' said the farmer, indicating the fire.

'But there's nothing to sleep on,' said Sophie. 'I don't suppose.' She felt sure these two kindly men knew what she and Luke would have been doing.

'It's very kind of you to come out on a night like this to rescue us,' said Luke.

'Yes. I really am sorry. I was very silly. If I'd known . . .'

'Well, hindsight is a perfect science,' said one of the men.

'And she only came to get a camera,' said Luke. 'I'd better get it.'

'It's in the attic. I think I know where it is,' said Sophie. 'Give me the torch and I'll fetch it.'

'I'll go, you've got nothing on your feet.'

Luke left the room and Sophie gathered up the things. She picked up her boots last. They were so sad now, soggy and crumpled. They seemed to symbolise her relationship with Luke: once beautiful and lovely, now fit for nothing but the dustbin, really. As she pushed her feet down into the slimy leather, she sighed, wondering if she'd ever be able to bring herself to throw them away.

Chapter Twenty-Five

❧

One of the farmers helped Sophie through the walled garden and up the hill to where the tractors were. The other was guiding Luke back to his car over the fields so he wouldn't have to wade through the ford. They'd leave her car until the morning; the floods were too fierce down there at present for anyone to risk their lives any more than they had to.

'I feel so awful putting you through all this, through my own stupidity,' said Sophie as she stumbled and slipped through the mud on boots that no longer seemed to fit.

'It's all right, my bird, you weren't to know.'

'And will Luke's car be all right? Will he be able to drive back to Moira's?'

'Reckon so. Are you and he "together" as they say these days?'

'No. Not at all.'

The farmer paused, possibly sensing Sophie's desolation. 'Soon have you up in the cab of the tractor, warm as toast and on your way home.'

'I just feel so guilty about all this.'

'Don't you worry about that! We're used to it in these parts.'

Moira was waiting for them when the tractor finally arrived at her front door.

'Are you all right?' She hugged Sophie to her.

'She's fine,' said the farmer. 'Cold though. Needs a hot

bath and something to eat. But I reckon you'll see her right, Moira.'

'I certainly will, Ted,' said Moira. 'And there's a meal in it for you and the family too.'

'Best get her inside now. I'll see you soon!'

'So, did you enjoy your ride in the tractor?' Moira asked when she'd led Sophie into the kitchen.

'Oh Moira, I feel so awful! Those lovely men could have been drowned because of me! And Luke!' She frowned. 'Is he back yet?'

'Not yet. I'm putting him in my office. There's a single bed in there. It's quite comfortable. I sleep there myself if I've got a lot of guests. Matilda and April have gone to bed,' she added.

Sophie frowned. 'You *have* got a lot of guests . . .'

'Don't worry. I've put you in my bedroom. I'm going to spend the night with my friend next door.'

'Shouldn't Luke have your bedroom? I'd be fine in the office. He rescued me. He should get the best room.'

'Maybe,' said Moira, 'but I'd have to spend hours tidying my room to put him in it. You can cope with the mess.'

Sophie came over and hugged Moira again. 'You're a lifesaver – literally.'

'Not at all! Now get into the bath. Use my bathroom.'

'What about Luke?'

'He can have a shower in the guest bathroom when he gets here. Don't worry! When you're ready, I've got some soup and I'll make sandwiches.'

'You're so wonderful, Moira, sending the rescue-pack and everything.'

'Get on with you, girl! You're making puddles on my kitchen floor.'

'OK, but sorry for being such an idiot.'

'Out!'

Lowering herself into the hot, scented water felt like the most delicious, luxurious thing Sophie had ever done. There was nothing more blissful in the world than a hot bath when you're cold and damp, she decided. Just for a moment or two the joy of it masked the sadness that had permeated her body more completely than any amount of physical discomfort ever could. She'd so messed it up with Luke. Of course he had Ali, but he had felt something for her once, she was sure. But somehow, she'd ruined it all.

Moira had a bath pillow and Sophie rested her head on it and closed her eyes, revelling in the wonderful heat. She could hear noises in the distance: Luke must have come back. Moira would be making a fuss of him, she realised, feeling guilty for taking the bath. Perhaps she should get out and ask if he would like to lie full length in steaming hot water? But he might not want pre-loved water; and he was American, they went in for showers there.

She realised she had actually dropped off but didn't know for how long. The water was cooler and she could leave it without minding too much. She climbed out and dried herself, hunting on Moira's shelf for some sort of body lotion. When she'd smoothed some on she put on Moira's bathrobe and then dithered. She was hungry but did she want Luke to see her, her face still red from the bath and her hair in rats' tails because she hadn't pinned it up properly?

She couldn't face it. She brushed her teeth and got into bed. She'd see him in the morning, when she had make-up on and had had a chance to get her head round it all. She slept.

Her cleaving stomach woke her at seven. Then she remembered why she'd gone to bed without supper and considered pulling the duvet back over her head for a bit. No, that was just silly. She had to face Luke sometime. It might as well be now.

She saw that Moira had put her bag in the room, and a foil packet of sandwiches. She must have come up with them last night and Sophie had not heard her. Sophie started on a sandwich while she rummaged through her bag. Her one skirt, tights and a jumper and she was ready – except for her feet. There was no way she could wear her boots again, and certainly not now, while they were still wet.

She was still bracing herself to go downstairs when there was a tap on the door. It was Moira.

'Are you awake? Oh good, you're dressed. If you're ready, could you come down? There's a bit of an emergency and we think you can help.'

'Of course! Anything I can do. I'll come immediately.' She paused. 'Can I borrow your slippers?' She indicated a pair of sheepskin mules.

'Help yourself.'

Matilda and April were sitting at the table, Moira was doing duty over the Rayburn but there was no sign of Luke. Sophie relaxed somewhat.

'Good morning! Sorry I'm late.'

'You're not late, honey,' said Matilda. 'But we're pleased to see you.'

'You've obviously been up.'

'Old people tend to be early risers.'

'Did you sleep well?' asked Moira, handing Sophie a mug of tea.

'Like a log, thanks.' She pulled out a chair and sat down. 'Did you? I hope your friend's spare room was as comfortable as your bedroom was.'

'It was fine,' said Moira. 'Now, what about breakfast?'

Sophie noticed that Matilda and April had used plates in front of them, indicating that they'd had theirs. 'Is there time? What about this emergency? What do you need me to do?'

'You've got time for toast,' said Matilda. 'If you eat quickly.'

Moira glanced at her. 'I cooked bacon for Luke.'

'Toast is fine,' said Sophie. 'And where is Luke? Or is he still asleep?'

There was a tiny pause. 'Luke had to go, dear,' said Matilda. 'You won't remember but he said yesterday he had to get to a meeting.'

'Oh.' Although she'd been dreading seeing him, now she knew she wasn't going to, Sophie felt desperately disappointed. 'I'm sorry I didn't get to say goodbye and thank him for rescuing me.'

'That's all right, dear, you will have the opportunity. If you're willing to help us out.'

'The emergency,' explained Moira.

'It's to do with Luke. He rushed off in such a hurry I wasn't able to give him a very important document. He needs to sign it.'

'Oh.' Sophie put butter on the toast Moira had put on her plate, wishing Matilda would get to the point. Now she knew she had to do something she wanted to get on with it. 'How can I help?'

'We need you to go in the car, my car, to the airport, get him to sign it, and bring it back,' said Matilda. 'Do you mind very much? I would be so grateful.'

As Sophie had noticed before, Matilda had not got where she had in her life by lacking charm and persuasiveness on top of a steely ability to get her own way. Sophie was resistant to bullying but Matilda's smile was fairly irresistible. Frantically she cast around for an excuse – the thought of

366

meeting Luke alone, away from other people, was terrifying. 'I would go but I've got nothing to wear on my feet. My only pair of boots is ruined. I'm going to have to buy some before I can go home.'

'I'll lend you my loafers,' said Moira quickly.

'Couldn't April go?' suggested Sophie, looking at her. 'If it's urgent. She's got shoes on already.' Sophie smiled sweetly to indicate she wasn't being unhelpful, just practical, as was her way.

'She has a headache,' said Matilda, also quickly. 'We've been feeding her all sorts of painkillers but nothing seems to be working. Really, April, why don't you just give in and lie down?'

'We can look after Matilda between us,' said Moira.

'And I don't need looking after,' said Matilda.

'Very well,' said April. 'I'll do that. I'm sure I'll feel better soon.'

'You definitely will,' said Matilda.

'I'll bring you some water when I've sorted out Sophie,' said Moira.

'I'll bring my own water, don't worry,' said April, getting up.

Something didn't seem quite right to Sophie but she could hardly accuse April of faking a headache. Everyone else seemed convinced. 'Well, I'd better find some shoes then.' When she got to the doorway a thought occurred to her. 'Actually, couldn't your driver take the document, Matilda? If he's got to take me anyway—'

'Oh, I couldn't possibly trust a stranger with it, my dear! It's very important! I only met him yesterday.'

Matilda was sufficiently appalled to make Sophie realise she would have to go, however reluctantly. Still, if time was short, she wouldn't have to speak to Luke, just get his signature and get the hell out.

367

Moira joined her in the bedroom. 'I'll find you some shoes. I think your feet might be a bit bigger than mine but these are fairly sloppy.'

'They'll be fine. I've actually got quite small feet for my height. Now I'll just put some slap on . . .'

'Why don't you do it in the car?' said Moira. 'Take your whole bag. It'll save time.'

'Oh, OK. I'll probably poke my eye with the mascara, but there's bound to be a bit of a hold-up somewhere. There must still be floods and things,' Sophie agreed, stuffing her make-up bag into her handbag. 'When I come back, I must organise getting another phone. Luke was lucky his wasn't drowned or washed away.'

'Absolutely, but he was better prepared for a trip into the storm than you were.'

She wasn't actually reproachful but this made Sophie feel guilty all over again about causing everyone so much upset by not thinking. 'I expect you think I'm an idiot for going but where I come from it can rain an awful lot and there aren't any floods.'

'I know,' said Moira, 'I wasn't telling you off, just explaining. Now hurry up. Matilda's got the document all ready and she's waiting.'

The drama of the situation appealed to Sophie. She got into the back of the car, the large manila envelope in her hand, enjoying the luxury of being driven and also pleased that Luke would see that Matilda trusted her even if he didn't. Then she thought that Luke would probably consider Matilda to be deluded and so it wouldn't help. He knew she was on her way though; she had checked that before she set off.

There were signs of the night's storms everywhere. Mud coated many of the roads and washed-away items and stranded cars did hold them up several times. At the time

Sophie had thought it was only the area immediately round the house that was badly affected but now she realised that she and Luke had been lucky. It was very chastening, she realised, to learn how much worse it could have been. Thankfully Moira wasn't too concerned about her car, claiming that she had a friend who could fix it up in a trice.

It took the chauffeur-driven car just over half an hour to get to the airport, and because he went there all the time, the driver took Sophie to the right part for the private jets.

She got out of the womb-like back of the car, clutching her paper, feeling she had been delivered into a fantasy land of people who'd never flown cattle class and felt that even business class was a bit infra dig.

An attractive young woman in a smart suit and high heels was there to greet her. She seemed to know the driver.

'Hello, how do you do? I'm Susie. If you'd like to jump back in, Bob will follow me and we'll get you straight to the plane. OK, Bob?'

Sophie had been prepared to walk to the plane but then realised it was probably dangerous. This was a commercial airport after all.

The car followed Susie's vehicle right to the steps of a plane that was much bigger than Sophie was expecting. She said as much to Susie when she'd got out.

'People always think "Lear jet" but you need something quite a bit bigger if you're going to cross the Atlantic. Now, I'll just see if Sheila's there. I expect she is. The plane seems ready to roll.'

Before she could call, another glamorous woman appeared. 'Are you Sophie Apperly? Mr Winchester is expecting you.' She smiled a welcome. 'I'm Sheila.'

As Sophie climbed the steps Susie and Sheila had a quick

369

chat and then said goodbye to each other. They seemed to know each other well.

'We used to fly together years ago,' Sheila explained as Sophie stepped aboard. 'Mr Winchester is on the phone.' She indicated Luke's back; he was obviously talking. 'You just take a seat while you're waiting. Would you like some tea or coffee or anything?'

The luxury of the plane enveloped her and with it an atmosphere of soothing calm. Everything was covered with something that looked like honey-coloured suede. The seat Sophie was offered was supremely comfortable and she saw that with the flick of a lever it would turn into a chaise longue. In spite of herself, Sophie couldn't help appreciating her surroundings and the thought that she was actually in a private jet distracted her from her turmoil. A cup of tea would help, even if she only had time for a few sips. 'Tea would be lovely.'

She felt in a strange limbo. Part of her felt swaddled in comfort and calm while inside a little turbo of panic whirred away, muffled by the padded softness of her settings.

'All the papers are there,' said Sheila. 'That tea will be with you in a jiffy.'

Longing for *Hello!* magazine, Sophie riffled through the broadsheets and financial journals and was pleased to find a copy of *Vogue*. She didn't often buy it but was always pleased to have an opportunity to see what the latest trends were.

Except she couldn't concentrate. Luke had known she was coming; why was he being so long on the phone? The stewardess and the pilot, who had smiled a welcome, seemed preoccupied with pre-flight checks. Engines were running; the plane seemed set to take off at any moment.

'Would you mind fastening your seatbelt?' said Sheila. 'We'll be taxiing in a moment.'

'Oh God, you won't take off with me on board, will you?' Sophie fumbled for her seatbelt and Sheila laughed.

'We haven't had a stowaway yet!' She closed the door at the end, deadening yet more sound. Sophie hoped both that she wouldn't have to wait too long for her tea and that the car would be able to find her to pick her up.

It struck Sophie that she wouldn't really qualify as a stowaway because she wasn't hiding, and stowaways would want the plane to take off. She was considering getting up and having a discussion about semantics when the plane started to move.

Now she panicked. She'd been told they were going to move, but surely the plane wouldn't wait if it was all ready to go? But Luke was still at the back of the plane, having the longest telephone conversation on record, and her document was still unsigned. Supposing the car couldn't find her? She'd have to walk miles across runways, and it was raining again.

She fiddled with her belt buckle but just as she got it loose, Sheila came back and sat next to her, buckling it up again. 'Not while we're moving. It's not safe.'

'But I need to get off! The plane is about to take off!'

'Not immediately. I assure you Mr Winchester has it all under control.'

Sophie calmed down a little. Luke was very conventional. He wouldn't do anything untoward and, while he might be annoyed with her at the moment, he wouldn't commit her to a long and possibly dangerous walk back to the terminal.

The stewardess got up as the plane seemed to speed up. One rule for staff and one for passengers, thought Sophie, in the safety stakes. Sheila closed the door behind her and Sophie was alone in the cabin.

Suddenly, Sophie could bear it no longer. If the

stewardess was safe to walk around, so was she. She got out of her belt and her seat and marched to the back of the plane.

'Luke!' she demanded. 'Sign this paper! I need to get off!'

Luke, still on the phone, turned to her and smiled. 'Don't panic, it's all going to be fine. Just sit down and wait. And do up your seatbelt.'

Sophie had thought she would die before she saw Luke smile at her again. It made her want to cry. There was so much unfinished business between them. Everything had all gone wrong but she could never deny how magical those short hours had been when they'd been together, heart and soul and mind. She sat back down and did up her seatbelt and looked out of the window, watching the rain dash against the glass, raindrops racing as the plane speeded up and then to her relief, slowed down again.

'OK.' Luke came and sat down opposite her and did up his own belt. 'Sorry that call took so long. Give me the paper.'

It was actually a manila envelope and was looking quite tatty now. It had been clutched in Sophie's hand for a while. She handed it over. 'Hurry up and sign it! The plane's going to take off in any minute!' She glanced out of the window. 'Oh my goodness, we're going backwards!'

'That's right. We don't want to miss our slot.' He had taken the paper out of the envelope but he didn't seem to be reading it, let alone getting out his pen.

'But I need to get off before it takes off! Tell them to stop!' Why didn't he understand the urgency of the situation?

'You're all right.'

'No I'm not all right! I'm on a moving plane that is going to take to the skies at any moment! I want to get off!'

'Can't let you do that. It's too late. And besides, I'm kidnapping you.'

'No!' she roared. 'You are not! This is not a film where the hero carries the girl out of the factory at the last minute!'

'Do you judge all life by whether you've seen it in a film or not?'

Sophie breathed. 'Seriously, Luke, tell them to stop the plane. I want to get off.'

'I'm not letting you go, Sophie, ever.'

Sophie thought she was going to faint, a sensation not helped by the fact that the plane was now going very fast indeed. She really couldn't get off now. A second later they were in the air. Her mouth was dry and she felt slightly sick. 'Luke, what have you done?'

Chapter Twenty-Six

❧

'Seriously, Luke. It's not allowed! It's hijacking or something.' Addled by the horror of the situation, Sophie's brain refused to work properly.

'No, hijacking is when someone takes over the plane,' Luke explained gently. 'Now, have you had breakfast?'

Just for a moment, Sophie couldn't think what breakfast was, let alone if she'd had it or not. Then she remembered the toast she hadn't finished. 'I don't know,' she said cautiously.

Luke nodded to Sheila, who had appeared with a tray. She set it down on Sophie's table. There was the promised tea, a glass of orange juice and a basket filled with warm croissants, some butter and a dish of cherry jam.

'You planned this,' said Sophie.

'I'm sorry. I've messed up so badly, I felt I had to work out a strategy.'

'Champagne?' said Sheila, producing a napkin-covered bottle from somewhere, behind her back probably.

'Certainly not!' said Sophie.

'Maybe later,' said Luke and the stewardess took the bottle and herself away.

'This is a dreadful thing you've done,' chided Sophie, looking at the croissants and suddenly wanting one.

'I know, but it's not the worst thing and I felt I might not get an opportunity to apologise or explain – so I kidnapped you.' Luke sat down opposite her, picked up a

374

plate, put a croissant on it and tore it apart. Then he put a smear of butter on it and some jam. He held it out to Sophie.

'I don't like jam. Thank you,' she added as an afterthought. Then she remembered she usually loved it.

Luke prepared another bit of croissant for her, leaving off the jam this time. Sophie took it.

'You went to bed without supper last night. You can have the Full English afterwards if you like.'

The way he said 'Full English' made Sophie smile inside a little. He offered her half a croissant and she ate that too. She drank the orange juice.

'Tea?' she said.

'Certainly, tea,' Luke agreed. He picked up the pot and poured tea into a china cup. 'Milk?'

'Just a little.' She took a sip of tea and realised that there was something about the food and Luke feeding it to her that made her feel a little more human, less as if she'd been swept up into the sky by a giant. 'Aren't you eating?'

He shook his head. 'I did have supper and breakfast, and a large dose of humble pie, even if you haven't eaten it yet, sort of takes away your appetite.'

Sophie looked at him questioningly. Her mouth was full.

'Oh yes. When we got back last night, after you had gone to bed, Matilda and I had a long talk.'

'What about?' The croissants were heavenly.

'Well, she said, "Have you and that lovely girl got together yet?"'

Sophie stopped chewing, swallowed and had to take another sip of tea to chase the croissant down. 'Did she really?'

'Yes, she did, and when I told her that no, I'd just shouted at you, she was not pleased.'

Sophie smiled a little. 'I can't imagine she told you off, she adores you.'

'She does adore me and it's that that gives her the right to treat me to a bit of plain speaking, once in a while.'

Sophie laughed. He was obviously quoting Matilda word for word.

'Then she cross-examined me on my feelings for you.'

Sophie winced. 'And did you pass the test?'

'Oh yes. And then she helped me hatch this plan. I think Moira helped too.'

Sophie became serious. 'You do realise you've committed an illegal act. I haven't got a passport.' Although feeling much better disposed towards him now, she didn't want him to think he could just feed her croissants and orange juice and everything would be all right.

'Currently, you don't need a passport to get from Cornwall to London, although that may change.'

Sophie should have been relieved, but part of her was disappointed that she wasn't being swept over the Atlantic in this little bubble of luxury.

'Oh. And I've got Moira's shoes,' she added.

'I'm sure she doesn't mind them going for a little trip.'

Moira was probably fed up with her metaphorically and literally sobbing in her arms about Luke; she would probably be willing to sacrifice a pair of shoes not to have to do it again. Sophie hoped Moira hadn't wasted her shoes on a lost cause.

'We have about an hour to get things sorted out,' said Luke. 'I have an hour, I mean.'

Sophie swallowed. The flutter of hope that had been stirring in her stomach was increasing, but she couldn't let it get out of hand. There was still the matter of Ali to get over. 'Get talking then. Tell me what was in the paper that Matilda needed so urgently. Or was it just a ruse?'

Luke didn't answer.

'So it was a ruse?'

'I had to get you here somehow, Sophie.'

'Really? You didn't think you could have just stayed at Moira's and talked to me? Like a normal human being?'

He shook his head. 'I have this damn meeting and you might have run away. Besides, there were too many people in Moira's house for a proper discussion.'

Sophie acknowledged this was true by gathering up croissant crumbs with her finger as she always did.

'And I do have to be in London,' Luke repeated.

'And would it have been a big fuss to get your slot changed?'

Luke tried to imply with a look that such petty matters were of no concern to him but then just said, 'Yes.'

'I still think you should look at the paper. She did put something into the envelope and if it had just been a ruse, she wouldn't have bothered.'

Luke took the envelope, which was lying on the seat. 'I expect she just put some sheets of paper in to stop it feeling empty.' He opened it and pulled out a couple of typed sheets. 'Oh.'

Sophie watched his expression change as he read. First he seemed to be reading something familiar. Then he frowned and, finally, he smiled.

'What's funny?' asked Sophie when she couldn't wait for him to tell her a minute longer.

He looked up and handed her the paper. 'Granny has given you the house.'

Sophie snatched the paper in horror. She skimmed the first half, which seemed to be Matilda telling Luke how much she loved him, and then reached the relevant paragraphs.

I'm giving the house to Sophie. She told me back home that she'd always wanted to live by the ocean – she obviously loves it – and we both know that I don't need another property, although I do very much love that one.

Whether she decides to hook up with you is up to her, but my advice to you, young man, is to catch that girl and never let her go . . .

There was more but Sophie didn't read it. She let the paper slip from her fingers. 'This is awful!'

Luke frowned, rescuing the paper. 'Is it?'

'She can't give me the house . . . that's just not right! Just because I love it and everything—'

'And found it.'

'*We* found it, Luke! Together!'

'We wouldn't have if you hadn't looked for it, you know that.'

'But it's too much! Goodness, I felt guilty enough when she gave me this ring, I can't accept a house!'

'Can't you?'

'No! What sort of a girl would that make me? I know you haven't always thought the best of me, Luke, but I wouldn't do a thing like take a house from Matilda.' She paused. 'Do you remember, back in New York, when you told me about that young woman and her children who moved into a beach apartment or something? I thought that was a disgusting way to behave and would never, ever have done anything like that. This is worse!'

Luke leant across and took her hands. 'But you can't refuse it. Think how unhappy that would make Granny. She loves you, she wants you to have the house.'

Sophie clutched at his fingers. 'But it's too much!'

'How much money did your Uncle Eric give you?'

'Twenty thousand pounds. That was too much too.'

378

'But you accepted it.'

'Yes, and you told me off!'

'I wasn't thinking straight! I was mad with you – mad generally, I think. I was so confused.'

'Confused by what? I don't think I was ever confusing.'

'You were maddening and enchanting and wonderful and I suppose you're right. It wasn't really you that confused me.'

Sophie felt herself tense, knowing the answer but not wanting to be the one to say it. 'Who then?'

Luke looked at her, holding tightly on to her hands.

Sophie entwined her fingers in his and clung on. 'It's Ali, isn't it? The elephant in the room – or should I say plane.' She tried to smile. 'Elephants on planes probably aren't a good thing.'

'Ali and I were never together like that. She wanted us to be together; she behaved as if we were.'

'Did you sleep with her?'

'Once, before I met you. Sophie, I may not have behaved well there. It was just sex with someone I liked, but I never loved her. I never pretended I did. She wanted more from the relationship than I did.'

'Poor Ali. I can sympathise with that.' Sophie felt she could afford to be magnanimous towards Ali now.

'It's why she tried to keep us apart. She told me you were too young, too inexperienced, that you were after my money—'

'Which I am so not! I have my own money now anyway, and even—'

'I do know you're not after my money. I do know that you don't really need money. You have all your resourcefulness and practicality and ability to make one dollar do the work of five – and yet somehow, I listened.'

'Why?' Sophie was hurt but tried not to show it.

'You were like a creature off another planet to me, Sophie! You were so innocent, so lacking in guile. I'd never met anyone like you – I don't think I even knew girls like you existed. Everything Ali said made a sort of sense.'

As Sophie had also thought that Ali was perfect for Luke she didn't comment.

'Then I realised – when I thought you were drowned – how utterly joyless my life would be without you.'

'So you kidnapped me so you could tell me that?' She made herself sound disapproving because she still felt there was a lot that hadn't been explained, but in fact she thought it was very romantic.

'There didn't seem to be another way. I had to go to London.'

'OK, but you could have rung me or something.'

'Not to tell you all that, I couldn't. Besides, you have no phone.'

'You're finally calling it by its proper name!'

Then Sophie's hand flew to her mouth in horror. 'Oh my God! I've just thought – all my numbers! That's dreadful.' The vision of her phone swirling away in the water came back to her and at the same time came the realisation that there were many worse things in life than not having a mobile phone, even for a girl. 'Still, it can't be helped.' She suddenly felt a wonderful sense of freedom. What did it matter if she'd lost her phone? She was here with Luke, the man she loved.

'But you understand I had to say all this in person. Particularly after the way I behaved yesterday.'

Sophie found herself smiling. 'I suppose so.'

Luke regarded her, his usually confident expression almost diffident. 'I am so sorry.' He spoke softly. 'About everything. Not just yesterday, when actually I was perfectly justified. But before. I was trying to find excuses not to love you.'

'Why? Would loving me somehow demean you?' Sophie felt if he gave the wrong answer she would fight her way to the cockpit and demand that the pilot turn the plane and take her back to Cornwall. And the wrong answer could be almost anything.

'You know I was married before?'

'Yes.'

'My first wife not only humiliated me in a fairly public way, she also took me to the cleaners financially.'

This wasn't a good enough reason. 'You're very rich, you could afford it.'

'Yes, but the damage to my self-esteem was less easy to get over.' He paused. 'I had been very much in love with her. I learnt not to trust the emotion.'

'But you trust it now?'

'I know that life without you isn't worth living.'

'That's . . . nice.' How inadequate. She bit her lip. Her feelings were far stronger than her words suggested.

'Would the champagne be a good idea now?'

'I think it might be. I'm in shock, I think.'

'What about?' He pressed a button.

'Everything! This' – she indicated her surroundings – 'you, Matilda wanting to give me the house.'

Sheila appeared with the champagne, already opened, and poured two glasses. Then she left. A perfect professional, she didn't offer congratulations, or make a comment, or do anything except serve and leave. Sophie was so grateful. She took the glass Luke handed her.

'I've had an idea,' said Luke, once he'd clinked Sophie's glass and taken a sip of champagne.

'Oh?'

He nodded. 'I've thought of a way for you not to take the

house from my grandmother but for her to still give it to you.'

'That sounds very complicated and contradictory. Is it some sort of lawyer speak?'

'Not at all. It should work brilliantly.'

'Then tell me!'

'This isn't quite how I wanted it to be.'

'What isn't?'

'My proposal of marriage. I wanted to have a ring, take you somewhere romantic . . .'

Sophie's heart began to somersault.

'But will you marry me? I know you're awfully young and probably don't want to commit yourself – especially to someone like me, but if you do . . .' He seemed about to produce the carrot he'd been leading up to. '. . . then Matilda could give us both the house, as a wedding present.'

'Oh well, that would make it more acceptable, I suppose.'

'But will you marry me?' Luke said urgently.

Most of Sophie wanted to say yes immediately, but a wicked part wanted to tease him a little. 'I might, but how do I know you really love me?'

'Sophie, I'd do anything – Hell, I waded through a swollen torrent to rescue you!'

'That's true.'

'Tell you what,' said Luke after a few moments. 'Have another glass of champagne and think about it.' He topped up her glass. 'And consider how shocked my grandmother would be if we decided to just live together.'

Sophie snorted. 'I don't believe she'd be shocked at all! She's very modern – not like an old lady at all.'

'But she is quite old. If we put it off too long, she may die before it happens. Then she'd have to leave the house to you in her will and you'd have to pay all kinds of tax on it.'

'You're such a lawyer sometimes!'

'I know. And you're maddening, but I love you. Sophie, will you marry me? We haven't got long. I can't go into this meeting not knowing.'

'I could tell you after the meeting.'

'I need to know now. The meeting is about me setting up a full-time office in London, while you do your course, anyway.'

'You'd do that for me?'

'In a heartbeat.'

'Oh, Luke.'

'But only for you. You're unique.'

'Everyone's unique, Luke!'

A rueful smile made one corner of his mouth go up. 'Actually, I think a lot of the women I meet are clones.'

Remembering the women who'd surrounded him at the brunch, Sophie felt he had a point.

'So can you imagine spending the rest of your life with a rich preppy attorney who's not always very bright?'

Sophie was now beginning to smile. She picked up her napkin and hid her mouth. 'I guess.'

'So you'll marry me?'

'I guess. Just for Matilda's sake, though.'

He was out of his seat and next to her in a minute. 'Oh, Sophie, you don't know how happy – how relieved you've made me. I never thought you'd agree!'

'I love you too, you know. Have done for ages. I tried not to.'

'What's wrong with me?' Luke tried to look offended but was just triumphant.

'You said it yourself! You're a rich preppy attorney! And I'm not in your league.'

'You're way out of my league,' said Luke and then he kissed her. A few moments later he said, 'If you knew how much I want you . . .'

'I do hope you're not going to suggest we join the Mile High Club!' said Sophie, wanting him just as much but feeling she'd like a bit more privacy.

'I'm not actually sure we'd get to a mile high on such a short flight. I should find out.'

'Not on my account!' Then she relented a little. 'Someone in the wine bar told me that she had done it on her honeymoon, and when it came down to it, you were just having sex in a public loo.'

Luke narrowed his gaze. 'I hate to throw my indecent wealth in your face, but this is a Gulfstream. We would not be making love in the "loo".'

The way he said the word made her giggle; it sounded so incongruous. 'I think that maybe I might be able to get used to this lifestyle.'

'So can I tell my grandmother we're engaged?' said Luke.

'Uh-huh,' said Sophie from somewhere in his armpit.

'Here,' said Luke. 'Let's make ourselves a little more comfortable, at least until we have to fasten our seatbelts for landing.'

A few levers and a bit of rearranging later, they were lying next to each other and, although they both had all their clothes on, she felt she was Velcroed to Luke, and that nothing now would ever part them.

'So, what are we going to do when we get to London?' she murmured, setting her glass down.

'I propose I book you into the company suite at Claridge's and then go to my meeting. And when I come back, I'm going to show you what a rich preppy attorney can really do when he's got a mind to.'

Sophie sighed with happiness. It was a perfect proposal.

If you have enjoyed *A Perfect Proposal*, why not read Katie's wonderfully romantic new novel *Summer of Love*?

Sian Bishop has moved to an idyllic Oxfordshire village for a better life her herself and her young son Rory. With her roses-round-the-door cottage, the perfect school for Rory just down the road, and her very own vegetable patch she knows she's made the right decision. She's also struck gold in Richard – steady, safe, reliable, he is the perfect man for her and the perfect potential stepfather for Rory.

But little does she realise she's now living in the village, Gus – the wonderful, irresistible, dangerous, unreliable and straight-out-of-a-Georgette-Heyer-novel, Gus – grew up in. And her quiet life in the country is about to get a whole lot more complicated...

Published in March 2011, *Summer of Love* is the perfect gift for Mother's Day or simply as a treat for you. Go on, indulge in a little romance!

Turn over to read the first wonderful chapter!

Chapter One

✦

'Er, hello!'

Sian put down her fork and looked over the garden wall. A woman was smiling at her, holding a bottle of wine in one hand and a jam jar full of flowers in the other.

'Hello!' said Sian.

'I hope you don't think I'm appallingly nosy but I noticed the furniture van drive away yesterday and thought I'd pop round and welcome you to the village. I'm Fiona Matcham. I live in the house up the end.' She swung the wine bottle vaguely in the direction of the lane.

'Oh,' said Sian. 'Would you like to come in?' She suspected that her visitor meant the Big House, a beautiful building that her mother had raved about when she'd come down to help Sian move in.

'I don't want to stop you working, but I could come and watch you.'

1

Sian laughed and wiped her hands on her shorts. She'd managed to get all the strawberry plants in that her mother had given her. 'No, no, I'm quite happy to stop. I'm Sian Bishop.'

'Hello again, Sian.' Fiona waved the jam jar at her. 'Here, take these.' Fiona Matcham handed Sian the bottle and the flowers over the wall and then walked up to the gate and let herself in. 'Oh! You've got a boy! How lovely! I love boys!'

Rory, who was digging with his little spade in the soil his mother had softened for him first, looked up and stared quizzically at Fiona from under his blond fringe.

'You're doing good work there, aren't you? Are you going to grow something?' Fiona Matcham addressed Rory while producing a jar of jam from the pocket of her loose linen jacket.

'Yes,' said Rory seriously.

'We're hoping to grow our own vegetables now we're in the country,' said Sian. 'Rory's got that patch, and I'm going to have a bigger patch in the back garden. We've planted strawberries. Salad we'll do later. Rory, would you like to stop for a drink now? Or carry on while I make tea?'

'Carry on while you make tea,' said Rory, turning back to his digging and ignoring them both.

Sian knew her son felt shy and would probably join them when he realised the tin of chocolate biscuits his grandmother had left had been produced. 'You would like a cup of tea?' Sian asked her guest. 'I've kind of assumed . . . '

'Oh yes, tea would be lovely. If you don't mind.'

Sian had already decided that this woman, who seemed to be in her mid-fifties, wasn't the sort who would be critical of a house not in perfect order, or why had she brought the wine? The flowers, too, were artistic and original – and no doubt from her own garden, not a conventional bouquet. Sian was inclined to like her already.

Sian led the way into the cottage. It seemed dark after the bright June sunshine outside and smelt of damp. But, as her mother had pointed out, it was very cheap to rent, had a big garden and the landlady, who lived in France, had expressed herself happy for Sian to make necessary improvements provided they weren't extravagant. She found space for the flowers on the table and instantly everything looked better.

'Excuse the mess,' said Sian, removing a half-unpacked box of crockery off a chair. 'I couldn't bear to be inside when the weather is so lovely. Do sit down. And thank you for the flowers. They make the place look so much more homely, somehow.'

Her guest popped the jar of jam on the side with a 'For you', pulled out an unoccupied chair and sat at the table. 'Well, as this might be our entire summer it would be a shame to waste the sunshine unpacking.' She paused. 'I brought the flowers in a jar so you wouldn't need to hunt round for something to put them in. Nothing is more irritating when people turn up for dinner with flowers that mean you have to abandon your guests, the dinner and the drinks to find a vase. I no longer have a husband,' she added. 'Single-handed entertaining.'

'I'm a single parent, so ditto.' It wasn't really a test but Sian had discovered, in the four years since she'd had Rory, that people who were unlikely to become friends would flinch a bit when she said this.

'I've been that, too. The boys' father died when they were quite young. It's tough.'

Sian smiled at Fiona across the half-light of the gloomy hallway-cum-dining room. She had a feeling she'd made a new friend already.

'I'll put the kettle on. What kind of tea would you like?'

'I can't believe you're so organised as to have a choice already,' Fiona replied, perched on the chair as if ready to leap up and help at a moment's notice.

Sian smiled. 'My mother stayed with me for a few days. I drink builder's, she drinks Earl Grey. Those are the choices unless you want herbal tea.'

'Builder's is fine.'

'I've got some biscuits. My mother brought a huge tin of them. I'll be back in a moment,' Sian said as she disappeared off to the kitchen.

'I do think Luella ought to take that wall down and make this room into a big kitchen diner!' called Fiona. 'Why don't you suggest it?'

'Do you mean Mrs Halpern? She's been very co-operative and said as long as I don't go mad I can make changes. But I think she might consider taking down a supporting wall as going mad,' Sian called back.

4

She was no longer alone in the galley kitchen. Her guest, apparently not one to sit around and be waited on, had joined her.

'Look at the damp on the floor!' exclaimed Fiona. 'It's appalling. Mind you, it might only be the gutter that needs clearing. Would you like me to send someone round to look at it?'

'If it's only the gutter I can probably manage it myself,' said Sian. 'If I can't, I'd be grateful for the name of someone reliable.' Sian liked to be as self-sufficient as possible but she knew there would be things she couldn't deal with. Since she'd moved her dad was no longer round the corner to do those things for her.

'Well, just say. I've lived here so long – since Noah and Mrs Noah were courting – I know more or less everyone. Oh, hello, Rory,' she said as he appeared in the doorway.

'Can you take the biscuits?' Sian handed her son the tin. 'Why don't you take them out into the back garden?' She turned to Fiona. 'There's a table and chairs there. I'll make the tea.'

'Good idea. Rory and I can go and get settled and have a chat. My name is Fiona,' she said to the boy.

'Wouldn't you rather be Mrs Matcham?' asked Sian.

'Oh no,' she said firmly. 'Fiona is much better.' She smiled, possibly to offset the firmness.

'Would you mind taking the milk out?' asked Sian.

'Oh, just put it in the mugs in here, why don't you? Then when you and Rory come over to visit me, I can be my usual slutty self.'

Sian smiled and put tea bags in mugs. She could just imagine her mother's delighted reaction when she told her about Fiona. She would see her as a wise older friend and a potential babysitter, not to mention someone who lived in a lovely house and so might perhaps be a customer for her daughter as well. Richard would be pleased too. Although it was because of him that she had moved to this particular village, and he had taken her and Rory under his wing, he'd be glad that the neighbours were being friendly.

Fiona Matcham and Rory were up the far end of the garden when Sian brought out the mugs of tea. Sian sat down on one of the chairs and sipped hers, watching them together. She was pleased that Rory had forgotten to be shy and was making friends. She had been a bit worried about taking him away from everything he knew in a busy city out into the country, although, as Richard had pointed out, it was in a village, not a remote location miles from anywhere. There was a school, a pub, a church and two shops, one of which was also a post office. 'Which makes it a heaving metropolis,' Sian's father had said dryly. He was less sanguine than his wife about his daughter moving away with his only grandchild, although both her parents accepted she was moving for very good reasons. 'Tea's up!' she called. 'And biscuits!'

Rory turned and ran back down what would be a lawn one day – if Sian was able to stay that long of course, she thought wistfully, and her landlady didn't object –followed by Fiona.

'I don't suppose you could spare me some of that wonderful cow parsley?' Fiona said as she reached the table. 'I've got to do church flowers tomorrow and a huge display of just that could look stunning!'

'Oh yes, of course. Take anything you want.'

'Thank you. You could come and help me do them if you want. My opposite number is away so I'll be on my own. Rory can help.' She paused. 'Although not if you're busy, or morally opposed to church flowers.'

Sian laughed. 'No, I'd like to help. I don't actually go to church…'

'That's all right, just help me do the flowers.' Fiona picked up her mug and sipped. 'Your reward will be an introduction to the Yummy Mummies. There are at least three I know moderately well. Will Rory be going to the school later?'

Sian nodded. 'In September. He actually started last year in London but it was a disaster. Having a summer birthday he was only just four and it was such a big school. His teacher wasn't very nice either.'

'How awful! I can't imagine anything worse. Poor Rory. Poor you.'

Sian smiled. 'I'm glad you don't think I'm a dreadfully over-protective mother. One of the reasons I wanted us to move away from London was the schools. I home-educated him when I finally gave up

7

trying to get him to go to school, but we're going to start again here.'

'Our local school is brilliant. I was a governor for years. I'm sure he'll be fine there.'

'I am too. And when you get to the secondary stage, London schools are even more frightening.'

Fiona nodded. 'And you probably didn't want to send him away to school. Don't. I did – it was expected – and it broke my heart, nearly.' She frowned. 'Although maybe I wouldn't have minded so much if my first husband hadn't just died.' She drank some more of her tea. 'So what were the other reasons for moving?'

Sian made a gesture. Usually she was quite a private person but something about Fiona made her feel comfortable about elaborating. 'There are lots. The country life, wanting to grow vegetables, be more self-sufficient. A friend suggested we came down here and found me this house. His sister – who Rory knows well and loves – is starting up a nursery and play scheme here which means I can work through the summer holidays, which I really need to be able to do.' She paused. 'And I couldn't go on more or less living right next door to my parents for ever, even though they did do quite a lot of childcare.'

'No?' Fiona looked thoughtful. 'One of my sons is going to be living with me quite soon.'

'Oh no, it'll be fine!' Sian hurried to reassure her, although she had no idea what sort of relationship Fiona had with her son. 'What I meant was, if London was the wrong place to be living in every other way, I couldn't go on doing it just because my parents were so close. It wasn't fair on them in a way, me expecting them to drop everything if I had a lot of work. They have their own lives.'

'And how did they take the news you wanted to move away?'

'Obviously they were a bit unhappy but once Richard – he's the friend – found me this place they were fine.' Sian counted her new home's advantages off on her fingers. 'It's in a village so I won't be too isolated. There's a lovely school within easy walking distance. It's only just under an hour to London by train and the station's not too far away. It has a huge garden so I can grow vegetables and the rent is extremely reasonable.'

'Because the kitchen is cramped and damp,' said Fiona.

Sian laughed. 'I can put up with that, or even change it.'

Fiona laughed too. 'Luella probably isn't the most attentive landlady, but she's very nice.'

'She sounded nice on the phone and while we were arranging things.'

'She doesn't really need the money for renting this place and she'll probably sell it eventually, but she likes to keep a foothold in England while she's in France.'

'I've got a three-month lease that will probably be extended,' said Sian, suddenly chilled by the thought that she might have to leave her cottage if it was going to be sold. It might be damp but it was perfect for her and Rory.

'And I'm sure you can stay much longer than that if you want to,' said Fiona, suddenly realising she'd worried Sian. 'Last time we emailed she said she had no intention of coming back to the land where you drink tea instead of wine. I missed her when she went to France. She was my best friend locally.' She took a chocolate finger. 'I love chocolate fingers. There's something about them, isn't there? Nothing else tastes quite the same.'

Sian agreed. 'Would you like another one? Otherwise I think I should take the tin inside to stop them all melting. Rory? One more?'

Rory helped himself to another biscuit and then leant against Sian's chair, playing distractedly with a toy truck he'd retrieved from under the table, whilst his mother went off with the tin.

'So tell me your plans?' said Fiona once Sian had returned with a damp flannel for Rory's face and everyone's fingers. 'Or haven't you got any yet?'

'Oh no, I have plans. For one thing I want to get going on the garden. I've never grown vegetables before but I'm longing to try. It'll be quick-growing plants to start with, spuds and things later. Then I need somewhere to carry out my business in. I'm hoping to rent something.' She didn't mention the possibility of settling down with Richard. She was by no means sure she would, although sometimes the idea seemed tempting. He was a dear friend and definitely a 'catch', as her father would have said.

'What sort of business? I mean, do you need an aircraft hanger or a garret?'

'Something in between, but more hanger than garret. I paint furniture, customise it.'

'Oh?'

'If you're really interested I'll show you some pictures.'

'Oh do! I'd be thrilled. Rory, would you like to take me up the other end of the garden again while your mother gets the pictures? There seems to be a little house.'

'All right,' said Rory after a moment's thought. He clambered to his feet and they set off.

Sian found her albums easily and turned the pages on her own while she waited for Fiona and Rory to come back – they were engrossed in what looked like the remains of a summer house at the bottom of the garden. Sian hadn't had time to investigate it yet herself. She was pleased to have met someone so soon – she'd been a bit worried about her and Rory becoming too dependent on each other and Richard if they had no one else to talk to. She might meet some mums at the play scheme Rory was booked into, but she might not. And Fiona seemed so good with Rory, friendly without being patronising. She sighed. Richard was a bit of a worry to her. She liked him very much but she wasn't in love with him, not in the way he so obviously was with her, and while he knew this and accepted it, he clearly hoped she would come to love him as more than just a friend. Sian hoped that too, in a way. He was perfect in so many respects. But she couldn't marry a man she didn't love, not even for the financial security she longed for.

Rory dashed back when he saw his mother, Fiona following more sedately behind. 'That's my one!' he said, pointing to a picture of a chest of drawers covered with dragons, castles and seascapes.

Fiona inspected it. 'It's wonderful! What beautiful painting! How did you get the idea?'

'Well, Rory was obsessed with dragons at the time – still is, to some extent. My mother had bought this chest of drawers for half nothing at an auction – she's addicted to auctions – and as it needed something doing to it I decided to do more than just sand it down and put on a coat of white gloss.' She chuckled. 'I went to art college. I wanted to earn my living doing something that was actually connected to my degree but I could do from home. This is perfect – or it will be, when the business has built up a bit.'

Fiona turned the pages. 'But not all these are yours – your furniture, I mean?'

'Oh no. But when my friends saw the chest of drawers they started getting me to paint things for them. Now I have a website and stuff, but I need somewhere where I can paint bigger items. I've done one or two adult pieces, too.'

'So what sort of premises do you need?'

'Do you think you might know of somewhere? I

need a barn or something. Some of the paint is a bit toxic so I need plenty of air around if possible.'

'I might indeed know of somewhere – my own barn in fact, just by my house – but it's absolutely full of stuff.'

'Well, if you did think you wanted to rent it out, I could help you clear it first.'

'That would be worth it, even without the rent. I've been meaning to do it for years and have never been able to face it.'

'I think that sort of thing is fun.'

'I suppose I'd think it was fun if I didn't have to make decisions about everything, but if you can help me with that, well, I'd be thrilled.'

Fiona seemed a little tentative. Sian didn't want her to change her mind about the barn and so nodded enthusiastically. 'I'd love it. Apart from it being fun I might be able to buy some things from you that I could paint. It seems a waste to buy new when there's so much perfectly good furniture around that just happens to be hideous – before I get my hands on it, of course!'

'Personally I don't think if furniture is hideous it can be described as "perfectly good",' Fiona said dryly, handing back the album to Sian.

Sian laughed. 'That's just the sort of thing my mother would say.'

'I hope you mean that in a good way!'

'Oh yes, definitely. My mother and I have a lot of fun together.'

'Well, that's a relief.' Fiona put her hand on Sian's briefly and got up. 'I should go. Now, were you serious about being willing to help with the flowers?'

'Oh yes.'

'Then I'll pop by at about two tomorrow and we can pick the cow parsley and then arrange it. Will that fit in with nap times and things?'

'I don't have a nap now,' said Rory. 'I'm too old.'

'I have naps all the time and I'm much older than you,' declared Fiona. 'But we won't argue about it. Until tomorrow then?'

When Sian had seen her guest out and renewed her thanks for the house-warming presents, she rang her mother. She would be thrilled that Sian had a new friend already. Sian was thrilled herself.

'It's Fona,' said Rory the following afternoon, looking through one of the small front windows at the person on the front door step.

'Oh good.' Sian went and opened the door. 'Hello! Come on through to the garden, we'll get picking.'

Fiona was carrying a bucket in which there were a pair of secateurs and what looked like an old curtain. 'Good afternoon. Hello, Rory! Are you going to help us put flowers in the church? There are toys there if you get bored.'

The two women cut swathes of cow parsley, filling Fiona's bucket and another one they found in a shed, and then set off for the church.

'Can I carry the bucket?' asked Rory, anxious to be

involved. He'd been a little put out that he hadn't been able to help with collecting the cow parsley but Fiona had said the secateurs were too dangerous and only to be used by adults and his mother hadn't felt his pulling at the plants was achieving the desired effect. He'd had to watch them both and had got bored.

Sian thought about it. The bucket was heavy but she didn't want to start a row in front of Fiona. Rory was an easy child on the whole but he could get terribly offended if anyone suggested he was too young or too small for a particular task, and he'd already sulked a bit when they wouldn't allow him to help pick the flowers. 'OK,' she said casually, hoping he'd abandon the idea quite quickly.

'Actually, I could do with a hand with mine,' said Fiona. 'Your mum could carry that one but I'm not sure I can manage this one on my own. If you'd be a kind chap and carry it with me, I'd be very grateful.'

Flattered by this request for help, Rory took hold of the handle.

'It's quite hard to carry with all this cow parsley, isn't it?' went on Fiona.

'It's not heavy,' said Rory.

'Not for you, perhaps!' said Fiona. 'But you're a strong boy.'

Sian let herself lag behind her son and her new friend. It was nice that they got on so well. Fiona was very good with him. She thought Rory might miss her parents, being used to the company of adults. She locked the house and put the key in the pocket of her jeans. Fiona and Rory began to sing as the three of them lumbered up the lane towards the churchyard.

The church was cool and dark and Rory was a bit over-awed until Fiona put on some lights, chatting away as if she was somewhere familiar and friendly. It took Sian a few moments to feel it was OK to talk above a whisper but by the time Rory had been shown the toys, which included a train set, she was soon helping Fiona pull out the faded flowers from the stand of oasis and fielding the dead leaves that missed the curtain Fiona had spread out to catch them.

A little later she was taking the lower leaves off the cow parsley and handing the sprays to Fiona as if she'd always done it. There was something satisfying about flower-arranging, especially in the calm interior of an ancient building. 'It only has to look good from the back of the church. That's where most people sit,' said Fiona, stepping back and looking at the display with a critical eye.

'It looks good from here!'

'Thank you! I do hope you'll come back to tea afterwards,' said Fiona. 'I've made a cake and Jody and Annabelle are coming. Annabelle's about Rory's age and you'll like Jody.'

'That's so kind. We'd love to meet them and we love cake. Especially homemade.'

'Me too. I've trained myself to believe that shop cake isn't worth getting fat for, but I'm not sure I believe it really.'

'You really needn't have made a cake just for us. We're not proud about shop cake!'

Fiona laughed. 'Actually, I've got a bit of a favour to ask you. I thought I'd soften you up first.'

Sian laughed too, hoping she wasn't about to let herself in for something she wouldn't be happy doing. 'Well, anything you think we can do.'

'You don't really have to do much but it's not something I can ask Jody, for example.' Fiona bit her lip, frowning a little as she adjusted her arrangement. 'It is a bit mad and I don't want to ask anyone I know well.' Fiona stepped back from the pyramid of frothy white and green, which to Sian looked like a patch of starlight. 'Do you think that looks all right? People always say my arrangements are "unusual" and I'm never sure whether to take that as a compliment or not. No one's ever done anything like that as far as I know but I always remember my mother telling me about Constance Spry having a big jug of cow parsley in the window of her shop, in London, just after the war. I've always wanted to do it.'

'I think it looks stunning. Really simple and pure. And if it is unusual, it's lovely.'

'As long as it looks OK from the back of the church,' repeated Fiona, walking in that direction.

Once Fiona was happy with the arrangement and they'd cleared up and put the train set away, they headed back to Fiona's house. As they approached, Sian said, 'I don't suppose you could tell me your mad thing now? I'm dying of curiosity.'

17

'Well, we can't have you dying, although really I'd prefer to tell you with a paper bag over my head. And not a word to Jody.' Fiona plunged on. 'It's all your landlady's fault. She put me up to it.'

'But what is it?'

'Internet dating,' said Fiona. 'There, I've said it. And look, there's Jody.'

ALSO AVAILABLE IN ARROW

Love Letters

Katie Fforde

Has Laura met her leading man . . .?

With the bookshop where she works about to close, Laura Horsley finds herself agreeing to help organise a literary festival deep in the heart of the English countryside. But her initial excitement is rapidly followed by a mounting sense of panic when she realises just how much work is involved – especially when an innocent mistake leads the festival committee to mistakenly believe that Laura is a personal friend of the author at the top of their wish-list. Laura might have been secretly infatuated with the notoriously reclusive Dermot Flynn ever since she studied him at university, but travelling to Ireland to persuade him to come out of hiding is another matter.

Determined to rise to the challenge she sets off to meet her literary hero. But all too soon she's confronted with more than she bargained for – Dermot the man is maddening, temperamental and up to his ears in a nasty case of writer's block. But he's also infuriatingly attractive – and, apparently, out to add Laura to his list of conquests . . .

'A great fun countryside romp with engaging characters and a narrative thrust that had me hooked to the end.' *Daily Mail*

'Fforde's cosy style is strangely comforting and Laura's transformation from ingénue to confident and lustful young woman makes for an enjoyable summer read.' *Daily Telegraph*

arrow books

Wedding Season

Katie Fforde

All you need is love . . .?

Sarah Stratford is a wedding planner hiding a rather inconvenient truth – she doesn't believe in love. Or not for herself, anyway. But as the confetti flutters away on the June breeze of yet another successful wedding she somehow finds herself agreeing to organise two more, on the same day and only two months away. And whilst her celebrity bride is all sweetness and light, her own sister soon starts driving her mad with her high expectations but very limited budget.

Luckily Sarah has two tried and tested friends on hand to help her. Elsa, an accomplished dress designer who likes to keep a very low profile, and Bron, a multi-talented hairdresser who lives with her unreconstructed boyfriend and who'd like to go solo in more ways than one. They may be very good at their work but romance doesn't feature very highly in any of their lives.

As the big day draws near all three women find that patience is definitely a virtue in the marriage game. And as all their working hours are spent preparing for the wedding of the year plus one, they certainly haven't got any time to even think about love. Or have they?

'A funny, fresh and lively read' *heat*

arrow books